Kristine Kathryn Rusch

Kristine Kathryn Rusch is one of the best writers in the field.
—*SFRevu*

Whether [Rusch] writes high fantasy, horror, sf, or contemporary fantasy, I've always been fascinated by her ability to tell a story with that enviable gift of invisible prose. She's one of those very few writers whose style takes me right into the story—the words and pages disappear as the characters and their story swallows me whole….Rusch has style.
—Charles de Lint
The Magazine of Fantasy & Science Fiction

The SF thriller is alive and well, and today's leading practitioner is Kristine Kathryn Rusch.
—*Analog*

Praise for
Diving into the Wreck

The Diving Universe, conceived buy Hugo-Award winning author Kristine [Kathryn] Rusch is a refreshingly new and fleshed out realm of sci-fi action and adventure. And the latest offering…doesn't disappoint.
—*AstroGuyz.com*

A combination of first-person and third-person narrative and flashback segments makes this a complex and compelling story. It's like having three tales in one, with an added peek into the bad guys' activities, all of them intriguing, classic science fiction. It leaves the reader eager to explore this universe again and see what will happen next with these characters.
—*RT Book Reviews*

Praise for
DIVING INTO THE WRECK

Rusch delivers a page-turning space adventure while contemplating the ethics of scientists and governments working together on future tech.
—*Publisher's Weekly*

This is classic sci-fi, a well-told tale of dangerous exploration. The first-person narration makes the reader an eyewitness to the vast, silent realms of deep space, where even the smallest error will bring disaster. Compellingly human and technically absorbing, the suspense builds to fevered intensity, culminating in an explosive yet plausible conclusion.
—*RT Book Reviews* Top Pick

Rusch's handling of the mystery and adventure is stellar, and the whole tale proves quite entertaining.
—*Booklist Online*

The technicalities in Boss' story are beautifully played.... She's real, flawed, and interesting.... Read the book. It is very good.
—*SFFWorld.com*

Praise for
CITY OF RUINS

Rusch keeps the science accessible, the cultures intriguing, and the characters engaging. For anyone needing to add to their science fiction library, keep an eye out for this.
—Josh Vogt
SpeculativeFictionExaminer.com

Praise for
BONEYARDS

Rusch's latest addition to her "Diving" series features a strong, capable female heroine and a vividly imagined far-future universe. Blending fast-paced action with an exploration of the nature of friendship and the ethics of scientific discoveries, this tale should appeal to Rusch's readers and fans of space opera.
—*Library Journal*

Filled with well-defined characters who confront a variety of ethical and moral dilemmas, Rusch's third Diving Universe novel is classic space opera, with richly detailed worldbuilding and lots of drama.
—*RT Book Reviews*

Praise for
SKIRMISHES

... a fabulous outer space thriller that rotates perspective between the divers, the Alliance and to a lesser degree the Empire. Action-packed and filled with twists yet allowing the reader to understand the motives of the key players, *Skirmishes* is another intelligent exciting voyage into the Rusch Diving universe.
—*The Midwest Book Review*

Kristine Kathryn Rusch is best known for her Retrieval Artist series, so maybe you've missed her Diving Universe series. If so, it's high time to remedy that oversight.
—Don Sakers, *Analog*

Also by
Kristine Kathryn Rusch

The Diving Series:

Novellas

Diving into the Wreck
The Room of Lost Souls
The Application of Hope
Becalmed
Becoming One with the Ghosts
Stealth
Strangers at the Room of Lost Souls
The Spires of Denon

Novels

Diving into the Wreck
City of Ruins
Boneyards
Skirmishes
The Falls
The Runabout

Collections

The Diving Bundle: Six Diving Universe Novellas

The Falls
A Diving Universe Novel

Kristine Kathryn Rusch

The Falls

Copyright © 2016 by Kristine Kathryn Rusch

All rights reserved

Published 2016 by WMG Publishing
www.wmgpublishing.com
Cover and layout copyright © 2016 by WMG Publishing
Cover design by Allyson Longueira/WMG Publishing
Cover art copyright © Philcold/Dreamstime
ISBN-13: 978-1-56146-768-6
ISBN-10: 1-56146-768-5

This book is licensed for your personal enjoyment only. All rights reserved. This is a work of fiction. All characters and events portrayed in this book are fictional, and any resemblance to real people or incidents is purely coincidental. This book, or parts thereof, may not be reproduced in any form without permission.

ACKNOWLEDGEMENTS

Thanks on this one go to Allyson Longueira for being so very flexible on this project, Dayle A. Dermatis for helping with continuity (all mistakes, however, are 100% mine), and Dean Wesley Smith for keeping me sane. And the fans, who let me know how much they like the series.

THE FALLS
A DIVING UNIVERSE NOVEL

1

THE SHOES STARTLED HIM. Rajivk Agwu stopped at the edge of the black path and stared at them. Two pairs, both brown, smallish and well-worn, were neatly lined up against the black wall. Just beyond them, the water of Fiskett Falls churned, blue and gold and gray. A slight rainbow formed on the edge of the spray as the late afternoon sunlight hit the water just right.

Usually, Rajivk never stopped at this overlook. It was halfway up the Falls, and provided a view mostly of the water as it cascaded into Rockwell Pool below. A lot of people liked to study the water as it fell. It was dramatic and gorgeous and always powerful.

But this overlook was damp and cold, with very little light. It had been built by some of the first engineers to arrive in the Sandoveil Valley, hundreds of years ago. They were entranced with Fiskett Falls, just like everyone else who visited this remote part of Nindowne, and because the engineers were from the Fleet, they decided to make it easy and safe to view the Falls.

They built several overlooks, using the same nanobits that they would use to carve Sector Base E-2 several miles from here. The overlooks were solid, if a bit too slippery. The nanobits were designed to build underground caverns that could withstand thousands of years of constant activity. So they could handle the elements, even the elements as they were on the far part of Ynchinga, the tenth—and least populated—continent on Nindowne.

The weather was always active here. Twelve seasons, although most of the people who lived in Sandoveil, still using Earth Standard thousands of years after the Fleet had left their home world, liked to say they had four seasons—the Earth equivalent of fall, winter, spring, and summer.

Really, though, this part of Ynchinga had predictable variations: early-fall, mid-fall, late-fall—and the same for the other seasons.

It was mid-fall right now, the kind of day that made Rajivk grateful, because he knew the next few seasons would be stormy and difficult. The cool sunlight that created the lovely rainbow at the edge of the mist would become rare in the next week or two. Late-fall always brought rain- and ice-storms, sometimes so severe that the only way Rajivk could get to work would be to take the underground transports, which he hated.

It made him feel like he was on the *Qoraxda* again, unable to feel any wind on his face or smell rain in the air. He had been born in the Fleet, always traveling through space, rarely spending any time planetside, but he was not born *to* the Fleet.

The day that the *Qoraxda* came to Sector Base E-2 for the once-every-five-years overhaul was the day that changed his life.

This was another day that would change his life—or so most of the employees of the sector base had said. He hadn't believed it, because he thought the change a minor one. Although the news must have had some kind of impact on him because he had decided, at the spur of the moment, to take the upper trails around the Falls on his walk home. The upper trails added an hour to his walk. An hour and just a bit of treachery.

Viewed from a half mile away, the Falls looked symmetrical, the water evenly proportioned across its entire plunge to the pool below. Up close, it became clear that the looks were deceiving. The center of Fiskett Falls poured the most water below, and the edges were thin and clear.

The edges froze in late-fall or early-winter, making the Falls even narrower, and much more dangerous. All of the moving water squeezed into the middle section, shutting down the lower overlooks.

This overlook was always closed from the beginning of the freeze until mid-spring, but most of the locals stopped using this overlook in late-summer.

That was why the shoes startled him. They didn't look like tourist shoes. These shoes were nearly boots. He could tell just from a glance that the shoes had local modifications. It took some particularly strange footwear to climb the paths. The nanobits were too smooth, and impossible to reconfigure, so local footware designers modified boots generally used in zero-g. The boots would cling to surfaces, but not too much. They would adjust according to the conditions—if the path was wet, the boots would provide a different kind of traction than if the path was covered with a thin sheet of ice.

If locals decided to wear shoes like these, they still had the modifications. And these shoes did.

Then Rajivk shook his head. Shoes shouldn't have startled him, no matter how unusual they were. Maybe some hiker had set them here to wait for a return. Although they were getting wet.

And climbing up the trail in mid-fall could be dangerous. Those thin sheets of ice were invisible to the naked eye. Many a hiker tried to take the upper paths around the Falls, only to slip and break a limb. Some of the local guides only took tourists up the paths if the tourists wore basic environmental suits, the kind that space tourists had to use to prevent easy injury.

Rajivk walked the upper paths as much as he could, and hadn't worn an environmental suit up them ever. Once he moved here, fifteen years ago, he made it a point to learn everything he could about Fiskett Falls and its trails.

And the first thing he learned—the thing he reminded himself about every single spring—was that the Falls were dangerous. They could kill if he didn't pay attention every single second.

That was probably why he shouldn't have come up here today. He was distracted. For the first time since he started working at the sector base, everyone had been required to attend a meeting. Usually information got recorded and shared, or trickled down through departments.

The announcement made at the early morning meeting was simple enough: the base had finally received its closure date. Thirty years from right now, the base would shut its doors. It would stop taking Fleet ships for their every-five-years maintenance twenty years or so from now, depending on the rotations. And it would stop taking emergency repairs at least two years before closure.

Closure itself would take every moment of those two years. It would be better, the administrators said, if the base had five years to shut down operations. Everything had to be done perfectly, and no one wanted to leave some Fleet ship stranded, too far from Sector Base F-2 to have its *anacapa* drive make easy contact with the base's drive.

In theory, a Fleet ship could contact *any* existing sector base, anywhere, so long as the Fleet ship was in foldspace. In practice, the contacts became difficult once a ship moved several sectors away from a base.

The Fleet learned, over the years, to move the bases, along with the ships, mostly as a precaution.

Rajivk believed in precautions when it came to space. He was raised on Fleet ships, born in motion, as they liked to say, and he had chosen to stay at Sector Base E-2 even though everyone knew it would be the next base closed. The Fleet kept only three sector bases open at one time—at least for ship repairs. In addition, there was always one base (sometimes two) under construction at the far end of the Fleet's trajectory, and there was often (although not always) one base in the process of shutting down at the back of the trajectory.

Rajivk wasn't even born when Sector Base D-2 had shut down. As long as he had been alive, Sector Base E-2 was slated to close. The only difference today brought was an actual date—and that date was so far in the future, a good third of the crew would already be retired.

He ran a hand through his hair. The spray from the Falls had beaded on it. The sunshine and the warm(ish) mid-fall weather had kept him from noticing the growing damp. The spray wasn't really spray today, more like a fine mist. It smelled faintly of sulphur—the entire Falls did sometimes—and fresh air with just a hint of the decay that signaled mid-fall was nearly over.

Seasons changed. They moved forward, just like the Fleet did. The change of seasons was as reliable as the fact that the Fleet would eventually leave a sector. At some point, the Fleet would be gone forever. And then it would become a memory, at least in this part of this galaxy. Then it would become a rumor or a legend or a myth—or, as some said, forgotten completely.

Although the Fleet would leave, much of its tech would remain on this little corner of Ynchinga, and eventually, the people who lived here in the Sandoveil Valley would remember that some group had initially colonized this area, but they wouldn't remember who.

The rainbow was slowly disappearing. The sun was moving along the horizon. He needed to move too if he wanted to get home before dark.

But first, he walked over to the shoes. He had to investigate them. They bothered him. Anything out of the ordinary bothered him up here.

Annoyingly, his boots stuck to the path. The black nanobits weren't wet enough to make the first level of the boots' tech effective, but they were wet enough to activate that first level.

Another reason he rarely walked to this overlook.

His heart started pounding as he approached the shoes. He observed his own reaction as if he were outside himself. Sometimes the proximity to the Falls made his heart race. The roar of the water, the damp and cold air, the constant and hard vibration all around him sometimes grabbed control of his limbic system.

Rajivk wasn't sure if his increased heart rate was because of the Falls or because of the shoes. He couldn't see the shoes' owners anywhere. Leaving two pair of shoes behind, deliberately, was either symbolic or really stupid.

Apparently, part of him was worried that he was dealing with really stupid. Had two people taken off their shoes, climbed onto the smooth wall to see the water better, and fallen?

If so, he might find them on the other side of the wall, unable to get purchase to climb back up it. He knew of some kids who had fallen off this part of the overlook, but they were local kids. They knew that they couldn't climb back up. They threaded their way along the pointed rocks, moving slowly, and making sure of every step until they made it to the other side of the overlook, and crawled the last few feet to the path itself.

Of course, they had the proper shoes, and they had even brought hiking gear, so they had the right kind of gloves and rope and all kinds of tech that enabled them to survive the most treacherous part of their fall.

And none of them had been hurt.

His mouth was dry. He had been breathing through it, nervously. He didn't want to find someone on the other side, clinging to those rocks.

He braced his hands on the cool wall. Water had beaded on the top. He actually dislodged puddles that he hadn't been able to see. He wondered if this part of the wall was ever dry.

He leaned forward. He would have shouted, but it would have been impossible to hear his voice over the thunder of the Falls. He looked down, saw slick wet rocks the color of slate. Tiny runnels of water threaded down the sides of the rocks, as if creating their own miniature waterfalls.

He hadn't expected it to be so wet and violent on that side of the wall. He had known about the kids, had thought that they had landed on a dry patch, but of course they hadn't.

There was no dry patch on that side of the wall. Technically, there was no dry patch on this side of the wall.

Clearly luck—and fantastic equipment—had allowed those kids to grip the rocks at all. Sheer determination that enabled them to crawl away from the water. And even more luck that got them past the overlook, to the drier rocks on the side, before they finally reached the path he had walked up.

Whoever owned the shoes on the overlook beside him hadn't had the proper equipment. Shoes were good on the path, but to handle the wet side of the Falls would require full-fledged boots, maybe some kind of suit, and climbing gear.

Maybe the shoes owners' had removed the shoes and put on boots. But he saw no evidence of that.

And why would someone do it? There were people who tried to best the Falls, and some who succeeded, but that took more than good boots and a willingness to step into a wall of water, free-falling at the rate of thousands of cubic feet per second. Rajivk had never wanted to try. It seemed like certain death to him.

Rajivk wiped the water from his face. He couldn't even see into that wall of water. He didn't understand the attraction.

He glanced at those shoes, so neatly lined up, and felt a surge of anger. Maybe someone had left them to taunt him. Maybe they were supposed to signify something he didn't understand.

Whatever the reason, he hadn't asked to be the one to find them. He hadn't asked to worry about them.

And, he finally decided, the shoes were not his concern.

He backed away from them, and then when he reached the path—and only then—did he shake the water off his shirt and pants. If he had known he was going to get that close to the Falls, he would have worn his outdoor gear.

But he'd been thinking about the sector base's end date, the fact that he could envision his choices again—if he wanted to take them. He could stay here for the rest of his life, knowing he would retire in thirty years whether he wanted to or not. Or he could apply to work at one of the other sector bases. Or he could stay here, find some other job, and move even farther away from the Fleet.

Those thoughts were why he had chosen this upper path. Because he knew, deep down, that if he wanted to continue his career into the future, he would have to move.

He would have to leave the Falls.

And he couldn't imagine leaving the Falls.

Just like he couldn't imagine climbing into them.

He sighed.

He would have to do something about those shoes, and unfortunately, he would have to do it soon.

2

A DOOR SLAMMED TO HER RIGHT. Bristol Iannazzi raised her head from the diagnostics screen. She had been deep in the repair of an *anacapa* drive, the kind that required firm concentration or she would send the entire room into foldspace. Or something worse. She didn't like to imagine worst-case scenarios, not when it came to *anacapa* drives.

She stood in the middle of her lab, a deeply secure room in Sector Base E-2 on Nindowne. The base was miles beneath the surface near the city of Sandoveil. She'd been thinking about their location all day, weirdly enough, even though she shouldn't have been.

She probably shouldn't have been working on the drive, either, not after the morning's meeting. The entire staff of the sector base had to show up at the beginning of the morning shift—even third-shift workers who really wanted to go home and get some sleep.

They met in the amphitheater on the ground level, a space rarely used. It had smelled musty, which she had deemed appropriate once the administrators had made the announcement.

Sector Base E-2 would be closing thirty years from now. The date was set. By that day, all functions of the base would cease. The new base, Sector Base G-2, would have been running at full capacity for five years by then, and would take over Sector Base E-2's place in the rotation.

All the work that they had to do, all of it, from this moment forward, would be with the closure in mind.

She had known the closure was coming. Everyone did. They were informed in their yearly job review, and reminded that they could request a transfer to Sector Bases F-2 or G-2 at any point, and that transfer would most likely be approved.

The problem was that this base had existed for more than three hundred years, and entire families had built their lives around it. Iannazzis had worked at Sector Base E-2 for five generations, with a sixth in training. Bristol's daughter had just gotten a job here last year, and her granddaughter—all of ten—talked of nothing more than working in the base.

Which was closing.

The other two active bases weren't even in this sector. They were light years from here, in wildly dissimilar places, chosen by some Fleet engineers to meet some standard that Bristol didn't care about.

She, at least, had imagined life off Nindowne, but so many who worked here couldn't conceive of it. She had warned her daughter about the upcoming changes, and her daughter had scoffed.

Mom, they've been saying the base would close for years. It's not going to happen in our lifetime.

Well, it was now.

Bristol ran a hand through her short-cropped hair and set down the tiny screwdriver she'd been using. The light at the tip shut off as she set it down. She closed the casing around the *anacapa* drive, then put the drive in a specially built storage unit, to protect herself and the room.

She really wasn't concentrating enough to work on the *anacapa*. If she kept thinking about the base closure instead of the delicate work she'd been doing, she truly would be a danger to herself and others.

Her lab was one of two dozen such secure labs, built under layers and layers of rock, deep in the Payyer Mountain range. The walls were smooth and black, constructed by the same nanobits that made the spaceships used by the Fleet.

In theory, the thick black walls would hold in any explosion and protect the mountains themselves from catastrophe. Such theories had been tested in other sector bases, not this one, and Bristol was deeply aware that each sector base was different.

There had never been a catastrophic accident at Sector Base E-2, and if their luck held for another thirty years, there would never be one.

The room had no windows, although some of the walls had clear screens over their surface. The screens would activate if someone outside the room wanted her to see something important or if one of the major and unexpected DV-class ships arrived into the sector base. At that point, the ship's *anacapa* drive and the base's *anacapa* drive would activate at least one screen in every room on the base, so that the crew was notified of the ship's arrival.

Walk through the wrong area when a ship arrived, and you could die, horribly.

The screens rarely activated, though. She preferred to use the holographic screens on her equipment or little screens she could attach to her work area. There were shelves everywhere, and more tools than almost any other workroom.

Bristol liked using the best tool for the job, and sometimes the best tool was obscure.

Since she was one of the most experienced *anacapa* engineers in Sector Base E-2, she felt safest working alone. Besides, if she ended up making a mistake—and everyone did, no matter how good they were—then she wanted to make sure the only person who died in the blast was her, and not anyone else.

Which was why the sound of a door slamming bothered her. The door to her right wasn't an exterior door. It was a blast door, separating this room from the ship storage area. She wasn't working on a DV-class ship. She was working on an FS-Prime runabout from the *Ijo*, which had arrived for its five-year upgrade one week ago.

She had graduated from DV-class ships, under direct supervision, to handling the smaller vessels connected with the ships years ago. But she hadn't worked on anything like the runabout before.

It was an older technology, one that the Fleet now recommended be retired. Captains of the DV-class ships didn't have to listen to recommendations, however. They could maintain older equipment as long as they felt it useful.

She hated the runabout. The FS-Prime designation referred to foldspace. The geniuses in ship design way back when hadn't wanted to call these runabouts *Anacapa* models, so they hid it with the FS designation.

This model was the only runabout model with an *anacapa* drive. For most of its history, the Fleet did not put *anacapa* drives in ships smaller than a DV-class vessel. Then, those geniuses, working before she was born, decided to test runabouts with *anacapa* drives. Early in her career, those drives had been the bane of her existence.

But she, and several other engineers, had convinced most captains in the Fleet to retire their FS-Prime runabouts. Only a handful of captains had held out, including Captain Harriet Virji of the *Ijo*.

No surprise that this ancient runabout was malfunctioning. The problem was, of course, the *anacapa*, which was smaller than the average *anacapa* drive. The small size was also a hindrance, because it carried a lot of power, but didn't have some of the redundant controls.

Anacapa drives sent ships into foldspace. If the drive was used properly, it would send a ship into foldspace for a short period of time, and then the ship would return to the same coordinates in regular space. Ships could also use foldspace to travel across sectors, using beacons that the Fleet had set up in various sectors.

Sector Base E-2 had *anacapa* beacons, and could pull ships in trouble from anywhere in three nearby sectors—and maybe even farther away than that. No one had really tested the reach of the beacons.

But everyone knew of stories in which beacons malfunctioned at long distances. That was one of the reasons the base was going to close.

The Fleet had moved beyond this section of space, heading forward as it always did. In theory, by the time that Sector Base E-2 closed, there would be no more Fleet vessels within easy activation range. They would be better served by other sector bases, and that travel through foldspace would be safer.

She was always cautious when she spoke about foldspace. Not only had she never traveled in it, she didn't entirely understand it. No one in the Fleet did, and that made everyone who worked on the *anacapa* drives nervous.

Some of the captains believed that foldspace was a different part of the universe. They believed the *anacapa* drive actually folded space, allowed the ship to travel across that fold, and end up elsewhere. They cited the fact that the star maps were drastically different in foldspace, so different that they were completely unrecognizable.

But the theorists who studied foldspace believed that foldspace itself might be another dimension, something they didn't entirely understand. Some other theorists believed the foldspace was a different point in time—some*when* else, not some*where* else.

And a few of the theorists believed that the *anacapa* sent the ship into an alternate reality, and then, somehow—magically, Bristol thought—brought the ship back again.

She didn't even have a guess. She had been trained on the *anacapa* drives, so she understood what the interior of a drive should look like. She understood how to test it in the lab to make sure the drive was functioning properly.

But if she or her family were to ever be invited to travel via *anacapa* drive, she would respectfully refuse. She didn't like the fact that the drive could send her somewhere else, in a way that no one entirely understood. She knew, because she studied it, that ships got lost in foldspace all the time, and that terrified her even more.

The fact that she wouldn't go through foldspace was one of many reasons why she would never work at another sector base. To get to those bases, she would have to take a DV-class ship that traveled through foldspace. She would have to experience a working *anacapa* drive from the inside of a ship.

She wasn't willing to do that, which was rather hard to explain, since she worked on *anacapa* drives every day.

She sighed softly. Maybe she hadn't heard the door. Maybe she had misinterpreted another sound.

Or maybe she had been so deep in her work that she hadn't noticed someone else walking through her workspace.

That idea made her shudder.

She waved on one of the larger screens. She recorded her work from three angles. She recorded it from above, taking in the entire room, so she could see if she took the wrong tool for a particular job. She recorded it from the top of the *anacapa* drive so she could see what her fingers were actually doing. And she recorded it from the tools themselves, making a record of her every move.

The caution had saved her from catastrophic mistakes more than she liked to think about. Sometimes, viewing her work on the three separate recordings at the beginning of the following day made her revisit what she had already done. If she had started up from where she had left off, she would have probably destroyed the device or blown herself up.

Or blown herself—and the room, and part of the base—into some part of foldspace. Somehow. Somewhere. Or some*when*.

The idea compounded her off-kilter feeling. She had been this way all day. It was unusual enough to have an all-base meeting; the fact that it had started at the beginning of her workday had thrown off her routines, making her feel behind from the moment she set foot into the room.

Alone.

"Overview of the entire room, please," she said to the screen. She had set the voice command to respond to her voice only. Anyone else would have to use the access panel beneath the screen. But she liked accessing her work from here. "Show me the last hour at the usual pace."

The usual pace was a pretty fast scan. Her eye was good: she could see mistakes in her work at speeds where most people saw a blur. It felt intuitive when she worked like that, even though she knew it wasn't. She processed things quickly; she just couldn't always articulate what she saw.

This time, though, nothing caught her attention—until she thought she saw a movement at the door to the right.

She noted the time stamp, and let the replay continue all the way to the current moment. She saw nothing else unusual.

"Replay at one-half the usual speed," she said, and then gave a time stamp for the start five minutes before the stamp that she noted.

She watched again, and sure enough, the door to the right bowed open slightly, and then banged shut.

"Normal speed from the same point," she said. "With sound."

She usually had the sound off because she had learned, years ago, that when she concentrated deeply, she either hummed a tune or she talked to herself. She found neither trait attractive. In fact, she found them massively annoying.

But she wasn't going to look or listen to herself this time. She was going to watch, in real time.

She moved the holoscreen kitty-corner so that she could watch the door in real time while watching the replay. The fact that she moved the screen made her realize that she was deeply unnerved. She hadn't allowed herself to feel that before.

She turned down the sound on the replay. The door opened silently. And she heard nothing except the room noise, not even a hum from her, until the door slammed closed.

The sound, turned low, still made her jump. Her pulse pounded, and her mouth was suddenly dry.

She had a couple of choices. She could leave the room, then report this. Or she could continue to work as if nothing happened. She could check out the room herself. Or she could ask for security.

Only she didn't dare ask for security out loud. She would have to do it on some kind of private setting, on a screen.

She had never done that before. But she knew she couldn't work in here any longer. Even if she wanted to concentrate, she couldn't—not with enough focus to work on an *anacapa* drive.

If she left, then whoever it was (*what*ever it was) could escape.

If she stayed, then she might be in danger, although she wasn't sure what kind of danger.

Although she didn't want to think about what could be behind that door, something not human that had forced it open.

Because the runabout had a feature she hated: to remove and check the old *anacapa* drive, she had to replace it with a different *anacapa* drive. The runabout couldn't even sit idle without one. It would begin its emergency procedures alerts without a drive.

That was one reason the FS-Prime class of runabouts was no longer being made. They were delicate in a strange and unusual way, mostly about their equipment. And ships in space couldn't be delicate in any way.

Her skin crawled. What if the *anacapa* she had placed inside the runabout as a temporary measure was causing some kind of problem? What if what was going on in that room had no human agent at all?

Her heart beat even harder.

If that were the case, she needed to leave.

But she couldn't think of anything an *anacapa* could do that would cause a door to open and slam shut like that.

Except activate.

She backed away from the blast door. Then she went to one of the platforms, and stared at the controls for a moment. She could hit the emergency beacon, but that might start an alarm, warning everyone to leave the area.

And if an *anacapa* had been deployed, that would be important.

But she didn't know, and she didn't want to investigate on her own.

Because if someone were in that room with the runabout, then she had just given that person warning.

And who knew what that person would do to her?

She certainly didn't.

She keyed in a request for an immediate security presence, saying she couldn't tell anyone the nature of the emergency.

And, with a last-minute thought, she also asked for the security detail to arrive in environmental suits.

Then she signed off, and grabbed her suit from the container she kept it in. The suit looked dusty and a tad too small.

But she was going to squeeze into it.

She *had* to squeeze into it.

Because she had no idea what was behind that door.

3

Rajivk decided to contact Ynchinga Search & Rescue for the Sandoveil Region when he got home. Shoes, he thought as he made his way up the side of the mountain, were not a time-sensitive emergency. Let the YSR-SR determine what to do next.

Besides, he knew how the YSR-SR felt about errant clothing. He sometimes volunteered with the YSR-SR, and abandoned clothing runs, without any missing person reports, were usually annoying, not decisive.

He wasn't working with the YSR-SR at the moment, but he might work with them again, and he didn't want to upset anyone. So he'd tell them, and they might send someone out in the morning.

His strides had increased because his adrenaline was up. It didn't take as long as usual to reach the wall at the edge of the upper trail.

At the moment, the wall looked like a silly precaution, something an overzealous city official had placed in position to protect tourists from themselves. In mid-spring, when the snowmelt was mixing with the rain, the water often covered the rocks that blocked his view now, and made the wall at the edge of the upper trail seem like inadequate protection.

He always looked at the wall as an indication that he was nearly halfway done with this particular walk. This time, though, he felt a thread of disappointment. He really hadn't paid much attention to the austere beauty around him.

He had been thinking about the damn shoes. They irritated him. The fact that he had gone onto that overlook irritated him, the fact that he had to investigate the shoes irritated him, the fact that people had left them behind, probably for just that reason, irritated him.

Of course, he probably wasn't really irritated at any of those things as much as he was irritated at the overreaction of his colleagues to the morning's news.

All day, they had been acting like someone had died, as if their entire world had been destroyed. Apparently, they had believed—despite all evidence to the contrary—that Sector Base E-2 would never close, that they would have their jobs forever.

The thing that irritated him the most? Half of his colleagues hated their jobs. They always said they would work elsewhere if there were an elsewhere to work. The sector base enabled them to live in this beautiful place, and the base would continue to enable them to live in this beautiful place, with retirement packages and guaranteed income for life.

Not the income they had now, but a goodly portion of it. And they didn't have to work for it. The base took care of their own.

Or they could move. That option had been presented just that morning. The staff of Sector Base E-2 could move at any point, now that the end date for the base had been set. All anyone had to do was talk to their direct supervisor. They might not be able to move immediately, but they could set up a move date, when their job became less necessary to the base.

In fact, the administrators had said that morning that they would love it if half the staff left sooner rather than later. The best thing that could happen to Sector Base E-2 was that half of its staff would leave and be replaced by younger, newer workers. Those workers would be trained by the remaining staff of the oldest sector base in the Fleet's system, and then those workers would be sent to Sector Base G-2.

Rajivk had to admit he didn't like that part of the plan because he would be one of the people training the newcomers. But he accepted that as the price of remaining in the most beautiful place he had ever seen in his little corner of the universe.

He was slightly out of breath as he crested the top of the path. This part of the mountain was deceptive. It looked like an actual mountaintop, but the mountain itself actually continued upward almost two miles away. This plateau was two miles by five miles, flat as the ground in the Sandoveil Valley, except in the very center, where the waters of the Jeleen River flowed into Fiskett Falls.

At this time of year, the Jeleen River was slow moving. There was no snowmelt and the worst of the rains hadn't started yet. From this vantage, at the very crest of the plateau, the river mirrored Rockwell Pool below.

From mid-summer through now was the time of year that rescuers dreaded the most. It was the time of year when tourists would take off their shoes and wade in the river, the time of year when some gung-ho young adult would think he could swim across the river to the other side, the time of year when idiot parents let their kids splash along the shoreline.

Signs hovered everywhere, ruining the vista, warning people away from the water. But people never listened.

Every year, when the Sandoveil Council went over the budget and saw the cost overruns for saving idiots (or pulling their bodies out of the water), they talked about spending the money early and setting up actual barriers, preventing anyone from ever stepping in the water again.

The council talked about all kinds of barriers, from invisible barriers made of some kind of force field, to visible barriers made of modified nanobits that would turn dark as someone got too close, to a good, old-fashioned spiked fence that would injure anyone who tried to climb over it.

Every year, those proposals got voted down—and every year, Rajivk was relieved. He liked the view just the way it was.

This afternoon, the sun hit the river water just perfectly, turning the top layer golden. The current was barely visible, working its way around the rocks. To most people, the river looked placid at its low point.

To Rajivk, the river simply revealed its teeth—all those pointed rocks, all those eddies, all that treachery that usually hid beneath crystalline waves.

He walked to his favorite overlook. Tourists rarely used this one, even though it jutted over the Falls. You couldn't tell that from the path, though. It looked like an overlook that had a view of the Sandoveil Valley or maybe just the gray-blue sky.

But one visit to the overlook would change anyone's opinion. It had the best views in the entire area.

Rajivk smiled in anticipation. As he got closer, he watched the view come into focus. The view went from gray-blue sky to the sparkling water tumbling over the the edge. Sometimes the spray here was as thick as the spray at the overlook where he saw the shoes, but not at this time of year.

At this time of year, the volume going over the Falls was down by two-thirds from its seasonal peak in mid-spring. The water almost looked as unthreatening as water pouring out of a large tap.

But he knew better. Fortunately, the engineers who had built this overlook made it impossible to lean over the edge and dip a hand in the water. That much force—especially in mid-spring—could pull a person into the raging torrent without even much of a blink.

When he stood with his shoulders squared and looked directly forward, he could see the entire Sandoveil Valley spread before him. The valley seemed to extend forever, with houses and businesses growing like weeds. In the center of the valley was the city of Sandoveil itself, formed on a grid pattern, like most Fleet-built cities. The city, with its red, gold, and blue buildings and perfectly positioned green spaces, provided lots of color. But beyond the main part of the city itself was another set of mud flats. They had very few pools. The land burped mud, making gigantic mud bubbles that looked like tents in their own right.

And, just beyond that, a hint of the gray ocean, twinkling at its own jokes.

The waters of Rockwell Pool siphoned off in the spring to create their own stream (called, unoriginally, Rockwell Stream). But some of the water flowed to a much smaller, less impressive underground waterfall, which fed the springs that provided the city water.

Those springs—and their annual growth as the snowmelt covered everything—were the reason why Sector Base E-2 never got built underneath Sandoveil, the way that many sector bases were built under their cities.

Rajivk preferred the distance. He liked to think of the city as separate from the base. The city would become even more separate from the base in the upcoming years.

He approved of that, just as he reveled in this view of his favorite corner of this world.

He stepped up to the wall separating him from the Falls. Usually he kept staring forward, but on this day, he braced his hands on the wall's cool surface.

If he pushed his body up just enough to gain an extra foot or two, he could see the part of Rockwell Pool at the base of the waterfall. There was a smaller section of the pool there, a place where the water gathered, a place that seemed deceptively calm.

It was deep and it was dangerous and fortunately, it was inaccessible from any of the paths and lookouts.

But it was the one place that a reckless person who jumped from here, or the overlook below, might actually end up.

He leaned a little forward, felt his heart trip-hammer harder than it had in years. He hadn't told anyone he was coming up here. If he unbalanced, he would fall forward, and if he fell forward, he would die.

He tried not to think about that. Instead, he looked down.

The water fell in a stunningly organized fashion, only a few drops venturing away from the large gush of water. The sun had moved, so this side of the Falls did not have any more sunlight rainbows.

The water fell into the pool below, churning the water.

Except in the side pool. He didn't see anything there, thank goodness. He lowered himself, and let out a small breath.

Then he frowned as something registered on his brain. He *had* seen something. A bit of light brown.

There shouldn't have been any brown at all. The rocks were almost black from the constant wet. The water was frothy white, gray, and blue, and the pool itself a blackish-green.

There were no visible rocks in that part of the pool, nothing that would—that could—be brown.

He had imagined it.

He turned away, then caught himself.

At this time of year, there was a very slight chance that someone who stupidly (or accidentally) went into the Falls had survived. There was also a chance that all he saw was another shoe.

But he had to look.

He placed his hands on the top of the wall again, and levered himself up slightly. The water seemed to flow even faster, taunting him. His heart beat harder than it had before.

For some reason, looking the second time felt a lot more dangerous than the first. Maybe because he was going to focus more on what was in that second pool than on his own safety.

He coudln't really do both.

He leaned forward slightly, being very careful of his balance. His lower arms trembled underneath his weight.

The water churned and splashed, filling the side pool with eddys. He thought he saw more brown, and something else—yellow?

He needed to lean farther forward, but he wasn't sure he dared. If he were younger, or maybe if he wore the right gear, he would sit on top of the wall, but he didn't dare do that. Not alone.

And he wasn't sure he should lower himself down, then raise himself up, trying this again. So he only had this one look—for as long as his arms could hold him.

The trembling had moved into his elbows. He could actually feel his muscles burning. He walked everywhere, but he never did much with his arms. They weren't very strong.

He saw brown tendrils, canary-yellow something—soggy, like fabric.

Maybe whoever took off their shoes had tossed their clothing into the waterfall.

Maybe it had been some kind of ritual.

He could only hope.

And then an unmistakeable foot floated out of the water, attached to a leg wearing bright red pants. The foot floated toward the middle of the side pool, followed by a full torso (in yellow) and a bare arm. The brown tendrils were hair. The side of a face turned toward him as the body spun, revealing the remaining limbs.

A face. Buried in the water. Clearly not breathing. From here, it looked like the person was dead. He couldn't see any aparatus for breathing, not even those thin clear hoods that someone had designed for planetside environmental suits.

He couldn't see any protection at all.

And the feet were bare.

That really bothered him, given the shoes on the lower overlook. Who would do that? And why? Had they sat on the edge of the wall, dipping their feet into the waterfall? Had there been some other reason?

Was there someone else in the water?

His right arm bent involuntarily, and his hips hit the wall, sending a burst of pain through him.

He slid back down the side, then stood in the overlook, his heart pounding.

Someone had clearly died. A barefoot someone had died. And Rajivk had found two pairs of shoes.

He didn't like the implications. He didn't like them at all.

4

Security arrived five minutes later. Two men and two women, all of whom barely fit into the lab along with Bristol Iannazzi's equipment, the screens, and the boxed *anacapa* drive she had been working on.

At least this team knew how to maneuver in one of the labs. The team came in one at a time, each moving in a different direction, watching where they stepped so they could avoid any tools on the floor or open pieces of something she had been working on.

An experienced team, then.

Good. That meant whoever had received Bristol's message had taken her seriously.

She felt squeezed in her own environmental suit. Clearly, she hadn't put it on in months, maybe a couple of years, and she had gained weight in that time. The suits were designed to compensate for about twenty pounds, and apparently, she was just on the outside edge of that.

After she put it on, a recommendation did flash across her eyes, requesting that she purchase a larger suit. She told the suit to fuck off before she established working communications links.

The four security team members had the latest environmental suits. The security teams—both on the base and in the city of Sandoveil—had the best equipment. They were constantly updating everything, as they should.

The entire community relied on them.

This team wore clear hoods, so she could see their faces. She recognized all four of them, but in that casual *we-work-in-the-same-building* way. She didn't know their names.

She gave them the hand signal that everyone at the base had learned for *let's sent up a private communications link*. She had never set up one of those links, however, so she hoped one of them would do it.

She bit her lower lip, visibly, and made herself look like she was pleading with everyone. Maybe they would get the message without her having to resort to a real comm link.

Then a man said in her ear, "Okay. Can you hear me? I'm setting up a private comm band for the five of us."

"I hear you," she said. The hood of her environmental suit was so tight that it moved when she spoke.

Everyone stared at it, and she flushed.

"Sign in," he said to the rest of the team.

"DuBerry," said the tall woman near the door, her gaze on Bristol.

"Fitzwilliam," said the shorter man standing next to her.

"Tranh," said the muscular woman on the other side of the door.

"Wèi," said the man to her left, clearly the one who had started this all. "You're Bristol Iannazzi, right?"

He mispronounced her last name, but she didn't care. She nodded. Then when that was greeted with silence she said, "Yes."

"Good. Brief us."

She did. She had taken the security training every year since she started at the base, and she knew the essentials: tell the team what happened succinctly. Make sure to include what seemed threatening, unusual, or out of place, because they often did not have the scientific training that the people calling them did.

Bristol told them about the slamming blast door, which made Wèi lean his head back in surprise. And she thought about it for a moment, a chill running through her.

That door was too heavy to slam. It was also designed to ease closed slowly. No one wanted a door that heavy to hit them with that kind of force.

She should have thought of that, and she hadn't.

"Can you open the door manually?" Wèi asked.

"Yes," she said. "Would you like me to?"

"Not yet," he said. "Show me the recording."

She had the recording cued up. She showed it to all four of them, on one of the regular wall screens, not the holographic screen. They all watched without moving.

"It looks like the door was blown open," Tranh said. "Is that possible?"

"I've never seen it," Bristol said. "But with enough force, anything is possible."

They all remained in place, staring at each other. Apparently that idea unnerved them as much as it unnerved her.

"I can open the door," she said, even though the very thought of it made her heart pound even harder. "I know what I'm looking for."

"No," Wèi said. "We'll do it."

The woman, Tranh, shifted beside him.

He shook his head slightly. Then he corrected himself. "*I'll* do it." As if he didn't want to upset anyone on the team.

But wasn't that what the team was here for? Bristol didn't know. She didn't like working with a team, which was one reason why she had been so glad to get her promotion all those years ago.

"We'll do it," DuBerry said, and moved toward the door.

Bristol rubbed her hands together. The gloves pulled against each other, and she remembered why she hated wearing them. Why she hated wearing the suit in the first place.

"I-I…um, I should go with you," she said.

"You should wait right here," Fitzwilliam said as he passed her. "If there's a hostile in that room, we should deal with it."

"If there's a 'hostile' in that room," Bristol said, "wouldn't they have harmed me already?"

"People are most dangerous when they're cornered," DuBerry said, and flashed a smile at Bristol. Bristol thought the smile was weirdly inappropriate.

Tranh was the last person to walk past Bristol. The security team waited by the door.

"Do you need a code to get in?" Wèi asked. "I'd rather not override."

Overriding any of the door commands sometimes set off alarms too.

"Yeah, you do, sorry," Bristol said. "I can open the door from here. You want me to?"

"On my mark," Wèi said. He looked at his team. "Ready?"

They must have given him some kind of response because it only took a second before he said,

"Okay, Ms. Iannazzi. Here we go. Mark."

She swallowed hard and hit the command that opened the door. It remained motionless, which it wasn't supposed to do. It was supposed to open slowly, just in case someone might be standing nearby.

Then the door opened, but the movement was jerky, as if the mechanism were damaged.

The team stood to one side. They seemed to expect someone to rush out of the room or shoot at them or something.

She was standing in the same spot she'd stood in all along, which put her directly across from the door. She felt a sudden, violent anger that they hadn't warned her that she might be in danger standing there.

But she didn't move and she didn't act on it. Instead, she watched them.

Wèi went in first, followed by Fitzwilliam and DuBerry. Tranh remained outside. Bristol wondered if they had a private comm link as well, or if they were just following standard procedure.

She had a hunch it was both, in case they needed to discuss her.

She couldn't hear anything on the group comm link, and that worried her. She shifted slightly, so that she could see the area near the door more clearly, but she couldn't see anything behind the door.

Her heart was pounding harder than she'd ever felt it pound. It made her entire chest cavity vibrate. Her suit issued a warning and a question. *You're having an adrenaline spike. Would you like something to calm you?*

No, she sent back, then wondered if she should have made the decision so quickly.

It was normal to be alarmed, she knew that. She also knew that she had set up her suit to keep her calm. She was an engineer, and she didn't dare have an adrenaline spike when she was working on something as touchy as an *anacapa* drive. Her hands might shake or she might knock something loose.

Over the years, she had cultivated calmness. She needed calmness more than she needed the reliability of a fight-or-flight reaction. So this reaction bothered her.

She stared at that open door, at the lights, which had come up, and at part of the bare black floor beneath. Shouldn't she be seeing more? Shouldn't she be hearing from the team?

Shouldn't she be doing *something*?

"Ms. Iannazzi?" said Wèi's voice through the comm link. "Will you join us, please?"

She let out a breath—or tried to. She apparently hadn't been breathing much so she didn't have a lot to release.

She nodded her head before giving verbal consent, even though he couldn't see her.

Damn. If something had gone wrong with any of the tech in the room, she could have handled it calmly. But the idea of walking into the storage room, with the security team inside, made her palms sweat.

She wanted to ask him if it was safe. She wanted to ask him if he was all right. She wanted to ask him if the team was requesting her presence of their own free will.

But she knew (she hoped) she was making things up.

She said, "Yes."

That single word sounded choppy, revealing her nervousness. Her cheeks grew even warmer. She wasn't sure why she was embarrassed that she was frightened, but she was.

Apparently, she had imagined herself differently than this.

She walked across the workroom. The walk took longer than it ever had before, and yet it happened instantly. She wasn't sure how she had a dual perception of time like that, but she did.

She reached the door, her heart pounding so hard that she could feel it in her throat, her mouth, her ears. She half expected the suit to chastise her again, but it remained silent.

Apparently, the offer of calmness was a one-time thing.

First she looked at the blast door itself. It seemed bowed in the middle, just a little. She glanced at the edges and tried to remember: had it seemed off-plumb when she had been staring at it earlier?

Not that it mattered. She wasn't here to examine the door—yet, anyway.

She didn't cross the threshold. Instead, she leaned forward slightly and peered inside.

The storage room was larger than her main workspace. Small ships had to fit inside, and they often did.

There were fewer wall screens here, and no place to store an *anacapa* drive. If she wanted to do the delicate work, she did it in the main part of her lab.

However, the storage room usually looked cramped to her. It always had a ship that barely fit lengthwise or was almost too tall. Even the smallest of ships made it difficult to maneuver around them.

So when she saw the room, and registered how large it was, she frowned for a half a moment. The security team members stood on the edge of the lowered work platform. They formed a rectangle, whether they knew it or not.

And they were all looking at her.

"I thought you said there was a ship in here," Wèi said.

"Yeah," she said softly. "There was."

5

MARNIE SAR ARRIVED AT THE OVERLOOK ahead of her team. The Falls roared and threatened, like they always did, the water cascading over the edge down to its lowest volume of the year. Even that amount, though, seemed like more water than she would ever have thought possible.

She wasn't fond of the Falls. She'd seen too many people die here.

She had been on her way home, shift over. She did one weekly stint at the headquarters of Ynchinga Search & Rescue—Sandoveil Region. One weekly stint was required of anyone who had more than five years' experience with YSR-SR. Usually the stints were quiet, especially if they were in the middle of the night.

She had so much seniority, though, that her shifts were never in the middle of the night. She had her choice of days and times, and she always chose midweek because the tourists always arrived toward the end of the week and stayed for a few days.

She didn't like her shift to be completely quiet because she preferred to rescue locals. They at least had an idea that they were in trouble or they had done something stupid.

Tourists usually expected rescue and never apologized for the inane things they had done to get themselves in trouble.

She hiked up to the top overlook, gear on her shoulder. Rajivk Agwu leaned against the stone wall, arms crossed. He was not a tall man, but he was strong, particularly considering he was space-born. He had been part of YSR-SR off and on for years.

Right now, he was off, but he had followed procedure. He had contacted them, said he saw a body in Rockwell Pool, a body that was only visible from above, and that he would wait until YSR-SR arrived.

He had clearly known that he might wait longer than that: Sometimes witnesses had to go through a lot of hoops before they were allowed to leave.

His clothes were wrinkled and clung oddly to his skin, as if they had gotten wet. His hair was a mess as well, parts of it clumped together. He stood up when he saw her.

"Marnie," he said.

"Rajivk," she said. "Gotta tell you I'm recording."

She was, too, using two different pieces of equipment. The YSR-SR had learned long ago to make recordings of every call, just in case tourists sued or someone—even an YSR-SR member—died. Recordings didn't always settle the liability issues, but recordings could provide answers when, in the past, there had been none.

"I know," Rajivk said, as if he expected nothing less. He swept a hand toward the walls that jutted out over the water. "It's a two-part scene. There are shoes on the lower overlook."

She frowned. "That's what the dispatch said. Why are shoes important?"

"Because your body is barefoot," he said.

She sighed. Some dumb tourist, then, doing some dumb tourist thing.

"But that's not the curious part," he said. "At least for me."

Marnie made herself focus on him. She remembered him being a good volunteer, conscientious and hard-working. He wasn't the most fit member of the group, but he had always been willing to do what he was told.

"The curious part," he said, "is that there is more than one pair of shoes."

"So there's two bodies down there?" Marnie asked.

"I only saw one," he said.

Her gaze met his. He looked both sad and concerned at the same time. She understood: Either two people had died or someone was missing.

Either way, the YSR-SR would have to assume that one person was missing until they learned otherwise.

"How long has the body been there?" she asked.

"I don't know," he said. "I walked the lower trail on my way to work this morning. I haven't been on the upper trail for the past couple of days."

"What made you do it today?" she asked, although she could have guessed. The weather was lovely, and everyone knew that great weather would be disappearing in the next few weeks. It was as if the citizens of Sandoveil were batteries: They stored up the great-weather energy from the late-spring to mid-fall so that they could survive the travails of the winter.

"The announcement at the sector base," he said.

It took her a moment to parse the answer. She had been so expecting him to talk about the weather that what he actually said took her by surprise.

"You heard, right?" he asked.

She had heard. Her daughter had contacted her during lunch, needing to talk. Her daughter, all of thirty, was acting like the loss of Sector Base E-2 was the end of the world—as if she hadn't had warning that the base would shut down eventually.

"I heard," Marnie said. She had to ask, even though she didn't want to. "You upset about that?"

He shrugged. "I took a longer walk to think about it," he said. "But I wouldn't characterize myself as upset. The reactions, they bothered me."

"Reactions?" she asked.

"Other people's. They seemed strange." He shrugged again. "Although none of it is important when you get down to it. I mean, someone is dead."

Marnie nodded. This was where Rajivk's old YSR-SR training had failed him. His motives for coming up here weren't unimportant, any more than the way he felt about the sector base's closure. That was the biggest news Sandoveil had had in a long time, maybe in Marnie's entire lifetime.

The base closure would change the way everything would be done in Sandoveil, from the way people worked to the supplies they got to the way they thought.

The fact that the closure was thirty years out made it seem less important, but as Marnie's daughter reminded her this afternoon, the changes began now.

Nothing at the sector base would work toward the future. Everything would be focused on the closure.

The future was moving across the galaxy, along with the Fleet.

"You served with the Fleet, didn't you?" Marnie asked Rajivk.

"This isn't about me." He sounded testy. "There's a dead person in the pool."

Marnie nodded. "I can't do anything about the body until the rest of the team arrives."

"You could at least look," he snapped.

She let out a small breath of air. He was right about that. She hadn't even looked. Because he had been YSR-SR, she had trusted his observation. Had he been a tourist, she would have assumed he was wrong.

She inclined her head toward him, slightly embarrassed that she hadn't followed procedure to the letter, particularly when she could be the bitchest person in the city if someone else didn't follow procedure.

She glanced at the overlook. The black nanobit-formed structure looked a little dull in the late afternoon light. At this time of year, the spray was pretty minimal, so water didn't coat the surface of the overlook. The overlooks generally looked shiny and almost new, except up here, which was why she always considered the ones up here to be the most dangerous.

She walked across the overlook, her boots squeaking against the dry surface, and braced herself against the wall. She had a trick for looking over the edge without endangering herself.

First, she bent down and put her boots on the lowest *adhere* setting. Then she slid on a pair of gloves. She used the small control under the surface of each glove, setting them on a strong *adhere* setting. Then she placed her hands, deliberately, at the very center of the top of the wall.

She raised her boots and pushed their soles against the middle of the wall. Behind her, she heard Rajivk make a small sound of protest.

She ignored it. He didn't work with her anymore, and even if he had, he had never outranked her.

Still, she could hear him approach, as if he thought he could grab her if she slipped over the edge. To be truthful, his presence actually relieved her.

She hated doing this alone.

She leaned forward, looking to the side and down. The Falls thundered past her like it always did, but it didn't sound as fierce at this time of year. In the spring, the Falls sounded angry and powerful, as if it could break free of its setting and attack the entire city.

Marnie tried to ignore the Falls, a nearly impossible task. The water rushed below her, making her slightly dizzy. She always hated this perspective. The movement, the rushing water, the loud rumbles, made her feel off-balance, even though she wasn't.

It was hard to see through the spray. Some of that difficulty was caused by the dimming sunlight. If she had come here any later, she would have had to set up lights.

She looked at the deceptively calm water in the second pool. The water seemed to push away from the Falls. Only the currents really didn't do that. They swirled.

She knew that because she had pulled nearly a dozen bodies from the pool in her career with the YSR-SR, most of them accidental deaths or suicides.

Now she had one more. She could see the body, slowly turning as if someone were holding it from underneath, spinning it in a circle as if it were up for inspection.

Confirmation done, she nearly looked away. But something stopped her. She blinked, frowned, tried to figure out what had caught her.

Red pants. Bright red pants. And a yellow top.

She recognized that. It was the usual outfit of a woman with long brown hair.

Glida Kimura had worn that very outfit at the Sandoveil Sandwich Bar more than once.

Marnie stared at the body for a moment. She couldn't see the features clearly, but everything else was right.

She cursed softly, then lowered herself back on the nanobit base of the overlook.

"Did you see it?" Rajivk asked. He meant the body.

Marnie nodded. She wanted to tell him who she thought the body belonged to, but she knew better. Ten years before, someone in the YSR-SR had told a local the identity of a dead body and caused a panic, particularly when it turned out that the identification had been wrong.

Marnie hadn't seen the body's face clearly enough to identify it, and anyone could wear a combination of red and yellow. Not that just anyone would.

"You look shaken," Rajivk said.

She made herself give him a rueful smile. She was shaken, but she wasn't going to confess that.

"I'm going to make sure the rest of the team is on the way," she said, walking away from him. Her boots stuck to the surface. She had forgotten to turn down the *adhere* setting.

First she peeled off her gloves and shut them down. Then she shut down her boots, remaining bent over for just a moment.

She couldn't assume. She knew that. Assuming was the worst thing she could do.

But her mind wouldn't settle.

Because if Glida was in the pool, barefoot, and there was a second pair of shoes beside hers, then the only logical conclusion was that she hadn't come up here alone.

Glida had come up here with Taji Kimura.

Her wife.

6

"So that's what you heard?" Wèi asked. "A ship left and blew out the door?"

Bristol stepped inside the storage room. She held out her palms, then asked the suit to measure the room's environment. She wanted to know if it was safe to remove her hood.

No one else had removed theirs yet. She didn't know if that was because they were following procedure or if their suits had measured something.

"It's not that simple," she said, waiting for the suit to respond. "A ship couldn't leave here using its regular drive. It would either have to be transported manually or, in the case of the FS-Prime runabouts, it could use its *anacapa*."

"Yes," Wèi said, as if she were treating him like a stupid man.

Everyone at the base knew the only way in and out of the base was to use an *anacapa* drive. Small ships came in here only in the belly of a larger vessel. One part of the base used to open at the top, but no ship had used that exit in over a hundred years.

Besides, the entire base would have known if the old exit had been used. It probably would have been quite dramatic.

"You don't understand," she said. "I'm working on that runabout's *anacapa* drive now. The one in the runabout, the one that got used, was temporary."

"So?" Wèi asked. Even though he was challenging her, his tone had changed. Now he sounded on edge.

"So," she said, "I had simply installed it to make sure the runabout's systems continued to fire. It's a feature of these FS-Prime runabouts that they had technical issues if the *anacapa* was ever removed."

"What are you saying exactly?" DuBerry asked.

Bristol squared her shoulders, trying to look stronger than she actually felt. "I'm saying that the *anacapa* I put in that ship probably doesn't work properly."

"Why would you do something like that?" Tranh asked, as if Bristol had done something criminal.

"It's standard procedure." Bristol made sure her voice was level. "We have *anacapa* drives that we change in and out of older ships for just this reason. You're not supposed to launch a ship from this part of the base. Ever. We just transferred the runabout from *Ijo* to this storage room internally, using the base's *anacapa* drive. We never use those auxiliary *anacapa* drives."

"Then how do you know someone didn't just transfer the runabout out of here?" Fitzwilliam asked.

"I don't for certain," Bristol said. "But I received no notification of it. Did you?"

"No," Wèi said, his voice soft.

"We'll have to check that," Tranh said. Clearly something about this job bothered her.

"Yes, we will." Fitzwilliam spoke gently, as if he were talking down to a child.

"You think someone stole a runabout?" DuBerry asked.

"I don't know," Bristol said. "I just know that I'm the one in charge of that runabout. And I didn't authorize its removal. In fact, I thought it was here until you came back here."

"We need to track it then," Fitzwilliam said.

"I hope we can," Bristol said, doubting that was possible. "I really hope we can."

7

THERE WAS A TRICK TO GETTING BODIES out of the side pool at Fiskett Falls. Tevin Egbe had pulled more bodies out of that pool than anyone else.

And he hated it.

When the call had come in from Fiskett Falls, he had grabbed all of his gear, hoping that the body was in the water's edge on the upper Jeleen River. Of course it wasn't.

By the time he had arrived, Marnie Sar had contacted the team, letting them know the body was at the base of the Falls, in the side pool. So, Tevin made certain that the air van pulled up on the far side of the Falls, away from the overlooks where the body had been sighted and the shoes discovered.

Before he had left his office, where he'd been working when the call came in, he had contacted his best team. The Falls were scary on good days, and things rarely went as planned. It was always best to have the finest people beside him.

Ardelia Novoa had come with him. She worked only a few buildings down from him. He had picked her up and brought her along, stopping twice, once to pick up her gear and once to pick up Jabari Zhou.

Zhou had his gear ready. He had helped at the Falls five times in the past two years, and each time had scared him to death. Yet he continued to work it.

Tevin believed that Zhou performed better because of his fear—which wasn't usually the case with people who join the YSR-SR. But it made Zhou both more cautious and more insightful.

It had gotten to the point where Tevin hated working without him.

The fourth member of the team, Cherish Dinithi, had already arrived. She had her suit on, with her hood down. The main part of the suit was white, as the YSR-SR recommended, since they did so much work at night.

The suit they all used had been developed by the Fleet for water environments. So many underground teams developing sector bases encountered groundwater that someone whose name was now lost to the history of the Fleet had modified the environmental suits the Fleet used for working in space, and made them work in water.

The suits themselves were thin, with their own controlled environment. They compensated for water temperature, and often had to compensate for water pressure.

More than once, a member of Tevin's team (not this team) had gotten caught under the pounding waters of the Falls and had been gotten out safely, partly because Tevin would do damn near anything to make sure no one on his team died while recovering a dead body.

And so far, none of the calls he had gone to—at least for the side pool—involved any survivors.

"Let Marnie know we're here," he said to Dinithi as he got out of the air van. He spoke louder than usual, just to compensate for the noise of the Falls. The sound always overwhelmed him at first, although it receded slightly into the background as he worked.

"Already have," Dinithi said. "And she warned us. There's a good chance this body belongs to someone we know. So be braced."

Tevin didn't care, but he knew his team did. He wiped off his face. Spray had already sprinkled his skin with tiny drops of ice-cold water.

"Shit," Novoa said. She had gotten out of the van as well. "Did it have anything to do with the news today?"

"The sector base closure?" Zhou asked. "You think people are going to suicide already?"

The YSR-SR had been warned that one of the sad results of base closures was an increased suicide rate. The YSR-SR got briefed on all kinds of things about the base, and since Sector Base E-2 was the next slated for closure, the emotional results of the changes had been part of the briefings for the last several years.

"Suiciding this early would surprise me," Dinithi said, "but I don't get the mentality anyway."

"Some people don't handle change well," Novoa said. "Maybe the very idea that the Fleet will be leaving this sector for good has people upset."

"No way to know until we get into the water and see what we have," Tevin said, and then clamped his mouth shut. He shouldn't have said "what." He should have said "who."

But the "what" was a window into his mindset. He couldn't think about people, not at this juncture. Because he wasn't being asked to recover a person.

He was being asked to recover the remains of a person.

He removed his shoes and his dress clothes, leaving only his undergarments in deference to the rest of the team. If he were alone, he would have worn nothing underneath the suit.

The air had a bite to it, which meant that the water might already be early-winter cold. It shouldn't matter. The suit should protect him from the elements.

But he always thought about these things, just in case something went wrong.

He slipped the suit on, and then pulled the hood over his face. The hood was clear and had several different communications links built in. First he set up the environment, running the on-site test, something he demanded his entire team do.

They had all suited up as well, their expressions grim. They knew this task wouldn't be pleasant. Because Dinithi had suited up before everyone else, she had grabbed the equipment—a bag that they might or might not use for the body, and everything from an old-fashioned webbing gun to a catchall pole.

She held up two harnesses.

"Need these?" she asked out loud. She hadn't yet pulled up her hood.

Sometimes, on the mountains, the team had to harness the injured back to safety. It was different with the Falls, though, and made Tevin realize she had never worked this part of the Falls before.

Tevin touched his hood, indicating that she should put hers on.

She gave him a deliberate grimace, then pulled up her hood with one hand. The edges were unattached, but at least the presence of the hood would allow him to check the team communications link.

He used that now.

"No," he said in response to her question. "We should be able to hook and pull."

He was trying to be a bit more delicate with his language than he had been a moment before. The team communications were recorded, and often played back by a variety of officialdom. Particularly if someone thought the death was not accidental or a suicide.

He didn't want to put ideas in his team's head though. He wanted them to remember what they had learned about webbing. It caused extra marks on a body that were sometimes indistinguishable from the injuries caused by other means.

So he was going to avoid the webbing if possible.

"Everyone hear me clearly?" he asked.

Novoa nodded. So did Zhou. Their hoods were attached.

Dinithi had put the harnesses in Tevin's van, along with the rest of the equipment. Then she ran a finger along the neckline of her suit, sealing the hood in place.

"Cherish?" Tevin asked. "Did you hear me?"

"Yeah," Dinithi said with just a touch of sarcasm. She opened a hand toward the van, as if to say, *It's obvious, Tevs, because I put the harnesses away.*

She wasn't good at procedure, at least procedures she thought were stupid. She didn't like the communications check because she didn't like being recorded.

She had been a lawyer before she moved to Sandoveil to start over. Tevin had never understood how she had worked in law. She hated rules and regulations. She ran her own business now, creating signature beverages for locals and one-shot drinks for tourists.

He asked for her on the team, though, because she was his most creative thinker, and she had gotten him out of tough patches more times than he wanted to think about.

He turned away from her, not reprimanding her for the sarcasm. He doubted the other two had noticed. This team had been together long enough that they compensated for each other's foibles.

Before they started the mission, he checked the rest of the communications. First, he sent a ping back to headquarters, getting the usual response.

Then he contacted Marnie. "Situation the same?" he asked.

"Yeah," Marnie said. "No sign of the owner of the second pair of shoes. We're checking on those now, but waiting first for a firm identification from you."

"I'll send you a tentative one as soon as I have it," he said. He didn't do firm identifications. That was for the local death investigator to determine.

Unlike Dinithi, Tevin followed the rules.

He nodded toward the team. They fell in beside him. He double-checked to make sure their hoods were on firmly, and they wore their equipment belts.

Dinithi had a catchall. So did Novoa.

Tevin hoped two poles with their hooked ropes would be enough.

He led them to the edge of the trail. Then he glanced at the team.

This time, he didn't speak. They could see his face. They knew they had to do everything right, or this recovery mission might turn into a rescue—of one of them.

"Let's go," he said, and walked to the churning water of Fiskett Falls.

8

Bristol's suit notified her that the environment was fine. She pulled off her hood, then finger-combed her hair. Wèi watched her for a moment, then removed his hood.

Even though the hoods were clear, they distorted the features somehow. Wèi's face was broader than she had expected, his nose flatter. His eyes were brown, their expression sympathetic, something she wouldn't have expected.

She recognized him. She had seen him in the base many times; she just hadn't known his name until now.

She nodded at him. He gave her a bit of a smile, then turned his attention to the others.

Tranh's hood came off next, her face narrow, her chin slightly pointed. Her eyes were as black as her hair, which was cut very short. Bristol had seen her around as well. In fact, they both had lunch at the same time every day, and had had polite exchanges over the local concerts they both attended. They didn't have the same opinions about the music, except that they both liked that the city could afford to bring in musicians from all over Nindowne.

They smiled at each other, and Wèi looked at both of them in surprise.

DuBerry removed her hood as well. She didn't look much different, except that her reddish-blonde hair curled, like an out-of-control hat. Fitzwilliam had shaved off his hair, and his skull wasn't quite even, which made him seem as if someone had poked one side of his face just a little too hard.

Bristol frowned at that thought, then looked at the storage room for a second time. It wasn't just the emptiness that made it feel off.

She walked to the wall in front of her, and slowly ran her hand down the smoothness. In the very center, it felt gritty. And her fingers told her that it had bent outward just a little. The nanobits hadn't compensated yet, but they would.

"We need to measure this, now," she said.

"What?" Wèi asked.

"Something blew out parts of the wall. The nanobits are repairing it, but right now there's a bubble here. I'd like to send for more techs," Bristol said.

"Is that wise?" Tranh asked. "We don't know what's happened here."

"That's the point," Bristol said before anyone could answer.

"We have procedure, though," Wèi said. "Technically, I'm not supposed to let anyone else in here until we know what has happened."

"Well, we're not going to know if you don't bring more people in," Bristol said. Now that she knew she was safe, she wished she hadn't contacted the security team. She needed a tech team, and she needed them now.

"All right," Wèi said, even though he sounded reluctant. "Bring them in. Make sure that the team has a high clearance, and doesn't have a tendency to talk."

Bristol nodded, even though he really wasn't in the position to give her any instructions. It was her work space. She could call in help if she wanted, now that the security team had informed her that the area was clear.

"DuBerry, I need you to check the base's logs and see what they registered here," Wèi said. "Fitz, please go over the recordings of the entire area and see who entered this room."

"There's a possibility no one did," Bristol said, suppressing a sigh. "The *anacapa* could have been activated from anywhere."

"I know." Now Wèi sounded offended. "But I want to make sure it wasn't accessed from in here."

He had a good point. Bristol didn't add anything else though. She saw no reason to.

His mission was now different from hers. He had to find out who or what caused the runabout to leave here.

She needed to know what had happened technically. Because there was one other possibility, one she knew the security chief hadn't thought of.

The *anacapa* she had placed in that runabout might have activated on its own. Anyone who worked with *anacapa* drives knew that was one of the defects some of the older drives had. And an older drive in an older runabout might have caused some kind of interaction, particularly if the *anacapa* detected a signal from another ship built in the same era.

She had used the *anacapa* drive that she had put in the runabout a dozen times before, but never in a vehicle that old, and never in one that would lose its diagnostics if the drive were not in place.

Wèi had come up beside her. He touched the wall with his gloved hand, then he frowned and turned his head ever so slightly.

"Something big happened here, didn't it?" he asked quietly.

She was a cautious woman. She wasn't going to speculate—at least, not out loud.

"I can tell you only one thing for certain," she said.

He looked at her directly. "What's that?"

She did her best to keep her voice level and as low as his. "The blast doors worked."

9

Security officer Bassima Beck stopped in front of the tiny home, halfway up the mountain on the back side of Sandoveil. The homes here sat on a lot of land and had spectacular views of the city below. Most of the homes took up a large portion of the land, but not this one. Instead, a garden covered everything except a stone walkway leading to the front door.

The garden had approved plants from all over the sector (and beyond) as well as local greenery. On her left, Bassima recognized edibles. Everything on the edges and along the right were decorative.

And amazingly decorative. She didn't know the names of those plants; she specialized in edibles, not decoratives from off-world. But they had a pattern. They went from pink to red to purple to blue. Yellow flowers lined the edge of the path, and near the doorway, pots with hanging yellow vines tied everything together.

The net effect was to make everything feel homey and welcoming.

Except this afternoon. This afternoon, all this care and beauty made Bassima's heart sink.

The house had that quiet that empty homes often had. Bassima walked up the two carved rock steps leading to the wide, wooden wraparound porch. The door was made of mountain stone, heavy and solid. On either side, a narrow ribbon of opaque glass added drama to the door's design. A knocker, built over a digital pad, sent signals inside—probably from the moment Bassima had arrived.

Still, she grabbed the metal ring on the knocker and rapped three times.

Lights went on inside the house. She could see them reflected in the opaque glass. If she hadn't know how the knocker worked, she would have felt better. But the lights went on in the default pattern. Kitchen and stairs first, then hallway, then entry, as if someone were trying to come to the door.

She couldn't hear movement behind all this rock—the house had been built to blend in with the landscape—but she didn't see any.

Even though she had never been up here before, she had known the Kimuras for nearly a decade. They had met on the Sandoveil Botany Committee, when all three of them had served.

Locals had to qualify for the committee with either a year of training or degrees in botany and plant science. No new plant species could be introduced into the Sandoveil Valley without approval from the committee first.

Approval came after a year or more of rigorous testing to make certain that no alien plant would become a predatory species against something in the local environment.

So many communities (even ones elsehwere on Nindowne) used computer modeling to see if the new plant would become invasive. But Sandoveil protected its heritage and its local landscape better than any other place Bassima had ever heard of.

She loved serving on the committee, and she had loved working with the Kimuras, although they left a few years back. They didn't have as much time for community activities, not if they wanted to maintain their jobs and their own garden.

Bassima had missed seeing Taji Kimura on a regular basis. Bassima had long ago accepted that she had a strong attraction to Taji. Bassima had never understood Taji's love for Glida, who had seemed like one of the most difficult people Bassima had ever known.

But Bassima was old enough to recognize that attraction rarely made sense.

She could have that thought and still blame her own unusual height and extra weight for the fact that Taji wasn't interested in her.

Bassima knocked again, and took a step back from the door. She leaned sideways so that she could see the window that overlooked the porch. The window had shielded glass—no one could look in if the Kimuras didn't want anyone to look inside—but the house's designer had placed more opaque ribbons of glass around the windows, and hadn't bothered to shield that.

Bassima couldn't quite see inside, but she could get a sense of movement—or she would have, if there had been any.

She sighed, and walked around the left side of the porch, her shoes making the old wood creak. Two rocking chairs sat in front of the window, plants on the table between them, more yellow vines trailing onto the wood below. Some of the vines had bright red buds, which would probably become bright red flowers.

Glida favored that combination—a bold red with an even bolder yellow. She often dressed that way.

Bassima sensed Glida everywhere: in the design of the home, the placement of the plants, and the color scheme. In addition to the yellow vine plants, yellow pillows rested against the backs of the rocking chairs and a yellow-and-red checked chaise lounge pushed up against the side of the house, beneath another large, shielded window.

Bassima knocked on the glass, knowing she was probably triggering some kind of alarm. But the city security office were the ones who dispatched her, so when the alarm came in, they would know she had triggered it somehow.

They would only pay attention if she contacted them directly.

She peered around the back of the house. The porch narrowed here, more of a walkway than any place to rest and enjoy the great outdoors. There were also no windows on this side of the house, which made sense since it butted up against the mountain. One narrow door provided an exit from one of the back rooms, but there wasn't even some kind of mat in front of it to catch shoe dust or debris.

Clearly, that door wasn't used very often.

She walked the rest of the distance around the house, moving just a bit faster now. If someone had been inside, they would have contacted her by now. The two knocks, then the window alarm, would have had them peering out, seeing that it was her, and then asking what she wanted.

If only. She had had half a fantasy that they would be home. All three of them would laugh over the misunderstanding, and then they would get serious again, acknowledging that *someone* had died, just not one of the Kimuras.

She walked around the porch one more time, looking outward this time, into the garden. The garden wasn't one of those decorous things with tiny plants that encouraged walking and serious if trivial discussion. This was a working garden, the kind that harvested plants for others.

There were neat rows, visible to other gardeners, but not trails. And no evidence that someone had plunged into the garden in haste, destroying the Kimuras' hard work.

Finally, Bassima gave up. She hit the comm link on her uniform collar, and contacted the security office.

"No one's here," she said. "No way of telling when someone was last here, either, unless you give me authorization to tap into the private house's private systems."

"I can't give you authorization yet." The response came from Amy Loraas, head of the security office. That surprised Bassima. She had expected someone else in the office, someone of much lower rank, to answer her.

The fact that Loraas was now on this meant that someone was certain that the dead body belonged to Glida. They just didn't have official confirmation yet. And doing things by the book was what the entire city of Sandoveil was all about.

"You want me to wait?" Bassima asked.

"No," Loraas said. "You can always go back. Check downtown. See if anyone has seen either of them today. Maybe we just missed them."

"I hope so," Bassima said and signed off. Then she looked at the beautiful garden, the flowers turning their blooms toward the setting sun. "I really hope so."

10

Rajivk leaned on a rock a few yards from the lower outlook. The sun was going down. On the upper path, there would still be light, however grainy and indistinct. But down here, it had turned dark suddenly as the sun vanished behind the mountains.

Searchlights illuminated the overlook. Beyond it, the falling water looked like an ivory column filled with some kind of strange life.

He hated being up here at night. It was too dangerous. It didn't matter how much gear you brought or how well lit you were, one false step and you would tumble into the water, just like that person below had.

He'd heard the conversations. Marnie believed the body belonged to Glida Kimura. He could see that. She favored that kind of bright clothing. But wherever Glida was, Taji was as well. And, aside from the shoes, there was no evidence she had been up here.

If the shoes could be considered evidence.

The YSR-SR was treating them as evidence. They had bagged the shoes. He would have recommended taking DNA first, but he hadn't been down here the entire time.

Maybe YSR-SR had taken the DNA already.

He crossed his arms. He was getting cold. He'd felt a little chilled ever since he had gotten wet when he found those shoes. He had dried off, but the chill had already set in. What he really needed was to finish his walk, get home, eat something, and take a hot, hot shower.

The very thought of it made him even colder.

The YSR-SR wanted him to wait until they identified the body for certain. But procedure kept him standing here, waiting. Because they didn't dare let him go, in case he had been the one who had pushed the dead person into the waterfall.

They had to make sure they knew who they were dealing with, and then they had to make sure he had no real ties with that person. Or at least, no obvious ties.

Clearly, the YSR-SR couldn't examine all ties, not while he was waiting here. They would have to take him somewhere.

He hoped he wouldn't have to wait until they finished their investigation. If that was the case, he would ask—no, he would demand—to go to their headquarters.

The lights were set up just a few yards away from him, and a clear block had gone up so no one could accidentally wander into the overlook without clearance. Not that it mattered here. Because Rajivk didn't believe Glida or whoever that was had made it this far up.

It was almost impossible to hit that side pool from this overlook. He'd seen bodies of people who had jumped off of this overlook, and those bodies had usually gone down the main part of the Falls. Those bodies had been slammed down by the force of the water, and usually popped up a few hours later at the far end of the main part of Rockwell Pool.

If the bodies didn't get tangled in the currents underneath the Falls and end up there for a few days. Those bodies never came out looking good. They were always battered and bruised, often with so many broken bones that it would take the death investigator a few days to reconstruct the face. If, of course, there was no DNA on file.

From above, that body in the pool didn't look bruised and battered. It probably was, but not in the same way. The yellow shirt seemed to be intact, at least from this vantage, and the hair floated, rather than being tangled.

Rajivk sighed. He was speculating on things that meant nothing because he wasn't in the thick of it. People walked up and down the path, sometimes alone, sometimes consulting, rarely going into the upper overlook, although for a while, one entire team worked the overlook closer to the mountains, where the Jeleen River turned smooth.

If the body belonged to Glida Kimura, they could let him go right away. The only real thing he had in common with Glida was that they both worked at the sector base, just like 80 percent of Sandoveil. He and Glida didn't even work in the same department.

The only reason he had gotten to know her was that they sometimes passed each other on these paths. She'd be walking with her wife, and he'd be walking alone. Eventually, they would nod a hello.

When he got to work one morning, Glida had been heading inside at the same time. They had exchanged names and pleasantries, and had laughed about being the only ones in Sandoveil who loved the Falls enough to walk around it on a regular basis.

He didn't even know the name of Glida's wife. The only reason he had known they were married was because Glida had said they had wanted to hold the ceremony near the Falls, and the city had denied them a permit for it.

He had no idea where they had even had their ceremony, only that it hadn't been up here.

Voices came up from below, apparently loud enough to be heard over the roar of the Falls.

Another chill ran through him. Did that mean they'd found another body? Located another person? Or lost a member of the recovery team?

He wanted to ask, but at the moment, he was alone on this level.

And then his work handheld buzzed in the corner pocket of his shirt. He had forgotten he was even carrying it. This day seemed so long already that work had been a very long time ago. The first thing he usually did when he got home was to place the handheld in its little charger by the door, set on emergency notification only.

But he hadn't done that yet, which meant they could get to him for stupid stuff.

He hauled it out of his pocket. The handheld had a red border, which meant urgent. He sighed and placed the device on audio only. He didn't want them to see anything going on up here—even though, most likely, anyone looking at this scene through a screen would only see darkness.

There was a message for him to listen to before he contacted the base. *We have a situation. We need you at the base immediately.*

The message came from Bristol Iannazzi, who was one of his supervisors. Only he'd never had any real interactions with Iannazzi. She did her work and let the staff beneath her supervise everyone else's.

A situation. He couldn't remember ever hearing that language before.

But, on some level, the summons didn't surprise him. The day had started oddly. The reaction of his colleagues to the news had been even stranger. If someone was going to break and do something untoward, today would have been the day.

He stood up. He had to find Marnie.

He had to let her know that he was going to leave—whether she wanted him to or not.

11

More members of the YSR-SR had arrived as word spread. Either that, or Marnie Sar had called them. Tevin didn't have time to figure out which was the actual case.

Twilight had fallen, which meant the light at the base of Fiskett Falls was mostly gone. His team had set up large lights on this side of the trail, and someone—he had no idea who—had set up lights on the other side from either the path or the overlooks. The lights pointed downward.

He wished he had learned about this body earlier in the day, because they would be working all night now. Even with the best possible lighting, the brightness would change the entire look of the scene, making it seem deceptively safe.

If he reminded his team of that, they would get angry at him for telling them something obvious. If he didn't remind them and one of them died, he would regret it. So he opted for a statement that would remind them, but wouldn't upset them quite as much.

"Watch the shadows," he said.

He got no response at all. He glanced at his team. Even through their hoods, they looked grim. Apparently, they were as determined as he was to remain safe.

Dinithi had grabbed a light and put it over her shoulder. Zhou had some extra gear in a pack over his—and that probably had an extra light as well. Tevin had one large light and several built into his suit.

Only Novoa didn't seem too concerned. But she was the only one of them who had ever worked in space. Darkness didn't bother her as much as it bothered the rest of them.

Tevin slipped behind a pair of six-foot-tall rocks to the opening that led behind the Falls. The city had built a protective barrier here, making it look like the rocks continued, when in fact, they did not. In the early years of the city, too many people had died here, so the city decided to make changes.

At the same time they built the path, they barricaded off the most dangerous parts of the Falls. Some were barricaded permanently. Others, like this one, were useful for search, rescue, and recovery, so people with the proper codes could bring down the barriers.

He pulled off his glove and touched the side of one of the rocks. It was smooth, because it wasn't a rock. It was composed of nanobits, programmed slightly differently than the nanobits in the path.

The barrier here had a simple code, based on fingerprints from a living hand and an easy-to-remember pattern that changed quarterly. In theory, anyone at the YSR-SR could use the pattern to access this part of the Falls recreationally, but as far as he knew, no one ever had.

He placed his fingertips on the extra layer of nanobits. The usually smooth surface felt slightly rough; that was how he knew he was in the right place. He tapped his fingers in the set pattern for this quarter—three from his index finger, one from each finger, then three from his middle finger, and so on—until he finished the entire pattern.

The barrier slid down, disappearing into the path. It looked like someone had cleared rocks quickly or like they had gone to a completely different part of the Falls.

Dithini let out a breath audible in the comm.

"That's always so impressive," she said.

No one answered.

Tevin stepped across the barrier—always the most dicey moment, in his opinion, because he worried that it would rebound in place. It didn't, at least for him.

He stepped back, then watched as Dinithi crossed, followed by Novoa and, finally, Zhou. They crowded near him, waiting for the barrier to go back up. If it didn't reset within five minutes, he would have to do it by hand.

He hated waiting. If he had been even slightly convinced that they were heading toward a rescue instead of a recovery, he would try to reset the barrier right now.

But sometimes doing so upset the delicate mechanism. The barrier didn't come down very often, and its controls had been badly constructed. Fixing the barrier hadn't worked its way up any priority list, so any team who crossed that barrier had to waste precious time waiting for it to work or worry that they might leave it open for anyone to wander back here.

Finally, it bounced back up, making the path back to the vehicles look impassable.

"All right," he said. "One at a time to the pool."

The path here was wide and deliberately rough. It had been built by the original Fleet settlers hundreds of years ago. Everyone in the team activated their boots so that they clung to the rough nanobits with the same kind of power they would use if they were outside of a spaceship.

Right now, they didn't need that power, but they would in twenty yards or so. The path was wide here because it wound around the mountainside. There was plenty of room for the team to walk abreast, even though they didn't.

The path would narrow in ten yards and become treacherous ten yards beyond that.

Right now, it hugged the mountainside. The pool was a few yards away and nearly ten feet down from the path. The water in the pool was choppy from the Falls pouring into it, but there was no danger that the team would slip and fall into it—at the moment anyway.

The path wasn't even wet here. But the roar of the Falls made it hard to hear, especially since Tevin didn't shut off the outside noise when he had his hood on. The hood cut noise automatically, but not severely. He set it to let outside noise in when he was working in a natural environment so that he could judge hazards as well.

The path wound around one more corner. Spray rose up here, and the pool had gotten closer to the edge. No rocks or anything extended beyond the path. From here on out, the path was decidedly more dangerous.

Tevin rounded that corner and found himself beside the waterfall. This moment was always breathtaking. A wall of water, cascading in front of him. The first time he had walked here, he had removed his hood just to feel it all—the ice-cold spray on his face, the fresh and damp scent of the air, the crackle of power all around him.

He didn't dare be distracted by that this time. He inched his way behind the Falls, where it was deceptively calm.

To his right, the cliff face curved inward. It had eroded in the centuries since the Fleet's engineers had built the path. Some of the dirt still piled along the interior edge of the path. In theory, the nanobits should process the dirt and use it to make the path sturdier, but that function seemed to have failed years before.

Tevin always saw the dirt as something that made transversing this part of the path even more difficult, but Zhou, who worked as a geologist for the sector base, said the problem was worse than that. The entire cliff face was unstable. Either it could crumble bit by bit over years, or something could trigger an avalanche, which would bury anyone on the path and possibly fill in this back area of the pool.

That would be a shame, because Tevin loved this part of the pool. In daylight, it was an eerie brownish-green, and exceptionally clear. The turbulance from the Falls seemed to flow outward—toward the main part of the pool. While the pool back here wasn't exactly calm, it wasn't filled with as many eddies and currents either. Just the soft and somewhat predictable ripples from the water falling like a curtain before it.

In this light, the pool looked black. The lights from above, filtered through the moving water, shone on the surface, but didn't penetrate it. Tevin knew from experience that shining the lights the team carried on this part of the pool would make the water reflect more but look dirtier at the same time.

Tevin moved carefully past the fallen rocks. He kept his hands free and didn't touch any part of the cliff face. Ever since Zhou had warned him that the cliff face was unstable, Tevin didn't want to do anything that would initiate some kind of slide.

The roar of the waterfall seemed muted back here. He had known that was going to happen too, but he still didn't understand it. He once thought that the sound of the water would echo back here, along with the vibrations from the power of Falls, but it didn't.

It felt like a shelter, like a place he could hide forever, and no one would find him.

On this part of the path, he wasn't even getting hit with spray. It almost felt like he was in a cave, protected from the rest of the world. The waterfall formed a curtain of water that, in daylight, was opaque and comforting at the same time. Right now, it looked foamy and bright with the lights from above—as if someone were shining a spotlight through thick fabric over a window.

If it had been like this all the way along, the city of Sandoveil would have allowed this path to remain open. But as the path got narrower, it got lower as well. In the spring—all three parts of it—the water rose so that sometimes, it actually lapped against the edges of the path.

So far, Tevin had never had to cross this path during the worst of the spring rains and snowmelt, so he had no idea if the path was ever submerged, but he suspected that it might be.

He finally reach the last wide part of the path. It might have been an overlook in the days before this path was closed off, but if that was the case, the protective walls were long gone. He stood in front of the cliff face—not leaning against it—and waited for the rest of the team to arrive.

Dinithi came first, head moving as she observed all of her surroundings. Novoa peered at the water, maybe looking for clues or something to do with the body. Zhou brought up the rear, careful to check behind them as they stopped to make sure some civilian hadn't followed them.

"Okay," Tevin said. "This part will be tricky. Cherish, I need you to follow Ardelia through here."

"I'll be fine," Dinithi said.

And that was the reason Dinithi unnerved him. Because she sometimes (often) dismissed his orders.

"You haven't seen the next part of the path, and it's growing very dark," he said. "I want you to follow me and Ardelia. Jabari will bring up the rear because he knows the procedure down here."

"Seems like an excess of caution, Tevin," Dinithi said.

He smiled in spite of himself.

"Yep," he said. "That's why I'm team leader and you're not. We all need headlamps, people, but pointed downward so we don't blind each other."

Everyone reached up to the top of their hoods and manually adjusted the lights. That was learned through long experience as well. The adjustments happened quicker and were more accurate when done by hand. A flaw in the suits that, according to an YSR-SR team member, seemed to happen only in real gravity, not in the zero-g the suits were designed for.

The additional lights, pointed downward, revealed the moss growing on the rocks beside the pool, and the algae at the pool's edges. If Tevin pulled off his hood, he knew he would be able to smell it all, along with the unusual humidity in this place.

Instead, he got the metalic tang of the recycled air inside his suit.

He rounded the last corner, and peered at the path ahead. It was worse than he remembered. Parts of it had fallen away. Other parts disappeared into the growing darkness.

He was glad they hadn't had a rescue call. At this time of day, there was no way to hurry through this part of the path. Getting the body out would be another chore he really didn't want to think about.

"Okay," he said with more cheer than he felt. "Let's go."

12

THE PROBLEM, BRISTOL THOUGHT as she worked, was that this was a storage room. No one expected anything to happen in here. And unlike storage rooms on the surface, no one expected break-ins or thefts either. Everyone who had access to this part of the facility had high clearance, and knew better—or should have known better—than to steal something from such a remote location.

Plus, the storage room didn't have small items. It had housed a runabout, for godsake, as well as some smaller equipment used in repair. But none of the equipment could be easily carried from the facility.

She spent half an hour getting current readings from the walls and door, so she could compare them with the original readings. But the security system itself didn't surveil this room the same way it surveiled the others. It had a camera, like her main room did, but the monitoring for everything from the environment to the integrity of the room itself got bundled into the standard surveillance of her lab.

Her lab had two separate surveillance systems—the standard one, and the technical one. She usually used the system that focused on the tech because she wanted to know the details of whatever went wrong, if something did. The standard system was for security, and usually she thought that a good arrangement. She hated having anyone, be they human or computer, examine what she was doing on a micro level.

Right now, though, she would have loved it, especially if it had been focused on the storage room. Because she had no easy way to compare the room as it had been with the room as it currently was.

Bristol didn't want to think about the fact that someone might have snuck into her lab and stolen the runabout. She hoped, although she saw no evidence for it, that the someone had snuck in while she was working earlier in the day, and that was why she heard that door bang.

But if she paused and really thought about it, she *knew* that the door had banged as the damage occurred inside the storage room. If that blast door hadn't held, she would probably be dead now. Or so injured that she might never be able to function again.

She closed her eyes and took a deep breath, trying to calm herself. Even when she promised herself that she wouldn't think about the what-ifs, they rose out of her subconscious like water bubbling out of the mud flats.

She had come close to dying, through no fault of her own. She had always thought that if she were going to die at work, it would be because she had done something wrong, not because someone else had done something illegal.

She made herself open her eyes. Then she squared her shoulders, and walked purposefully into her lab.

It was full of people. Half a dozen people worked on the various stationary work stations, under the aegis of the security team. The team had questions. The techs might be able to answer them.

She had never had this many people in her lab before. They made her both claustrophobic and nervous. She didn't want them to touch anything or move anything, even though they would have to in order to work.

This place would be a mess for weeks after the crisis ended, and there was nothing she could do about it.

Bristol ended up beside the closed-off *anacapa* drive. She didn't want anyone to come near it. She had already locked off the *anacapa* drive she had been working on. She was going to be the only person who touched that.

She called up a holographic screen so that she could review her work. She needed to make sure she had done nothing wrong, as well. Eventually, though, she would have to either use one of the stationary screens or a handheld for privacy. She didn't want some of the people in this room to see what she had been doing for the past few days.

Her most trusted colleagues weren't here yet. She had called them back from whatever they did after their work days ended. She hadn't spoken to them, because she didn't like dealing with people one on one. She had received acknowledgement on her work handheld (which she hated) that everyone had seen the messages, though, and if someone failed to show up this evening, that someone would be fired, at least if she had something to say about it.

She needed the people whose work she knew, not these qualified, but unknown to her, members of the evening shift.

She returned her attention to the screen. Before she got into the details of the changes in the storage room, she needed to review the *anacapa* data, to see if anyone with clearance had switched out the *anacapa* in the runabout with yet another *anacapa*. Such an action would cause the kind of breach she had seen in that room, and there would have been a record of it.

Every *anacapa* that the base owned did a security update to the *anacapa* teams' systems. The security update—which was in the code used by all *anacapa*s—meant nothing to anyone else. No one knew how it worked except the teams. But updates allowed the teams to know if an *anacapa* got handled by someone not cleared to touch one or if an *anacapa* in its protective casing got moved to another part of the base without the teams' permission.

Both of those things had happened in the past, and both were firing offenses.

She half-hoped she would find something in the security data, but so far, she hadn't. She knew the security team had looked as well. They hadn't found anything that obvious. Yet.

Wèi stepped out of the storage room. Bristol stiffened. Watching everyone move through her personal space was slowly making her crazy.

Only he didn't move through. He walked over to her. He was holding a screen in his left hand.

The screen looked blank as it was held away from her, but as he raised it, she realized there was an image on it. Apparently this was one of security's screens, the kind that only allowed people with clearance to view it.

He swiped the image, then held it in front of her. It showed her lab, dark and empty. The blue lights from pieces of equipment blinked quietly. The pale, whitish overhead that she kept on low added to the blue tones. The equipment was in dark shadow, the pathways around it lighter.

Usually she stood in the lab after she had turned everything off for the evening, just soaking in the ambience. The lab almost felt like a live thing to her—a friend, a place of comfort. She liked it in darkness and in full light.

But she knew, she knew, that this day would change all of that. It would make her feel unsettled here.

She already did.

And "unsettled" was the wrong word. She felt unsafe.

She swallowed, watching the screen. Nothing looked different. It seemed to be the lab at night. She was about to ask what she was supposed to see when a triangular sliver of light indicated that the main door had opened.

A slight figure blocked the light, and then the door closed. The figure became a shadowy form that worked its way past the screens, almost blending against the back wall.

Bristol's breath caught as the figure headed toward the *anacapa* container. Bristol had one of two metal keys that unlocked the container's keypad. The head of security had the other key and, she supposed, all the other keys for the *anacapa* containers scattered throughout the labs in the sector base.

The head of her division knew that the keypad was a dummy pad. To open the container, the keypad had to be pulled down, and a flat screen in the back took fingerprints, as well as a tap-key. The final step in opening the *anacapa* container was entering the daily security code in the keypad *before* it was replaced into its position.

Bristol's poor heart continued to pound hard. She hadn't been this stressed in years, not since one of her team members accidentally broke off part of an ancient *anacapa* drive, partially activating it. Three days of severe stress and worry that someone would get unintentionally sent into foldspace.

This incident could evolve into the same kind of thing, particularly if that shadowy form knew how to open the *anacapa* container. Which would somehow mean that the form had a metal key.

Bristol bit her lower lip so hard she tasted blood. She leaned toward the image, praying she wouldn't see a break-in near the container. The image blurred a moment, or maybe that was her vision. She lost track of the shadowy form.

If someone had tampered with the container, Bristol would have known, right? Something would have shown up the next day as she opened it herself. Wouldn't it?

She actually didn't know the answer to that. She had always assumed that the security at the base knew what it was doing. Besides, no one from Sandoveil would ever break into the base. Sandoveil had a security force, but it mostly handled incidents with tourists.

And tourists had no idea that the sector base was here.

"This is what I wanted you to see in specific," Wèi said, and froze the image.

Bristol blinked again, unable to see anything other than her lab, filled with the black shapes of the equipment and the bluish glow of the walkways between. She couldn't even see the shadowy form anymore, because it was lost in the muddiness around the *anacapa* container.

"What?" she asked.

He tapped the farthest section of the image. She blinked a third time, then wiped her eyes. In her concern for the *anacapa* container, she had missed the fact that the shadowy form had moved past the container. The form had looked like another piece of equipment to her, but she now realized there was no equipment near the entrance to the storage unit.

"Oh," she breathed, startled. "It *was* someone breaking in."

Wèi frowned at her.

She flushed, not certain if she should have spoken aloud. But no one else turned around. They all seemed focused on their various screens, hands moving, lips moving, heads inclining forward.

"No," he said, his tone just a little condescending. "*This.*"

He tapped the screen again, and a section of the image grew. Suddenly she realized she was looking at a reflection in one of the screens near the storage room's door.

Half of a face, angular, pale, a strand of brown hair curling against the forehead. A hood pulled over the head, obscuring the rest of the image.

"Recognize that person?" Wèi asked.

The thing was, Bristol did. Or thought she did. The half face looked familiar. If she had to guess, she would say she was looking at woman, but she couldn't be completely certain.

"I'm not sure," she said, because that was the only truthful answer she could give. "Can't your systems make an identification?"

He didn't answer her. Instead, he tapped the screen, and Bristol watched as the shadowy form grabbed the storage room door and slipped inside, then pulled the door closed.

Bristol swallowed hard. She didn't like Wèi's sudden silence.

She wanted to defend the fact that the storage door had been unlocked. But the truth was, none of the storage doors in any of the labs had locks, unless the person in charge of the lab installed them. Since Bristol's team all needed access to the storage unit, she had never seen a point of installing any locks.

Besides, the team couldn't get in without going through several layers of security. She looked over at Wèi.

"Do you have a record of that person going through security?" she asked.

He didn't answer her, and she felt her adrenaline spike even more. Was the shadowy person someone in her team? Someone she had just called in?

Was there something going on here that she did not understand, but had, perhaps, facilitated?

"No," he said so quietly she almost didn't hear him. "We don't have any record of that person at all."

13

Tevin reached the secondary pool behind the Falls ahead of the rest of his team. The Falls sounded muted back here, the rocks somehow dampening the usual fierce roar.

The lights from above illuminated the slag rock behind him and the path, which glistened blackly. The area curved in here, a wide spot that butted against the cliff face. A *landing pad*, his own supervisor had called it, years and years ago, when Tevin had received his training in water rescues.

The landing pad had grown smaller over time. There had been rockfalls. Tevin didn't remember ever before seeing any boulders touching the path, and now an entire pile of them forced him to go around. Working here would be harder than he'd anticipated—and he hadn't expected it to be easy.

He didn't look at the water, not yet. He didn't want to make any decisions or get lost trying to figure out where the body was. He needed to set up first.

Dinithi and Novoa arrived next, almost side by side, with Zhou bringing up the rear. Zhou and Novoa set large lamps opposite each other, so that they cast light upward and out, covering the edges of the pool.

Dinithi should have put her lamp in the center, but there wasn't room for a lamp and for a person, not with the rockfall. Tevin moved her closer to Zhou and instructed her to set her lamp as close to the water's edge as she dared.

He put his large lamp closer to Novoa's. The lights created bright spots on the rocks behind them, and increased some of the shadows. He sighed, knowing that was the best they could do.

Tevin turned to the water and raised his headlamp, steering it so that he could use his forehead like a beacon.

The lights made the pool black, as he'd expected. To his right, the Falls tumbled, the lights illuminating that swirling water, making it gold and white and seemingly solid.

His team gathered around him. Dinithi held her catchall like a cudgel. She seemed subdued. Maybe she finally understood the difficulties of their task.

Zhou swept a flashlight over the water. The gold circle skated across the top, showing just a bit of sediment below the surface. Finally, the light caught something pale and bloated.

A hand.

No one said a word. No one made a sound.

Only Zhou moved. He shifted the light slowly, so that it moved along the red-clad arm toward a torso. The center of the light hit the stomach, but the edges of the light illuminated the entire body.

It seemed to be intact. The hands were outstretched, the bare feet pointed. The yellow pants and red top made it look like it belonged to Glida Kimura, who was known around town for her gaudy clothing.

But there was something wrong with the hair. Reports had said that the body here had brown hair, but in this light, the hair looked black. The face was impossible to see, half submerged, one milky eye open and staring.

Not for the first time, Tevin felt relieved that fish avoided this pool and birds found it impossible to get to. He hated seeing bodies that had been in the water and then picked apart by Ynchinga's wildlife.

"Is that Glida?" Novoa asked quietly.

"I don't think so," Dinithi said, just as quietly.

"Let's not jump to conclusions," Tevin said. "Let's just get her out, as carefully as possible."

14

Six layers of security on his way to the labs. Rajivk had never seen the security department this active. At each checkpoint, he had to answer questions from four different officers. He walked repeatedly through the detectors instead of being waved past. And before he took the stairs to the laboratory level, he had to stand under the examination light, normally used for guests and visitors with high clearance.

After he went through the first two layers of security, he thought maybe they were spending more time on him because he was disheveled from his attempted walk home. After the next two layers, he wondered if security was always this tight at night. After all, only a skeleton crew and a handful of stubborn techs worked at night. So therefore, anyone who came down here would be considered suspicious.

By the time he reached the last two layers of security, though, he realized that this level of response was unusual. Everyone was on edge, and it seemed to get worse the deeper he went into the sector base.

Down here, it actually felt like he was in a series of caverns. The black walls seemed to absorb the light in a way they didn't above. The ceilings were high, but that still didn't help the claustrophobic feel of the lower labs.

He didn't work down here regularly. He had requested and received a small lab on the second level of the base. He came down here occasionally because his supervisors asked him to repair the small ships that the DV-class ships used to land staff on planets or to explore parts of a new system.

But this level of the base was reserved for *anacapa* work, and he tried to avoid that. He hated *anacapa*s, and it showed. His discomfort with them actually caused his hands to shake whenever he had to touch them.

It wasn't an unusual reaction to the *anacapa* drive. A number of employees had similar issues.

But very few of those employees had ever traveled with the Fleet. Rajivk had. He knew that little bump-shift a DV-class ship would make as it activated its *anacapa*. He remembered the ever-so-slight increase in tension around the ship as it traveled in foldspace.

Everyone knew that some ships never returned from foldspace. And everyone worried that this time would be their time.

The relief when the ship left foldspace was always palpable.

He could never get those memories out of his head when he worked on *anacapa* drives. Those memories were what caused his hands to shake. That, and the worry that he might accidentally activate an *anacapa* and send himself into foldspace. Or do something he didn't entirely understand.

He preferred to repair every other part of a small ship. Those parts made sense to him. He could take them apart and rebuild them. He could construct a piece brand new. He could add new bits of technology and know how they would interact.

The *anacapa*…

His stomach clenched. He hadn't really thought it through when he got a summons from Iannazzi. She worked almost exclusively with *anacapa* drives. The fact that she had sent for him meant that he would be going into her lair, where there was never just one *anacapa* drive. Sometimes there were several.

The thought made him shudder as he passed through yet another detector. He wished he could turn around and head home. This time, he would take the underground transportation. He didn't want to see what was happening at the Falls, and he really didn't want to know what was happening here.

As if he had a choice to avoid it.

No one spoke as he passed through the last security point. At the others, there had been desultory conversation about the base closure, but nothing here. The silence bothered him almost as much as the beefed-up guard.

The security checkpoint here was several yards from the door to the *anacapa* labs. There was no signage, of course. The doors had numbers that only appeared for workers who had the security clearance to be down here.

He went through the main door and was surprised to see more security in the hall near the door to Bristol Iannazzi's lab. A woman, wearing a security-issued environmental suit, had her hood down. She was examining some recessed places near the door, places that had to house camera lenses.

A male security official who was not wearing an environmental suit examined the entrance locks. And still another security official, whose gender was impossible to determine, had taken apart a section of wall that housed even more equipment, a section that Rajivk, at least, hadn't realized was there.

His gaze went back to the environmental suit. His entire body stiffened. He no longer wanted to enter the lab at all.

"Excuse me," he said in his most authoritative voice. "Can someone tell me what's going on?"

The man handling the locks stood up. "And you are?"

"Rajivk Agwu. Bristol Iannazzi sent for me. I'm part of her team."

The man pulled out a handheld and tapped it. Apparently, he had information on the entire team on that thing.

"All right," he said. "You can enter."

Rajivk didn't move. "I'm not sure I want to. Do I need an environmental suit?"

He sounded scared, which surprised him. He hadn't realized he was scared until he spoke up. But he was. All those years of worrying about the *anacapa* drives had now come to this.

"No," the man said. "You're clear."

"Then why is one of your team wearing a suit?" Rajivk asked, wishing he could gain more control over his voice.

"An excess of caution that's no longer needed." The man stepped aside. "Go ahead and go in."

Rajivk's heart rate increased, and this time, the pounding of his heart felt different than it had at the Falls. There, he had known the dangers. He had protected himself from them, and he had done his best.

Here, he was walking into the unknown, and he was doing so for a paycheck.

He couldn't move his feet. He didn't want to die because someone had called him in for an emergency.

He'd had no idea that he was this deep-down terrified of the *anacapa* drive.

"Really, it's all right," the man said. "Apparently Iannazzi wants her team to examine data from the last few days. We're trying to figure out what happened."

"But *something* did happen, right?" Rajivk asked.

"Yeah," the man said. "And no one's exactly sure what it was."

15

WITH TINY PADDLES AND SOME EXPERT SCULLING, Tevin's team managed to ease the body to the edge of the pool.

"We caught a current," Dinithi said, loudly, over the sound of the Falls.

She was right. The body had reached the right position at the edge of the falling water to enable the group to slide it toward them using the strength of the water instead of fighting it.

The recovery of the body couldn't have gone better, although it wasn't entirely done yet.

Tevin wasn't going to call this a victory until he had the body back at his van.

Zhou had opened a body bag. It was spread out at the edge of the water, waiting for them to place her into it.

Her gender was certain, but little else was. The body had rolled as they pulled it toward them, the face going underwater.

A bit of a stench accompanied it as well. Not the bright, fresh dampness of the Falls, but something a little rotted, as if a dead fish were caught on a nearby rock.

The pool did have a slightly brackish odor that Tevin had noticed in the past. He had to assume that he was smelling a version of that odor right now.

Although smells could be indicative of cause of death. He remembered to turn on the analyzer on his suit as he crouched over the body itself. The analyzer sampled the air and stored a small sample for later testing. The analyzer also did an on-site reading, in case the scent or problem had been carried on a breeze and couldn't be captured easily.

He hoped the others had their analyzers on as well. He didn't want to mention it, though, not while they were concentrating on recovering the body.

Dinithi had crouched near the feet. Novoa was near the head. Zhou held the bag open, making sure it maintained its position.

Tevin, as the most experienced person on the team, had the torso. He gently slid his hands under it, even though standard procedure called for him to use a flat brace. He'd found that the edges of the brace caught on clothes and skin, making an autopsy even harder.

Not every body found in this pool was autopsied, but this one would be. No one had observed her going into the water, so there would be no way to know if the death was voluntary or involuntary. Murder, suicide, and accident—the death investigator had to take all three of those things into account now.

The watery clothing felt squishy against his gloves. He remembered to have the gloves' analyzers on as well, so that everything would be recorded.

This time, he would speak about it.

"Make sure your analyzers are all on," he said to his team. "We need a record of what we're finding here."

They didn't respond. They didn't have to. They knew the drill.

Tevin's gloves registered the frigid temperature of the water, warning him about it. He didn't need the warning. He couldn't feel the cold, but he had a sense of it. Something about his gloves felt different when they were in cold. He never could identify what that "something different" was, but he knew it existed.

He slowly worked his arms underneath the body. It was too close to shore for him to shove his hands beneath it. He had to touch the clothing and skin, but he did so gently.

He had no idea how long the body had been in the water, and sometimes skin sloughed off, loosened by the water itself. He didn't want that to happen here.

He finally reached the body's far side, and then eased his arms upward, actually holding the body in place.

"Now," he said. "Gently and carefully."

He had to say that for the record, in case something went wrong. He wanted the YSR-SR covered against all contingencies. The tourists had become litigious lately. He needed to make sure there was no real liability here.

Both Dinithi and Novoa verbally acknowledged him. Dinithi grabbed the body's ankles—gently, Tevin hoped—and Novoa placed her hands underneath the head.

On the count of three, they lifted the body.

He was braced, fortunately, because the body weighed more than he expected. He leaned ever so slightly forward, a little startled at the effort moving the body took.

Water poured off every surface, running like a minifalls into the pool. The team held the body over the pool until the water went from pouring to dripping. They didn't want to carry extra weight back with them if they could help it.

Then they levered the body over the bag and slowly lowered it onto the bag. Zhou continued to hold the bag in place.

Water gathered around the body itself, despite their precautions. The body was facedown as well, which was usually not an issue. They usually closed the bag and then carried it, remembering which side needed to face upward.

But they needed to do an on-site identification if they could.

"Let's roll her gently," Tevin said. He placed one hand on the body's shoulder.

Novoa kept the head stable. Dinithi moved away from the feet and crab walked until she was behind Tevin, so she could see as well. She grabbed Zhou's flashlight.

Tevin eased the body backward slightly. Novoa gently moved the head so that he could see the features. She had to smooth the hair away from the skin.

Tevin frowned. The face was bloated and blotchy. Even though the skin color was grayish-white like the water in the Falls itself, he was beginning to think the skin wasn't pale at all.

One eye was open and clouded, the other closed. The nose was lost in the water-swollen flesh. The lips were parted, revealing small white teeth.

He tried to compare in his mind that destroyed face with Glida's face. He couldn't. And he didn't dare remove a handheld and compare image to corpse. That would show a predisposition toward an identification, which had been a problem in the past.

"Do you recognize her?" Novoa asked. Implicit in her tone was the answer: *Of course you recognize her. Stop stalling and tell us.*

But he wasn't stalling. And Dinithi and Zhou were silent behind him.

"Do you recognize her?" Novoa asked again. This time, her tone was a straight inquiry, mixed with just a little confusion.

Dinithi and Zhou didn't volunteer their opinions, so Tevin spoke for all three of them.

"I'm not sure," he said. "I'm really not sure."

16

THE SANDOVEIL DINER SMELLED of onions frying with spicy mountainside greens. The air had a snap to it that meant the cook was frying the onions in toolique oil, conjuring mistura, a local delicacy that only a few could manage to make without setting the entire kitchen on fire.

Bassima Beck's stomach growled. She hadn't eaten since she'd had an early lunch. She'd spent much of the day searching for the Kimuras, on instructions from the security office. She'd spent enough time at the Kimuras' house to realize they were nowhere nearby, and for the last few hours, she'd been trying to trace the Kimuras' routines.

One of their routines had included eating regularly at the Sandoveil Diner. Or so Bassima had told herself when, really, she was just hungry.

Besides, the Kimuras had changed their routines greatly in the last few years. Bassima hadn't seen them much at all.

The diner was full this evening. The low hum of conversation didn't hide the interest the patrons were taking in Bassima. By now, everyone would know that something was wrong—that a body had been found. If she wasn't careful, everyone would ask her.

From the area near the door, she heard the telltale sizzle of water being added to the oil, the final step before the mushrooms, cheese, and egg that gave the dish its signature taste. Her stomach growled again, and she finally gave in, heading to the counter.

The tourists loved this place because it looked like something from Ancient Earth. The diner had been designed to look like an old Earth place, the interior taken from some old history that the Fleet had left behind.

The Fleet had originated on Earth millennia ago. If it weren't for the documentation, for the Fleet's history, Earth itself would be considered a myth. Some actually believed that, even now. And, if Bassima were truthful with herself, she half-believed it as well.

There were Fleet officers and crew in this diner. They didn't wear uniforms, except for formal occasions, but they looked different. Most of them were thinner than the locals—not in weight, so much, but in build. Despite all the precautions taken on the ships, those who had grown up shipside always looked more delicate. Their bones were thinner—strong, yes, but not as dense.

She could spot someone raised shipside with a single glance—at least among the tourists. Sometimes the locals surprised her. Privately, she believed they changed after living in Sandoveil for a decade or so. But the one time she had mentioned that to someone, they had accused her of judging people unfairly.

She hadn't thought she was judging anyone unfairly, although that was the moment she realized she had been judging people. Of course, judging them—sometimes at a glance—was part of her job.

Just like she was doing as she walked deeper into the diner. Two tables to her right were crammed with people from the latest Fleet ship to visit the sector base. They talked and laughed with a familiarity of people who had spent a lot of time together.

A table to her left had real tourists, probably from somewhere else on Nindowne. They ate quietly; plates of local food sat in the middle of the table, with everyone serving themselves and picking tentatively at the dishes.

One of the tourists noted the laser pistol on her hip, then looked up, saw her uniform, and turned away.

It was late enough in the day that the locals who were here were here for some kind of dinner. Locals nodded at her or smiled or looked away.

Bassima respected all of those reactions. When someone invited her to sit—which two different groups did, by patting the chairs or the empty place near them—she shook her head gently.

She needed time to think. She felt like she was missing something.

Hardly anyone sat at the counter. It wound its way through the entire restaurant, providing seating for people in a hurry or people who preferred to eat alone. She picked a seat on one of the curves that was mostly hidden from the people in the restaurant, but she had learned long ago that the seat actually provided a view of everyone and everything.

As soon as she sat on one of the round, padded stools, a servo unit rose in front of her, blinking its questions about her order. Someone had set the thing on mute, for which she was very grateful. She tapped in an order of mistura because it had smelled so good, some coffee since it would be a long night, and added a side of meringue plum cake for dessert.

Usually she didn't indulge like this when she was investigating, but the office had slowed her down twice now—the first time at the Kimuras' house, and the second time when she wanted to dig into their financial accounts to see when they were last used.

All of that was standard behavior when someone might be missing. Sometimes the best way to find out where they had gone was to see what they were currently spending money on.

Or not spending money, as the case might be.

But the office told her to hold off, to find out how their day went, and maybe, Amy Loraas had said, find one of the women and call this entire search off.

So far, Bassima hadn't found anything, and it frustrated her. Taji's company, a small consulting, information, and legal business, hadn't been open all week, which was odd. Taji always had her doors open when a Fleet ship was in town.

Many in the Fleet had no idea how planetside behaviors worked and so sometimes paid for help with that. Others just needed to consult on what was normal—at least in this place. And still others needed help with legal advice from someone who wasn't part of the Fleet but understood it.

Bassima wasn't certain how Taji became an expert in both Fleet customs and planetside behaviors. She wasn't even sure how much of an expert Taji was, except that she was *the* expert for Sandoveil.

The servo unit brought a sizzling plate of mistura. The oil still popped and the greens had turned so bright they almost seemed alive. All of it rested on a bed of cheese and eggs ringed by thinly sliced onions and mushrooms.

Bassima dug in, trying to sort the information she had gathered. Taji's business was closed. No one had seen either woman most of the week, not even at the grocers or any of the restaurants.

Although Bassima hadn't asked here. She would have to go into the kitchen to do that. The chef was the only working human on the premises. Everything else was done by automation or servo units.

Bassima ate slowly, savoring every spicy bite. Behind her, the conversations were mostly about the base closing and the decisions every single family faced now. Did they leave their established life on Sandoveil or did they try to find new employment here?

The servo unit finally brought her coffee, but it was too hot to drink. She stared at the dark liquid, then frowned. It wasn't just the people at the sector base itself who would have to make choices.

Taji's business was based entirely on Fleet visits. She didn't cater to the average tourist. She specialized in assisting Fleet crews, and she seemed to understand all the vagaries of Fleet rules and regulations, which seemed to vary from ship to ship.

She never said whether or not she loved her job, but she had done it for years and years. She had to enjoy it on some level, or she would have shut it down. Right?

Bassima had no idea how to answer that last question to herself. She had always worked for other people, although she had only worked on things she loved. She assumed everyone else made similar choices.

She finished the mistura and waited for her plum cake, although she wasn't sure she wanted it anymore. She wanted to check out Taji's business the way she had checked out the house. She had gone by the business before, but she hadn't really examined it. She hadn't given it much thought.

And it deserved a bit more of her time.

She had a hunch she might find some answers there.

17

Two members of Bristol's team still hadn't arrived. The other four hovered in the back of her lab. She didn't want to brief her team until everyone was here. Talking to people was stressful enough for her without having to repeat herself six times.

Still, waiting meant the lab was even more crowded than it had been just an hour ago. Her skin crawled. She wanted the unnecessary security personnel to get out. She half-wanted even the essential personnel to get out.

She rubbed her hands together and glanced at the door into the lab, willing the remaining two members of her team to arrive. But they didn't. Instead, someone touched her right arm. She jumped, and turned at the same time.

Wèi.

"Come with me," he said.

She took a deep breath, nodded at her team, and then walked with him inside the storage room.

She didn't want to be in there. She could see the walls glistening as they continued to repair themselves. The fact that it was taking hours to repair the damage—whatever it had been—meant that the damage had been extensive.

She tried not to look at the walls. Instead, she focused on Wèi. Two other members of his team were in here: Fitzwilliam and Tranh.

"We found a new image," Wèi said.

He put up a holoscreen. A human-sized image floated in the center of the room. The image was of a woman. She was slight, with sharp features, and long brown hair pulled away from her face.

In spite of herself, Bristol took a step backward. It was as if someone else had walked into the room. She had already had enough of people. Another stranger made her uneasy.

Then she swallowed hard and made herself walk around the image. Usually these holographic images were the same size as the actual person.

She had been wrong, earlier. She didn't recognize this woman at all. Not from the front, and not from the back. Bristol didn't think she had ever seen the woman in person, but she was aware that holographic images were not the same as actually seeing the person, particularly when the image was static.

"Who is this?" Bristol asked.

"You don't know?" Wèi asked.

Bristol shook her head. "I've never seen her—that I can remember, anyway."

"She's the person who spent thirty-six hours inside this room," he said.

Bristol moved away from the image. It made her queasy. She had known, since she saw the shadowy figure, that someone had spent a lot of time in her lab. She hadn't really put together that it was more than a day.

"I thought we couldn't identify the person," Bristol said.

"It took some imagery manipulation," Wèi said, "and a bit of carelessness on her part. Not here, but at the upper levels of security."

Bristol walked back to the door, staying away from the glistening walls.

"She works here," Bristol said, as the realization dawned. "That's why you think I know her."

"Not in the lab," Wèi said. "At the base."

"Yeah, her and most of Sandoveil," Bristol said. "I don't know all of them either. I don't even see all of them. I'm not very social. I don't go into town much—"

He put up a hand, stopping her. She made herself take a deep breath. She was sounding as stressed as she felt. And the stress was veering into panic.

They weren't going to blame her for this, were they? That was her biggest fear, that they would somehow pin whatever happened here on her, and take her work away from her.

She didn't want to lose her work. It was her life.

She drew in a shaky breath.

"She works in security," Wèi said quietly.

It took a moment for Bristol to process that sentence.

"What?" she asked, but more as a filler than an actual question. Security? That meant this woman was Wèi's responsibility, not Bristol's. "She works for you?"

Wèi tilted his head slightly, as if he didn't even approve of the question. "She works in a different department. Sector Base E-2 has one of the largest security staffs in the Fleet, primarily because Sandoveil became a major tourist destination."

Bristol wasn't sure she knew that. She wasn't sure she knew much about security at all, except that it existed, and it was a pain in the butt to go through when she came to the lab. This afternoon had been the first time she had contacted security, although she'd been through sweeps before.

"But you know who she is, then." Bristol wasn't sure if that made her feel better or not. She was still jittery, and some of that was the storage room.

"Yeah," Wèi said. "Her name is Glida Kimura."

He paused as if Bristol should know the name. She didn't.

"She's worked at the base for more than thirty years," he added.

"What part of security did she work in?" Bristol felt like she was behind in understanding what he knew.

"That's the thing." Wèi glanced at the holographic image. It didn't move, of course, making it look like a woman frozen in place, a woman who thought she couldn't be seen simply by not moving.

Bristol made herself look away from the image, and look at Wèi.

He seemed to have been waiting for that, to get her full attention. She wasn't sure why, exactly, except that he felt what he was going to say next was extremely important.

"Kimura worked as an information manager," Wèi said, as if Bristol should know what that was too. "She had been reassigned."

Bristol shrugged, then shook her head.

"She didn't leave her office. She could work at home with some of the non-classified stuff." Wèi was speaking louder with each sentence. Tranh glanced over at him, as if he were making her nervous. "If she was in her office right now, we would probably farm some of this information up to her."

Bristol frowned. "I'm sorry. I still don't understand."

Wèi took a deep breath, as if speaking the next sentence aloud put a huge burden on him.

"She shouldn't have been able to come down here. With her security clearance, she was limited to the upper part of the base."

Now, Bristol was really confused. "Then how could she work on secure materials?"

Tranh gave Wèi an exasperated glance as if she believed he was making all of this too difficult.

"The security team has several different kinds of clearances," she said. "Some are information-based, some are location-based, and some are both."

Bristol let out a small breath. She wasn't looking at Wèi any longer, and she tried not to look at that holographic image. The longer she stood near it, the more it upset her.

She was watching Tranh. Tranh had come closer, as if she knew that Bristol felt more comfortable around her. Maybe Bristol did. At least Tranh was a familiar face.

"So, Glida Kimura had information clearance," Bristol said, "and nothing else."

Tranh nodded.

"She used to have overall clearance, though." Fitzwilliam spoke from the back. Both Wèi and Tranh turned at the sound of his voice.

Bristol couldn't entirely tell, but it seemed to her that his words surprised his teammates.

"How do you know that?" Wèi asked before Bristol could.

Fitzwilliam's uneven face broke into an uneven smile. "I used to work with her," he said. "A long, long time ago."

18

Tevin sent Zhou and Novoa back to the van with the body. Because it was so waterlogged, it was heavier than the average female body. But Zhou was strong and could have carried it on his own. Novoa was just as strong, and would back him up if he needed help getting the body out of here.

Tevin trusted the two of them to handle the path back to the van on their own. He didn't trust Dinithi. She was too inexperienced with this part of the Falls.

He kept her here, beside him, partly because she was a hard worker, and partly because he needed to teach her when the rules were more important than her rebel spirit. Back here, in the side pools behind the Falls, rules trumped everything.

The lights were still on from above, making the pool water seem greenish-gold, and the Falls ice-gray. The falling water wasn't as much a sound as a vibration: he could feel it in his teeth, and all the way through his bones. He knew he would feel it in his dreams for the next two or three nights.

He and Dinithi were using scanlights, catchalls, and good, old-fashioned water rakes to make sure they hadn't missed anything. He had two small underwater probes in his equipment bag, but he didn't want to use them. The probes cost money, and no matter how skilled one of the team was at deploying them, they always ended up getting caught in the currents in this pool and eventually getting destroyed on the rocks.

He would use the old-fashioned equipment first, then, if he had a hint that he had missed something, he would send out a probe. If the probe saw something, he would send in divers to recover it—if he couldn't do it with more equipment.

All judgment calls, and all based on what he knew, what he was told, and what he could see.

He and Dinithi needed to make certain that they hadn't missed anything. After all, there had been two pair of shoes on that overlook, which meant there could easily have been two bodies in this pool. His big concern was that one had floated and the other had sunk.

"You know they think that the body belongs to Glida Kimura," Dinithi said softly.

Tevin wished she hadn't spoken, because her words were now on the record. His entire team was still wearing their hoods, ostensibly so that they could continue to communicate. He had other ways to communicate with the team that didn't require wearing the full environmental suit. But it was dangerous back here, and he wanted both himself and Dinithi protected if one of them accidentally fell into the pool.

He didn't answer Dinithi. He was using one of the rakes to stir up the water. The rakes could extend and go deep. They also had cameras attached to the tines. No one was examining the live footage. He would go over it himself when he returned to YSR-SR headquarters.

"You could have told them what you saw," Dinithi said. Clearly, his silence was irritating her.

He wanted to tell her to shut up. He hated on-the-record speculation. He glanced at her. She was using one of the scanlights toward the edge of the Falls.

The scanlights floated, pointing downward, illuminating what was beneath them. She had to have a small window open on her hood visor so she could monitor what the light was showing. She wouldn't turn up much that way because the water was constantly churning, but it was the only way to safely examine that part of the pool.

At some point, he would have to decide whether or not to send divers into the pool to see if they could find another body. He wanted to avoid that if possible. The surface of this part of Rockwell Pool looked calmer than the rest of the pool, but no part of the pool was calm, particularly below the surface.

He'd only been down there once, but the currents, crosscurrents, and eddies were so strong that he had felt pulled in a thousand different direction at once.

It was the hardest dive he had ever done, and he didn't want to repeat it.

"Why didn't you tell them?" Dinithi asked.

She clearly wasn't going to let this go.

"I don't do investigations on the fly," he said, more for the record than for her.

"That's not true," she said. "I've been with you on several recoveries where you identified the body right away."

He grated his teeth together, then wondered if the sound would show up on the record. Maybe he shouldn't care. But he did.

He raked harder. The water in front of him was filled with sediment, but none of it looked like human detritus of any kind.

He made himself focus on that, instead of answering her.

"I mean," she said, "they think it's—"

"It doesn't matter what they think," he snapped, cutting her off before she repeated the identification for a second time. "What matters is what they know. They were basing their opinion on hair color and clothing. No one was down here until us."

At least, that was what he hoped they had based it on. He never really questioned it. He hated knowing the assumptions before he went into a scenario. Sometimes he hated it because he didn't want to know the details—*the deceased is a family man, three children, all under the age of five. Raising them alone*—and sometimes, he didn't want to know because knowing pushed the identification in the wrong direction.

This, clearly, was one of those wrong-direction times.

Which he didn't want to explain to Dinithi, not on the record, not in the ways that might actually make some kind of difference in some kind of investigation.

"Tevin," she said. "If you know—"

"That's just it, Cherish," he said. "I *don't* know. I didn't know. I couldn't tell, not from the kind of examination we did. Sometimes you can know. Sometimes you can guess. I didn't know and I couldn't guess."

"But you could have used an image—"

"No." He stood up. His back ached from the pulling and raking and the lifting of the body. He winced, and wished he hadn't. "It's not my job—it's not *your* job—to identify the person we recovered. It's our job to recover that person. We've done that. And now we have to see if she was alone down here. That's all."

Dinithi didn't answer, which was typical of her behavior whenever he spoke sharply to her. He loved her work, but he had to remember she was, like everyone else on the crew, a volunteer. She was supposed to have training, but she probably didn't have as much as some of the other volunteers had when they were new.

He actually had no idea, because training quality depended on the training instructors. Everyone saw the recorded stuff and went through the same tests, but when it came to the in-the-field hands-on work, it all depended on who the trainer was and what kinds of calls the young volunteers went on.

"It looked like Glida Kimura to me," Dinithi said sullenly.

Tevin felt his heart sink. He did *not* want that on the record at all. When they returned—hell, when they got off the communications equipment—he would remind her not to have these kinds of speculative conversations when they were being recorded.

"Did you know her?" he asked, because he had to ask that now, because she had forced his hand.

"No," Dinithi said, and he cursed silently.

"Then what makes you say that?" He needed to ask that question as well, now that she had forced him into it.

"I called up her image when I heard the speculation. The features match up," Dinithi said.

He almost asked how she could know that, given the distortion from the water, but he didn't want any more of her opinions on the official record.

Instead, he said, "The features were hidden in the bloat, the skin was damaged by the cold water, the eyes were cloudy. We can't make identifications based on visuals when that happens. It's not allowed by the death investigator, and frankly, it shouldn't be. So stop speculating, Cherish. It does no one any good."

She didn't respond again. He was glad for that. This conversation was over, as far as he was concerned. He'd have to shut her down even harder if she tried again.

But she didn't say anything. Instead, she was running the scanlight back and forth over the same patch of water.

He hoped that was a mental glitch on her part.

"Tevin," she said in an entirely different tone of voice. "You need to look."

He sighed and piggybacked on the scanlight signal she was working off of. A window opened in his hood visor. He saw sediment, white and powdery, then shadows of the water as it forced its way down toward the bottom of the pool.

He almost asked her what she was talking about when he did see something, something glittery that caught the light, something that was not a natural part of the environment.

"Move the light again," he said, coming over to her side.

Then he leaned as far forward as he could, pushing with the rake. Whatever it was didn't budge. It was wedged down below.

He was about to give up on the rake entirely when it grated against something. The little window on his hood visor showed him that the rake's tines had snagged a bit of chain, raising it up just enough to reveal fine links, tiny ones—not something to hold equipment, but something ornamental. A metal lanyard, maybe, or maybe a necklace. A long one.

He couldn't tell what it was attached to, if it had fallen free from the corpse's neck or if it had been dropped a decade ago by some long-lost visitor. The scanlight didn't penetrate any farther into the gloom.

All he could see below were rocks and shadows.

He cursed, under his breath this time.

He was going to have to send in the probe. And generally, when a probe went into the water, divers followed.

"Okay," he said, gently dislodging the tongs from the chain. "On to phase two."

19

Rajivk stepped inside Bristol Iannazzi's lab. He had never seen it so crowded. People he didn't know, some in environmental suits, worked at the lab stations against the wall. Others carried tablets, and still others worked with holographic screens, all examining data.

He didn't see Iannazzi at all, which surprised him. She was usually at the center of this lab, like a spider in the middle of a web. He'd always hated coming down here. She usually had an *anacapa* drive open and half-disassembled on the platform in the center of the room. The lab usually smelled like some kind of spicy incense, even though she didn't burn any here. She probably burned it at home, and it came in on her clothing. Because she didn't dare have fragrances in here that would interfere with the *anacapa* drive.

He looked at the center of the lab, the *anacapa* table and storage. The table was folded up, forming part of the container for the drive. The container was locked, and a red light blinked on the console, signifying that the lock was encrypted as well.

At least no one had gotten into that, yet. It didn't quite relieve him, but it did make him feel incrementally safer.

The only thing that calmed him were the members of Iannazzi's team—his team—hunkered in the back like refugees in a foreign land. Five of them, clustered together, watching the others work as if the lab had been invaded by a foreign army.

He didn't see Iannazzi anywhere. But he went to the rest of the team. Three women, three men, counting him, with Iannazzi above all of them, although that really didn't count. Rajivk's immediate supervisor wasn't Iannazzi. It was Jasmine Pereyra.

She stood slightly in front of the team, as if she were guarding them against intruders. She was a tiny, plump woman with hair that changed color almost daily. This day's color, fading as the day had faded, was a peachy purple. It made her dark skin seem sallow. Or maybe that was her reaction to everything going on.

"Where's Bristol?" he asked quietly, instead of saying hello.

"In the storage room," Pereyra said just as quietly.

"What the hell happened?" he asked.

"From what we can tell, a break-in and possibly a theft."

He immediately glanced at the *anacapa* container. His throat closed with the panic that had threatened since he realized all the security had been bolstered because of the crisis—whatever the crisis was. A stolen *anacapa*, particularly one from this lab, was beyond a crisis.

It was a disaster. The *anacapa*s here were malfunctioning. Iannazzi was the expert on repairing the small *anacapa*s. The rest of the team backed her up, did research on lost *anacapa*s or on the ships that worked with the *anacapa*s. The ships were his specialty, but half the team, those huddled behind Pereyra, did the *anacapa* work.

"No," she said, following his gaze. "That's okay as far as we know."

He frowned at her.

"The runabout in the storage room is gone," she said, "and the room is damaged." She swept a hand at all the people around him. "Everyone here is supposed to figure out what happened."

Security investigations. That explained it. But his brain was having trouble figuring out what was going on. The runabout in the storage room was being retrofitted. It had many working problems. It should have been retired decades ago, but the captain of the *Ijo* liked those old-fashioned runabouts and wanted to keep them in service.

"If they're all investigating what happened," Rajivk said, "then why are we here?"

"Because Bristol thinks this might be a tech issue," Pereyra said.

Rajivk started to ask another question, but Pereyra raised her hand, stopping him.

"That's all I know. She's in the storage room. Now that we're all here, we're to report there."

He stiffened. The room was small and wouldn't hold the six of them, plus Iannazzi and the runabout.

But the runabout had been stolen. His frown grew. To steal a runabout from a storage room at the deepest security level of a sector base, the *anacapa* had to be activated. And Iannazzi had removed the *anacapa* drive, replacing it with an even older one.

He hadn't been present for that, but he had known about it. That was one reason why he had refused to work on that particular runabout until its regular *anacapa* drive was repaired. In theory, the regular drive wouldn't malfunction while he was on the runabout.

He had been lobbying to have Leroy Sheldenhelm work on the interior of the runabout—on-site—while Rajivk remained in his lab, studying the data. He had delayed the decision, though, by asking Iannazzi (through Pereyra) to wait until the original *anacapa* was restored.

Sheldenhelm stood near the back wall, head down, fingers laced together in front of him, as if he had just finished praying. He looked terrified.

Rajivk didn't need to see that. He looked away.

"Come on," Pereyra said, and then headed toward the storage room.

Rajivk waited until the others followed, then brought up the rear. He hated that storage room. It was larger than some—big enough to handle the runabout—but the room had always felt slightly claustrophobic to him. The idea of working in there, along with five other people, and Iannazzi, made him nervous. He hated being in that room with anyone else.

As he threaded his way around the closed *anacapa* storage container, his skin crawling, he wished he were anywhere else. There were too many people in the lab, let alone in that storage room.

What a strange day. The announcement of the base closure. The shoes. And now this.

Pereyra opened the storage room door, and voices filtered into the lab, voices that stopped the moment they noticed the door was open.

Rajivk tensed. Just what they needed: even more people inside that storage room.

But, he knew, Iannazzi was in there. Why would he have expected her to be alone?

The team walked through the door, and moved to one side. Rajivk entered last, startled to see four others besides Iannazzi and the person she was talking to. Iannazzi and four of the others were wearing environmental suits, with the hoods down. But the remaining person was dressed casually—and, he realized, she was frozen in the middle of the floor.

The door banged behind him, and he jumped. One of the women in the environmental suits had pulled it shut. He glanced at her, recognizing her from security, but he didn't know her name.

And still, the woman in the middle of the room hadn't moved.

It was a holographic image, someone in mid-movement.

His mouth went dry. It was Glida Kimura.

"What the hell?" he asked, his worry about overcrowding forgotten.

Everyone in the storage room turned to him. He didn't look at them, but instead walked toward the image of Glida. She was mostly solid, but he could see the glimmering of the black nanobit walls behind her.

The walls were supposed to glimmer. No wonder Iannazzi had brought the team in here. The room was repairing itself.

Still.

Which meant the damage to this room had been extensive.

That crawling feeling under his skin had grown worse. He suddenly wondered if it was more than simple aversion to the situation and all the other people. Was that feeling also being caused by something in this room? Something he couldn't see? A remaining chemical reaction? Something to do with the explosions? Some kind of electric charge in the air?

He suddenly wished he had an environmental suit, for protection or something. But he didn't say anything.

Instead, he walked toward that image of Glida.

"What's going on?" Pereyra asked the question, not Iannazzi. Iannazzi, as head of the team, should have been the one to corral her teammate, but Iannazzi had never been very good with people.

"That's Glida Kimura," Rajivk said. His voice sounded hollow even to himself.

"Yes," said one of the men wearing an environmental suit. He was the one standing closest to Iannazzi. His brown eyes snapped with intelligence, and his tone was flat, as if he were humoring Rajivk somehow.

"But I thought..." He let the words trail. He wasn't supposed to know that the YSR-SR believed—that *he* believed—the body in the pool belonged to Glida.

"You thought what?" The man's tone sharpened.

Rajivk sighed. He had already started, and they were in an enclosed environment, dealing with some kind of confidential emergency. By the time he got out of here, the situation at the Falls would probably be resolved.

Or so he told himself. Because he didn't think he dared keep this information back.

"This is going to sound so strange," he said. His voice still didn't sound like his own. "This afternoon, after I left work, I went walking up the trails at Fiskett Falls."

One of the women just at the edge of his vision shifted from foot to foot. Everyone was uncomfortable in here, and no one wanted to be here, and now he was prolonging their torture.

So he shortened the story.

"I...um...saw a body in one of the pools. And honestly, I thought it was Glida's."

"What?" the man asked. He looked at Iannazzi as if she had an explanation.

She looked like she was about to burst into tears. She had always struck him as the most nervous department head he had ever met, someone who preferred to be alone. And now she was in a small room with nine other people. That alone would probably make her lose it after a while.

But with the added stress of this crisis, she seemed to be barely holding on.

Rajivk made himself look away. He didn't have a lot of sympathy for her, and he probably should have.

"You saw her up close?" the woman who closed the door asked.

Rajivk shook his head. "Just the clothes. Her hair."

And, he realized as he looked at this image, the hair had been off. Or this image was older. Because that hair was long, and the hair here was short.

"What?" Iannazzi asked. Her voice shook. "What-what-what's making you so uncertain?"

Rajivk's gaze met hers. He had forgotten how perceptive she could be. Maybe that was why he never really liked her. She was odd and perceptive.

"When was this hologram made?" he asked, pointing at Glida.

"From an image in the last twenty-four hours," the man in the environmental suit said. He was clearly in charge in some way.

Rajivk swallowed hard. He mentally compared the woman in the water to this woman, and realized he had no idea who he had been looking at in the pool. Was he supposed to think that Glida Kimura had died? Was it some kind of setup?

He shook his head. "Something's really wrong here."

"Clearly," said the woman who had closed the door.

The rest of the team was watching quietly, as if they didn't know what to make of this.

He didn't know what to make of it either. He was confused. She was dead, but she had been at the base twenty-four hours ago? He didn't understand.

"Why exactly do you have Glida's image down here?" Rajivk asked.

"She's the one who broke into the lab," the man in the environmental suit said. "She might even have stolen the runabout."

That very idea made his brain hurt.

"Glida?" he asked. "Really? You think she could have done that? She's completely harmless."

"You're basing that on what?" the other man in an environmental suit asked. He had shaved his head, and clearly not for aesthetic reasons, since he didn't have a symmetrical skull.

Rajivk didn't ever remember seeing him before. Or any of them, besides the woman in the suit.

He looked at Iannazzi, who nodded at him, her lips thin. The nod could be interpreted any which way, but Rajivk chose to interpret it to mean *go ahead and tell them*.

He shrugged. He wasn't sure why he thought Glida was harmless. He just did. He usually prided himself on having a good sense of people.

"It's not based on anything, really," Rajivk said, and realized just how stupid that sounded. "I mean, I've seen her around. I know she works here, and I know that she wanted to get married up at the Falls. I'm not sure if she did, but she and her wife walk around the Falls a lot. I figured they love it here as much as I do."

The words hung in the air. They didn't quite echo, but Rajivk could feel them, as if they hadn't dissipated.

"None of this makes any sense," Iannazzi said, her voice trembling. "This Glida woman doesn't have security clearance to get down here."

"But she used to," the man with the shaved head said.

"Rajivk, who is a good and honorable man, thinks she died in a pool near the Falls," Iannazzi continued as if the man hadn't spoken.

Rajivk felt his face heat. Iannazzi had never given him a compliment before. If he had been asked a few hours ago what her opinion was of him, he would have said she didn't have one.

And she probably hadn't even realized she had complimented him. Because he finally recognized her tone. It was one she used when she was brainstorming an idea.

"That's not quite what he said," the woman in the suit said.

Rajivk glanced at her, unused to being discussed in the third person. "No, that is what I said. It's just that the identification was based on the appearance from above."

"What you said," Iannazzi continued in that same tone, "was that everyone *thinks* the body in the pool belongs to Glida. Which is just brilliant."

The three people who had been in the room with her looked at her in surprise. Pereyra smiled just a little, as did Sheldenhelm. They had worked with her, just like Rajivk had.

Iannazzi liked to think out loud, and whenever she came across something that was smart, she labeled it as such, even when it got in the way of some theory she was proposing or something she was doing.

"Why is it brilliant?" the first man asked. He sounded almost offended.

Iannazzi blinked at him as if she had forgotten he was here.

"Well, think about it," she said, and then didn't say another word. Her sentence wasn't a rhetorical twist. It was an order.

Rajivk felt an inappropriate giggle rise in his throat. The fact that the inappropriate response was a giggle—something he probably had done three times in his adult life—told him just how very nervous he was.

He knew that look of confusion the first man had. Rajivk had had the same look on his face the first few times he worked directly with Iannazzi. She expected everyone to keep up.

When she said *think about it*, she wasn't going to explain any more. She was going to let the person *think* about it, and come to their own conclusion.

"I have thought about it," the man said, even though he really hadn't had a lot of time to consider it all, "and I have no idea why *you* think this is brilliant."

He sounded both annoyed and offended, as if he hated having his own stupidity pointed out to him while expecting her to spoon-feed him whatever it was she had been thinking.

Rajivk had a hunch he knew, but he'd learned over the years that his hunches were never as complete as Iannazzi's. Which was why she had her own lab and team, and he was on the team—avoiding Iannazzi whenever he could, because she made him feel stupid sometimes too.

But, as usual, Iannazzi didn't consider how her words made other people feel. Although the man in the environmental suit's annoyance had gotten through to her. Strong emotions sometimes did.

She leaned back, looking at the man as if she were seeing him for the first time.

Rajivk braced himself. He knew how this next bit would go before she said a word.

"Well, it's obvious, isn't it?" she said to the man.

"If it were obvious, I wouldn't have asked you," he snapped.

Most people would have smiled at that, thinking they had won some kind of rhetorical battle. But Iannazzi hadn't been battling. She had actually expected him (and the team) to keep up.

"This Glida woman," Iannazzi said as if she were speaking to a very young child, "faked her own death, probably to buy some time."

"Time for what?" the man asked.

Iannazzi looked at the man, a slight frown on her face. "Time to steal the runabout. We wouldn't be looking for her if we thought she was dead."

Iannazzi said that last as if anyone would do the same thing in the same circumstance. And maybe she was right. Because it seemed logical now.

But Rajivk felt a chill run through him.

"You're saying Glida would have had to kill another woman and toss her body into the pool just to buy some time," he said, but even as he spoke, his brain was whirling. Of course. That explained the shoes.

Two people didn't take off their shoes and then fall to their deaths. Someone—Glida—put both pair of shoes in the overlook, and then put a body in that pool. She knew procedure. She knew that the YSR-SR team would search for the owners of both pairs of shoes.

She had also known that if they misidentified the body as Glida's, they would think the other missing person was her wife.

Rajivk shook his head a little, not liking the way his own thoughts were going.

But apparently, he wasn't walking down this mental trail on his own, because Pereyra put her hand on his arm.

"Were you there long enough to see the rescue team bring the body out?" she asked.

He shook his head.

"So we don't even know if what you saw was an actual body," Pereyra said.

"What?" the man in the environmental suit asked. "He just said it was a body." Then he looked at Rajivk. "It *was* a body, right?"

"I looked down on it from the top of the Falls," Rajivk said. "I assumed it was real, but I don't know if it was."

The very idea that the body wasn't real made him feel uncomfortable, and the fact that he was uncomfortable made him even more uncomfortable. If the body was fake, he had called out the YSR-SR team for no reason, and that bothered him. Former YSR-SR volunteers knew better than to send in a false alarm.

But how was he to know?

And did he really want that body to be real? Because if it was, then someone was dead—and they had probably died badly.

"I didn't think we had murderers here," said Pereyra. She sounded perplexed.

Rajivk realized that he was feeling perplexed too. He couldn't remember the last murder in Sandoveil. If there had ever been a murder in Sandoveil.

If there had been one now.

"We don't know if she did murder someone," Rajivk said. He wasn't sure why he was defending Glida. He wasn't even sure if he *was* defending Glida. Maybe he was defending himself, what he saw, and what he had perceived.

"All we know," the security woman said, "is that she stole the runabout."

"We don't even know that," Iannazzi said. "That's why I called the team in here. This room is still repairing itself. There's a good chance the runabout never left."

Rajivk let out a small breath. He hadn't thought of that either.

But, if the runabout was still here, then it would be shielded, and still in the center of the room. He should have been able to touch it—well, *someone* should have been able to touch it.

"We would have bumped into it by now," the man in the environmental suit said, using that same condescending voice Iannazzi had used on him.

She didn't seem to notice. She never noticed rhetorical games. It was one of the things that was most annoying about her.

She was shaking her head. "I know it's not shielded. It's obvious that the runabout is no longer intact."

The color drained from the man's face. It clearly hadn't been obvious to him until just then. And Rajivk wasn't sure a non-scientist would understand the implications.

So he said them aloud, to Iannazzi, as kind of a way of explaining things to everyone else. "You think it exploded."

Her gaze met his. Her eyes were glistening slightly, as if she were overstimulated and just a little terrified. Her lower lip was bleeding in the center. She must have been biting it.

"That's why I called you in here," she said, then swept her hand at the whole team. "Whatever happened in here was bad."

Her words hung in the room. That crawling feeling increased underneath Rajivk's skin. Now he knew at least part of it was nerves. But he had no idea what part.

Sheldenhelm glanced at him, eyes wide. Pereyra was biting the cuticle on her left thumb, apparently not even realizing she was doing it. The other members of the team looked as stunned as Rajivk felt.

The idea of standing in an *anacapa* blast zone made his heart pound even harder.

"The question," the man in the environmental suit said, "is whether that bad thing was intentional or accidental."

"That's not the question," Iannazzi said curtly. "The question is, did the runabout go into foldspace or did it explode?"

"I got that," the man in the environmental suit snapped again.

"No, you didn't," Iannazzi said. "Because if it did explode, we have even more questions. Did the temporary *anacapa* drive malfunction? Did it destroy the runabout, or did the malfunction send the runabout into foldspace? And if it did, was that foldspace the foldspace that Glida had planned to go to?"

Rajivk felt a shiver run through him. He had never heard anyone discuss the various ways that foldspace could malfunction—at least, not in an official capacity.

"Or," Iannazzi was saying, clearly not finished, "did something else malfunction on the runabout? The thing was old and poorly maintained. There were a dozen ways that it could have obliterated itself. Which is why I want my team in here, why I want us to investigate what happened, before the nanobits repair it all and ruin our best evidence."

She looked at Pereyra, then at Rajivk, and that look couldn't have been clearer. *Get to work*, it said.

Rajivk took a deep breath. She was right: they needed to act fast. He nodded at Pereyra. They had to start reviewing everything that happened, as well as scraping information off the walls before it all went away.

He returned to the team. They all looked determined.

But apparently, the man in the environmental suit wasn't done with his pissing contest with Iannazzi.

"That's the question *you* have to deal with," he said. "But you're acting on an assumption. You believing she came in to steal the ship."

"Of course I am," Iannazzi said. "Why else would she go through that elaborate ruse and come down here?"

"And I thought assumptions were an anathema to science," the man said.

Iannazzi opened her mouth, apparently to rebut him, but he continued.

"What I want to know," he said, "is did this Glida woman intend to steal the runabout? If so, why? And if she didn't, did she come down here to steal something *off* the runabout? Did she accidentally triggered something? Or, did she come down here intending to blow up the runabout? And if so, why?"

"If she did intend to blow it up," said the man with the shaved head, "how come she didn't know that the blast doors would protect the base?"

"Or maybe she did know that," the other man said.

"Then why would she want to blow up the runabout?" one of the women in the environmental suits asked.

Iannazzi was watching all of them, shaking so hard that it looked like she was vibrating. For the first time since he met her, Rajivk felt some sympathy for her.

"We always speculated that the blast doors might not hold," she said quietly. "At least if something happened with an *anacapa* drive."

Everyone looked at her.

"The idea was that *anacapa*s would link together, create something bigger." Her voice was firmer than Rajivk would have expected it to be, given what she was discussing. "That's why each lab is on its own level, and why they're not stacked one on top of the other."

Her gaze met Rajivk's. He knew, at that moment, that she had always understood his fear of the *anacapa*, and maybe even respected it. And yet she had continued to work around them.

"Maybe the question is," Iannazzi said, clenching her hands together so hard that her knuckles had turned white, "why had she waited so long inside the storage room? Had she waited for me to arrive?"

"I hate to be blunt," the man said in one of those snide tones that actually meant he didn't hate it at all, "but there would have been much easier ways to kill you."

"Oh, I know that," Iannazzi whispered. "But I work on *anacapa* drives. And the one in my lab would have been unshielded after I arrived."

Rajivk's throat went dry. "You think she was trying to destroy the base?"

"I thought that was impossible," Sheldenhelm said. "All those safeguards—"

"Safeguards can be worked around," said the same woman as before. "If it was completely impossible to circumvent them, there would be no need for security."

"Why would anyone want to blow up the base?" asked Pereyra. "Especially today."

She clearly meant after the closure meeting. There would be no point. The base's future had become finite in a very concrete way.

"She didn't go to the meeting, right?" Rajivk looked at that man. "I mean, you said she was here."

"She was here," he said softly. "While everyone else was several stories up. In the same room."

20

HE ALWAYS FOUND THE PROBES to be unbelievably tiny, given the amount of work they had to do. Tevin held the probe in his right hand. The probe was round and gray, with ridges along each side. The entire thing had redundancies upon redundancies upon redundancies. It contained a multitude of sensors, lights, cameras. It read every kind of information it possibly could about its environment—everything its designers knew about environments, and everything the designers could anticipate.

Designed for space and space exploration, the probe had more power than any other tool in his YSR-SR arsenal. Very few on the staff could use the probes. He was the only one on his team approved to carry one—partly because the damn things were so expensive.

Dinithi was still working her scanlight over the small circle of water where they had found the human-made chain. She also held his rake, her arm trembling just a little.

He hadn't wanted to set the rake down. He had wanted to keep it in the exact same position, so that they wouldn't lose the chain in the rocks or break it by trying to pull it up to the surface.

He brought the probe to her side. She glanced down at it, her mouth pursed in a bemused smile.

"It's smaller than I thought it would be," she said.

He had had the same reaction the first time he saw one. Then he had picked it up. The probes were dense and heavy, which more than made up for their small size.

The water lapped at their feet. He had actually become used to the roar of the waterfall, although he did know if someone tried to yell at him from above, he wouldn't be able to hear it. He had his hood off, so his cheeks were damp and chilled.

With his free hand, he put his hood on again. Before he had left the YSR-SR office, he had synched the probe to his own comm system just like he was supposed to do. He was rather amazed he had done so. Sometimes he forgot.

Perhaps the idea that he was coming to the waterfall made him think of synching before he left. Or maybe the thought that he might know whoever had died here.

Although he wasn't entirely sure the thought was conscious. He had just done so, as part of putting his gear together.

Still, now that he was on-site, he checked the gear again. He flicked the probe to active by hitting a tiny ridge with his thumb. A red light appeared in a holographic screen in the center of his vision. The red light and the square screen overlaid the dark pool with its patches of yellow light, and the constantly moving wall of water beyond.

It made him slightly dizzy.

"I don't see anything," Dinithi said.

"I'm not going to loop you in," he said. It was a last-minute decision, but the dizziness made his choice clear. If either one of them lost their balance and fell into that pool, the other needed to start a rescue, not try to undo a synch and lose the holographic screen.

She grunted with disgust. "I'd like to see this. I thought it's always better to have two pair of eyes on everything."

"It is and you will," he said. "Just not right away."

He was a little more curt than he probably should have been. Much as he liked how she worked, her constant demands and questions were beginning to irritate him. Maybe he was just getting tired.

He activated the hands-off controls of the probe, so that it would respond to the commands he gave it through the environmental suit. The probe glowed slightly in his palm.

The holographic screen showed a blackness on one side, and something shaped like a black mountain. It took him a moment to realize he was looking at part of his palm, with the lower part of his thumb appearing at the far side of his vision. He'd never quite had a literal hands-on perspective like this before.

It also made his dizziness increase just a bit.

He made the holographic screen smaller and moved it to the left of his vision, so it didn't dominate what he saw. Then he gently tossed the probe into the water as near to the scanlight as he could get it.

The probe landed with a splash he couldn't hear. He watched the probe sink, then slip forward, following its initial instructions to approach the end of the rake.

The probe turned its lights on full, which made him blink hard. The water was greenish-brownish-gray, with a lot of sediment.

"What do you see?" Dinithi asked. Her arm was still shaking.

When he had gotten the probe from his gear, he had also grabbed a small screen and tucked it into the side of his equipment belt. He pulled the screen out now. That screen was set to the probe's frequencies, but allowed no real command of the probe. He had kept that for himself.

He held out the second screen, then tapped it so that it came alive.

Its imagery mirrored the imagery in his hood, but staring at both of them gave him an instant headache. That's when he remembered his training: he was supposed to look at one screen or the other, but not both.

He couldn't make the holographic screen in his hood visor go away, so he didn't. He just held out the small screen, so that Dinithi could look at it while she waited.

"What a mess down there," she said.

He agreed. The probe had gone to the edge of the rake's tines and then, as per his initial instructions, started scanning downward.

A flood of information scrolled past on the left side of his holographic screen—temperature, water pressure, composition of the water, the rate of current and movement. He couldn't keep up with all of it and didn't even try.

He focused on the imagery first, and he would worry about the other stuff later.

The small links in the human-made chain loomed large in the probe's cameras.

"When do I get to let go of the rake?" Dinithi asked.

"We can't let go," Tevin said. "I'll hang onto it."

He moved the screen to his other hand, careful not to look at the images, and grabbed the rake. Its tines, below the surface, bobbled, but the chain stayed on them.

The movement made him a bit dizzy too.

Then he passed the screen to Dinithi. She held it up, and he could just barely see it out of the corner of his eyes. He had to look away.

"The light's weird down there. I'm thinking I should set the scanlight down," she said.

The scanlight recorded things, though. And he wanted something other than the recording from the probe.

"Keep using it," he said.

The probe followed the program he had given it, slowly following the chain to the rocks below. In the whitish light from the probe, the rocks looked gray and brown, but they didn't have any sediment on them that Tevin could see. Maybe the lack of sediment was due to the churn in the water. There was sediment everywhere else, making the water look thick and grainy.

Still, the rocks looked jagged to him, something he normally didn't associate with rocks that had been underwater, particularly rocks with this kind of churn constantly wearing at their surfaces.

As the probe got farther down, he realized the chain wasn't trapped between the rocks. It had come up alongside them. The thing at the bottom of the chain was hitting against the rocks, but it looked—at least from this angle—like he could pull it up.

He wasn't going to do that yet. He moved the probe a little closer to the swirling water, careful (or at least hoping) to keep the probe out of a strange little kaleidoscopic eddy the water had created.

The light caught something waving in the moving water. Closer to shore, he'd seen some seaweed doing that. He wondered how close these rocks were to the bottom. He supposed he could use all that information flowing from the probe to figure it out, but he didn't really want to.

He would lose his focus on the images and on what to do next.

"What is that?" Dinithi asked. She brought the screen closer to her face. It illuminated her dark skin, and somehow removed its luminescence. She was still moving the scanlight, but slowly, clearly not paying attention to it.

Exactly the way he didn't want his own attention to wander.

"I'm not sure what that is," he said, but he didn't like it. Something in the way it moved bothered him. Plants usually moved more. They bent in a variety of places, and sometimes rippled with the current. This wasn't rippling. It really was waving.

He let the probe sink farther down. The water here had a different composition. The numbers had changed along the side. He forced himself not to watch them.

The water also seemed a little darker here, but that might have been the fact that the lights from the surface weren't penetrating as well this deep.

The probe finally reached the side of the rocks where the chain was hung up. Only it wasn't quite what he expected. He had thought he would find some kind of jewel or nametag or bauble slamming against the rocks.

Instead, he realized, the chain hadn't fallen free. The thing that held it wasn't whatever hung from the end of the chain. It was the thing the chain hung from.

Someone's neck.

21

Bassima wished she hadn't eaten the plum cake. She kept burping the meringue. Someone had decided to add a hint of strawberry to the egg whites, and it hadn't mixed well with the plum.

But she had eaten it, of course. When she got nervous, she tended to eat everything in her way.

She had left the diner and walked to Taji's office, partly to see what kind of walk Taji often took during the week. Most of the businesses on Sandoveil's main street were tourist businesses, some catering to the Fleet arrivals and others to tourists from the rest of Nindowne. It was easy to tell the difference between the two.

The Fleet shops had a lot of basics—clothing, underwear, boots—made to last, because no one would be able to return to replace those items.

Or, rather, if the Fleet did return, it would do so years from now, and those items (made by the same company with the same materials) might not be available any longer.

The Fleet items were blindingly expensive unless the buyer could prove that they were involved with the Fleet somehow. Bassima wasn't, so she had no idea what kind of discount the Fleet members got, if indeed it was a discount and not some kind of donation.

The tourist shops for the Nindowne locals had cheaper items, souvenirs that had no real worth, posters and mugs and all kinds of things that simply weren't practical on a spaceship. The clothing was cheaper as well, and more cheaply made—bought for an emergency on a trip across the planet, rather than bought for life because the owner would never return.

Bassima never shopped in either kind of store. When she went into the places on Main Street, it was because she was being official. She didn't pay attention to her clothing, getting most of it used. And her office provided her uniform, which was feeling a little tight after that meal.

Everything felt tight. She hated having her hands tied by regulations. If only the office had let her investigate properly. She would probably have found the Kimuras by now. Or at least Taji.

Bassima tugged on her shirt and headed past the tourist shops. The entrance to Taji's office was on a side street, but she had one small window that overlooked Main Street. In that window, a sign blinked: *Consultations, Advice—Legal and Informational*, followed by a small symbol that anyone with the Fleet recognized as Fleet-approved.

Most people on Nindowne had no idea the Fleet used Sandoveil as its base. To most regional tourists who came through, the day-to-day operations of the city seemed a mystery. No one mentioned the city's largest employer, and according to official documents, the slot for biggest job creator was the tourism industry.

Bassima stopped at the window first, noting that the lights were off, just like they had been when she had come by earlier.

But there was no notice that the office would be closed. The hours, which were a small, steady yellow beneath the sign, hadn't changed—and showed that the office should still be open.

She cupped her hands around her face and peered inside, but the light from the sign made it hard to see anything. She squinted, thought she saw a blanket trailing off a couch, and wondered if she was just making that up.

She stepped back. The street was empty. No one had come by. Most of the shops were closed now, and people were going about their business. Besides, the local tourist trade went down in mid-fall, so the only strangers on the street should have been from the Fleet. Who knew what they did in the early evening.

Bassima's heart was pounding, and she wasn't sure why. She trusted the feeling, though, because she had learned that she observed things and processed them without actually being conscious of them. She had seen something this time; she just wasn't sure what it was.

She glanced up and down the street again. Most of the lights were out in the other businesses, and nothing went by. She slipped onto the side street. It curved, like many of the side streets in Sandoveil. They followed the path of the river on the south end of town, all moving toward a bigger road that went just under the mountain.

The businesses back here got less traffic. Some were artisanal shops, bakeries, and small restaurants. And a few were lawyers or accountants.

Taji's was the only business that advertised consulting as well as information and legal advice.

The window overlooking the side street was large and rectangular. It had a gray shutter that Taji clearly kept closed after business hours. It was closed now.

When Bassima went by the first time, she had noted the hours, the lack of a sign explaining the closure, and the fact that the shutters were closed. She had peered through the square window over the door, but only saw the hallway, and it had told her nothing.

This time, she rapped on the door again, then pushed the door to see if it would open.

It did.

She stood in front of it, feeling a surprise she hadn't expected. Doors to businesses like this should have locked automatically at a certain time, especially if the shutters were down.

But she didn't see any obvious computer controls, or any overrides, at least not outside the door. The system looked different from the one at the Kimuras' house. Maybe it had come with the building rental.

Bassima activated the evidence-capture feature on her regulation shoes. Then she stepped inside. No lights came up, and they should have as she entered.

She swallowed, stepped back out, and flicked on her shoulder comm, contacting the office. This time, she got dispatch.

"I'm outside Taji Kimura's office," she half-whispered. "There's no one about and the door is unlocked. The automated lights aren't working. It looks like the system is down. I'm going in, but I would appreciate it if another officer checks on me."

The dispatch muttered something about anything to do with the Kimuras required approval from Amy Loraas. But Bassima ignored it, signing off.

Every time she had spoken to Amy Loraas, she had been discouraged from doing anything.

Bassima wasn't going to be discouraged this time.

She stepped inside the door again. Even though she expected the darkness to remain this time, it still unnerved her. Lights came on when people walked through doors. That was simply how everything worked.

When it didn't work, it made her nervous.

She didn't draw her laser pistol, although she kept her hand on it. The office felt empty. She wasn't sure why she had that opinion, but it felt exactly the same way the house had felt near the edge of the mountain—as if it had been abandoned.

She did activate her scanlight on her belt. The sudden yellow made her blink. It revealed a layer of dust that surprised her. She would have thought a busy office like this one would stay clean just from the traffic.

But she had no idea. She always operated on foot.

She kept the scanlight on her belt. The light would record what was in front of her and little else. She didn't want to hold the light, not as she was going into the darkness.

The office smelled musty. The computer system had to be down. Every building in Sandoveil had an automated environmental system that not only maintained temperature, but kept the air at a certain level of cleanliness—one of the many things the Fleet engineers had given the community when they had built it centuries ago.

A lot of the buildings used Fleet technology, just as if the owners were still on board a ship.

Which meant the air shouldn't have smelled musty and a little decayed. That disturbed her as well.

Her heart was pounding as she rounded the corner.

The office, in the strangely focused light, looked odd. She made herself focus. A desk near the door, with two chairs on one side for clients, and a chair on the other, presumably for Taji. But the desk was crammed across from the window, between a table covered with food containers and a door that clearly led to the office's only bathroom.

On the wall beneath the shuttered window was a couch that was too big for the space. It had a flat surface that could fit Bassima—which was saying something given her height and girth.

A pillow was scrunched against one arm, with another pillow on the couch's back. Blankets and sheets were bunched at the door side of the couch, as if someone had just kicked them back. Another blanket had slid to the floor.

She had seen that after all through the Main Street window.

The musty smell didn't come from the food containers. They would have been self-cleaning if they had come from any of the nearby businesses.

But something had spilled along the floor. Something that looked black and haphazard.

She stepped around it and peered into the bathroom. No one was there.

Then she grabbed the scanlight on her belt.

"Hello!" a male voice shouted, and she just about jumped out of her skin.

She whirled, saw Reginald Udhe hovering just inside the office door. Apparently, he was the backup she had asked for not all that long ago.

"Hey," she said, by way of greeting. "Stay there, would you? Don't let anyone else in."

"Okay," he said. "Not that there's anyone on the street."

She nodded, noting that. She crouched, and held the scanlight over the blackness.

As she got down close to it, she realized the blackness was the source of the musty smell. This close, it smelled foul, like something rotten. Whatever environmental system was in this office had been turned off, but the systems still worked in the neighboring buildings, probably cleaning out the air here, just a little bit.

But not this close. Clearly, nothing else had been this close.

The scanlight revealed how thick the blackness was, how it had pooled. She could have flaked it off with her finger if she were so inclined. She wasn't.

Because she knew what she was looking at. She was looking at blood.

A lot of it.

More than anyone could afford to lose at one time.

"Let dispatch know we have a death scene," she said to Reginald. She didn't want to contact them, because they'd put her through to Amy.

And Bassima was going to investigate this, no matter what anyone else said.

22

Tevin leaned forward, as if movement would make it easier for him to see what the probe was showing him. The images the probe was sending back were playing on the holographic screen on his hood visor. Dinithi was using a handheld screen for the same imagery, and she had moved it closer to her face.

She had already seen the neck, but hadn't identified what it was. Or maybe she had and hadn't really allowed that to sink in.

He wasn't sure he had allowed it to sink in, either. Maybe he expected to see a neck, so what he saw was a neck. He moved the probe just a bit toward the rocks on the left side, a little distance away from the waterfall, and farther from the chain that had led him to the neck in the first place. He wanted a perspective that he hadn't had before.

"Oh, no," Dinithi breathed. "Is that what I think it is?"

Finally, she understood what her eyes were showing her.

He wasn't going to answer her, though. Not until he was certain.

He made himself catalog what he was seeing.

First, the waving thing. It wasn't human. It was some kind of plant, with filaments that also waved in the constantly moving water. The plant was thin and supple, bending in ways human beings did not.

As he looked, he slowly realized that there were several plants, all of them rising between the rocks, growing up like weeds. Maybe they were the same plant, with lots of tendrils.

He didn't know, and he couldn't exactly identify it. That was a problem for a later time.

Right now, he needed to focus on the thing attached to that chain, the thing he assumed (correctly: he just knew he was correct) was a neck.

He blinked several times, trying to clear his vision. Neck, arched slightly, leading into a torso. He thought he saw a collarbone, but that might have been a trick of the light. The torso arched as well, and disappeared under the rocks.

The arms weren't floating alongside, like he would have expected. And there didn't appear to be any hair floating upward, either. If the clothing was loose, he saw no indication of it because it didn't fan like the plants did.

He guided the probe along the far edge of the rocks, hoping it wouldn't get caught in the inevitable riptide this close to an eddy like that. He would lose the probe altogether if he did that.

He wasn't quite shaking, though. He was holding his breath.

"Tevin." Dinithi's voice was different. Serious. Hushed. "Is that a person?"

Not anymore, he thought, but didn't say. They were on comm now, and he didn't want such a callow comment recorded.

He couldn't tell if this body was newer or older than the other one, although it appeared to have intact skin. After some time in the water, the skin would have worn away, and instead of a neck, he would have seen neck bones.

He shuddered just a little, and moved the probe closer to that neck. The top of it bent backward unnaturally, and finally he saw a somewhat delicate chin, and black hair that caressed what was apparently the sides of someone's face.

"That *is* a person," Dinithi said. "Trapped under the rocks."

He hadn't put that together, but she was right. The body was being held down by those rocks. "Trapped" was a good word, maybe the best word.

The question was, had the rocks been in place long before the body (and whomever the body belonged to) had swum or fallen and got caught underneath because of that riptide? Or had the body gone down with the rocks or at the same time as the rocks?

He couldn't answer that, not from here.

He moved the probe across that strange neck and over to the face. His breath caught.

He recognized the delicate features, the open eyes.

Taji Kimura.

His heart twisted.

He didn't say anything about the identification, though. He knew it only because he had been there when Taji had gotten a thin scar just beneath her chin, a scar that she liked, a scar she considered a badge of a landlocked life.

The scar glowed whitely under the water, beckoning him to come get her.

It was beginning to look to him as though someone had deliberately stashed her corpse down here. He couldn't tell if she had been alive when they had done so. He was no expert, despite the relatively large number of bodies he had pulled out of this water over the years. He had no idea what distinguished a drowning victim from a waterlogged corpse.

Either way, he needed to let Marnie know. They could call off the search.

He had found two bodies. He was now becoming convinced that the first body belonged to Glida Kimura.

He would have thought the deaths a dual suicide if it weren't for those rocks, holding Taji down. Had something worse happened? Had someone targeted the two of them?

If so, why?

"You know her, don't you?" Dinithi asked.

He raised his index finger to his lips. He didn't want to make an identification on the comm. Even if he had wanted to do that, he didn't dare. His voice would have wobbled.

His emotion would have showed.

Dinithi nodded, just once, to show she understood what he was indicating.

He stared at the face, the plants waving above it, the watery sediment flowing past like snow on a windy day.

Then his gaze traveled to the rocks.

Not a double suicide. Maybe a murder suicide. But why the rocks, then?

A chill passed through him. Something awful had happened here.

Something he didn't entirely understand.

Oh, Taj, he thought, using all of his restraint not to speak aloud. *What the hell happened to you?*

And why?

23

Bristol looked up at the ceiling of the storage room and did some computations in her head. Each layer of nanobits had been designed to hold extreme amounts of pressure. They had also been designed to prevent collapse from above and explosive decompression from below.

Each floor had the standard nanobit layer, and the floors between here and the top also had blast protection.

Then Bristol looked down at Wèi, who was watching her warily. Fitzwilliam leaned slightly away from her, arms crossed. The only member of Wèi's team who didn't seem hostile was Tranh. She remained in her place near the door.

Bristol's team huddled together, except for Rajivk, who was still standing beside the hologram of Glida Kimura. Bristol hated the way that hologram was in mid-movement. She almost wanted to start it up, so she could see Glida move forward or out of the frame or just leave them alone.

That last thought left Bristol shaken. She hadn't realized how angry she was, beneath the fear.

She glanced at the glistening walls. Before she said any more, she turned to her team—to Jasmine Pereyra, who always seemed to know how to make Bristol's desires into commands that the team understood.

"Every minute we stand around talking," Bristol said, "we're losing evidence."

Pereyra nodded, even though Wèi cringed as if Bristol were reprimanding him. Maybe she was, in an offhanded way. She hadn't exactly meant to.

Pereyra leaned into the team and spoke so softly to them that Bristol couldn't hear, despite the close quarters of the room. Rajivk gave the hologram a regretful look, then headed toward the team.

Bristol turned to Wèi.

"Glida Kimura wasn't trying to kill everyone," Bristol said. "There are much more efficient ways to do that, if she so desired. I'm sure you've planned for them—"

"We block all the easy ways," Wèi said.

"If she worked security," Bristol said, "then I'm certain she knew how to unblock those easy ways, just like she knew how to get down here without the proper clearance."

Fitzwilliam raised his eyebrows. They looked out of place since he had shaved his head. She could tell, though, that he agreed with her.

"Besides, even with a massive *anacapa* explosion, there would be no guarantee that anyone would die several stories up. This is Sector Base E-2. *Anacapa* explosions have been part of our history from the beginning."

Wèi opened his mouth as if he were going to interrupt her. Bristol didn't want him to. She really wanted him out of her storage room. He could do whatever it was he was supposed to do, somewhere far away from her.

"If we were in Sector Base A or maybe even Sector Base M, I would completely believe that she was trying to destroy the base with a large *anacapa* explosion. However, over the centuries, we have constantly redesigned sector bases. After all that we've been through, and all the history that we have, and all the fail-safes—"

"Don't you think they're just like the fail-safes for the rest of the base?" Wèi asked, a little too forcefully. Apparently, he had decided he disliked Bristol as much as she disliked him. "Something someone from security could override."

Bristol couldn't help herself. She smiled.

Rajivk looked over at her from the team meeting and rolled his eyes. Then he returned to the meeting. Clearly, he understood what she was feeling.

She tried not to sound too patronizing. But she didn't really know how. And rather than let that statement stand, she had to answer it.

"Well," she said, "I suppose someone from security could try to override all of the protocols we've established over the years to prevent a massive *anacapa* blast."

Wèi's expression had become wary. He glanced at Fitzwilliam, who shrugged.

"But," Bristol said, "that would mean disassembling huge parts of the base, destroying many of the nanobits, and figuring out how to breach not just security but the very integrity of the base itself."

Wèi tilted his head a little, as if he wanted to ask her to stop, but didn't know how.

She couldn't help herself: she had to finish.

"I would think," she said, "*someone* would have noticed all of that activity, don't you?"

Wèi's mouth thinned. "That's not what I meant."

That was a defense Bristol loathed. It was the defense of small minds, who seemed to always believe they were being misunderstood. Sure, he might have misspoken, but she doubted it.

"Well," she said, "let's assume that your scenario is correct, that this Glida woman snuck down here and planned to create some kind of *anacapa* chain reaction at the very moment the meeting was going on several stories above us."

Wèi tensed. All of Bristol's team watched now, as if they were watching a particularly interesting show.

"How did she know the meeting was going to happen?" Bristol asked. "We were all told that the decision had come from the Fleet itself. Which means that the administrators of the base didn't even know they were going to hold a meeting this morning, until they got the news about the date of the closure—"

"Which probably came last night," Wèi said.

"We don't know that," Bristol said. "Not that it matters, anyway. Because the entire time that all of this was happening, this Glida woman was in the storage room. Doing...what? Waiting for a meeting she couldn't even have imagined twenty-four hours before?"

Wèi's skin flushed. "Point taken."

He sounded surly.

"It is a good point," Tranh said, "and one we should explore. What could she have been doing in a runabout for that many hours? Or was there something else stored here in the room, something none of us know about?"

Bristol froze. What else had been stored in here? The backup *anacapa* was in the runabout. There were some tools, but for the most part, she had cleaned out the room when Captain Harriet Virji from the *Ijo* made it clear that only Bristol's intervention would cause the runabout to be decommissioned.

Bristol looked at Pereyra.

"We moved everything to the storage room near the big lab," Pereyra said, reading Bristol's mind.

The secondary lab. Where Rajivk worked. Where the rest of the team did whatever it was they needed to do that allowed Bristol to focus on the *anacapa* drives.

"We should investigate that, then," Wèi said.

Bristol nodded. They should. Because there might be something in that room that should have been in this one. Although—

"We didn't leave a lot here," Pereyra said. "It wouldn't have taken Kimura more than a day to figure out we had taken everything out of the room. It wouldn't even have taken her an hour."

Bristol crossed her arms and stared at the spot in the center of the room where the runabout had once stood.

"Then what exactly did she want?" Bristol asked. "And why is that so very hard to figure out?"

Wèi shrugged. "We've never encountered anything like this before. In my tenure, at least, no one has stolen anything from the base."

Bristol leaned back slightly, then glanced at the frozen holographic image. No one had stolen anything.

He was right: she couldn't remember hearing that anything had been stolen ever.

Why would anyone want to or need to?

Everyone who worked at the base had all of their needs taken care of. They lived in a beautiful place. If they didn't like living here, then they had choices—they could move to one of the other sector bases, including Sector Base G-2, which was going to replace this one—or they could apply to return (or go to) the Fleet itself.

If they wanted to leave Fleet employ, they could do that as well, working in Sandoveil or leaving the area entirely. And if they left the Fleet's employ, they did so with the understanding that they could return to the Fleet at any point.

They also received enough money to cover their moves and their expenses for years to come. It was a safe way to let people out of the Fleet, and made them less likely to reveal secrets or to take the kinds of risks that people who needed basics like food and shelter sometimes took in order to care for themselves.

In fact, the only thefts she knew about happened in Sandoveil proper, and they usually were perpetrated by tourists or the children of tourists. If they were children, they stole because they were badly brought up or because they were bored.

"How could someone work for security and be a thief?" Bristol asked Wèi. "Don't you vet your employees?"

He bristled. "They're not *my* employees. I don't work with everyone there. I do vet my team, though."

As if his team mattered at the moment. Although the defensiveness of his comment made her look at them. They watched her as well.

Her gaze caught Fitzwilliam's. He raised his chin defiantly. She had no idea what he had to be defiant about.

"But you worked with this Glida woman, when she had really vast security clearance," Bristol said. "Hers was reduced. Isn't that unusual?"

"No," Wèi answered before Fitzwilliam could. "If you no longer need to visit some parts of the sector base, you don't need clearance there."

Bristol frowned. Some of the rules were different for different types of employees. The techs kept their clearance until they left the base altogether.

Which, she supposed, made sense. Techs had no idea if they would be called in elsewhere in the facility, either for some emergency or because whatever was causing the problem might be immobile.

If someone could no longer do the difficult work of overall security and was restricted to information-duty, that person wouldn't need to have a clearance for parts of the facility outside of the information area.

"Was she trustworthy?" Bristol asked Fitzwilliam.

He glanced at Wèi, as though trying to see if Wèi was as surprised at Bristol's bluntness as Fitzwilliam clearly was.

Wèi shrugged one shoulder almost imperceptibly. Apparently that meant, *I have no idea why she's asking this, but you can answer it.*

Bristol felt a momentary surge of irritation. Wèi did not have charge over her. She was the head of her department, in charge of things that would frighten the crap out of Wèi if he understood them.

"Was Glida Kimura trustworthy?" Fitzwilliam asked. "The base clearly thought she was."

As if the base were a person. As if the base was trustworthy.

"But you didn't?" Bristol pressed.

He frowned at her. "I didn't say that."

"That's right," she snapped. "You didn't say anything at all. You told me something I already knew. I was asking your *opinion*."

Bristol's team exchanged looks, all except for Rajivk. Sheldenhelm lowered his head, but not before Bristol saw a tiny smile on his face.

Apparently, they recognized her tone as something they had encountered in the past.

Fitzwilliam's eyes had grown wide.

"Did you trust Glida Kimura?" Bristol asked, making her question even clearer.

Fitzwilliam bit his lower lip, then licked the spot as if he had hurt himself. He tilted his head, first to the left, and then to the right. Not quite a shake, meaning *no*, but close enough.

"Did you?" Bristol pressed, not caring how uncomfortable she made him.

"I didn't like working with her," he said after a moment.

"Why not?" This time Wèi picked up the questioning. He had finally caught where Bristol was going.

This time, Fitzwilliam did shake his head. "She was…odd."

Everyone knew that. From her clothing to her insistence on getting her own way in public, Glida Kimura got attention. Bristol hadn't even known her, but she had seen her around Sandoveil, and she recognized that the woman was one of the stranger residents.

She just hadn't realized that Kimura worked in this building.

"Odd how?" Bristol asked.

Fitzwilliam shrugged again. "Her…responses…just weren't what I would expect," he said, more to Wèi than to Bristol. "And she was really easy to anger. I avoided her as much as I could."

"Do you think that's why she was moved? The anger?" Bristol asked.

Wèi looked at her in surprise. Clearly, he hadn't thought of that.

"It's possible." Fitzwilliam didn't glance at everyone else in the storage room, but he might as well have. It was clear he didn't want to be overheard. "I asked that I not be partnered with her, if it could be at all avoided."

Wèi's gaze met Bristol's, and he nodded just a little, as if acknowledging that she had asked the right questions.

Bristol didn't say any more, at least on this. She'd worked at this base all her life. She knew that sometimes those in charge took the easy way out: rather than confront a difficult employee, the people in charge sometimes moved the person laterally and restricted that person's access, just to keep the peace.

"Do you think she's the type of person to steal?" Bristol asked.

"Clearly," Fitzwilliam said, a little too fast.

Bristol held up a hand. "I mean, thinking about what you knew about her before today's incident. Was she the kind of person who would steal?"

"I don't know," Fitzwilliam said, and the exasperation in his tone told Bristol he wasn't really considering his response. He wanted to stop being the focus of the conversation. "I tried not to think about her, unless I had to work with her."

"She was that unpleasant?" Wèi asked.

"She was that unpleasant," Fitzwilliam said.

"But not in any way you could document," Wèi said, as if he understood. Or was he coaching Fitzwilliam? And why would Wèi be coaching Fitzwilliam?

"Not in any way I could document, right," Fitzwilliam said. "Not that I would have. I didn't see how she could jeopardize anyone or threaten the base."

Bristol snorted, in spite of herself. She looked at the blast doors. "Until now, that is."

"Until now," Fitzwilliam agreed. His tone was no different than it had been with Wèi. It sounded like Fitzwilliam was simply a man of few words, and needed prodding to get them out.

Bristol didn't like the idea of anyone being difficult—unpleasantly difficult—at the base. She didn't like working around others, but she figured they were all people she could trust in one way or another.

When this night was over, she was going to have to reassess everything she had thought about this place.

Bristol looked at her team. They were scattered around the storage room. Some were taking samples from the walls. Others were using handhelds to take readings.

Rajivk kept glancing at that hologram of Glida Kimura, as if it bothered him personally.

Pereyra was standing where the runabout had been, taking measurements, and speaking softly to Sheldenhelm.

These were good people: Bristol had to think that they were good people. She had never had any problems with them, they had done their work well, and they had always done more than she asked of them.

She hated to think that they too harbored secrets, but she supposed they did. Everyone, it seemed, harbored secrets except for her.

That holographic woman looked tiny and ineffectual. Her black clothing probably made her seem thinner than she was, and that pose—in the middle of a movement—made her seem furtive.

How could one person cause so much mayhem?

And why was Bristol worrying about it? She had to worry about what had happened in this storage room, not about who had done it.

The loss of the runabout was serious, but even more serious was the loss—or the triggering or the explosion or *whatever* happened to that *anacapa* drive.

The room was repairing itself, but from what? And would the runabout come back? Sometimes they did.

"Jasmine," she said to Pereyra. "Don't stand there."

Pereyra raised her head, as if surprised that Bristol had spoken to her.

"If the runabout returns…" Bristol said, not wanting to finish that sentence.

Pereyra moved so fast to the side of the storage room that it seemed like she had jumped there. The rest of Bristol's team moved away from the area where the runabout had been as well.

Tranh still stood there, but when she saw the others move, she walked closer to Bristol and Wèi.

"You don't think the runabout was destroyed?" Wèi asked.

It was Bristol's turn to shrug. "I don't know. It might have been. But anything else could have happened. That Glida woman might have climbed on board somehow and then touched the wrong panel. The *anacapa* in FS-Prime runabouts is always left low-level active, and as a result, the runabout could have simply taken off on its own, to some preprogrammed place. It might have been a rebound maneuver."

"A what?" Wèi asked.

"Um…it…um…" She didn't know the military term. She never thought about it because she worked on *anacapa*s here in the base, not in space. "It's the maneuver that the Fleet uses the *anacapa* for most often."

Wèi and his team were frowning at her. They clearly hadn't served in space either.

"It's—um—that military maneuver where they hop into foldspace for a few minutes foldspace time, and reappear hours later in the same place."

Wèi glanced into the center of the room as if the runabout would arrive right now. He cursed.

"I hadn't thought of that," he said. "Do you know what the standard setting is?"

"No," Bristol said. "The standard settings vary from ship to ship. Some ships have them, and others don't. We'd have to ask the crew of the *Ijo* what they do with the runabouts."

Then she let out a breath. The *Ijo*. Had anyone spoken to the *Ijo*?

"What?" Wèi asked.

Apparently, her dismay had shown on her face. "Have you contacted Captain Virji of the *Ijo*?"

"No," Wèi said. "Why would I?"

"Her runabout is missing, maybe destroyed," Bristol said. She couldn't help herself. She just used that tone again, that tone which said—*You blithering idiot; can't you do your job?*

Rajivk's gaze met hers from the other side of the room, and then slid away. He didn't seem to be focusing on his work, and she needed him to focus. Maybe he would get *the tone* shortly.

"I thought you were the one who is supposed to contact her." Wèi matched Bristol's tone. Apparently she didn't intimidate him.

"Only if one of my people harmed the runabout or if there were problems we couldn't resolve," Bristol said, even though that wasn't entirely accurate. If there were problems, she spoke to the *Ijo*'s engineering staff first to see if they had done anything or needed anything.

Then, if the problem couldn't be resolved, she spoke to the captain or the captain's designated representative.

"Yeah," Wèi said. "You're supposed to contact her."

"This Glida Kimura isn't one of my people," Bristol said quietly.

Wèi turned pale. "I don't deal with captains. That's not part of my job description."

"Well, someone has to," Bristol said. "Because her runabout is not here."

"Can't we just wait until we know what happened?" Tranh asked. She had moved closer to the group.

"And what if the runabout is programmed in a particular way? Something we might need to know?" Bristol asked.

"If you need to know it, then contact her," Wèi said.

"Oh, for god's sake," Fitzwilliam snapped. "Stop worrying about your jobs and start worrying about the base."

Bristol looked at him. Wasn't he a subordinate? Should he even be allowed to talk to anyone like that?

Wèi closed his eyes for a moment. He looked vaguely ill. That surprised Bristol. She had thought him stronger than anyone else she had met this evening.

He shook his head slightly, then took a deep breath and opened his eyes. "I'll contact her. I have to. *We* have to. The runabout was in the custody of the sector base, and now it's not. It was stolen. By one of ours."

Bristol suddenly understood his reluctance. Not just one of the employees of the sector base, but one of the employees in security. This had gone very wrong, very fast.

She sighed, suddenly calmer, and in that moment, understood why her own subordinates disliked her.

She hadn't needed Wèi to contact Captain Virji. Not really. She just wanted Wèi to admit that the loss of the runabout wasn't the fault of Bristol or her staff. And he had just done that.

"I'll contact her," Bristol said.

"You just said I needed to," Wèi said.

"Yes, I did," Bristol said, keeping her voice calm. "But I was wrong. I just realized I needed to ask her if the runabouts had special settings, especially for the *anacapa* drives. I could have you ask, but you wouldn't be able to convey the answer to me in any way that would be useful."

Wèi flushed, and his eyes narrowed. There it was, that look she got from others when she was being particularly difficult.

She felt a tiny bit of triumph.

Yup, pure bitch.

Not that it mattered. Because they did have to resolve this, together somehow. And before Bristol could get to the parts she loved, she had to do one last thing.

She had to make one last contact. And she had to use diplomacy, which, as this little interaction reminded her quite clearly, was not her strong suit.

24

THE WORST THING ABOUT BEING AWAKENED to go to a death scene was being awakened at the beginning of the sleep cycle, not in the middle of it. Mushtaq Hranek had just fallen asleep when the security office had contacted him. He had gone to bed early because he had just returned from vacation, and all that travel had left him exhausted.

He was still exhausted as he arrived at the small office on a side street, just off Main. A security officer he didn't recognize stood at the intersection on Main, as if he were keeping riffraff away.

They were the only two people on the street. The rest of Sandoveil was either in bed or at home or doing something interesting with their evening.

He wished he was too.

Hranek nodded at the officer, then walked down the side street to the address that he had been given. Hranek was carrying his small kit, just in case he had to do some investigation on-site. In fact, he preferred doing just a bit of investigation on-site. Not only did it save time, it often provided the one piece of information that usually resolved a case.

The side street was dark. A blocked window, a malfunctioning overhead light—already this small stretch of city block was making him feel uncomfortable.

Bassima Beck met him at the door.

Hranek had always found Bassima Beck to be the most attractive of all the security officers he had ever worked with. She was tall and statuesque, her high cheekbones and large eyes as dramatic as her body.

He tried to keep his gaze averted from her because he didn't want his attraction to her to show. The city of Sandoveil had strict rules about employee interactions, and they had a zero-tolerance policy about some kinds of violations.

He'd only learned of these things after Sandoveil had hired him. And then he had learned that Sandoveil's main industry wasn't tourism as he had understood it, but a large, rather secretive base that had been sponsored by an organization known as the Fleet—something he had found mysterious in his first few cases, and now found simply annoying.

The Fleet was military, but in its own way, a way he understood as clearly as he could for his job only. Mostly, when something ended up having to do with the Fleet, he was able to pass the death—and the problem—off to the base's security operation.

Early in his career here, he had done that with reluctance. Now, he did so simply because following two (and sometimes three) sets of rules gave him too many headaches.

He was the chief death investigator for the region. Each community in the Sandoveil Valley had its own death investigator, all of whom answered to him. He also had two assistants here. It sounded impressive, but it really wasn't.

A lot of people died before their time in the Sandoveil Valley, mostly because of all the natural wonders. The waterfall enticed too many young people to act foolishly, the mud flats could suck in the unwary—and if the unwary happened to be drunk, then the unwary could die. The ocean had its own trials, mostly from swimmers who believed themselves strong enough to buck a serious riptide, and the mountains entranced hikers and climbers to try things beyond their abilities.

Tourists did a variety of stupid things. And there were dangers inside the base as well, which he mostly did not have to respond to, because—he'd been told—he usually did not have the kind of security clearance to deal with them.

He got unexplained deaths very rarely, and he preferred it that way. Unexplained deaths, particularly in small, tight-knit communities, usually caused rifts. Sometimes those rifts fell into his purview as well. He'd had to handle feuding family members, violent friends, and sobbing victims of the various deceased.

Over the years, he had become the kind of man who preferred things quiet and simple. Unexplained death was never quiet and simple.

He had known this unexplained death would be a problem the moment it woke him out of that much-needed sleep.

And now here he was, just off Main, which felt like a metaphor in and of itself. He hoped this unexplained death wouldn't be a highly visible one, but he doubted that as well.

From the expression on Beck's stunning features, she doubted it too.

Beck was half a head taller than he was. He had to look up to meet her gaze, something else that he found uncomfortable. He felt grimy from his exhaustion, as if the sleep he'd been rousted from still gathered around his eyes.

"Wow," Beck said. "Amy called *you*."

As if that had been some kind of procedural mistake, as if he didn't belong here at all. But Amy Loraas never made procedural mistakes. She was aware that her job as Chief Security Officer for Sandoveil Valley was partly political, and could be taken from her at a moment's notice. She was the most cautious person that Hranek had ever met.

"I thought you had a dead body," he said, and wondered if he sounded defensive. He felt a little defensive, as if the fact that someone—the office, dispatch, Amy Loraas, *someone*—had called him in was his fault and his alone.

"No, I don't have a dead body, that's the thing." Beck sounded slightly annoyed. And she wasn't the one rousted from a nice warm bed. "I have a lot of blood and some suspicious circumstances."

Hranek suppressed a sigh. She was right, then. He shouldn't have been called until they knew there had been a death or until someone found a body. He supposed he would have to file a complaint, although, if he were being fair, he had no idea what Loraas should have done.

He couldn't ever remember dealing with something like this—blood, but no body. At least not in Sandoveil. In Ynchi City, where he had gotten his training. But not in a place as beautiful and pristine as this.

Ynchi City had had a completely different governmental structure, with a variety of death investigative services. Not only was there an actual police force, run by the government itself, but there were dozens of detectives, an on-site analysis unit, lots of investigative technology issued to everyone from the lowest police officer on the street to everyone in the Office of the Death Investigator.

Sandoveil only had a death investigator because tourists whose family members had died in the Sandoveil Valley had professed shock when one hadn't existed. That history was before his time, but not that much before his time.

He was only the fifth death investigator the city had ever hired.

"So you don't think I need to be at this scene?" he asked Beck, wondering what he would do if she said that she believed he didn't. He had been called in, after all. He did have a job to do.

"I didn't say that," Beck said. "Everything is suspicious around here right now."

And then she launched into the strangest summation he had ever heard from a security officer. First she mentioned something about a dead body in a pool near Fiskett Falls, information that irritated him the moment he heard it.

A *real* dead body meant he should have been called to that scene, and he hadn't been. Yet, somehow, Loraas and her team had contacted Beck and told her to investigate the Kimura family. Hranek wasn't quite sure why—although he was gleaning from Beck's description that *someone* had assumed the dead body belonged to Glida Kimura, again taking over the job from him.

He was the only one who made the official identification of the dead in Sandoveil, and it wasn't something you simply did by eyeballing the corpse. Sometimes corpses surprised you. They looked like one person but really were another. Or they looked nothing like the person their

DNA said they were. Or they were so disfigured a visual identification was completely impossible.

He nearly interrupted Beck to say these things, but he stopped himself. She was not the person who called him here, nor was she the person who *hadn't* called him to the Fiskett Falls death scene.

His irritation was getting the better of him. He shifted from foot to foot.

Finally, he couldn't take it any longer.

"How did you end up here?" he asked.

"I'm unofficially looking into the Kimuras," Beck said.

He hated that word, *unofficially*. "Meaning you're doing this on your own or someone put you up to it?" he asked.

"Meaning we don't have an ID of the body in the waterfall yet," Beck said, "but everyone was certain enough—"

"I got that," he snapped, then felt his face heat. He didn't want to yell at Bassima Beck. She was a woman he admired, and he didn't want her to think he was as unpleasant as he actually was.

She nodded, as if understanding how she had lapsed into too much description.

"The office belongs to Taji Kimura," Beck said. "Glida's wife."

Well, finally, something that made some kind of sense. And it also intrigued him. Blood but no body? And a body in the Falls. More than one person had thought that tossing a body into the river above the Falls would destroy that body or at least make it unrecoverable.

But it wasn't. It was amazing what the YSR-SR could do, given time.

"Just show me the blood," Hranek said, overwhelmed by all the detail. He would determine if someone had died here.

He was happy now that he had carried his kit with him, instead of fetching it after seeing the scene. He hated returning to a death scene. It was usually trampled and destroyed when he got back—often because the local security office didn't have the same kind of training he did.

He'd learned how to operate in a large city filled with crime. Here, a small city without a lot of crime, no one really knew or cared about following procedure to the letter.

Beck nodded and extended her hand into the narrow hallway. The lights did not come up as the two of them moved toward the main room.

"Did you shut everything down?" Hranek asked, feeling just a little annoyed.

"The systems aren't working," Beck said. "I thought whoever investigated would want to know that, because turning the systems back on or repairing them would alter the scene."

Hranek looked at her in surprise. He had never really worked with her on an investigation; he was pleased to realize that she had a forensic mind.

"I have lights if you need them," she said. "I was careful not to trample anything, pick up anything, or change anything. I also have a video record if you need it."

"I probably will," he said, "but not yet."

He pulled his own lights from his kit. He had scanlights, like the YSR-SR team had, but he had splurged. His scanlight recorded and analyzed. It didn't just record the visuals, but the chemical composition of the environment, the ambient temperature, and more. His scanlights also interacted with the building's computer system, if the system was the standard one used in Sandoveil.

He suspected this building's system was standard, but Beck had said it wasn't on. He flicked off that feature on his scanlight. He'd had lights malfunction when they tried to synch with a system that wasn't working properly.

He placed one scanlight in a holder on his belt. He held another scanlight in his left hand. Then he stepped into the doorway between the narrow hall and the main room, and stayed in one position.

The air itself smelled of old blood. If he were in a more modern city or if he worked in space, he wouldn't know that smell. But he did, because so many tourists died in the Sandoveil Valley, often in enclosed spaces like small caves or whatever vehicle they had used to travel to their destination.

This old blood smell had a twist of decay, but the decay wasn't as pungent as it could have been. Often when he encountered old blood, particularly in a hot, moist environment, the blood had rotted.

The blood was probably decaying here, but it wasn't as evident by the smell. And the room was warm—perhaps 75 to 78 degrees Fahrenheit. The heat felt trapped here, as if the air in the room had not recycled in some time.

"Is something wrong?" Beck asked.

"Just taking in the ambience," he said, not expecting her to understand what he was really doing.

"It looks like someone had been sleeping here," Beck said. "I'm wondering—"

"Forgive me," he said with less curtness than he usually used for talkers at a death scene. "I don't need that kind of detail. I'm examining other things."

He didn't want to explain what those other things were. He didn't like talking his way through death, particularly when his initial impressions were sometimes wrong.

To her credit, Beck said nothing else. She just waited behind him. He could see her out of the corner of his eye. She had folded her hands in front of herself, and she was not moving.

He squared his shoulders and adjusted the scanlights but didn't move them yet. He made himself forget that Beck was beside him.

The windows were shaded. One seemed partially blocked, as if someone did not want any chance of anyone looking in. Blankets on the couch, chairs at an angle—Beck was right: this looked less like an office, more like a temporary sleeping facility.

Food containers from a nearby restaurant sat on a table. He was familiar with those containers, having examined them in several investigations. Once opened, they would start self-cleaning within four hours if not closed and refrigerated again.

He'd tried to break the self-cleaning function on the containers several times and failed. If someone had wanted those containers to malfunction, that person would have to work very hard at it.

Therefore, he didn't even have to examine the containers. He knew the musty odor did not come from them.

"Did you examine the bathroom?" he asked Beck.

"Examine, no," she said, and he felt his heart start to beat a little quicker. "But I did glance in there. There's no body or injured person. I made sure of that much before I called this in."

He nodded. His heart rate lowered. So the blood was the only thing that didn't fit. He examined the floor in front of him, then ran a scanlight over it. Blood splotches had blended into the old carpet. Someone had walked over them, just recently. Probably Beck.

"Do you have evidence-capture shoes?" he asked her, without turning around. He didn't want to see her expression change as she realized she had contaminated his death scene.

"Yes," she said.

He started, surprised. Not many Sandoveil officers would have thought to do that. He couldn't remember the last time a security officer working alone had thought to turn on the evidence-capture feature of all their standard footwear. Hell, most Sandoveil officers didn't wear standard footwear because, they claimed, it was uncomfortable.

When he didn't say anything, she added, almost defensively, "I turned them on when I stepped inside the office. I had no idea what I might find here, and I wanted to be able to walk freely."

"Good," he said. He didn't want to tell her that she had already stepped in some of the blood. In the half-darkness, she probably hadn't realized it. He hadn't seen it either until he had used the scanlight.

"When would you like me to transfer the evidence?" she asked.

"When I tell you." He made sure his tone invited no more conversation.

Hranek looked at the dried blood spatter under the light. The splotches were huge—fist sized. Whoever was bleeding was bleeding badly. But first, that person had rested in one place. Perhaps the splotches of blood came from blood on clothing.

It wouldn't do to speculate. He would need to follow the evidence.

He had to spend hours here. Every square inch of this small room needed to be examined, as well as the hallway they had traversed and the sidewalk outside.

"I need an assistant," he said.

"I'll be happy to do what you need," Beck responded.

That was when he realized he had spoken out loud.

"No," he said, still looking at the floor in front of him. "I need *my* assistant. Get Glynis Okilani for me, please."

There was a momentary pause. He realized then that he had spoken to Beck the way he spoke to the people who worked for him.

He silently cursed himself. He had planned to treat Beck with a bit more respect. Hell, with actual respect.

"Sure, I'll contact her," Beck said. "Would you like me to stay?"

He couldn't take back the harsh tone now, and he found that even though he was a bit peeved at himself, he didn't want to. He had a job to do, and the damn woman was going to ask him question after question.

"Someone carried either a severely injured person or a dead body out of this room," he said, without looking at Beck. He was still staring at the splotches. Evenly spaced, but the splotches themselves weren't even.

"Yes." Behind Beck's calmness, he heard an impatience that matched his own. Apparently, she was smart enough to realize what had occurred here, even without the forensic evidence.

He said, "There should be surveillance all over the streets. Some camera should have caught whomever it was carrying that body away. Find that footage."

"All right," Beck said, and this time, she didn't sound like she was humoring him. "Is it possible to give me an estimate of how many days or hours I should go back?"

"No," he said. "I don't have enough evidence yet."

And he wasn't sure he would. Except, perhaps, if the system kept a log of when it was shut down. He had a hunch it had been placed on a timer, to shut down at a particular time.

Whether or not that timer was activated by the killer or by the victim was a question he couldn't yet answer.

But he was going to try.

25

Marnie Sar crouched over the body bag. It rested on the ground between the vans and the edge of the trail itself. The area smelled of seaweed and damp air and, maybe, just a hint of her own sweat.

She was getting tired. She had been on-site for hours now, and they hadn't made a lot of progress. And now she had come down to the ground level to view the body Tevin Egbe's team had pulled from the pool.

Just as she arrived, he had contacted her: He had found a second body, still submerged. Marnie didn't want to think about that, not yet. Because this body was creating its own problems.

Two members of Tevin's team, Ardelia Novoa and Jabari Zhou, had carried the body here and then had contacted Marnie. She had come down here, expecting answers.

And all she had gotten were more questions.

When Marnie arrived, Novoa had opened the body bag, then stepped back. Zhou had stood just behind her, as if guarding the body—against what, Marnie did not know.

They had placed ground lights all over the area. Marnie had initially decided to identify the corpse using those lights, but after she had looked, she took out her own flashlight and pointed it at the face.

The face was a strange, grayish-white that reflected the light in unpleasant ways. The milky eyes were something Marnie had seen before, so they bothered her less than the bloating around the lips and nostrils. The lips looked just a little blue.

She didn't recognize the face. She had expected to. She had known Glida Kimura—not well, but well enough. And from above, that body had looked like Glida's.

From above.

Marnie sighed, put the flashlight back on her belt kit, and closed the bag. A waft of decaying flesh reached her as she disturbed the air around the corpse.

Then she stood, her knees cracking painfully. She didn't hear the sound, just felt it. It was nearly impossible to hear small noises this close to the Falls. The roar of the cascading water seemed to have grown louder as the night progressed, even though she knew that wasn't possible.

It was just the way she was responding to exhaustion and stress.

Tevin let her know that the positioning of the second body was no accident. This person, whoever she was (and Marnie was pretty sure this was a she), might have died accidentally, but the other person hadn't.

Not that the distinction mattered. The presence of two corpses, one clearly murdered, meant that the entire investigation now belonged to the death investigator.

Marnie had to secure the scene and make one more decision. She needed to decide if she wanted to continue a search, or move everything from rescue to recovery.

Normally, she was very decisive about these things, but she'd had the wrong information all afternoon and evening. She had operated as if all she needed was a formal confirmation of Glida Kimura's death, when in actuality, she had no idea who this corpse belonged to.

Which put those shoes in a completely different light.

If Tevin had discovered the second corpse before he had recovered this one, Marnie would have assumed that the second corpse belonged to Taji Kimura. Then Marnie would have called off the search, thinking the mystery of the two shoes had been resolved.

But now, with an unidentified corpse here, cause of death unknown, and another corpse still in the pool, cause of death suspicious at best, Marnie had no idea what to do.

Her teams had been searching half the night for clues about the body in the pool, with another set of teams exploring the trails with the idea that they might be searching for a missing person.

Marnie had been very clear about all of that: sometimes, when a person observed another person's sudden death, the survivor behaved erratically—running from the scene or trying to backtrack and forgetting how they came.

She had tracked down tourists who had become horribly lost after such a tragedy.

If one of her team had asked her three hours ago who they were searching for, she would have said, *Unofficially, I suspect we're searching for Taji Kimura.* But her team was well-trained. They hadn't asked any of that.

They had done what she asked. They had searched. They continued to search.

She sighed.

Two pairs of shoes. Two bodies. No one would fault her for moving the operation from a rescue/recovery to a full recovery.

She ran a hand through her hair, startled to find it damp. She hadn't realized the Falls gave off that much spray, even this far away from the wall of water.

Novoa's gaze met hers. Zhou was still looking down at the now-closed bag.

Marnie's shoulders slumped.

"I don't recognize her," she said, and her tone sounded even more defeated than she felt. Not that she had wanted Glida dead. But Marnie had wanted to wrap this up quickly and easily.

There was going to be nothing easy here.

Novoa nodded, as if the news hadn't surprised her.

"We'll take the body to the death investigator, then," she said. Standard procedure for this kind of death. Usually they had to leave the body *in situ,* but that had been impossible here.

If Marnie knew Tevin—and she did—then she could trust that he had recorded everything before pulling the corpse from the water.

"I'll let Hranek know it's coming," Marnie said. And as she spoke those words, she realized what she was going to do next.

She was turning over the entire investigation to him. She would block off the paths, mark the scene, and let him determine how to handle everything from now on.

Including the recovery of the second body.

She would let Tevin know.

He would not be pleased.

26

Captain Harriet Virji sat on the edge of the bed, head bent, fingers tangled in her short brown curls.

So much for time off.

She had been sound asleep when an engineer from Sector Base E-2 contacted her with the startling news that one of the runabouts was missing. The engineer—Bristol something—had wanted to know if the *anacapa* drive was programmed for a quick launch away from a site, with an automated return programmed in.

It was not. Virji did not believe in preprogrammed settings. Even though it seemed like they caused less work, in reality, they caused *more* work. They had to be unprogrammed and then reprogrammed, sometimes in the middle of a difficult situation. Why add something for convenience that wasn't going provide any convenience at all?

She needed to sit up straight and reclaim her identity. She usually wasn't a woman easily defeated by bad news.

She wasn't defeated now, but she was tired. The last year had been one crisis after another, though, and even the most highly trained officer with the highest possible stress tolerance got tired.

She had gotten tired.

She had been looking forward to this trip—her reward—for six months now.

She had booked this lovely cabin in the woods in the Payyer Mountains, just outside of Sandoveil, because it seemed as far from the *Ijo* as she could get.

The fact that Illya Markosian had to be in Sandoveil at the same time was simply one additional perk of the trip.

She ran a hand over her face. Illya. She had promised him three weeks of bliss after he finished his work here. He finished this afternoon, and they had had a lovely evening.

She had cooked, something she rarely did. But the kitchen had spectacular views of the Jeleen River. She had watched the sunset while the fish baked, the windows open so she could hear the rumble of nearby Fiskett Falls.

Then she and Illya had spent the rest of the evening in bed.

He had gotten up when Bristol something had contacted Virji. Both Virji and Illya had jobs that required them to hold almost everything they did close to the chest. She knew that Illya was one of the directors of Sector Base Operations for the Fleet, but she hadn't known why he needed to come to Sector Base E-2 until he had finished his task this afternoon.

Then he told her that he was the one who let everyone at the base know they now had a firm date for shutdown. He called it a rough time for any community, and warned that he might have to leave at a moment's notice.

And yet she had been the one who had received the middle-of-the-night contact.

A missing runabout.

She leaned her hands back on the soft sheets. The bedroom had an option to shield the windows against any light from the outside, something apparently designed for starship crews, because they weren't used to daylight at all times.

She had set the window shield when she and Illya went to bed, not to keep out the light, but to keep any potential hikers from peering in at them. Even though the rental agent had told her that this cabin was about as isolated as it got this close to Sandoveil. He had actually warned her that she might not see another human being for days.

Her eyes had become accustomed to the darkness. The rental agent had described the bedroom as small, but it was twice the size of her bedroom on the *Ijo*. She had a full suite, of course, and that took up a lot of room. The actual sleeping area wasn't much bigger than the room she had had as a cadet on the *Brazza Six*.

Here, the bedroom had a double-large bed, two comfortable chairs that faced the windows she had currently shielded, end tables, and an entire entertainment wall if she felt like she needed to remain in bed for several days.

She also could have had her meals prepared for her, an option she hadn't ordered.

A missing runabout wasn't a crisis in and of itself. But it would become one. She knew that as clearly as she knew her own name. Something was off here.

Something she would have to deal with very carefully.

"Was that something important?" Illya entered the bedroom, carrying a tray of food. While Virji had been dealing with Bristol something, Illya had cut up some local cheeses and cured meats, along with fruits Virji didn't recognize. A rich, warm chocolate smell wafted over to her, and she sighed slightly in disappointment.

She would have to forgo the lovely meal, shower, get dressed, and make herself official again. Instead of drinking sweet warm chocolate, sampling local cuisine, and then sampling Illya again.

Their relationship wasn't new, but it felt new. They saw each other so rarely. His job with Sector Base Operations kept him moving between five different systems, constantly monitoring things.

It was rare that she and he got assigned to the same area.

Each time she saw him, he seemed just a little older. His back was still straight, his shoulders broad, but he always had more care lines on his face and a little more silver in his well-trimmed black hair.

He set the tray down on the bedside table and sat beside her. She leaned against him. He felt solid and strong, just like he always had.

He often kidded that she was the adventurous one in their relationship—heading off here and there on some important and often dangerous mission—but he had a steady consistency, the kind she valued in her own support staff. If there was a problem, he would solve it, quickly and with a minimum of fuss.

The food, the supportive shoulder, that was fuss, for him.

He had asked if something important had happened, but the tone of his question implied that he already knew something important *had* happened. After all, who contacted a captain in the middle of a vacation except someone with an emergency?

"I have to go to the sector base." She smiled a little at the irony of it. They had been together in this cabin for a week, and she had hardly seen him.

He had spent every day, and almost every evening, at the sector base. He had just told her at dinner this evening about the shutdown date. She hadn't understood why it was such a big deal. He had tried to explain—something about planning and raising entire families in the same place for generations, and the expectation of consistency for generations more.

She understood that—intellectually. She had some consistency in her life. The Fleet was consistent. It flew together, ever forward, heading to new systems and new worlds. The people were mostly the same, although some did retire near sector bases, some grew up and decided to leave the Fleet, and some disappeared on dangerous missions.

But the Fleet never remained in the same place for long. The sector bases got shut down because the Fleet would move so far past the old bases that the only way to get back to them was via *anacapa* drive. While it could be done relatively easily, the Fleet had set up its system millennia ago.

She had been taught that it was easier to build a new base than it was to maintain an older base, but since she'd been involved with Illya, she learned that wasn't true. If she had thought it through, she would have realized the falseness of that teaching. A new injection of nanobits, some reprogramming, maybe some additional buildings somewhere, and an old base would be retrofitted just fine.

But this system, the new bases, kept the Fleet fresh. It also kept Illya and his entire staff incredibly busy.

He'd dealt with one other base closure in his long career. He said he had stories for her about how difficult it was, about the ways that people went somewhat crazy in the years leading up to the actual shutdown.

He said the first difficult day was the day that the base staff was informed that it would close some time in the future. That day was, in his words, a "bumpy one."

But the first dangerous day, he said at dinner, was a day like today. That day when the base would close went from "sometime in the future" to a particular date. It became real.

And people went slightly—or majorly—crazy.

He wouldn't like this news. *She* didn't like this news either. Primarily, though, because it inconvenienced her.

She usually skated through changed plans. But not on vacation. Vacation was her time.

"Your ship okay?" he asked.

She took a slice of some kind of ham off the plate and took a bite. A little sweet for her, but no matter. She wouldn't be eating much of it anyway.

"My ship is all right," she said, although as she spoke the words, she realized she didn't really know if her ship was all right. "But one of my runabouts is missing."

He had been taking a piece of cheese, but froze when she got to the phrase "is missing."

He looked at her sideways, his silver-blue eyes narrow. "Missing? How the heck does that happen? I thought they were with the ship."

She gave him a small smile. He knew a lot about sector bases and almost nothing about the way that ships worked.

"My runabouts are an odd model class." She couldn't tell him that she wanted to get rid of them. She no longer told anyone that. There were some things you couldn't share with a sometimes-lover, particularly one whose entire life was spent in officialdom, not in shipboard operations. "I have them checked every time we do a major shipwide check."

"Because?" he asked, sitting beside her.

"Because they can be dangerous, and I want to make certain that we take the proper care of them."

That wasn't quite a white lie. When she had become captain of the *Ijo*, she had gotten in trouble for requisitioning too many new small ships for her crew. No one in Fleet Shipboard Operations ever thought that through, no matter how many times she tried to clarify.

The *Ijo* had been the first DV-class ship built at a much larger size. It had two small ship bays instead of one. Everything on the *Ijo* was bigger and better than the previous DV-class models, and while the ship itself had been meticulously planned, some of the aspects around it hadn't been.

Such as filling those two ship bays. Apparently the Shipboard Operations didn't want to send out the *Ijo* half empty, so they had assigned her a lot of the older, smaller ships to fill out the secondary bay. The smaller ships in the first bay were state-of-the art, so she usually used those.

But the smaller ships in the second bay had their issues, and as she learned them, she tried to get rid of the ships. She had succeeded too much at first, and had caused that line item on her ship's budget to be ten times higher than the recommended amount.

As a result, she had gotten a reprimand that to this day she didn't feel that she deserved. A black mark for making sure her crew was safe.

Since she couldn't exchange bad ships for good any longer, she now tried to keep the bad ships in as best repair as possible, until whatever sector base she visited recommended the ships get retired.

So she wasn't saddened to hear that the runabout was missing. But she was sad that her vacation was ending.

"So the runabout was in the base," Illya said, popping a small red berry in his mouth. The movement made the berry's scent reach her—a cross between watermelon and brandy, if she didn't miss her guess.

"The runabout wasn't just in the base," Virji said. "It was in one of the lower tech levels of the sector base, getting its *anacapa* drive repaired."

He shifted slightly so that he could face her. "*Anacapa* drive? On a runabout?"

"Told you it was an odd model," she said.

"Good God." He thought about it for a moment. She knew where he was going mentally, and she didn't want to go there. She reached across him for more ham, knowing she had to shower and leave, knowing that once she did, she might not make it back to this isolated place—and that marvelous sense of calm that had just started to overtake her.

"I doubt that the disappearance is connected to the sector base closing," she said to forestall him. She didn't want to have that conversation.

"Still," he said, "you have to admit that it's some kind of coincidence."

She sighed. She had known he would say that. And, if she were honest with herself, she had thought it. But, she had rationalized, she had had that thought because of their dinner conversation, about the things that people near the sector base did when the closing became a reality.

She grabbed another slice of ham and stood up. "It seems rather odd to steal a runabout as a protest against a base closure. Especially an expected base closure."

She sounded harsher than she had planned to. She hadn't meant that as a criticism of him. He had his focus; she had hers.

This wasn't the first time someone had stolen a runabout during her tenure as captain of the *Ijo*. It probably wouldn't be the last.

"I'm sorry," she said, half turning, just so that she could see his expression. "I didn't mean to be critical. It's just that with the *anacapa*, the runabout—"

"Could be anywhere, I know."

Her breath caught. He had interrupted her when she was talking about her ship's business. When was the last time someone had interrupted her like that? Especially when she was speaking in her capacity as captain?

"It's just that," she said more slowly, her tone deliberately harsh this time to let him know that the interruption was both unacceptable and incorrect, "with the *anacapa*, the runabout might not have been stolen at all. If the *anacapa* drive had malfunctioned, the runabout could have been obliterated."

"Taking the base with it," he said. Clearly he hadn't heard her tone, or if he had, it hadn't concerned him.

She felt a flash of irritation. She couldn't remember the last time she had felt that way about him, if ever.

"You, of all people, should know that sector bases are built to withstand *anacapa* malfunctions," she said.

He froze midway through reaching for another piece of cheese. Her tone got through this time.

"Yes, I'm sorry," he said in a tone of voice she had never heard before. It sounded official. "I was incorrect. Wouldn't it be odd, though, to have an *anacapa* malfunction the day the base learned the date it would cease to exist?"

"Odd, yes," she said. "Unusual, no. *Anacapa* malfunctions happen. They are the stuff of nightmares, at least for ship's captains."

Then she pivoted, and headed for the shower, her heart pounding. Had that been a lover's quarrel? An actual fight? The beginning of the end of something fun?

She didn't have the time to find out.

27

Bassima ended up in her office. Even though she had eaten hours ago, she was still burping strawberry-flavored meringue. That dessert had really been a mistake. She would have to remember that next time.

But of course, she wouldn't. This night would become a blur of images, not her own.

Her investigative office was small, little more than a chair that she had to have custom-made because she was so tall, and a desk that she had placed on blocks to accommodate her knees.

Mostly, she worked on holographic screens, scattering them around her so that she could follow the imagery, but the desk itself had become a kind of catchall for everything from gloves to bits of paper to small rocks that she brought to remind her of the great outdoors.

One reason she had volunteered for the shift that began in the afternoons was to avoid office time with her more jovial coworkers. Most of them worked mornings. She did her rounds early in the afternoon to avoid the other officers who hung out in the office too much. Then she did any work that she had to be in the office for late into the evening.

On this night, however, she had moved past evening work long ago. She was officially here after hours. She would have to fight to get paid for the time she spent sitting here, but she would argue that Hranek had deputized her as one of his assistants. She would also say that he had implied that the work needed to be done immediately.

He hadn't actually said that, no, but it had felt urgent. Even though the death scene was old, and no one, as far as Bassima could tell, was in jeopardy.

Bassima smiled grimly at herself. She was making excuses for her own thoughts, because no one would end up caring how much time she put in or how much it cost. The Sector Base funded everything in the Sandoveil Valley, so there was an amazing amount of extra money in this community. She'd had after-hours time approved for events less significant than this one.

She was just nervous and worried in general. That blood pool had startled her. The evidence collected by her shoes and moved into the collection bags upon her arrival at the security office had even more blood in it than she had expected. So she had stepped on the blood trail without meaning to.

That embarrassed her. She didn't like to think of herself as an inexperienced investigator, but when it came to death scenes without a body, she was. She couldn't remember ever seeing a death scene like that before. Every time she found blood and signs of something awful, the scene was on the mountain or near the mud flats, and the something awful was usually something that had occurred because of the environment, not because of another person.

Bile rose in her throat, and she swallowed hard. Her stomach ached. Maybe the discomfort she was feeling was coming from the potential loss of the Kimuras, not because of her rather overstuffed dinner.

She rubbed her eyes and leaned back.

Because she was working here alone, she had holographic screens surrounding her. Screens of all different sizes, all set on 2D at the moment, and opaque along the back. Usually, if she was working on something important, she worked on fewer screens and kept them only in her line of sight, so that she would know if someone approached her.

The screens all showed different angles of the surrounding streets. She had taken one square mile's worth of footage over the past week. There was a lot of footage, from almost every building, from most vehicles, and from the street cameras at every intersection.

Most people didn't mind that their entire lives were recorded. Most people didn't even think about it. Recording daily life was common on starships and many, many of the residents in Sandoveil had grown up in Fleet families, even if no one in several generations had served on a Fleet vessel.

Surveillance was simply a fact of daily life for anyone connected with the Fleet, and that had become part of daily life in Sandoveil as well.

Bassima hadn't even noticed how common recording was until she became a security officer. Then she realized how much of her own life was on some kind of public record. The only place she was guaranteed complete privacy was inside her own home.

She was running the images on the screens backward from her arrival at the scene. Initially, she had the images stop or slow and notify her any time a person entered the street. But as the images reached the close of business, they were all pinging her and letting her know that there were dozens of people on the streets.

So she left that warning in place only for the evening hours. In fact, at the moment, she was scanning over the daytime hours, figuring that the killer (if, indeed, that blood pool meant someone was dead) had moved the body after dark.

Bassima would examine daylight hours once she had gone through all of the nights.

She hadn't expected to find anything on this night, but she had hoped to discover something the night before. She did learn that a number of local residents window-shopped after they finished their dinners at nearby restaurants.

At the moment, she found that habit irritating. She wanted the street clear except for the killer.

Nothing suspicious had happened the previous night. Walkers went by, then the window-shoppers, and then nothing for hours at a time. Employees of various businesses started showing up around dawn, especially at the bakeries and restaurants.

Most people did not use their private vehicles to get to work unless they parked outside of her one-square-mile radius. Most people walked or took the underground transport, and most of them acted like they had done nothing out of the ordinary. They didn't seem distressed or uncomfortable; they weren't looking around as if searching for stores or landmarks. The early morning locals simply seemed like people everywhere on their way to work—paying more attention to the destination than they were to buildings, vehicles, and others around them.

Later in the day, though, most people did not act like locals. Most of them acted like Sandoveil's downtown was unfamiliar territory.

Some of those daytime people were locals, but if she had to guess, a goodly number of the daytime people were tourists.

She did not suspect a tourist killed Taji, although perhaps she should have. After all, Taji ran a business that catered to people who did not live in Sandoveil. Perhaps one of them had killed her…and then what? Carried her body away in a fashion that made it hard to track?

Or was the blood at the scene Glida's? Had Taji killed her and then taken her body away? Taji would have known how to shut off the environmental system and how to get across parts of Sandoveil without being seen.

Bassima shook her head slightly. She trusted her instincts, and her instincts told her that Taji wasn't a killer. But everyone could become a killer, given the right circumstances. Or so Bassima had been taught.

She continued to scan through the images, heading backward. She hit the darkness of two nights previous, and saw nothing before the early morning people started to show up.

Until the early morning hours, when her gaze caught a shadow. It was at the blurry edge of one of the cameras. She backed up the image and froze the frame. Then she saved her place on the other screens and momentarily shut them off. She expanded the holoscreen with the shadow, and moved it to a 3D image.

The shadow was the tail end of a vehicle. Bassima recognized it: some kind of medium-sized aircar with a bubbled back. Cars like that were made just outside of Sandoveil and usually sold to businesses that had to haul things around town.

She moved the image backward at half-quarter time, hoping to see more. The tail end of the car was all she could see, but the reason she had noticed the shadow at all was because someone was moving beside it. She slowed the image even more, saw a flash of color reflected in the car's shiny surface.

Her heart was pounding as if she were actually on-site, about to catch a criminal by herself.

She made the image even bigger so that it was life-size. Then she stood up and walked toward it, examining the sides.

The back of this particular vehicle had no windows, so she couldn't see inside. But it looked like the flash she had seen had been some yellow caught in the light.

She moved the image backward farther, but didn't see any more. So she went forward again, trying to get the system to show her whether she was actually seeing something yellow or another reflection.

She couldn't tell.

She let out an exasperated sigh, then moved the image backward farther than she had before. No movement, nothing. Just the vehicle, sitting on the side of the road, barely inside the one-square-mile radius.

Of course. Anyone would think to use a standard measurement in a search, like one square mile.

She changed the search parameters to one-and-a-quarter square miles.

The entire car appeared before her—life-size, slicing into two nearby desks and completely absorbing one of the chairs. She didn't move anything, and she didn't bring the image down.

Instead she went back and forth over that small window of time.

Someone approached the vehicle from the front, not from the back like they would have if they had been coming directly from Taji's office. Yellow flashed again, and this time, Bassima realized she was seeing some kind of fabric.

The cameras didn't record sound. Normally that would have pleased her, but in this instance, she wanted to hear what was going on. The vehicle rocked as a door on the far side opened, away from the camera. She saw feet, small feet, wearing women's shoes. Locals' shoes.

A surge of triumph ran through her. She had known she was dealing with a local.

And then the triumph faded.

She had no reason to tie this vehicle or anything about this vehicle to the crime scene at the office. For all she knew, the owner of the vehicle was picking up a delivery from a nearby business or adding something to the vehicle to take elsewhere. And the shoes—they were common in Sandoveil. Many local women wore them.

Assumptions were the death of investigations. Bassima knew that, and she was getting lost in this one.

Bassima brought the image size back to 2D and made it the size of a tablet. She now knew where to look. She even knew what to look for.

She needed to expand the search just a bit more, see who approached the vehicle from the other direction, and then go back even farther and see who actually parked the vehicle in this spot.

It would take a little time, but she would get some answers—even if they might not be the kind of answers she wanted.

28

Rajivk finally figured out how to slow down the nanobit repair. He stood in the middle of the storage room, sweat trickling down one side of his face. It was hot in here, partly because so many people were still standing around. The security team was watching as if they expected everyone inside the room to run off with the room itself or something.

Rajivk had no idea what was left to steal in here.

Most of his team stood near the walls, taking readings, doing the kind of research that Iannazzi had asked them to do. He hadn't consulted with her about shutting off the nanobits. He had simply done it.

The nanobits, by doing their job and repairing the damage, were destroying the very information he and the team needed to solve the mystery of the missing runabout.

He had never needed to shut down nanobits in the midst of a repair before, and he hadn't been certain he could do it. The nanobit system was pretty self-contained. He had worked with nanobits throughout his career, and essentially, all he had to do was activate one of several programs, and they did the rest of the work.

There were fail-safes that, in theory, protected techs from activating nanobits incorrectly. He usually complained about all the times he had to confirm that he wanted to inject new nanobits into a system or he wanted to have nanobits create a small part that he needed for repair.

He did understand why he had to do so, though. Nanobits were powerful technology. They could transform the interiors of mountains, create caverns where there were none, and create material so strong that it could protect human beings against all of the hazards of space.

But just because he and the other engineers couldn't imagine using nanobits without extreme caution didn't mean that others had the same attitude.

So there had to be some kind of mechanism that overrode human error. What did people do if they programmed nanobits to repair something that didn't need repair? Or to repair something that was beyond repair?

At first, he thought that something would be simple to find, but it hadn't been. There were very few manuals for nanobits. There were textbooks and lectures on the nanobit, similar to the ones he had taken for classes a long, long time ago, but he didn't have time to go through those right now.

He would have thought that it would have been in some basic instructions on the nanobit, only he discovered as he did his quick search that there were no basic nanobit instructions, not connected to Sector Base E-2. The base was so old that Sector Base Operations believed that the beginning how-to-build-a-base information didn't need to be here.

And considering the day's events, they had been right.

Besides, the base itself didn't need repair often. Ships did, but, generally speaking, their nanobits worked automatically, just like the nanobits had done here. And if the nanobits ceased to work properly, they got revitalized or replaced with a new batch of nanobits, which would then take over the job.

He had finally stepped back, taken one single nanobit, and examined it, finding what he was looking for in its operating system. He hadn't looked in a nanobit's operating system in decades, probably not since he had been in training.

And even then, he couldn't recall doing it.

But he found the way to pause the nanobits—not shut them off—which would allow them to continue their cleanup when the team had finished with their investigation.

Pereyra was doing her best to reverse-engineer the crisis, using information from the nanobits as well. She was downloading the repair records, seeing what the nanobits had done since the incident happened.

Rajivk grabbed a cloth and wiped the sweat off the side of his face. The environmental controls had been partially shut down since the team was working with nanobits. No one wanted nanobits from this room to get sucked into the air system. There were filters and capture equipment, but he hated relying on that.

He stopped work and took a deep breath. He would have to take some kind of break soon. He hadn't eaten in hours, and he was tired. This was the middle of his night. He needed to attend to himself—food, since he couldn't have sleep.

He glanced at his colleagues. Pereyra was standing near one of the walls, her hands cupped in front of her, a holoscreen floating on one side. Two other team members were using scanners on the blast doors, which had clearly taken some kind of terrible hit. Sheldenhelm was measuring the room for the umpteenth time.

And that damn image of Glida Kimura still stood, completely frozen in the center of the storage room. The image bothered Rajivk. Her form—twisted slightly as if caught doing something wrong—looked as if it were trying to escape. Even though it couldn't.

Some of the security team was still here as well, guarding the room, for reasons he didn't entirely understand. He wished they would leave. They were adding to the room's heat. Plus, they were watching everything (and probably not understanding any of it). Rajivk didn't like being watched while he worked.

Iannazzi had returned a while ago. She had vanished shortly after she had given everyone the order to get to work, and then she had returned, looking frazzled. She had informed the team that that the *anacapa* wasn't preprogrammed. Which meant that even if it had activated automatically, it wouldn't have taken the runabout anywhere predictable.

As Rajivk had pointed out, the *anacapa* could have simply reactivated its last known program and sent the ship there.

Iannazzi had nodded—perhaps that was part of the reason she looked frazzled—but Sheldenhelm frowned.

"You'd think we would have heard if it showed up on some other base or somewhere in the Fleet," he had said quietly.

"Has anyone checked the interior of the *Ijo*?" Rajivk asked. "It might have returned to its normal bay."

"Good thought," Iannazzi had said. "I'll check."

And that had ended the meeting. He hadn't heard if the runabout had returned to the *Ijo*, but he doubted it had. He knew Iannazzi. She was the kind of woman who hated having anyone in her lab, and he knew she considered this storage room part of her lab.

The quicker she resolved all of this, the faster she could clear the area. He had to trust that she would do all she could to clear the room.

He knew part of the reason he wanted to double-check her was because he was so very tired. He hadn't been this exhausted in a long time. His eyes ached as if he had been rubbing them too hard. But that was because he had been staring at small things—small screens, small sections of wall, small representations of nanobit operation systems.

He needed to connect with the team before he decided his next move. He didn't want to duplicate work they had already done, unless, of course, he needed to on this side of the room. Information might differ here.

He started toward Pereyra, avoiding the center of the storage room, just like everyone else. Iannazzi's point had been a good one: that runabout could return at any moment without warning, particularly if the *anacapa* wasn't working properly.

He had just taken a few steps when the blast doors banged open, startling him.

Harriet Virji, Captain of the *Ijo*, strode in. She seemed bigger than everyone else here. Tall, straight back, square shoulders. She wasn't wearing her uniform, but she just as well might have been. The black shirt and pants made her look official, even though her brown curls were still damp and her face was ruddy with the cold.

She did, however, have a laser pistol strapped to her hip as if she were going into battle.

For one brief moment, he worried whether she had clearance to be down here, and then he almost smiled at himself. He *was* a lot more tired than he was willing to admit. Of course she had clearance.

Starship captains could go anywhere in sector bases.

Virji glanced around the room as if she was startled that so many people had been packed into such a small space.

Everyone stopped working and stood at attention, or what passed for attention in a sector base where half the staff didn't consider itself part of the Fleet at all. Just employees of the base, sir, as Rajivk would've said if she had asked him.

And of course, she wasn't going to ask him.

She gave the image of Glida Kimura a hard look and then said, "At ease."

She didn't reassure anyone, like most captains did, that this visit wasn't official. Of course it was official: her runabout was missing.

"Forgive me, sir," Iannazzi said, sounding a bit breathless. "I must have miscommunicated. I was going to contact you when we had information. We could—"

"Did you think that I was going to ignore the loss of a runabout?" Virji snapped.

"Um, no, sir," Iannazzi said. To her credit, she didn't apologize again.

Rajivk didn't move. He didn't want to call attention to himself. He hated dealing with captains or anyone from Fleet vessels, really. Their culture was very different from his, even though, in theory, they were part of the same organization.

"I take it there's no news since you contacted me?" Virji asked.

"No, sir. We're making progress, but it's as small as the nanobits." Who knew that Iannazzi could be so poetic? Rajivk hadn't thought it in her.

"I'll be honest with you," Virji said to Iannazzi as if no one else was in the room, "the runabout isn't worth much to me or the Fleet. I had hoped to retire all of my FS-Prime runabouts, but due to some reasons

I won't go into, I wasn't at liberty to do so if the sector base staff felt the runabouts were still space-worthy."

"Are you saying that we should stop searching for the runabout?" The head security guy—Wèi, was it?—sounded weirdly nervous for someone in his position.

Rajivk repressed the urge to roll his eyes. Clearly, Wèi did all his work around sector base employees and not around the crews of the Fleet ships, or he would have known, first, how to address someone of Virji's rank, and second, how ridiculous the question was.

Virji gave him a withering look. "You are?"

"Karter Wèi."

Rajivk wanted to whisper, *Sir. Add sir,* but he wasn't close enough.

Wèi seemed to sense that he needed to say something more, but he clearly wasn't certain what it was. "I head security for this section of the base."

"Well, you've done a piss-poor job, haven't you?" Virji said. She didn't wait for his response. She walked over to the image of Glida Kimura.

No one else in the storage room moved, not even Iannazzi, who was nominally in charge.

Rajivk turned slightly so he could see Virji's face as she reached the image.

"Is this our thief?" Virji asked.

"Yes, sir," Iannazzi said as Wèi spoke as well. He said, "We don't know if she's a thief—"

His voice was the one that carried.

"Really?" Virji's sarcasm was withering. She didn't even bother to look at him. "She broke in and a runabout is missing. Even if the *anacapa* activated and took the runabout somewhere unexpected, this woman had no business on one of my ships."

Then she inhaled, almost as if she had stopped herself from speaking further. She bent over slightly so that she could peer into the face of the holographic image.

"This woman is…?"

"Glida Kimura, sir," Iannazzi said. She didn't move as she spoke, as if she wanted to add more, but didn't dare.

Rajivk wanted to tell the captain that Glida had been thought dead until a few hours ago, but he didn't say that either. He didn't want to get into the middle of this discussion at all.

"Glida Kimura," Virji repeated, almost as if she were trying the name on for size. "Glida Kimura."

She shook her head.

"No," she said. "That's not right."

"Beg pardon, um, sir," Wèi said, clearly catching a clue about his methods of address, but not yet figuring out how to talk to someone of her rank. "But that woman is Glida Kimura—"

"Oh, perhaps here she is," Virji said. "But she served on my ship, decades ago."

The room grew exceptionally quiet, as if everyone held their breath. Rajivk frowned at Virji. She didn't even seem to notice him. She was staring at Glida's face, as if memorizing it.

Then Virji looked up. Wèi had been watching her.

"Sir," he said, slowly. Carefully. "We have no record of her ever serving on your ship."

Virji nodded. "Because she did not go by Glida Kimura then."

"But her DNA should have been on file. We should have had a record of her, no matter what name she served under." Wèi sounded so distressed that he forgot the honorific.

Even though Rajivk noticed, it didn't seem that Virji did. Or perhaps she didn't care.

"Yes, it all should have been on file." Virji pulled herself away from the image and turned toward Wèi. "I assume you are not the man in charge of the entire security division."

"No, sir," he said. He sounded very polite, but color had crept into his face. Either he was getting annoyed or he was embarrassed. Or perhaps both.

"I would like to speak to the person who runs security. You'll make the contact for me?"

"Yes, sir," Wèi said.

Virji nodded once. After a quick glance at the image, she turned to leave.

No one was telling her about the death on the Falls. No one was informing her that there seemed to be more to this than a simple break-in and a possible mistake.

Rajivk didn't know if it was his place, but he couldn't keep quiet.

"Sir," he said, his voice shaking just a little.

Iannazzi glared at him. Wèi's lips thinned, not that Rajivk cared what Wèi thought. After all, Wèi had already screwed up his encounter with Virji.

Virji looked at Rajivk as if noticing him for the first time. Of course she was. He had done his best to be invisible until now.

There was a question in her eyes, and he suddenly realized that she wasn't certain if he had spoken to her or not.

"I'm sorry, sir," he said quietly, "but there's one more thing you should know."

She stopped before him and clasped her hands behind her back. "And you are?"

"Rajivk Agwu," he said.

She waited.

"I, um, work as an engineer on Bristol Iannazzi's team."

Virji continued to look at him. Iannazzi raised her chin slightly, as if daring him to make her appear stupid.

"But, um, this has nothing to do with the base, at least, I think it has nothing to do with the base," he said.

"You have me intrigued, Agwu," Virji said. But she didn't add anything else. No question, nothing. And it was intimidating. That silence—he had heard people could use it as a weapon. He'd never been subjected to something like that before.

His heart had started pounding. He felt nervous, even though he didn't know what this woman could do to him. She was the captain of a ship. She did not have the power to fire him, although she could probably make his life difficult here.

Still, he felt the power that she had. It was a personal power, the kind that controlled an entire room.

And she was certainly doing that. Everyone was watching.

"I—um—walk home near Fiskett Falls," he said.

She raised her chin slightly, as if he had gotten her attention.

"I found a body in a pool near the Falls earlier today. The YSR-SR—that's the—"

"Search and Rescue service," she said. "I have come to this base before."

And clearly had an interaction with the YSR-SR. Which made him even more nervous for reasons he didn't understand.

"Um," he said, "they tentatively identified the body as Glida Kimura's. That was before we found out about the incident here."

Virji turned slowly—not toward Iannazzi, but toward Wèi. "And no one was going to tell me of this?"

Wèi's flush deepened. "I—ah—." He glared at Rajivk, as if this situation was suddenly Rajivk's fault. "It clearly wasn't Glida Kimura, so we felt that it was not important."

"Really?" Virji said. "Why did you know it wasn't her?"

"Because she never left this room," Wèi said.

Rajivk resisted the temptation to close his eyes against Wèi's stupidity.

"And yet, she's not in this room, is she?" Virji said.

Rajivk wanted to jump in, to say that the body probably wasn't Kimura's, but he didn't.

Everything felt fraught, and he wasn't quite sure how to behave.

Virji turned back to Rajivk. Her gaze met his. "You're certain that the body did not belong to Glida Kimura?"

"I'm not certain of anything," he said. "I got called away before there was a firm identification, only to find she had locked herself in this storage room. The timing of the security breach—or what we noticed as a breach—"

He didn't know how to refer to the blast doors, exactly. Or anything else.

"—suggests that it wasn't her." There. He had thrown a bone to Wèi.

"But we don't know that either, do we?" Virji asked. Then she looked past Rajivk, at the image of Glida Kimura. "A dead body near the Falls. A missing runabout. Humph. The past always seems to repeat itself."

She squared her shoulders, then nodded at Rajivk. He had no idea what she had meant. He knew better than to ask.

"Thank you, Agwu, for your candor. I needed that piece of information before I see the head of security." Virji took a step toward the door, then stopped and looked at Wèi. "You will set up that meeting within the hour."

It wasn't a request.

"Yes, sir," he said.

She swept out of the room, and everyone relaxed visibly. Everyone except Rajivk. What had she meant about the past? Something more was going on here, something that none of them had the information to.

None of them, except Glida Kimura herself.

29

Hranek worked silently in that stuffy room, going over each inch, examining each bit of carpet, every table and chair leg. Evidence had spattered and moved, DNA coated everything, and he wanted all of it.

Eventually, he no longer noticed the musty smell. The blanket bunched up on the couch had become a pile of fibers, the pillow a DNA feast. He hadn't even made it to the table yet, where the food containers actually were, but he knew they would tell him something as well.

He had gotten past his early annoyance at being awakened, at coming to a scene with no body at all, at not being contacted about the actual body found near Fiskett Falls. This room was giving up its secrets one by one, and he was enjoying finding them.

He hadn't done this kind of investigation in nearly two decades, and never had he done one in Sandoveil. Here, the YSR-SR tracked missing people. Sometimes they showed up dead, but they were always presumed to be alive as the search continued.

Sometimes he had to reconstruct what happened to them, but he worked from the body backward, trying to figure out how it got to wherever it had gotten to.

This time, he was working from the blood pool forward. In Ynchi City, they called investigations like this *ghost investigations* because they involved shadows and ghostly images and things seen out of the corner of the eye.

Often, there, the reconstruction of a death scene occurred because most human beings were not master criminals, but they always tried to be. They hid bodies or destroyed bodies or burned bodies, taking them away from the place of death to some other place, thinking that would fool the death investigator, or the death investigator wouldn't catch them at all.

But death investigators always caught them. Most people on Nindowne did not know how advanced technology had become. It could shadow a human being, if it knew where the human being had been previous to arriving in this spot. It could recreate events out of splotches of blood and smatterings of DNA.

It could approximate what happened without anyone testifying to what happened.

Testimony was always flawed. Human memories did not work as well as science. Whenever Hranek had a suspicious death, he always used technology to verify the testimony. Technology told him the truth each and every time.

His favorite assistant, Glynis Okilani, had arrived without fanfare. Good investigator that she was, she had contacted him from the intersection half a block away, asking him what he wanted her to do.

He told her to use double evidence-gathering equipment on her shoes as she walked toward the scene. He knew the killer had to go somewhere with the body, and given how quiet Main Street was after dark, he figured the killer wouldn't really worry about being seen.

Sure, the killer probably had transport, but whether or not the killer had parked that transport close was another matter altogether.

He would work his way backward from the death scene, but he wanted to make certain that Okilani was working her way forward from the building's exterior.

Until Beck told him where the killer had taken the body—if Beck told him—he would assume the body went out the front door. He hadn't seen another exit, and before Beck had departed, he had asked her about one.

She didn't know either, but she had promised to check. He told her not to interrupt him with that information. He would contact her when he needed it.

This blood pool, this actually harked back to his past in Ynchi City. Homicides had a depressing sameness, no matter how clever the killers thought they were.

He had to focus, however. Because the difference between a homicide in Ynchi City and a homicide in Sandoveil was one of degree and practice. The last time he had dealt with a homicide here had been five years before, and the killing had been a straightforward one. A simple shove off one of the overlooks—a shove witnessed by six people. Yes, it had been a homicide, but it hadn't really needed much of an investigation.

He had just made it to the blood pool when Okilani told him she had arrived at the side of the building. So far, she said, she hadn't found any spatter.

He actually hadn't expected her to.

"Please continue forward," he said. "Let me know when you reach the exterior door."

He broke off the communication without a word, and concentrated on the blood pool. Although to call it a pool was a misnomer. It probably had been a pool once.

Now it was a thick stain. He didn't touch it, not yet, so it might still be damp or even wet in the middle. That depended on how long it had been sitting in the unrecycled air.

The pool covered most of the floor from the edge of the couch to the table. The pool had even edges, which led him to believe that the pool had flowed from a body, rather than dropped downward. The flow was probably fast and relatively uniform from a large point of origin, like a slit neck or a severed blood vessel.

He saw no arterial spray near the ground, although he had seen a mist along one wall. He hadn't investigated that yet, so he had no idea if it was even tied to the blood pool.

He used the scanlight to measure the size of the blood pool. Then he had his handheld scanlight examine the edges, to see if the pool had receded or expanded in the carpet itself.

The pool had receded—at least from what he could see with the naked eye. A large portion of it near the bathroom door had soaked into the carpet, becoming nearly invisible.

Beck had walked across that, even though it was clear from the placement of her footsteps that she had thought there might be blood or evidence she couldn't see. Her steps were very far apart, and as close to the wall as they could get.

She had leaned on the ball of one foot as she had peered into the bathroom. He knew that because her footprint had a deep indentation on the front.

He scanned the rest of the pool, looking for something he couldn't quite find.

Whoever removed the body had to have stepped in the blood pool. Or that person (persons?) had to use some kind of tool to get the body out of the blood pool.

Either way, he should have found evidence of that person in the blood pool or on the carpet leading away from the pool.

He frowned and looked up. Had the body been lying across a chair and bleeding downward? If it had exsanguinated that way, the blood pool itself would have absorbed the splatter left by the drips.

Both extra chairs were too far from the blood pool to have been used in that way. Unless they were moved. But again, the room was not that big, so moving the chairs would have shown up in or around the pool.

He looked at the couch with its bunched pillow and blanket. Perhaps there, on the end nearest the bathroom.

But that made no sense, since the deepest part of the blood pool was in the very center of the room.

He would have to look at that part of the couch, though, when he got there. Sometimes evidence could lie as effectively as a human being. Like any lie, evidentiary lies were easily exposed upon closer examination.

He made a mental note, flagging that possible exception.

"I'm at the door."

He started, not expecting to hear from Okilani so soon. Then he checked the time. It hadn't been soon. He had been standing in the same position, moving only his arm, for nearly an hour.

At that thought, his neck and back ached. Pain shot through the muscles in his shoulders. He hadn't been moving, and he hadn't been thinking about it. Only with thinking about it did he feel how stiff he had become.

"Have you found anything?" he asked.

He tilted his head from side to side, hearing his neck creak. He did this at every interesting death scene and he always paid for it later.

"Yes," Okilani said. "I've found microscopic blood drops heading south."

South from that door on the curved street. He had to close his eyes, picture the street's layout and then pull back, as if he were designing a mental map.

South—away from Main.

Of course. That would be the best solution, the easiest way to hide a vehicle. There were even places to park off some of the side streets.

"Follow the blood trail," he said. "See where it leads."

He said that, in part, because he wanted to remain alone in this room.

He moved his shoulders in tight circles, listening to the pop as the muscles loosened. The aches and pains eased enough that he could shove them into the background again as he crouched to look deeper at the blood pool.

Even though the scene looked like it was disorganized, he had a hunch he was dealing with a planner. He would guess, just from the placement of the blood pool and the lack of footprints or any visible way that the body was removed from this site, that the planner was either local or had studied how death investigation was done in Sandoveil.

The killer knew that his office had a small staff, but that he had experience with larger cases. He had not kept that secret. He had done presentations—tasteful ones—at every organization in Sandoveil, from the schools to the obscure social clubs that half the city seemed to join. He particularly loved talking about the cases of the moment—the ones that anyone who followed newstainment originating in Ynchi City would be familiar with. He would explain how he would have handled those cases, had they come to him, or if they were older cases, how he *had* handled some of them.

He wasn't a local celebrity—a death investigator failed if he allowed himself to become a celebrity—but he wasn't unknown either. And he always made it clear that he was a stickler for science and the scientific method.

A muscle in his back spasmed, and he had to stand upright to loosen it.

As he stretched, he realized he had never really discussed death scenes—not at most meetings. He usually talked about corpses, what they could explain or couldn't explain. He often discussed how important it was to find them at the site of their death, not just because of the trace evidence, but because the body in its final repose revealed so many secrets.

If the body were removed from its final repose, he often said, many secrets would remain lost forever.

He let out a small breath. He liked to say he hated hunches, but that wasn't entirely true. He hated *other people's* hunches. His were often stellar. He'd studied where hunches came from, and among the scientific, hunches were usually the brain working with evidence at such lightning speed that the conscious mind couldn't keep up.

Whoever killed the person who lost all of this blood had heard his talk. The killer knew that he preferred a body on-site, so the killer must have thought that removing the body would thwart him.

If, indeed, there was a body.

He took a deep breath and made himself take a mental step backward. He didn't know if the blood belonged to more than one human. He did not know if the blood in the pool was human at all. Nor did he know if the blood had been poured here, perhaps as a misdirect, or perhaps on purpose as some kind of study.

Then his official comm link activated.

He hated being interrupted at a death scene.

He answered without looking at who had the temerity to contact him in the middle of the night.

"What?" he barked.

"Mushtaq, it's Marnie."

It took him a moment to come out of his examination of the death scene and into the present. Marnie. The head of YSR-SR.

"What?" he asked again, letting her know she had disturbed him. She had worked with him for years. She knew he could be prickly. Not that he cared what she thought.

"I'm sending a body your way," she said.

"The one from Fiskett Falls?" he asked, not hiding his displeasure.

"Yes," she said. "Who told you about that?"

"You're supposed to contact me when you find a body," he said. "Not inform me after you've moved it."

"It was in that pool behind the waterfall. It was hard to reach. I had a team extract it. There was no reason to have you hike to the pool itself." She didn't sound distressed at his rudeness. She could be tough as well.

"I would want to see the body as close to the site as possible," he said. "You should know that."

"They put it in a body bag on the shelf in the area they call the landing pad just outside the pool. Behind the Falls. We've cordoned off the area where we believe the body went into the water—"

"I will determine that," he said. "So cordon off as much as you can."

"I know." She sounded calm. "It's already done. The body, in its bag, is coming your way."

He moved his shoulders in circles again. "Have you seen this body?"

"Yes," she said.

"Has it lost a lot of blood?" he asked, still staring at the blood pool.

"I—I have no idea." She sounded surprised. "It's pretty damaged."

"Of course it is," he muttered to himself.

"I'm sorry?" she asked.

"What?" he asked, wondering what she was apologizing for.

"You spoke," she said.

"I did," he said, not giving her any more. He needed her to leave him alone so he could get more done. Now he had two cases to deal with.

Or not.

If someone had heard his lectures, they would know that water immersion was one great way to get rid of evidence. He hadn't really discussed it much, but he had mentioned it over the years. He both loved and hated the preponderance of water in the Sandoveil Valley. The water made the deaths more interesting, but many of the deaths were interesting only because determining the exact cause was challenging.

"I have one more thing," she said.

He tried not to sigh audibly. "What?"

If anything, he made that single word even more curt. He really wanted to get back to his work here, particularly if he had more work waiting for him at his office.

"It looks like we have a second body," she said.

That snapped his attention back to the conversation. "It *looks like*?" he asked.

"Yes," she said.

He closed his eyes for just a moment. Sleep had just become a thing of the past.

"I'll be there shortly," he said, his reluctance in his voice. He needed to calm down. This scene would wait, although he had no idea how much evidence he would lose to decay. He would need to take readings—

"No," she said.

He froze. Did she just tell him not to come to a death scene? Was she hampering *another* investigation? The fact that he hadn't been present for the first body annoyed him beyond reason. The idea that she would do this *again* made him angry.

"Tevin Egbe's team will dive for the body in the morning," Marne said.

"Dive for it?" Hranek made sure he understood exactly what she was saying. "It's underwater?"

"He was following your procedure, making sure that evidence hadn't sunk to the bottom of that pool. He was recording everything, so that you would have it, along with the body. As he used the scanlight, he found indications of a second body. He wanted to dive immediately, but I said there's no reason. It's best to do something like that in daylight."

Even Hranek knew that. He preferred his teams to be safe. He hated dealing with the bodies of his friends. That had happened too much on this job, and it was the thing that discouraged him the most.

Hranek glanced at the time, realized that dawn was at least six hours away. That was six hours in which the water would damage more of the corpse, but that was better than trying to bring it up in near darkness.

Besides, he might be able to finish in this space.

"I'll be there at dawn, then," he said.

"There's no need," she said.

That anger surged again, and he bit back a harsh retort. He was beginning to think she was deliberately excluding him. Why would she do that? Was he some kind of suspect? Was there something she didn't want him to know?

He straightened his spine and heard crackles all along his back. Two more bodies—two bodies, he mentally corrected himself. Strange how he was continually thinking that this site had a body in it.

"Marnie," he said, making himself speak slowly, and consider every word, "I have told you before. I must be there to see the corpse *in situ*."

"And I have told you," she snapped, "that some sites aren't amenable to you. Unless you've learned how to dive…?"

She was deliberately provoking him. He knew that. And yet, yet…he had to answer her. He had to.

"You know what I mean," he said.

"I do," she said, "and frankly, I think you're being a ridiculous perfectionist. The body is underwater, and Tevin's team will film the entire extraction. You won't be able to see the body *in situ*, at all. You'll—"

"My people will have to examine the death scene. That body got there somehow," he said.

"Yes," she said. "it might have been dropped over the Falls or it might have been tossed off an overlook. You have no way of knowing, at this moment, if the body was carried into that pool behind the waterfall. In fact, that's least likely, because—"

"Of the barriers, I know," he said. "And someone could have breached those barriers. You think your security is so great, and there it is not."

She didn't respond. For a moment, he thought she had cut off the communication. Then he heard her sigh.

"Come if you want. Dawn. But I would think, with two bodies, you'd want to get started on the first one rather than stand in the cold, watching people disappear under murky water."

"Noted," he said, and then *he* was the one to shut off the communication.

He stood for a moment, letting the anger flow through him. She had a point. He would have a lot to do once the bodies arrived. He had this site as well.

For the first time in years, he actually faced a true challenge—not of extraction or figuring out an unusual type of death. But a challenge that would test *him*. He would have to work as hard as an Ynchi City death investigator. And he would have to determine which jobs he would hand off to his assistants, or which part of the job he would have to skimp on, just a small bit.

The very idea of skimping made him frown. He would not skimp. And he wasn't sure his assistants—good as they were—were up to the task.

Yes, he had trained them, but they had never worked anything like this.

All right. The next several hours would be about pace and priorities. He would need to organize himself and his tasks.

The first thing he would do was finish here, because this site was decaying right before his eyes.

His staff, even his middle-of-the-night staff, knew how to receive a body. He would give them instructions on what *not* to do, given that the body from the Falls might be a homicide victim. He didn't want anyone to touch the corpse until he arrived.

His staff knew how to do that.

He would finish here, go to the death investigator's office, and then go to Fiskett Falls to supervise the extraction. In between, he would need food and a bit of sleep.

He had enough time to do it all, if he kept on pace.

Before he returned his attention to the blood pool, he had to get his staff ready to go. That would only take a few minutes.

And then the challenge would begin.

30

Bassima used six holographic screens, all at eye level, to monitor the footage from the area near the car. Behind her, she ran footage on several other screens. Those programs were checking for people moving around the downtown area. The programs would ping her when they found something—which was more often than she would like.

She had a seventh screen to her left, which was compiling all of the images from the six screens into one composite image. At the moment she wasn't looking at it, but she would if she found something.

For the past hour, she'd been eyeballing the six screens, seeing if she could find anything. The computers knew how to sort the information, but they gave her only what she asked for, and sometimes she wasn't sure what she wanted.

She wasn't sure here.

She was about to give up and let the computers look while she searched for something to settle her stomach. She had been sitting for hours now, which wasn't something she usually did, and the lack of movement made her antsy.

The silence in the office bothered her too. Usually she liked it quiet, but on this night, she was finding the silence eerie—perhaps because she was looking at the quiet streets of her city, realizing just how small this entire place was.

Her stomach wasn't the only part of her that had become unsettled. She had as well. That notion she had, that she was dealing with a local, had given her emotional whiplash. First she had felt triumph, then uncertainty, and now unease.

She always prided herself on knowing the locals—at least by sight. She had always believed she would know which ones were likely to do something illegal, and she had been certain she would know which ones would do something horrible.

Those shoes made her feel like she hadn't known anything at all.

And then she would chide herself for being stuck in assumptions—all over again.

She was stuck in some kind of emotional cycle, unable or unwilling to break out of it.

And it was all about her, which also bothered her.

Since the death—and that blood pool—were not about her.

She rubbed her eyes. She was tired, that was all.

She stood, just as one of the screens pinged behind her. She turned. The screen had freeze-framed on someone standing near Taji Kimura's office. That someone had a pile of clothes under one arm.

Bassima looked at the time stamp on the image. The middle of the night. Why would anyone be carrying clothes? Was this when the fight had occurred that had led to Taji (or someone) sleeping in her office?

Bassima expanded the image. She couldn't tell who the person was from the back. The person was wearing dark colors and wore a hat that covered half the head.

Bassima changed the image, expanded it to life-size 3D, and realized that whoever she was looking at was small. Someone who barely came up to her shoulders. Small and slight, as most women were. But there were some men that fit that description as well.

Bassima didn't need a composite to see what the image was holding. The clothes reflected off some light from an overhang from a nearby building. Both bright yellow and bright red caught the light; they didn't absorb it.

Her heart started pounding again, just like it had done earlier. Before she moved the image around—going forward and backward in time—she crouched and looked at the shoes.

They didn't catch the light as well, and there wasn't as much information in the security feeds as she needed to see the entire shoe. But what she did see showed her that the shoes were the same general shape and style as the shoes left at the overhang.

She made herself breathe evenly. She couldn't think she had caught the person, but at the same time…

Then she took a deep breath and held it, considering. Maybe it was Taji or Glida. One of them bringing clothes to the office after a major blow-out—either to take care of the person who had gone there alone, or to take care of themselves.

But Bassima didn't remember seeing any red and yellow clothing inside that office. She would have noticed. Wouldn't she? She had been looking for Taji, after all.

She let out that breath, made herself focus, and then toggled the image very slowly. The person never turned toward the camera that provided the image. Instead, the person found her way (his way?) toward a dark portion of the street and then walked out of the frame.

This time, Bassima could give clear instructions to the various computer systems. She wanted them all to follow that image, to figure out where it went.

She shrank it back down from life-size, making it the size of the composites. The image—the person—was walking in the right direction, toward the car. Bassima found that interesting all by itself.

Then she leaned back and checked the time stamp on the image that had first caught her, the one of the rocking vehicle and the shoes. Ten minutes after this one.

About as much time as it would take to walk.

"Caught you," she whispered.

She wasn't entirely sure who she had caught or what catching that person meant.

But, for the first time that evening, she knew she was moving in the right direction.

Where that direction would take her wouldn't be up to her. But it would provide her with answers—finally.

31

Virji stepped into the larger lab. To her left, an *anacapa* box protected the malfunctioning *anacapa* from the runabout. Two people worked near it, as if they had no cares at all.

Several other people stood in various places throughout the lab, some working on stationary screens, others using holographic screens, everyone so busy that they didn't see her at all.

Which was good, because her legs had nearly buckled beneath her. That woman, that image, that half-feral frozen movement, it all looked familiar. Virji had let the information slip, but she doubted anyone in the storage room picked up on it.

They were all concerned with figuring out what happened and with covering their collective asses.

Except that one man—Agwu? At least he had been honest with her.

And his news made her even more uncomfortable.

Virji called up a holographic screen, putting some generic code on it so that she had something to stare at for just a moment, so that no one could see her face or her distress.

This all felt so damn familiar. She'd been through something similar before.

And she hadn't covered her ass, so she had come extremely close to losing her commission.

She hadn't realized until much too late that she had let a murderer go free.

She let out a breath, then scrolled the information ahead of her.

Glida Kimura hadn't been Glida Kimura when she had served on the *Ijo*. She'd been a difficult recruit, who'd been disciplined numerous times as a teenager, and who'd served some time on the *Erreforma*, the Fleet ship that acted as a school for troubled Fleet kids. It had taken years to clean Kimura up, years before the Fleet believed she could do anything that even remotely resembled work on a Fleet vessel.

Three other captains on three other ships worked with her, praised her, promoted her.

When Virji got her, she'd already been approved for short piloting stints, usually ship-to-ground missions or keeping a ship in orbit.

And Virji had given her runabouts.

Virji's stomach ached. She closed her eyes for a moment, but then she saw an image that had haunted her for decades. Young Sloane Everly, standing before her, head bowed, long brown hair pulled back, riotous curls tamed.

Let me at least clean out the runabout, she had said. *It's been a second home to me. Then you can send me wherever you plan to send me.*

Sloane Everly, now Glida Kimura.

Virji's mouth tasted like dust. She had lost all saliva.

I will send someone to supervise you, Virji had said, thinking she was being magnanimous. *And then we will discuss your future on board the* Ijo.

She remembered stalking out of the room, remembered feeling both angry and self-righteous, knowing that she should remove the damn girl from the *Ijo* and take away her piloting privileges forever.

But she hadn't—at least, not quickly enough. Virji's carelessness would allow Everly to escape, and then disappear, and now reappear here, under a different name, working *security* of all things, and leaving—again—in a runabout, assigned to the *Ijo*.

Virji's stomach twisted painfully.

She had barely survived that incident, particularly when the murders came out.

She wasn't sure she would survive this one either.

Then she took a deep breath. Not true. What happened in this base had more to do with the base than it did with her. Sloane Everly—or Glida Kimura, or whatever she was called—should never have gotten work here in the first place.

Virji frowned, then tapped the screen, making it opaque to anyone but her. She needed Kimura's security file, along with her entry interview and her DNA.

Maybe Virji's guilt on letting a murderer escape once before was coloring her vision now. Maybe Kimura was a woman who had snapped.

But Virji didn't think so. Over the years, she had learned to be humble, and in her humbleness, she had learned to be observant.

She knew in her bones that Glida Kimura was Sloane Everly. Which then begged the question: How had she gotten work here?

Virji had sent notices throughout the Fleet to arrest Everly on sight. Every base had received those notices, just like every ship had them. They were in the Fleet's database, along with Everly's DNA.

Then Virji sucked in a breath.

Everly had been a smart woman. She had taken that first runabout without anyone catching her. The same thing had happened here. The situation had repeated itself.

But what if there was one more missing piece of the puzzle? One piece Virji hadn't put together until now.

Glida Kimura had worked for security here on the base. Her clearance was limited. And yet she hadn't been flagged when she had come down here, into the most secure area on the base.

"Son of a bitch," Virji said out loud. Three people standing near her looked at her in alarm.

She ignored them. She collapsed the screen and walked back to that storage room, pressing open the blast doors.

They wobbled as they opened. They desperately needed repair.

The team was still working. Only Agwu had moved. He was closer to the group from the base than he was to the security team.

"Wèi," Virji said in her most commanding voice. "Come here."

He nodded at her, finished saying something to the dark-eyed woman next to him, and then walked to Virji—not fast, but not deliberately slow either.

"We need to check Kimura's DNA," Virji said. "We—"

"We already did," Wèi said, interrupting her.

Virji gave him her coldest glare. "I've been ignoring your insubordination," she said, mostly because she didn't have the time for this petty shit, not anymore. "Do I need to go over your head to find someone I can actually work with?"

His skin flushed, darkening it, and making his eyes brighter. The flush actually made him attractive, something she wouldn't have thought possible an hour ago.

"No, sir," he said. Somehow he didn't sound contrite, although he did sound chastened. "Forgive me. Please, continue."

As if she had been the one in the wrong.

She didn't like Wèi, and if he continued to treat her this way, she would report him. Right now, she was willing to give him the benefit of the doubt, trust that he was overworked or worried because of this situation, and work with him.

"You've set up a meeting with the head of security, yes?" she asked, because she needed to get Wèi back in line.

"Yes," he said. "One hour from now, his office. I can take you there, sir."

No chance of that. She didn't even acknowledge the offer. "Before the meeting, I want you to check Glida Kimura's DNA."

He opened his mouth. If he told her *again* that they had already done so, she would make sure that he didn't have a job in the morning.

He must have seen that thought run across her face, because he closed his mouth quickly.

"I need you to make sure it's been checked against something of hers from outside the base," Virji said.

"Sir?"

She had confused him. Good. Time to treat him the way he seemed to treat everyone else.

"Check the DNA on file," she said. "Make sure that it is her DNA."

"You think she knew how to tamper with those systems?" Wèi asked. "I'm not sure *I* would know how to tamper with those systems."

And I'm sure you're the best at everything, Virji thought, but didn't say. Instead, she said, "Just check. Bring that information to the meeting in an hour."

"Yes, sir," he said.

She nodded at him, then started to leave.

"Sir," he said quickly, quietly. "What makes you think she tampered with the DNA?"

Finally, a good question. One worthy of someone running an investigation.

"Because," Virji said, deciding to offer him a small bone. "I have a hunch she's done it before."

32

IT DIDN'T TAKE LONG to find all of the footage of that one person. Bassima was convinced she was looking at a woman, although why she believed that, she still wasn't certain. She had never seen the person's face, nor did the person's body give much of a clue.

The dark clothing the person wore was baggy, so the person's general shape was obscured. Bassima was beginning to think the person also had some kind of security filter over her (his?) features, so that no matter how she turned, the nearby cameras wouldn't pick up her face.

Security filters were sophisticated pieces of equipment, not something the average person in Sandoveil had access to. That alone made this person different.

Bassima had gotten rid of all of the other screens, for the moment, anyway. She had stepped away from her desk, taking the consolidated images into the widest spot in the room. It was the area that acted as a de facto snack bar, with a hot water dispenser, and a drop-down table for any food that someone wanted to put out for the group.

Bassima couldn't remember the last time anyone had used the dispenser or dropped the table down. If anyone wanted food, they got it at one of the many restaurants nearby and bought it to their desks.

So the entire area near the drop-down table was empty. She set up the consolidated images at life-size, but restricted them to the space around the table and made sure the images focused only on the person in dark clothes.

Bassima had already skipped through the consolidated images to make sure that it was worth the effort of moving everything to the open part of the office. She decided that it was.

Now, she stepped back and leaned on the nearest desk. She had created a small keyboard so she could use hand commands rather than vocal commands. Some of the security images had sound, which the programs had also consolidated.

She didn't want to be talking over something important. She wanted to hear everything.

She dimmed the lights until the lighting in the office matched the lighting on the images. The images came into sharper focus.

Late on the night in question, the car pulled into its parking place. A restaurant down the street still had lights. A band played something with very heavy bass—probably very loudly, since Bassima was picking it up.

She couldn't see who had driven the car, nor could she get any identifying numbers, although she would make the system try. She called up a small second screen for her notes. She doubted she would remember everything otherwise.

Whoever drove the car sat in it for more than an hour. The music stopped at the restaurant down the street, people exited, some passing the car. None of them looked inside. It wasn't clear from the outside that anyone was inside the car.

Bassima watched each excruciating minute of this footage. She wanted to make sure she didn't miss anything—a small gesture, a smile, maybe a word exchanged with the person in the car.

But there was nothing.

Fifteen minutes after the restaurant's lights went out, a door on the car opened. The person got out. Finally, Bassima got a good view of the shoes.

At this point, the person carried nothing. She closed the door slowly, hand on the side to make sure there was almost no sound. Bassima thought she heard a click, but she wasn't even certain of that.

After the person moved away from the car, she (he?) stepped into the street and did a slow, 360-degree turn, making certain that no one was around. This time, the security lights hit the person's face full on, and it still remained in darkness.

Bassima nodded. A security filter, then. Not only was she dealing with a local, but she was dealing with a local who had access to some very rare equipment for the Sandoveil Valley. Security filters were necessary items in some of the major cities, particularly for high-profile individuals.

But there were no high-profile people in Sandoveil—unless they were visiting from elsewhere.

She sighed. The security filter put an outsider back on the table as a suspect in this case.

Her disappointment didn't last long, though. Because the security filter also increased the likelihood that the person (whoever it was) intended to do harm or something illegal.

Bassima made that note as well, even though she doubted she would forget it.

Then she let the footage continue.

The person walked quickly across the street. There were gaps in the imagery, which the consolidated file played as a small purple blotch. Bassima had requested that, when the program asked what it should do when its subject went in and out of frames.

Bassima had studied enough of those images to realize that the person had deliberately avoided the security cameras that she (he?) knew about. Apparently, the person didn't know about all of them, however.

The person took ten minutes to walk to Taji's office.

Lights were on in the office. It was easy to see them on the 3D life-size image. The lights filtered out of flaws in the window shading. Apparently the window's shading was as old as the building itself.

Maybe the environmental system hadn't been shut off deliberately. Maybe it had failed.

Bassima let out a sigh.

The person stopped just before reaching the door to the office, and reached up to her (his?) face. Hands cupped the face, and then lowered, thumbs together as if holding something.

The security camera from across the street caught a quick flash of skin. It was impossible to tell exactly what color—not too dark, clearly, or it wouldn't have shown up in that moment, but not so pale that it reflected the light back.

Bassima stopped the consolidated image, tried to see if anything about that quick flash of profile was familiar.

But the movement was a blur, and the person had turned as she (he?) removed the filter, as if aware of the cameras on the other side of the street.

The person slipped the filter into a pocket, then approached the office door, and waited. Bassima couldn't tell how the person contacted the occupant inside. There was no movement on the person's part, no knock, no touch to some kind of bell or warning system. Just a pause, as if the person were either waiting for someone inside to answer or for the system to introduce him (her?).

After several minutes in which the person remained utterly still, the door opened. Bassima caught a glimpse of someone just as tall as the person outside, with dark hair, dressed informally.

But not in yellow and red. Instead, the person inside wore browns and tans.

Bassima watched as the person who answered the door let the visitor inside. Then the door closed tightly.

Bassima ran the image back. She got up, and walked over to the hologram. Two people, both shorter than her, one standing in a doorway, the other in that narrow hall.

This time, Bassima wasn't looking at the person outside the door, but at the person who answered the door. She asked the system to give her the clearest image of the person's face, only to be told she *was* dealing with the clearest image.

So Bassima enlarged it, and peered at it as if she were right next to the person, leaning in.

Skin a light brown, hair darker than that, a slightly upturned mouth and a delicate nose. Bassima couldn't see the eyes, but she had a sense of recognition.

That was Taji. It had to be.

Bassima caught that *it had to be* and made herself ignore it. One of those assumptions again. The person at the door probably was Taji. The person at the door looked like Taji—maybe, in some superficial ways. But it didn't have to be Taji. It could be one of Taji's relatives or a tourist who looked like Taji or someone else who looked nothing like Taji except in Bassima's fevered imagination.

However, the most likely person to be behind that door was Taji, and Bassima couldn't ignore that.

She tried to look at other angles and saw nothing. There wasn't even any reflection in nearby windows or walls.

Bassima stopped searching. She would let the programs do that. Maybe they could even construct a face based on the partial. She would have them try.

For the moment, though, she needed to continue the footage. She started it up again.

The person behind the door stepped back, out of the way, and the visitor walked through the door. Then the door closed, seemingly of its own accord.

After that, nothing happened for two hours. Bassima didn't watch the footage for two hours. She scanned through it, hoping she would see more. Then she told the consolidated program to search for anomalies. It didn't seem to find any.

Finally, the lights inside that office went out.

And Bassima didn't see the person emerge from the building. Not anywhere.

However, an hour after that, the person showed up at the vehicle, carrying red and yellow cloth. Clothing, or something like it. Bunched in a way that the cloth couldn't be a body.

Bassima stared at that footage. The person had come again from the wrong direction. Which meant that the person had exited in a way that Bassima hadn't been monitoring.

Bassima sighed, then set up several more screens. She expanded the search range again, taking in the entire downtown. Only now she had a figure for the system to focus on.

That person—the person from the car—was connected to this. The shoes weren't a coincidence. Neither was the clothing.

What Bassima needed to do was follow that car. She didn't just need to look for the person carrying a body or *something* from that office. She needed to find out where the person went after leaving the area, and where the person had been before.

The information was in Sandoveil's security systems and its records. She just had to find it.

And she was finally beginning to believe that she would.

33

THE BLOOD TOLD AN INCREDIBLE STORY. Hranek stood up straight, his back aching. He put a hand on his spine and made himself lean backward just a little, listening to the cracks and pops, just like he had heard before.

He should be tired, but he wasn't—not like he had been when he first arrived. The work intrigued him. The stuffy little room held a wide variety of secrets, and he had found most of them.

But Okilani had found a few as well. She had entered after she finished exploring the path from Main Street, and she had found a very faint blood trail that led into what appeared to be a wall.

It wasn't. It was a door designed to look like a wall. The door looked like it had been built that way, not added later. It blocked the narrow corridor.

The faint blood trail wasn't visible to the naked eye. To call what Okilani had followed *spatter* would be to mislabel it. She had followed microscopic drops that only her equipment could pick up. She figured out how to open that door, and then went through it with no trepidation, ending up nearly a block away, where the trail continued.

It disappeared across the street from the exit, not because the tiny drops had stopped dripping, but because they had gotten scuffed or washed away or picked up by regular shoes—evidence destroyed by day-to-day living.

Still, Hranek had found that all exciting. He had answers. And, apparently, in one part of that passageway that led to the hidden exit, the environmental systems were on so he could actually measure the decay in a controlled environment.

He loved working off specks of blood. He had done so a hundred times over the years, and had refined the technique for doing so at a death scene. Actually, he'd been more overwhelmed by the large blood pool than he had been from the specks.

He had worried that the large pool was not all one person's blood. But blood didn't necessarily mingle and mix the way that some liquids did. If he tested the wrong part of the pool, he would miss any secondary (or tertiary) source. If he tested the entire pool, he might waste half of his night.

So he did a quick cursory test, and it seemed that the blood all came from the same source. When he was done, he would have Okilani test different patches of the pool, just to double-check him. This death scene was so odd that he wanted to make sure he got everything right.

His night's work did get him a lot of information, though. The bulk of the blood (if not all of it) belonged to Taji Kimura. The DNA in the pool—at least the areas that Hranek tested—as well as the tiny specks that Okilani had found was all Kimura's.

Hranek had also been wrong in his early assumptions, which was why he tested everything. He had thought there had been no spray or splatter when the incident happened. But he discovered through his patient work that the blood had misted when Kimura was fatally injured, but most of the mist had been covered by the pool of blood.

As he methodically searched, he had found mist on the side of the couch, the legs of the table, and in certain places on the carpet. But the mist's pattern told him a lot. The mist had blown backward (forward?) onto—he assumed—the person who had attacked Kimura.

The mist had gotten on that person's shoes and clothing, leaving blanks in the impressions on the furniture and floor.

Using those blanks, Hranek had been able to construct part of that person—thin, not too large, with a relatively small shoe size. As Kimura had bled out, that person had walked to and fro inside the room, probably moving things. The blood pool covered most of it, but in odd ways. It filled in the indentations left by the shoes, but Hranek could measure those indentations in the depth of the blood.

That person had left the body in place for some time—the length of which he couldn't entirely determine, but long enough to make a slight impression in the carpet.

Then that person had picked up the body, wrapped it in something—maybe even a regulation body bag—and carried it from the room, using the hidden exit.

Either the bag hadn't been closed properly or it had a small leak, enabling those tiny droplets of blood to escape, forming the path that Okilani would follow.

The specks told Hranek that all of this had happened at least forty-eight hours before. The blood pool itself was decaying oddly, and he wondered if the environmental system had been on for a while after death and then shut off. He had no real way to prove that, except to do some on-site tests for decay rate, which he did not have time for.

He would leave Okilani here, though, to conduct some of those experiments. By noon, he would have all the information he could get from this small space.

He hoped it would be enough to put a killer away. Because that ghostly impression in the blood mist had told him that he did have a killer, and that killer had watched Taji Kimura die.

The thought did not anger him. He'd seen too much human death to have a reaction to that death during his investigation. When he reflected later, he might be appalled or upset, but right now, he was intrigued.

Besides, he needed to remain calm since his staff rarely was in this kind of situation. They hadn't seen enough violent, deliberate death to be able to compartmentalize it.

Part of him was grateful for that, and part of him wished he had a more emotionally experienced team. It would make his job easier. Or rather, it would make *this* job easier.

He had a few more items to check before he went to the death investigator's office. He needed to check on that corpse, which, according to Beck, probably belonged to Glida Kimura.

Something had happened to the Kimura family, and it had been sudden and tragic.

Ah, he felt the thread of an emotion there, and he needed to separate it.

He took a deep breath. The room was getting stale. Even though he had been here for hours, the rotting smell registered, which meant that it was growing quite strong.

Then he returned his attention to one errant blood drop. It was on the wall, near the side of the couch and the gap in the mist. This drop wasn't part of the mist. The drop was tear-shaped, and it had actually hit the wall as a globule, then slid down, slowly congealing and stopping a few feet from the floor.

He leaned forward and carefully used a tiny extractor to kiss the edges of the drop, without moving or ruining the drop itself. The extractor tested on-site, comparing the DNA to the DNA on file from all the residents of Sandoveil.

He didn't have the latest tourist information in his equipment, nor did he have access to anything from the nearby regions. But this apparently did the trick.

The device registered a DNA match.

Glida Kimura.

He frowned. Beck had told him that the body in Rockwell Pool belonged to Glida Kimura, or so everyone had assumed.

Then a surge of anger ran through him before he could prevent it. *That* was why *he* had to identify the bodies. *That* was why there were systems in place.

The YSR-SR on-site had misidentified that corpse, and it was already interfering with investigations.

His investigation, to be precise. Because his first reaction here was one of shock. How could Glida Kimura be here when her body had been in that pool?

And then he separated the emotion and let his brain kick in.

Glida Kimura could have been here. She could have been injured in the attack on her wife and then taken elsewhere. Just because he hadn't found traces of a third person didn't mean one hadn't been here.

Or conversely, Kimura killed her wife and then, in despair, flung herself off that overlook into the water below.

But how did that fit with the second body that Marnie had found in that pool?

He closed his eyes and tried to control his errant mind. He was speculating without evidence. He couldn't do that.

All he had to do was keep his mind open to possibilities.

Possibility: Glida Kimura had been here when her wife died.

Possibility: They *both* had died here, and were taken to the Falls.

Marnie had said the first body was badly damaged, although he wondered. How could the on-site investigators recognize Glida Kimura if the body were badly damaged? Those two pieces of information did not jibe.

Another possibility: the bodies were not the Kimuras and he had at least three deaths on his hands.

He stood, tired now. He felt slightly overwhelmed. That was what speculation did—it made all the possibilities real, made him feel like he had actual choices.

He did not. He had one more duty here before returning to the death investigator's office.

He had to check the environmental system.

And, given the situation here, the way the site was decaying, he would also have to see if any part of the environmental system could be salvaged.

He wanted to preserve this death scene as best he could. An intact environmental system had features that would allow him to do that. He just had to get to them.

34

THE CAPTAIN'S ARRIVAL AND ABRUPT DEPARTURE unsettled everyone even more. The security team scuttled around Bristol's lab like little crazy rodents, the extra researchers were talking among themselves, and she was so stressed that her hands were shaking.

That simply would not do.

She slipped away from all of them into the storage room, which looked more like its old self with each passing moment. Her team, at least, was focused, working hard on the information they could gather from the walls and the very air itself.

That horrid holoimage of this Kimura woman or whatever her name really was stood in the center of the room. The security team and, in particular, Wèi, had gone into Bristol's lab, trying to do whatever it was that Captain Virji had asked for.

Bristol put her hands on her hips and stared at the image of that woman, the woman who had ruined Bristol's day, the woman who had thought she could endanger the entire sector base for some odd reason.

According to the captain, this woman had served on a Fleet vessel. This woman had used runabouts before. And, more pertinently, she had used one to vanish.

The Kimura woman clearly understood *anacapa* drives. So starting the runabout had been no accident. She had known what she was doing.

What she wouldn't have known was that Bristol had switched out the *anacapa* drive with an older model. This Kimura woman would not have known that the older model hadn't been used in decades for anything but backup. It certainly hadn't sent anyone into foldspace.

On the holoimage, the woman's face was clear. She had beady eyes and a weak chin. Bristol stared at the image for a long moment, then decided that she hated this Kimura woman. Hated her. And wanted her gone.

With the flick of a finger, Bristol shut down the holoimage of Kimura. Let Wèi bitch. Bristol no longer cared. She had work to do.

At that moment, Sheldenhelm beckoned her. He was standing next to Pereyra, their heads together.

As Bristol walked over to them, Sheldenhelm said, "I think we have some results we can trust."

Bristol wouldn't let herself feel relief. There were too many wiggle words in what he had just said. "I think" did not count for any kind of certainty. But he wouldn't have brought anything to Pereyra without some kind of confidence, and Pereyra wouldn't have involved Bristol without even more confidence.

Still, Bristol had to push, not for research's sake, but for her own.

"You think…?"

"Yes, sir," Sheldenhelm said. "We'll need to run a few more tests and make some comparisons for complete certainty."

Bristol's gaze met Pereyra's. Pereyra's jaw was set, her dark eyes serious. She nodded slightly.

She agreed with whatever Sheldenhelm was going to say. She clearly approved it.

"All right," Bristol said. "Let's hear it."

Rajivk tilted his head. He was standing on the other side of the small room, but he could clearly hear them, as could the rest of the team. They were probably feeling a bit left out that they weren't consulted, but Bristol didn't mind.

They would be consulted in a minute. Bristol would have them double-check whatever results Sheldenhelm was about to present.

"I've run several scenarios as to how that runabout would have exploded," Sheldenhelm said. "In all of them, bits and pieces of the runabout would have scattered through the storage room. Even with the nanobits on full, making certain everything was cleaned and repaired, we should have discovered a little bit of the runabout as we took samples. We've discovered none of it."

Bristol frowned. She wasn't sure she accepted anything that Sheldenhelm was telling her, and she felt a twinge of annoyance that Pereyra let him waste her time.

Pereyra must have read Bristol's expression. Pereyra put her had on Bristol's arm, maybe to head off Bristol's response.

For whatever that would do.

"*Anacapa* explosions are by their very nature unpredictable," Bristol said. "No computer can predict what happened here. The *anacapa* drive might have obliterated the entire runabout. Or it could have sent half of the runabout into foldspace. Or it could have sent all of the runabout into foldspace. It could have exploded—I hate to use the term, but it's the only one that comes to mind—normally, sending out shrapnel like you mentioned. But that's only one scenario among many."

She turned to Pereyra, ready to tell her not to send anyone to her with only half-formed opinions when Sheldenhelm said, "I understand all that, ma'am. I ran every scenario that we have on record, not for what could happen, but for the debris left behind."

That caught her attention.

"The debris and the damage are the only things we have," he said. "I ran the models of the various possible explosions with a runabout of that make, and an *anacapa* with that kind of instability. Then I cross referenced all of those with the readings we took off of this room."

"We're not done with the readings." Rajivk had left his post and joined them.

Bristol felt another surge of annoyance. He had been useful talking to Captain Virji, but he was not being useful now. He was butting in. He should have known how much she hated it when anyone butted in.

"We have enough to get a pattern," Pereyra said quickly, apparently trying to keep Bristol from snapping at another member of the team.

"I would disagree. Your side of the room—"

Bristol held up her hand, stopping Rajivk midsentence. It was too late. The conversation was underway, and Sheldenhelm might have had a point.

Debris was debris was debris. Except when it was cleaned up. And even then they had started their work soon enough to capture at least some of it.

"If the runabout exploded," Sheldenhelm said, "we would have debris, even if ninety-percent of the shrapnel went into foldspace. That ten percent should have scattered around this storage room. Some of it would have still been in the air when we arrived. Jasmine was running an algorithm that showed how quickly this storage room's environmental unit cleaned up any mess it found, and we were in luck. This is a storage room, and most of the equipment here is lower grade. The theory is that the system will work slower here. We haven't double-checked that part, but the history of the environmental system shows that's the case."

Bristol nodded. She understood the theory, and she knew that environmental systems worked differently in different areas.

"So, based on all of that," Sheldenhelm said, "we believe that there still would have been particulate in the air when we all arrived—had the runabout blown up."

"It sounds like a lot of supposition," Rajivk said.

"Supposition is a start," Pereyra said.

Supposition wasn't something that Bristol usually liked, but she had known when she decided to find out what happened in this storage room that supposition might be all they ended up with.

"You have found no particulate matter," she said to Sheldenhelm.

"None," he said, "and no shrapnel or damage that suggests the runabout exploded outward."

"What about the blast door?" Rajivk said. "It moved, after all."

"I ran that," Pereyra said. "It would move if the runabout had been facing this wall."

She pointed to the wall opposite the blast doors.

"The sudden displacement of air would cause it," she said.

"When the runabout arrived, there was a similar movement of the blast doors," Bristol said.

Everyone looked at her. Some had accusing expressions. She could read them easily, which was unusual for her. They all wondered why she hadn't said anything before.

It was a bit of information she was keeping in reserve. One of the things her team hated about her was the way she always tested them. Withholding information, making them work harder than any other team in this part of the sector base.

But, the one thing she never told them was this: the fact that she did test them was what made them the best team in the base. One she was proud to have at her side, no matter how much they irritated her.

"You *knew* this?" Rajivk said.

Pereyra made a small gesture that Bristol wasn't supposed to see, trying to get Rajivk to calm down.

Bristol didn't care that the Rajivk had spoken up. If one person thought it, they all had.

"An explosion would have caused something similar," Bristol said. "So the movement of the blast doors told us only one thing: that something had happened in this room. What that something was could not be deduced by the movement of those doors."

Rajivk let out a small breath, as if he had been holding it. "We'll have to double-check this information."

"Yes, of course." Bristol's tone was curt. She wasn't sure if he was saying that about the blast doors, about Sheldenhelm's research, or about both. She wasn't sure she cared. "In fact, you'll have to triple-check."

But, given what Captain Virji had said, given the fact that this Kimura woman—whoever she was—knew how to pilot a runabout, and given the fact that the runabout was operational, just not at optimal levels, probably meant that it had left of its own accord.

"I think we should split up the team," Bristol said. "I want half the team to double- and triple-check the results. I want the rest of you to help me figure out where that runabout went."

"How can we do that?" Rajivk asked. "We have no idea what course that woman could have set."

"If she set one," Bristol said. "That *anacapa* was not very powerful. I deliberately use small and weak *anacapa* drives in repair work. It's just safer."

Although she could never consider an *anacapa* safe. She didn't have to tell her team that, however.

"She might simply have used the *anacapa* to get the runabout to orbit. If that's the case, we should be able to find a record of it. Someone needs to check that," Bristol said. "I want Sheldenhelm and Pereyra to help me determine the runabout's possible locations."

She wasn't rewarding them for their work, although they might take it that way. She was simply making certain she was using the team most efficiently. It was never good to have the same people who did the work double-check the work.

The team was still looking at her. No one was moving.

"Let's get to it," she said. "Right now."

35

THE CONTROLS FOR THE ENVIRONMENTAL SYSTEM in Taji Kimura's office were behind a panel in that narrow hallway. Hranek found them after more searching than he had planned on.

Time was slipping past him. He wanted to be at that dive at dawn, and he wanted to see the body in his office before that.

But letting himself feel the passing of seconds would only make his work incredibly sloppy. He wasn't quite sure why he was having to work on his emotions so much on this death scene.

He suspected it had nothing to do with the scene and everything to do with all of the bodies that had suddenly cropped up in his small town. He wasn't used to having a workload like this, and it was impacting his thought processes.

It only took a moment to override the command controls on the environmental system, using codes from the YSR-SR. The environmental controls were holographic. They flared yellow as they formed before him.

He studied the display for a moment, frowning at it. Everything was normal, except that the environmental systems had been shut off. He had rarely seen environmental systems off. The Sandoveil Valley was temperate compared to some other places on Nindowne, but the temperature did vary a lot, and it was easier to let the environmental systems control the differentiation than it was to do so by hand.

People did tamper with the environmental controls, often in a murder or a suicide, but usually when they decided to use the environmental controls as the *source* of the death. And that took both technical expertise and access, because the system was designed to veto a change in the oxygen mixture or the introduction of some kind of noxious gas into the mix.

But something about these controls was not right, and he couldn't see exactly what it was—not yet, anyway. He was about to shut it down and let Okilani work on the controls when he realized what it was.

The environmental controls had not been shut down manually. That was what had caught his eye. The controls were off, yes, but they had been shut down using a remote system.

He had to press his way through layers of menus to get to the proper remote system. The system the killer used—and he had to identify the tamperer as the killer simply because who else would have done this?—had been internal. The killer hadn't used a remote device to shut off the system once the killer had left the area. Nor had the killer used the remote shut down offered to vacationers or someone who planned to keep a building empty for long periods of time.

Those remote programs left a level of environmental control on—a certain remixing of the air, a steady temperature control.

This system had been shut down entirely, which Hranek had never seen before. He knew this part of the program existed, simply because buildings that were going to be remodeled or torn down needed to have the environmental system shut off before it was removed.

And to say that the shutdown was remote was incorrect. The shutdown was timed. It was set up so that the system would shut off piece by piece after the building was permanently vacated.

Only this building hadn't been permanently vacated.

He double-checked the controls to see what parts of the building they covered. The command for complete shutdown was given only to Taji Kimura's office system, not to the entire system.

So it wasn't a building-destruction command; it was a remodel command, designed to activate after the building was emptied and before the machines arrived to tear that part of the building down.

He looked through the other parts of the environmental system and saw a barrier between this system and the one in the other offices. That barrier had been reinforced, so that nothing—no air, no heat, nothing—moved through the walls.

If the killer had left the body here, no one would have been able to find it, maybe not for weeks. The smell would have been contained inside the room.

Except, perhaps, someone on the street might have smelled the decay. Since the environmental system was off, the window controls were off as well. Air would have seeped outside.

He had no idea if that was carelessness on the part of the killer or if the killer didn't think about the windows or the front door. He reserved judgment while he poked around the environmental systems some more.

Because he had one more question he needed answered.

There were hidden commands in every environmental system in Sandoveil. He had asked that they be implemented shortly after he arrived here, and he had to get special permission from the city to do so.

He wanted the system to maintain an automated backup, one that the homeowner or building owner did not know about. He wanted that backup to cover one week's worth of information, minimum, and he wanted it to be hard to access.

If the killer knew about the automated backup, that would limit the possible identities of the killer. It would have be someone who worked on the environmental systems or someone in his office or someone who had worked for the city when he had applied for this upgrade.

It took him almost ten minutes to access the backup on this system, but he found where the backup should be. For one frightening moment, he thought it had been erased.

But it hadn't.

He let out a small breath. So, good news and bad news. Good news in that the killer had not found it at all. Bad news in that the suspect pool became wide again.

A large number of people in Sandoveil knew that you could shut off the system before a remodel. He had no idea how big that large number was, but he knew it was a great deal bigger than the number of people who knew how to get rid of the backup.

He downloaded the backup into his own equipment, but he left the backup in place because the best place to do playback was on-site.

The backup wasn't a faithful reproduction of the minute-by-minute activities in a room or a building. The backup didn't record conversations (although he suspected they could be recovered in part by a skilled engineer), and they didn't record exact visuals of what had occurred in a space.

However, they tracked changes in temperature as well as the chemical composition of an area. They also tracked humidity, dampness, and a thousand other small things that an environmental system would concern itself with to make life easier on the people inside the building.

Including spill monitoring.

His hands shook. He wasn't interested in the backup for the spill monitor at the moment, although it would tell him where the spill originated (six feet up, in the middle of the room, on the floor itself), as well as some other choice details.

What he wanted to see were the movements inside the room on the night of the death.

He would have to turn the system on to have it play back inside the room.

He hesitated for just a moment. Either way, the blood would decay. If he set up the environmental system to his specifications, he could monitor the decay from this point forward.

That thought was the one that tipped him over. He set up the system, double recording the information about how he did so in several of his devices so he could share that with his assistants later.

He then opened the security backup and searched it to find when the spill occurred.

Two nights ago, after midnight. The spill registered relatively quickly. He then set up the playback as a holographic overlay on the room itself, so he could watch it in the space where it all occurred.

Movement replays disturbed some of his techs. That was why he often ran the replays himself. The replays did not show the actual people doing the actual deeds, but when speeded up, showed the changes in the air, light, and temperature.

He had a way of setting up the replays so that they didn't show him the actual heat signatures of bodies or the chemical compounds as the air mixture changed. Instead, he watched for gaps and changes in surroundings. If he set the playback fast enough, the changes actually took on shapes.

He could make the changes in the program quickly, and he did. Then he set it to start five minutes before the blood spilled. He didn't need to see how long the people had been in the room or how they arrived.

He simply wanted to see how the victim lost all that blood—if he could—from this.

He moved away from the panel to the arched door into the office proper. He saw two human-sized shapes cut out against the backdrop of the room. The human-sized shapes were both smaller than he was, and thinner. They looked like water that had risen up out of a pond and become a mobile, living creature.

That was in part due to the heat signatures, which he leached of their standard colors. He could never set up the playback so he could see through it, but he could set it up so that it didn't distract.

The wobbly air around each person was the way that the motion sensors reported changes. And there were other, subtle things that contributed to the sense of watching water creatures enact a play written by humans. He usually paid attention to those subtle things, but he wasn't going to tonight.

Tonight, he just wanted the general overview.

One shape stood near the window while the other stood near the table. If Hranek had to guess, he would have figured that one of the two had been eating before this drama began.

Arms flailed, the way that people did when they were animated talkers. Or when non-animated talkers (like him) had gotten very angry.

The person near the window took several steps to the person near the table. The person near the table backed into the center of the room. The person near the table swiped a hand over the table, and several things on the table jiggled.

Hranek made a mental note of it all. He had no idea what the jiggly things were, because they didn't correspond with anything on the table at the moment: nothing in real time occupied that space.

He squinted. Something had changed about the person who had swiped the hand over the table, but he couldn't tell what that was.

Then the person jabbed her arm forward, and the other person brought her hands to her neck. She stepped backward one more time, then tripped over something that also was no longer there, and fell onto her knees.

The person who had hurt her stood in the same spot, watching for just a moment, arm down. The gesturing had stopped. She just watched.

The injured person fell onto her side, jolting her hands away from her neck. That bounce was when the blood arced—spraying upward, creating its own little watery image.

Because of the body's placement, the blood spurt did not hit anything, but that must have been when the mist sprayed the couch and some of the furniture, as well as the killer.

The blood spray didn't touch the killer, though. So maybe he had that one thing wrong: maybe the tiny blood drops that Okilani had been following hadn't come from a poorly sealed body bag, but from something on the killer's clothing, something that she hadn't seen.

The victim was losing blood quickly. Clearly, the killer had hit an artery. The hands flopped a little, then lay still. The blood pool grew, and the killer watched.

That surprised him. Someone who killed accidentally usually tried to help the victim. Or the killer ran.

This one did neither.

She just watched.

He scanned the room to see if he had missed any other shape, any person coming out of the bathroom or standing closer to him. No one did.

Only two people stood here, which meant he was looking at Taji Kimura on the ground, and Glida Kimura standing.

He didn't see how Glida ended up bleeding as well, but that might have been something very simple.

Because, ultimately, the entire death was simple. And classic.

Glida had picked up a knife from the table and stabbed Taji. Knives sometimes injured the user as well as the victim, which was probably what happened here.

What was unusual was that Glida—Taji's wife—just watched her die. In a fugue state? But the rest of the evidence belied that. Because Glida (or someone) had cleaned up the body after it bled out.

He had seen enough. The details of the cleanup and the hiding of the body would become someone else's issue.

He now knew he was dealing with a murder, and a somewhat vicious one at that.

Even though he normally remained calm when he investigated a death, this disturbed him. The watching. What kind of person did that without trying to help? Or without fleeing?

He understood those: had seen them many times. But he had never seen the perpetrator stand, immobile, and observe.

He had studied it, though. He knew that natural predators, those who enjoyed the act of murder, often watched their victims die.

But those people were rare. What was more, they usually killed many times.

Glida Kimura had lived in Sandoveil for a very long time. If she had been killing people, he should have known.

At the very least, he should have suspected that *someone* was murdering others.

But he hadn't. Sandoveil did not have an abnormal number of murders.

Although it did have a higher than average death rate, which he—and his predecessors—had all attributed to the landscape. But what if it wasn't the landscape? What if…?

He checked the urge to hurry back to his office and look up how long Glida Kimura had lived in Sandoveil, and how long the death rate had been abnormally high for a city of this size.

He had no concrete proof that the killer was Glida Kimura, although logically it probably was. He didn't see how that one little drop of blood had gotten onto the wall, not as he watched the watery forms repeat their movements in that enclosed space.

He had supposition, not fact.

Although the fact had become a lot more concrete.

He now knew for a certainty that Taji Kimura had been murdered. He even knew how she had been murdered.

And right now, he had a body in the death investigator's office that someone had identified as Glida Kimura.

To throw him off his own investigation?

Or had she died after killing her wife?

The bodies would tell him.

All he had to do was listen.

36

THE *IJO* SEEMED LIKE A GHOST SHIP. Virji hated visiting her ship at a sector base. The lights were low, the environmental systems at minimum, and the crew at its lowest level possible.

Mostly, her engineering and repair crews were the only people on board, cycling in and out as needed. Some of the sector base employees worked around the ship as well, doing repairs and requested additions.

Even the family quarters were empty. Virji had learned early to make sure everyone took a vacation at the sector base, whether they needed one or not.

She also made it mandatory that the crew and their families vacate the ship while the ship was at the base. She claimed it was because it was easier to work on the ship when it was empty—which was true—but it was also because a good third of her crew wouldn't take time off unless she made it mandatory for them.

She headed through the darkened corridors to her rooms. She hadn't expected to come back here for another week at least, but she suspected her vacation was over. She just hadn't told Illya yet.

Fortunately, she hadn't had to go far to get to the *Ijo*. It was in one of the main repair bays in the sector base, not too far from the security chief's office.

She would probably be late to the meeting, but she didn't entirely care. If arriving on time had been important to her, she would have had someone on her crew look up this information.

But she wanted to do it. She wasn't sure she would believe it if someone else brought it to her, anyway.

Normally, the doors to her suite irised open as she approached, but she had reset them before she left. She wanted to make it hard for anyone to access her personal area.

She had not requested any repairs or upgrades here. In fact, she hadn't had any sector base touch her quarters in years. If she needed upgrades or the occasional touch-up, she had her own crew do it. That way she could check every night.

She opened the door, and stepped inside. The air was stale. She had set it to refresh twice per day while she was gone, which wasn't quite enough. The odors of everyday living—the scent of her shampoo, the smell of old coffee, the faint scent of the sandalwood sculpture she had attached to her wall—seemed even stronger than they usually did.

She didn't normally catch the scents of her living space: she was using it too much, and the ship scrubbed the system enough so that odors didn't linger. But her nose had acclimatized itself to that lovely cabin near Fiskett Falls.

She longed for it, as well as the bed—not because it was more comfortable than hers was here, but because Illya was probably in it, sound asleep, making that adorable little half-snore when he inhaled. Whenever she was with him, she had a sense of another life, one she could have had if she had opted for a different career in the Fleet.

Illya traveled as much as she did, saw many new places, and made hard decisions. He just didn't command a ship to do so.

Then she smiled to herself. She would have hated his job. Managing personalities on the ship worked for her—she saw them all as part of a tight unit, almost an organism in and of itself—but managing a different group every month, getting to know them, learning their foibles? That did not appeal to her.

Rather like dealing with that Wèi person. He either didn't respect rank or he didn't know protocol. And he was very full of himself. She had rather quickly figured out how to control him, but not how to best work with him. Her curtness and disregard for his feelings might have made her an enemy for life.

Or he might not have noticed.

She had no way of knowing.

She had a small office off the living quarters. The office was keyed to her DNA. She also added a retinal scan, along with a blink pattern, and a small keyboard code as well. Everything had to be performed in the proper order.

She did so now, and the door slid open.

The air in here constantly refreshed. She had a mini bridge in this little room. She could run the ship from here if it were boarded or they were in some other kind of trouble. She wouldn't be able to run the ship *well* from in here, but she could do so.

She sat down in her chair. It squeaked under her weight, a familiar sound that she had missed.

She shook her head slightly. So much for the longing for that cabin.

She used the database to go back decades, to the entire Sloane Everly mess. Virji had ordered a lot of protocol changes after Everly stole the runabout, but Virji hadn't thought about DNA until this very evening.

She accessed Everly's school records, particularly the ones from the *Erreforma*, and downloaded the DNA on file. Then she compared it to the DNA left on file for Everly here on the *Ijo*.

The DNA did not match.

Virji let out a small breath. She had expected that, but the confirmation irritated her. She didn't want to see it. She didn't want to know how completely they had been fooled.

How completely *she* had been fooled.

Again.

She sighed, and then, as a precaution, called up the images from Everly's *Erreforma* records. Virji did an image cross-comparison with the woman who had taken the runabout all those decades ago.

That woman, according to the image cross-comparisons, had been Sloane Everly.

But the DNA did not match. Somewhere along the way, Everly had changed the DNA records on the *Ijo*.

To function on the *Ijo*, she would have either had to do it when she came on board or just before she left.

Virji was banking on the fact that Everly had done so just before she left.

Virji had the system search for any changes in personnel records around the date of Everly's theft. That might take some time to find, time Virji didn't have.

She needed to use that time for one more task.

She reached into the pocket of her shirt and removed the tiny data chip she had brought from the base. She wasn't going to tie her system to theirs. This system remained completely autonomous—touching only the *Ijo*'s systems.

She uploaded the information, which took less time to load than it did to think about. Then she ran a cross-comparison—Sloane Everly's original DNA compared to Glida Kimura's.

They did not match, which Virji had expected.

The Kimura DNA did not match the *Ijo* Everly DNA either. As far as the computers were concerned, Virji had just included the DNA of three different people.

She probably had—and one of them had probably been the DNA of Everly/Kimura.

She put the different DNA profiles on the chip, then stood. She glanced at her system, wondering if she should shut down the search. But even as she wondered, she shook her head.

She wasn't done with this woman. Finding her would close a dark chapter in Virji's life.

She would be happy to leave it behind.

And with that thought, Virji smiled. She hadn't realized how much that original theft of a runabout weighed on her.

But of course, it was about so much more than a runabout.

Just like this one was.

37

The death examiner's office was at the north end of the city of Sandoveil, where the valley narrowed and the mountains began their climb to the famous, impossible peaks. Fiskett Falls was to the west, and so were the mud flats. All the drama at the north end of the city came from the mountains themselves, an ever-looming presence that shadowed everything.

There were no real views here, because the mountains rose precipitously. But a lot of locals had houses on the mountains' edges because of the isolation in this part of the valley.

When the death investigator's office was built, the office stood alone. It had been built by the same Fleet engineers who created the sector base, probably because they wanted a place to store dead bodies.

Initially, Hranek had hated the nanobit building. The Fleet didn't differentiate its nanobits: it used the same kind to make starships as it did to build underground facilities. No one gave thought to color-coding or even comfort. Hranek was certain someone could program the nanobits to make soothingly colored walls and floors with a bit of give, but no one had.

Either the Fleet engineers of three hundred years ago liked the black walls and incredibly solid floors, or those engineers simply believed that being on a planet was that much more preferable to being in space, and everyone should be grateful for life here, in Sandoveil, as opposed to being crammed into a starship.

Hranek wasn't grateful. He found the building gloomy and dark. It had the faint odor of rot. He noted that every time he walked in. The environmental controls could detect nothing: they scrubbed the air religiously of odors and harmful chemicals.

But he still smelled it, and, he knew, it was probably all in his head. He identified the place with death and so he constantly smelled death, even when that smell wasn't present.

The thing was, he didn't mind death. He found it fascinating, in all its infinite variety. Some deaths were easy, some were long, some were hard, but none were the same. He suspected that throughout the millennia of human history, no human had ever died in the exact same way as any other human. There was always something a little interesting, a little different.

He logged into his own office by touching the arrival panel near the door, pausing for a moment as it read his vitals, his features, and his DNA. The door was invisible to the naked eye until someone authorized touched the panel. Then the door outlined itself and, if the person was allowed inside, the door would click open.

He had set up the office so that he had an outer area with chairs and a large table, which allowed him to talk to families while sitting down, with something between him and them. Unlike the death itself, one person's reaction was often exactly the same as someone else's reaction. He could put them into categories—from the violent disbelievers to the calm acceptors.

The problem was that he could never predict which person would fall into what category until he broke the news. And if he wasn't prepared for all eventualities, he could be in serious trouble.

Behind that outer area was his private office, alongside a door that led into the death examination rooms. He went into his private office, put most of the equipment he had used onto a shelf reserved for the latest case, and then changed out of the clothes he had put on to go to the office. He bagged those clothes, in case he had picked up some trace, and showered in the small bathroom he kept for just that purpose. The shower drain captured and filtered the water for any more trace.

He stepped out, dried off, and put on a pair of work coveralls. Then he went into the death examination rooms.

They were chilled, but not as cold as the area where the bodies were stored. He had yet to find a better way to preserve the corpses that didn't compromise something—not that keeping them cold kept them pristine—but he was used to what the cold did.

Okilani was still at the Kimura death scene, and his other assistants didn't realize Hranek had returned. He liked it that way. He wanted some time to examine the new corpse himself.

As he approached the corpse storage drawers, a holographic screen flared yellow, offering him choices. He had a full list of every corpse in the building, including the unidentified ones that had been here for months.

The latest corpse, in keeping with custom, was marked with its arrival number, composed of the date, time, and the code for the location from which it was recovered. It also had a second standard identifier: *Female, Fiskett Falls [Rockwell Pool], Pending Identification.*

He tapped the screen for that corpse. The screen brightened as it approved the request, then disappeared. One of the drawers opened as a nanobit gurney appeared below. The gurney rose, attached itself to the bottom of the drawer, and then the drawer's bottom opened, automatically transferring the corpse.

Some corpses were too fragile for that maneuver, but that fragility was always logged into the system. (If it hadn't been, whoever had logged in the corpse would have been fired immediately.)

The gurney made its way to the examining theater. He followed.

There were dozens of theaters in the series of death exam rooms that went deep into the building. During his entire tenure, he had only used three of the rooms and a handful of the theaters.

It always unnerved him a little. Ever since he started here, he wondered why the Fleet builders felt they needed so many examination rooms. Was building a sector base that dangerous? Or did catastrophes happen on a grand scale back when this particular base was built?

Or had there been something in the history of Sandoveil that had required dozens of rooms, and some enterprising tech had revived the nanobits so that they built even more rooms?

As he watched a corpse head to the proper theater, he always wondered about the history of this place. He used to vow to look it up, but he never had.

He had a hunch—which he would never explain to his assistants—that he was afraid of the answer he would get.

The death examination theater mimicked the operating theater in the hospital here. Once all the pieces were in place—here it was the corpse and the assigned death investigators; there it was the patient and the medical team—the walls would close around the examination table. Standard equipment boxes would rise out of the floor unless the death investigator programmed for more exotic tools.

Hranek had no idea what he would need yet. He knew that this corpse had been found in water, but he knew nothing else about it. He didn't even really know its identity, and he was trying not to think about the possible identification.

He dipped his hands in a solution near the door. The solution cleaned off his own sloughing epidermis. Then he slipped his hands in the first round of gloves. These adhered to his skin and had little impact on his sense of touch. He used that sense a lot while working with corpses. He liked to feel what was going on inside a body. It told him a lot.

The gloves also took readings from the body—everything from the DNA (always a double- and triple-check) to the chemical composition of the areas he touched to an examination of whatever fluids were left inside the corpse. Each blood cell was analyzed, hormones (those that hadn't decayed) examined, and bones measured.

In some ways, his tools did much of the work for him, but he still found human interaction with the corpse essential. Sometimes an area caught his eye, a discoloration that the first scan missed or a small cut that, along with some other injury that caused massive bleeding, might have gotten overlooked.

He had to step down to get into the death examination theater proper. He walked over to the corpse as the soft lighting fell upon it. The lighting, set at the same level at this stage for every corpse he saw, provided information as well.

The light rose from the floor, the ceiling, and the sides of the gurney itself. He could change the intensity any time he wanted. He wouldn't do that yet.

He wanted to look at the corpse in the most familiar setting possible—at least to him.

The assistants hadn't undressed or cleaned her yet, according to his instructions. He wanted to do that. He found things at times when he carefully handled and cleaned a corpse.

This one had seaweed flopped over one arm. The skin was bloated still from the water, but it seemed to be intact. There were small creatures in Rockwell Pool that liked to nibble on soft flesh, and they hadn't taken any bites out of this corpse.

That alone told him that she hadn't been in the water long.

The still-soggy clothes dripped on the black nanobit surface. Water pooled on the floor until he gave the command for the receptacles there to mop it up and store it. He would see what microbes were there—again, later, when he had the chance.

He studied the corpse for a moment, tilting his head, taking in the entire thing. Small female, with brown hair, wearing yellow and red, just like Glida Kimura preferred.

The shaky identification must have been based on the size of the corpse and its clothing. Because the face was unrecognizable. It looked a little too flat, the nose sideways, and the eyes milky.

The damage to the face seemed off, unless the corpse had landed face-first from a great height. Even then, that kind of damage should have shown up in the neck and shoulders—obvious compression injuries.

He didn't see any, although that didn't mean anything. The compression injuries just might not have been easily visible.

Still. He stared at that face. In all of his years here, he had never seen any corpse that fell from the top or one of the overlooks at Fiskett Falls land primarily on its face.

Often the corpse would land on its torso or back, but the body would take the brunt of the injury before the face had any impact. And even then, the impact wouldn't smash the features the way they were smashed here. Even if the face collided with a sharp rock, the injury wouldn't be even. It would be more severe where the collision happened, often leaving a rock-shaped imprint on the face itself.

The injuries were always different if the corpse had been alive when it had gone off the Falls. People who jumped often went feet first and stayed upright on the way down.

People who were tossed usually went head first, and rarely could right themselves. There wasn't enough distance.

People who were unconscious when they went off the Falls landed on the planes of their body—torso front or back or the sides as the body spun.

Never the face.

He started there, before he even dealt with the clothing. He gingerly touched the forehead and cheekbones. They were squishy beneath his fingertips, not rigid like they were supposed to be. He ran his fingers along the bridge of the nose (squishy), the edges of the eye sockets (squishy), and the hinges of the jaw (squishy).

Gingerly, he touched the mouth. His fingers could have pushed inside if he wanted to. There didn't appear to be any teeth. The jaw itself didn't feel squishy. It had been shattered in the way that a jaw shattered when someone was punched in the mouth.

He removed his fingers, then had the gloves check the corpse's DNA. The result took a moment longer than he expected, and when it arrived, it was deeply unsatisfying.

Subject Unknown.

To be thorough, he compared the DNA to Glida Kimura's DNA. The gloves reported that the DNA on the corpse had no alleles in common with Glida Kimura. They weren't relatives, although they were of similar builds.

He paused over the corpse with that news. The clothing was unusual enough to catch anyone's attention. No one else in Sandoveil dressed like Glida Kimura.

And Glida Kimura—or someone of that same build—had just killed Kimura's wife.

These were not coincidences, but he didn't know how the puzzle pieces fit together. And he wouldn't know until he did a closer examination of this corpse.

He stepped back, removed these gloves, and contacted his assistants. He would need someone here to observe and perhaps finish the investigation when he had to head off to the dive.

He had a lot of work, but he welcomed it. For the first time in years, he was intrigued enough by something to let it consume his entire attention.

He smiled, knowing that a smile later would be deemed inappropriate by his staff. He couldn't very well explain to them that he lived for moments like these. He loved the challenges of the work. He had thought he would encounter more challenges here, but he hadn't.

Until now.

38

SHE WASN'T LATE FOR THE MEETING AFTER ALL. Virji found the security office with ease. She had never been here, not in all her years coming to Sector Base E-2. If there had been some kind of security problem that the Captain of the *Ijo* had to attend to, the security people had come to her.

The security division of the sector base was filled with activity, even though it was the middle of the night. Probably because of the theft or destruction of that runabout and all of the breaches.

Dozens of people filled the corridors, walking somewhere with great purpose.

All of them glanced at her, running their gazes from her face to her toes and back to her face again.

They had some kind of scanning equipment over their eyes or activated by their eye movement. She knew that every time they glanced at her, they were checking to see if she belonged here.

She did, just in a different way than they did. The moment after they identified her, they would look down or look away. She outranked all of them, and apparently, they figured that out as well.

The head of security's office was at the end of a tangled maze of corridors. If Virji hadn't had specific instructions on how to find it, she wouldn't have been able to.

The door opened as she approached and an androgynous voice welcomed her by name, instructing her to take the first left, which she did.

She found herself in another maze of corridors, all apparently leading to meeting rooms. The door to one room opened.

Gian Nicoleau, the head of security, stood near the entry. He was a short man with black hair peppered with gray. His weak chin and prominent eyes were his most distinctive features, and probably led people to underestimate him.

He smiled when he saw her, but the smile wasn't a happy one. It was apologetic and thoughtful at the same time.

Heads of security, she had found, were diplomats as well as the smartest people in the room. Nicoleau was no exception.

"First," he said, "let me apologize for—"

"No need." She didn't like apologies. Apologies tried to close the door on an event, rather than move forward. "I think this is more than a simple theft. I would like to speak to you alone."

He frowned ever so slightly. Apparently he, like her, wasn't used to being ordered about. Then he glanced over his shoulder at the room itself. Her gaze followed his.

Half a dozen people sat at a round table, tending to small screens before them. All except Wèi. He was watching her and looking nervous.

When her gaze met his, he nodded just a little. She didn't know him, so she didn't know exactly what he meant. She assumed he meant he had the DNA she had requested.

"Let's bring Mr. Wèi as well," she said to Nicoleau. Nicoleau raised his eyebrows in surprise but said nothing. He seemed to understand she had some kind of agenda.

She appreciated that.

But she wasn't going to discuss it in this corridor, so close to the room filled with people.

She asked, "Do you have access to a secure system somewhere in this little maze of rooms?"

This time, Nicoleau's smile was genuine. "As if you have to ask," he said.

He led her past two more doors, sweeping one open. The room lit up as they both walked inside. It was identical to the room she had been standing outside of. It had a round conference table that could fit at least ten people, some shelves and a sideboard, and all kinds of equipment built into all of the surfaces.

"Make yourself at home," Nicoleau said. "I'll get Wèi."

Then Nicoleau disappeared down the hallway.

Virji stepped deeper into the room. The round table was a great design. No one sat at the head or the foot. There was no automatic leader in a room like this.

It felt a little close for her tastes, which she supposed someone who hadn't been aboard a DV-class ship would have found odd. But most of the public rooms on the *Ijo* had windows that either showed the corridors or nearby rooms or had views of space. She rarely shielded the portholes when the ship was just traveling from one place to another. She liked the ambient light of deep space, and the view of distant stars.

She liked thinking about the possibilities.

This room had no possibilities. Even with the lighting up, it felt dark and oppressive. For the first time since she had come here, she realized just how deep underground she was.

That usually didn't bother her, but now it did.

Maybe because she wasn't just visiting on the way to somewhere else. Maybe because, for the first time since she'd been coming to this sector base, she would be having an official meeting here.

Virji took a deep breath. She had never spoken of the events on the *Ijo* to anyone outside of the command structure of the Fleet and her own team. Some of the details she'd been asked to keep to herself, and some—ones she had learned years later—she had never shared with anyone, except to update the already-existing file on Sloane Everly.

It felt odd to discuss Everly now.

Nicoleau returned with Wèi. Wèi looked at the chairs around the table as if he was so exhausted all he wanted to do was sit down. Maybe he was. It had already been a long night for him.

But Virji couldn't sit with this news.

"Did you check Glida Kimura's DNA?" she asked Wèi.

Wèi glanced at Nicoleau, as if asking for approval to speak. Nicoleau executed the tiny half-nod of command, the one that most people never saw.

Wèi walked to the nearest chair and sank into it. Apparently, he had taken Nicoleau's nod to mean that he could do what he pleased.

Virji crossed her arms and looked down at Wèi, waiting.

He licked his lips. "We got the DNA from her home." He glanced at Nicoleau, addressing this next part to him. "We really weren't authorized to do it, but we felt we had to—"

"We'll deal with the technicalities later," Nicoleau said curtly.

Virji wondered if he had been briefed on all the aspects of the incident. She liked to think he had, but she doubted it. When there were this many layers of command, information always got lost.

"You were right to be suspicious of it," Wèi said to Virji. "The DNA we got from the house—and we took a lot of it—wasn't a match to the DNA we had on file for Glida Kimura."

"If her DNA profile at the base didn't match her actual DNA," Nicoleau said, "how did she function here?"

"Well, that's the thing," Wèi said. "She used three different profiles."

He swallowed hard, and squared his shoulders. Virji wondered if DNA recognition fell under his purview or if Wèi just didn't like giving bad news to his superior.

"The first profile was the one she used to apply for the job. We ran that—or rather, someone did. She's been here so long it was before my time with security." He sounded relieved about that, at least. So maybe this was about his relationship with Nicoleau.

Virji glanced at Nicoleau's face. His expression hadn't changed. He had mastered that blank look most people who were effective in command had.

"The second profile was actually hers," Wèi said. "She had uploaded it separately shortly after she was hired. It overrode the initial file, at least for security identification throughout the base. So she didn't need to use trickery or anything. She could touch a screen and it would properly identify her as Glida Kimura. If that is proper, I mean."

He looked at Virji for confirmation of that.

"We'll get to her identity shortly." Virji wanted to hear the rest of this.

Wèi nodded. "The third profile—well, it's not really fair to call it a profile, because she didn't use it as hers. It belongs to Rhonda Touré. She has access all over the base, so no one thought twice when she entered the labs on the *anacapa* level."

"What can you tell me about Touré?" Virji asked.

Wèi shrugged. "I don't have much interaction with her. She works a different shift. I couldn't find anything in a cursory search of her files. I couldn't even find evidence that she and Kimura had much interaction."

"She looks like Glida Kimura," Nicoleau said. "Same height, same hair color. She was probably chosen for that reason."

"But you don't know that," Virji said.

"I don't know it," Nicoleau said. "You can rest assured we're going to start tearing about her life and associations as soon as this meeting ends."

Virji didn't even feel any empathy for the woman. If she had no real connection to Kimura, then Virji might spare some sympathy. But until Virji knew for sure, Touré was an accomplice and should be treated as such.

"Have you brought her in yet?" she asked Wèi.

"No." He looked up at Nicoleau, clearly panicked. "Should I have?"

"Yes," Virji answered, even though the question wasn't aimed at her. Anyone connected to Kimura should be in custody until they knew what exactly was going on.

Wèi glanced at Nicoleau, to see if Virji was out of line.

"Bring her in," Nicoleau said. "We need as much information about what's going on as possible."

There was a momentary silence. Apparently Nicoleau had no idea what to do next.

But Virji did.

"Thank you, Mr. Wèi," she said. "That will be all."

He looked startled. His gaze shifted from Virji to Nicoleau and then back to Virji.

"Do you want me to get Touré?" Wèi asked, clearly not sure who to address the question to.

"Wait for a few minutes," Nicoleau said. "Join the others."

And possibly lose Touré if she was involved in all of this. But they were all so far behind in this investigation that they had probably lost Touré anyway. A few hours wouldn't matter.

Virji hoped, anyway.

Wèi stood, then glanced at both of them as if he expected them to ask him to stay. When no one spoke, he headed out of the room.

Virji closed the door behind him.

"Can we sit now?" Nicoleau asked.

That restlessness still held her. She wasn't sure a chair could contain her.

"Do what you like." She realized, as she said that, that she wouldn't sit down at all.

He leaned against the table, but faced her, not sitting exactly, but not standing either.

"So what do you have?" he asked.

"A history," she said. "A long one. With Glida Kimura."

He frowned at her. She shrugged. There was no easy way to tell him all of this.

"Glida Kimura served on the *Ijo* decades ago," Virji said. "She used a different name. Her birth name. Sloane Everly. Her service ended when she stole a runabout and vanished into foldspace."

Nicoleau drew in a breath. Clearly he hadn't expected that.

"I did not know until today that she had changed out her DNA profile on the *Ijo*. I had reported the theft of the runabout—I had reported everything she had done, and there is more—to the proper authorities inside the Fleet. You should not have been able to hire her here, with that profile on file. But it was the wrong information. I checked just before I came here. She changed the DNA in her profile just before she stole the runabout."

"She stole two runabouts from the *Ijo*," he said, as if he couldn't quite wrap his mind around that. Virji barely could either.

"Yes," Virji said. "Two runabouts separated by decades."

"The question is why," Nicoleau said.

"No," she said. She'd been giving this some thought. "The question is why now? She should have remained on the run."

"Not with the DNA profiles changed," he said. "She had no reason to run—"

Virji held up a hand. "You don't have all the information. You see, we're pretty certain that Sloane Everly—or Glida Kimura—or whatever she's calling herself now—is some kind of mass killer."

39

A WAVE OF EXHAUSTION HIT HER. Bassima rubbed her eyes with her thumb and forefinger. She could hear her colleagues laughing as they came into the office, carrying their coffees and teas and pastries and fruit. She didn't look up from her desk. In fact, she set everything on *mute* so that she wouldn't call attention to herself.

None of her daytime colleagues had desks near her, so they wouldn't notice her unless she actually moved or talked to them. Or rather, they wouldn't notice her right away. They would sit and talk before they would actually get to work. Eventually, someone would see her and, maybe, talk to her.

They would think she had arrived early rather than having been there all night. She wasn't sure if any of her colleagues had spent an all-nighter at the office. She had done all-night work before, but never at the desk.

All-night work at the desk actually felt like work. Her back hurt from sitting too long, her eyes were filled with sand, and her head had become fuzzy.

She'd been staring at images too long. She had brought most of the screens down, and the two she still had up were floating inconspicuously near the front of her desk, the backs opaque so that no one could see what she was actually looking at.

She could probably bring those down as well.

She had a lot of information, and she had it stored in several places. It would help Hranek and the YSR-SR, even if it did discourage her a little.

What Bassima had found disturbed her more than she cared to think about.

It appeared that Taji had moved into her office some time ago. She had left it only to get takeout meals or to use a shower at one of the nearby clubs. She carried her clothing in a duffel, and she never seemed to smile.

The last time Bassima had Taji on camera—it seemed—was that middle-of-the-night image answering the office door, the image that Bassima had found in the middle of her long night. It had to be Taji. Bassima had dismissed that thought earlier, but she kept it now.

No one else ever went in or out of that office. Apparently, it hadn't been open for business for at least a week, maybe longer. Taji had moved in and the business had, for all intents and purposes, stopped.

Something had happened between the two of them—Glida and Taji—and Bassima couldn't tell what it was from security images of downtown. She had looked for security images near the Kimura home, and found nothing.

The nearest security camera that Bassima could tap was at an intersection off the side road to the house. There she hit her first pay dirt.

That car, bubbled and looking somewhat new despite its years, was headed off the road, which meant it had to have been in the vicinity of the Kimura household, if not at the Kimura household.

Bassima couldn't see who was in the car, but she trailed it through public security footage. She watched it wend its way through the south side of Sandoveil, then head down the biggest road in the entire community, the one that led to the sector base.

The vehicle parked in one of the employee slots, and a woman got out. She wasn't carrying anything. After she left the car, she walked down a flight of stairs to the main employee entrance at the base.

An image caught her face.

It was Glida, heading to work.

That one moment had confirmed everything Bassima suspected. She had then stopped following the car and had gone back to the footage of that night.

It had taken a while, but she had finally been able to reconstruct Glida's actions.

Glida had gone to the office and disappeared inside of it. Then she had come out from an exit a block away, an exit that wasn't intuitive, that probably only the office renter or owner or someone connected to the person who ran the office knew about.

Glida had gone several blocks out of her way to get to the car. She did not take a direct route at all. On this circuitous route, she was not as successful as she had been in avoiding cameras.

Bassima had gotten several good glimpses of her face. Apparently, Glida had left off the filter as well. Bassima had found that curious, especially since Glida had been so cautious about arriving at the office.

Of course, all Glida had been carrying at this point was clothing. She had brought that to the car and dealt with the clothing from an angle that Bassima couldn't see.

Glida had spent an unusually long time inside that car, and it rocked oddly.

When she left again, she was wearing the security filter. Bassima had been unable to see Glida's face anywhere on the way back. And Glida had been equally cautious about her trip back. She took the long way and entered through that same door she had used to exit.

Then she had stayed inside for thirty minutes. When she exited the second time, she had something large and long over her shoulder. She didn't stagger under the weight of it, though, as Bassima would have expected if she were carrying a body.

She methodically worked her way to the car, head down again, and this time, when she got there, she made sure she wasn't visible on any camera.

The only way that Bassima knew Glida had arrived was the car shook in that same way it had earlier, as if someone were inside it.

Halfway through Glida's trip to the car, as she carried whatever it was (a body? It looked big enough to be a body, even if it didn't seem heavy enough), the lights went out in Taji's office.

If they were on some kind of timer, they would have gone out. But Bassima knew of no way to shut down an environmental system on a timer. That didn't mean it couldn't be done.

She just didn't know how to do it.

"Hey! Look who graced us with her presence!" The male voice echoed throughout the office.

Bassima closed her eyes for a moment, swallowing her irritation.

The voice belonged to Harland Wuhan. He was a good officer and a pain in her ass. He always paid a little too much attention to her, which drove her crazy.

She opened her eyes to find him in the doorway, still behind her screens. He wasn't bad looking. He was as tall as she was and a little fleshy. Keeping himself in good physical shape seemed to be a bit more than he could manage.

Or maybe he liked food as much as she did.

"Whatcha working on?" he asked.

"Something for Hranek," she said. "And I have to finish today."

"In other words, piss off, Wuhan." He grinned, shoved his hands in his pockets, and headed back to his desk. Halfway there, he stopped. "You know, you could ask for assistance."

Normally, when he made an offer like that, she said something dismissive. *My job, my assignment, no thanks.*

But this time, the thought of food had made her stomach growl. "Would you mind picking up some breakfast for me? I've been here all night."

"Oh, hey, Princess," he started, then stopped and tilted his head. His smile didn't leave, exactly. But it went from flirtatious to serious. "What's going on?"

"I've been here all night," she said. "And dinner was a long time ago."

Someone closer to Wuhan said something. She couldn't make out the words, but the tone was snide.

He waved his hand in that direction, shutting the person up.

"Sure," he said. "This is serious stuff, huh? Related to the big YSR-SR presence on the mountain?"

"That's what I'm trying to find out," she said.

"You need help?" he asked.

She sighed. He was a good investigator. In fact, he was a better investigator than security officer. He liked being at the desk, focusing on small pieces of information.

"I'm not sure," she said. "Let me think about it."

"I'll give you until I come back with your fried okra omelet," he said.

She started, a bit surprised that he knew she liked that weird specialty from one of the nearby restaurants. "I have an account there," she said. "You can charge it to that."

"Nah. You can just buy me lunch sometime," he said, and disappeared out the door.

She sat still for a moment, surprised at his willingness to help. No one else in the office seemed to think much of it. One of the women in the back corner smiled at her, somewhat wistfully.

Bassima smiled back.

Then she turned her attention back to the screens, thinking about what she knew and what she didn't.

After that second trip, Glida did not return to that office. The car drove off, and Bassima tracked it through the city just fine. But the car eventually turned off the road, heading toward the mountains—not toward Fiskett Falls, as Bassima would have expected.

But she hadn't had time to search all the nearby security footage for the vehicle. And there were no actual security cameras on the mountain or near the Falls. So if Glida had taken a different route, one that led her to the Falls on a back road, Bassima wouldn't see it.

She had the various computers scan through all the footage on both office doors to see if anyone had entered or left in the days between Glida's visit and Bassima's discovery of the body.

Bassima's programs didn't find anyone going into the building at all, and Taji didn't leave—not even for food as she had done before.

Bassima didn't like any of that. She knew, deep down, that Glida had killed Taji that night and carried the body to the car. Then she had taken the body to the Falls and dumped it in the water.

So far, though, Bassima didn't have enough to prove it.

"Here." A bag of food, smelling sharply of onions and okra, landed on the desk in front of her.

She looked up. Wuhan was standing behind the screens, holding coffee. He set it down with a flourish.

"Need anything else?" he asked.

She opened the bag, saw silverware and napkins. She took the food out, her stomach growling, and opened the food container. The omelet was golden brown and still steaming, kept fresh by the container itself. Cheese bubbled on top as if the omelet was still being cooked.

She grabbed her fork and took a bite, her entire body relaxing just a little. She had been even hungrier than she realized.

He stood still. She wondered if he had intended the coffee for her, but she didn't ask.

Instead, she asked, "Do you know if the standard environmental systems around here can be programmed to shut off at a specific time?"

He set the coffee down in front of her, as if it was an award for asking him a question. He was still a major pain in her ass, but one she was rather fond of.

"They can be programmed by the owner of any building to change the environmental conditions at specific times," he said. "I would assume that also means they can be shut off, particularly if the building wasn't going to be used."

"It seems scary to me to allow people to do that," she said.

"Raised in space, were you?" he asked.

"No," she said. But her parents were. And she suddenly realized that she might have adopted this attitude from them.

"It's scary in space. I would think that systems couldn't be tampered with like that in a contained environment. But here, the oxygen levels remain safe even with the environmental controls shut off, and the gravity remains constant. So you can breathe and you're not in danger of floating away. You might freeze in the winter, but that would take a long time, and you could probably go somewhere else."

Then he asked, "Hey, Eleni, do you know if it's easy to shut down environmental controls on a timer or remotely or something like that?"

Of course he asked Eleni. She had the most technical knowledge of anyone in the security office. Bassima opened the lid on the coffee. It smelled bitter and sweet at the same time. It had the right amount of cream, which would have unnerved her if she didn't already know that the restaurant kept her usual order on file.

"You have to be listed on the control panel," Eleni said. Bassima couldn't see her, but she'd recognize that nasal voice anywhere. "It's hard to get listed most places unless you own the building. And being listed only lets you program. You can't control any environmental systems remotely. Too easy to tamper with them that way."

"Thanks," Wuhan said, and rocked his chair forward. "See why it's nice to work in the morning?"

Bassima was halfway through the omelet. She was hungrier than she even realized.

"So, what's the concern with environmental systems?" he asked.

Bassima shook her head. "Just information to give Hranek." She picked up her coffee and tilted it at Wuhan as if offering a toast. "I appreciate this."

He smiled, nodded as if recognizing the dismissal, and then stood.

"My pleasure," he said, and walked back to his desk.

She watched him until she couldn't see him around the screens. He was probably trying to make her feel guilty for not sharing the case, but she didn't feel guilty. Hranek had asked her to deal with the footage and she had.

She only had one other thing to determine: where the car was now. She asked the system to find it for her.

It took only a few seconds.

An image came up on half a dozen screens of the car, parked in its usual place at the sector base.

Bassima hadn't expected that. She expected to find the car parked somewhere near the Falls or maybe not even on any grid at all.

And there it was. As if the morning were an average day.

She shoveled the last of the omelet in her mouth, put the screens down, shut off the programs, and grabbed her coffee. She had to tell Hranek this.

Together they would decide what the next steps would be.

Bassima wanted Hranek involved because he could work with sector base security so much better than the Sandoveil Security Office could. He was the death investigator for both, and if she went with him, it would require no documentation, no filing of intent for a joint investigation—nothing like that.

Only smooth movement forward.

Movement that might answer some of the questions she was developing even as she threaded her way through the desks, nodding at her colleagues' greetings.

How did that car get to the sector base? Did that mean whoever drove it had access to the base? Why would someone kill Glida? Why would Glida kill Taji?

Bassima let herself out the main door and blinked at the morning sunlight. It refreshed her aching eyes.

But she no longer felt tired. Tired was for other people. She felt invigorated by the questions and the discoveries.

She headed for the death investigator's office, feeling like a solution might be around the corner for both of them.

40

Of course, nothing was easy. Why would it be easy? Bristol leaned against one of the consoles.

Sheldenhelm and Pereyra had determined that the runabout did not end up in orbit around Nindowne. In fact, there was no trace of the runabout anywhere in the solar system—at least, anywhere the sector base's systems could measure.

Bristol suspected that the *Ijo* might be able to gather more information. She had tried to contact Captain Virji, only to learn that Virji had gone into a meeting with the head of security.

For a moment, Bristol had felt left out. She should have been in that meeting. But then she realized how glad she was to be excluded. She needed to work here. It was much more important.

She had cleared the secondary security team from her lab. A few of them waited outside because Wèi didn't want the lab to be empty, not yet. But she needed it to be empty. She had sent the extra researchers back to their own labs so that they could work there.

Her team was still inside the storage room, following her instructions, checking and double-checking each other.

She had glanced over Sheldenhelm's work herself and concluded he was right: there had been no explosion. The one thing she had done that he hadn't was review the footage from the moment the runabout had arrived in the storage room.

The blast doors had moved then, too. In fact, they might have had some damage from years of receiving small ships, damage she hadn't noticed because most of those small ships arrived in the storage room during the off-hours when she was at home.

She hadn't told anyone she had found that, but she did make a note in her report. She also flagged the doors for special attention. Clearly, they needed more repair than the automated nanobit response could give them.

The fact that the runabout's substitute *anacapa* had activated was going to cause more problems than she had told anyone, including her team.

No two *anacapa* drives malfunctioned in the same way. And some of the malfunctions were not really *mal*-functions. They were more *inadequate* functions. The drives underperformed or they *over*performed, sending a ship too deep into foldspace or not sending it far enough.

Sometimes the *anacapa* didn't get the ship all the way to foldspace, a nightmare she had only seen once. That *anacapa* drive had activated inside the sector base and was to move the small ship to a storage area, much like the runabout had done.

Only that *anacapa* had misfired, and the ship hadn't ended up in the storage room. It had ended up in the mountain itself.

Bristol cursed slightly as she remembered that. She opened the door to the storage room and gestured to Pereyra.

Pereyra finished whatever she was doing on her small holographic screen and then walked over.

"I need someone to move to a different area of research," Bristol said softly.

"Who do you want?" Pereyra asked.

"I'll let you decide." Bristol didn't always pay attention to which of her team was best at what. She had Pereyra for that. It was the only habit that Bristol got in repeated trouble for from her superiors. She was supposed to be an excellent scientist *and* an excellent manager.

And she wasn't. She was too good at her tech/science job to fire, so everyone looked sideways when she let Pereyra manage the team.

Except when moments like this happened, and the administration of the sector base expected Bristol to know administration stuff.

"What's the job?" Pereyra asked.

"We forgot to look up one thing," Bristol said.

Pereyra frowned.

"We thought maybe the runabout exploded or it went far away using foldspace or it went into the solar system after a burst of foldspace." Bristol paused, not for effect so much as to choose her next words.

"Yes," Pereyra said, as if she felt like Bristol was wasting her time.

Bristol decided not to reference the ship-in-the-mountain incident. It was too graphic, and it might send whoever Pereyra assigned on the wrong mission.

"We didn't check the base itself," Bristol said.

Pereyra sighed in recognition. "Of course. The short hop."

Which was what the runabout had done to get to the storage room.

"I'll put Rajivk on it," Pereyra said. "He's great at this kind of work."

"Thank you," Bristol said, no longer caring. She knew that Pereyra told her things like that so that Bristol could make the assignment if Pereyra wasn't around, but Bristol saw all of that as unimportant information, not worth wasting the brain space on.

Bristol went back to the lab. She had something else to investigate. It would be harder to do. She needed to investigate both *anacapa* drives—the one she had in its box, which had been part of this runabout until a few days ago—and the other *anacapa* drive, the one she had used repeatedly to be the placeholder while she repaired the runabout's actual drive.

She paused for a half second, uncertain where to go first. The *anacapa* drive from the runabout would tell her how the runabout interfaced with the *anacapa* drives. The information from the placeholder drive would tell her how that drive had worked in other ships.

For a moment, she wished she could bring someone on this project to help her. But she had no idea how to do it.

Ninety percent of what she needed to do was in her own mind, impossible to access for anyone else, because she couldn't communicate it well.

She had to do this on her own, which meant figuring out how to make the data reveal what she needed to know. It meant figuring out a structure that she could follow quickly.

She headed to her favorite spot near the *anacapa* casing. Then she called up her personal screen and made a list of what she needed to know.

She needed to know what the placeholder drive's quirks were. Then she would look at the runabout's quirks. She needed to subtract what she knew about the *anacapa* that she was working on here—the runabout's actual *anacapa* drive—to see what quirks of the runabout remained, if any.

She had a lot of data on the idiosyncrasies of the *anacapa* she'd had in storage here. It would take a bit of an effort to subtract that from the problems the runabout had had over the years, but probably not as much as she would have thought.

The toughest part of all of this would be to figure out what the placeholder drive would do when it was fully activated. According to her records, it hadn't been fully activated in decades.

And she couldn't find who had last worked on that drive. Not fiddled with it to make it a placeholder drive. (That had been her, more than once.) But who had actually worked on it to try to repair it before deciding to retire it.

Those decisions were often hard. Because *anacapa*s were difficult to build and deploy. Weak or very old *anacapa* drives, without a lot of problems, were selected to become the placeholder drives.

They were also selected because they didn't have enough power to activate on their own.

She let out a small breath. Which meant that she now knew for certain that this Kimura woman (or whoever she was) had *chosen* to enter foldspace—not to get out of the base, but to travel very far away from here. Bristol had made the underlying assumption that the Kimura woman had wanted off Nindowne, but would only use the *anacapa* to get out of the base, not to travel a long distance.

Because anyone with half a brain would realize that the runabout was being repaired, which meant it was dangerous. *Anacapa* drives were dangerous even when they weren't being repaired, so a runabout that didn't work quite right combined with an old *anacapa* drive spelled disaster.

Besides, runabouts were built for short trips.

And short trips did not mean long periods of time in foldspace.

But if this woman had another agenda, then maybe she would risk entering foldspace, for whatever reason.

Not that it mattered. The Kimura woman's motivation was someone else's problem.

Bristol's problem was figuring out what happened to her—using the available data and a bit of deduction.

Glida Kimura (or whoever this woman was) had probably achieved a perfect storm of disaster. The runabout had problems, and the placeholder *anacapa* drive had problems. Those problems would most likely have made accessing foldspace either impossible (which Bristol's team was working on) or, more likely, unpredictable—at least for the person flying the runabout.

If Bristol had to guess right now, based on the information she had, she would guess that the runabout was probably in either an uncharted part of foldspace or in a part that hadn't been accessed for decades.

All of which presented some problems—and not just for the Kimura woman. The *Ijo* would want its runabout back. And the sector base was going to want to make an example of Kimura, since she had cost everyone in the base both time and money.

They would all want her back.

Which meant a foldspace rescue.

Foldspace rescues were difficult on good days.

And this was not a good day.

But it could be done. It would just take a lot of calculations and some educated guesses.

Bristol was up for the task.

If Bristol couldn't find her, then absolutely no one could.

41

THE PAST SEEMED VERY CLOSE. Virji hooked her thumbs in the top of her pants and paced across the small room. She had known she wouldn't be able to sit while telling Nicoleau her history with Sloane Everly, but Virji hadn't realized just how many emotions even thinking about it would arouse.

The worst emotion—and the strongest—was shame. She had let someone get the better of her, someone whom she should have been watching closely, someone she had thought she *was* watching closely and she hadn't been.

People had died.

Maybe more people than she realized.

Virji took a deep breath. Nicoleau didn't need to know all of it. Just the highlights—the lowlights—whatever she wanted to call it.

"I haven't heard that phrase 'mass killer' in years," Nicoleau said. "And never concerning someone who worked for the Fleet."

Virji nodded. "Everly was trouble ever since she was a child. But she went through behavioral courses on the *Erreforma* and it seemed like they had taken. She went through test after test, and passed."

Virji was pacing, but Nicoleau hadn't moved. It was as if this information froze him.

"She became one of our pilots. We trusted her to go planetside after a few years." Virji's voice broke. She willed it to remain strong. That shame was rising, and she couldn't let it. Because it would cripple her.

"Planetside," Nicoleau breathed. She could tell that he understood.

"She only killed when we let her stay for longer than two days. And never anyone the Fleet had contact with." Virji shook her head. This was the part she didn't entirely understand. "It was sport for her. I assume it still is."

"Sandoveil is a small community," Nicoleau said. "The Sandoveil Valley doesn't have a large population. We would know if someone has been routinely murdering people here."

"Would you?" Virji said. "Because I've heard since I first started coming here how dangerous the natural environment is around Sandoveil. People die here. I was supposed to tell my crew that, every time we stopped here, whenever I ordered them to take a vacation. I also had to warn them to take precautions so that they wouldn't go over the Falls or get trapped in the mud flats or drown in the ocean."

Nicoleau let out a small breath, then tilted his head back and closed his eyes. As head of security for the sector base, he would partner with the security team in town. He might even run it. That was how some of the towns connected to sector bases worked.

"She can't be that crafty," he said, eyes still closed. His voice was flat.

Virji remembered feeling like that—the disbelief, the denial. The anger would come later, and then the shame.

But she wasn't here to take care of Nicoleau.

"She's very smart," Virji said. "She thinks everything through. We didn't find out about her murders until after she had stolen the runabout. I used to think we should have known, but…"

She let her voice trail off. She didn't want to tell him that her superiors and her own counselor had told her that even she couldn't anticipate everything.

Everly had chosen her victims at random. She had often traveled to a different city or township to kill them. She used different methods for each kill.

It wasn't until Virji's own security team started backtracking Everly's movements hoping to find her that they discovered the murders at all.

Nicoleau was watching her now. He clearly knew there was a lot she wasn't telling him.

She also suspected he would look up Everly's files as soon as Virji left the area. The files wouldn't tell him much, though. When the Fleet wanted to keep a secret, it did so very, very well.

"Anyway," Virji said, letting him know she wasn't going to expand on that, "we might not have figured out that she committed murder at all if she hadn't run."

"Why did she?" he asked.

"Because she lost control," Virji said. "She had a lover onboard—Tom Harkness. They were planning a wedding. The next thing we knew, he was dead from a dozen stab wounds. We didn't find him for two days after the runabout went missing."

"He was her lover," Nicoleau said. "No one thought to contact him when they realized she had stolen the runabout?"

"For a while, we thought he was with her," Virji said. "She had ghosted the system, created a double image and then used it to mislead us."

"I know what ghosting is," Nicoleau said in a tone that told Virji he had experienced it.

She hadn't, not in that way. She was a straightforward woman. She couldn't quite imagine why anyone would lie about anything.

"She made us think they had gone away together," Virji said, partly because she was feeling like she needed to justify her actions. She always felt that way at this point of the story.

It was the part that made her feel the most inadequate.

"We thought—"

"He was on the runabout, I get it." Nicoleau's voice was dry. "Then you found his body."

"And some footage she didn't have the clearance to tamper with. We don't have images of the murder, but they were fighting so loud that some of their shouting could be picked up in the ship's corridors. Then she started to leave his suite."

That image of Everly was burned on Virji's brain, which was probably why she had recognized Everly so quickly from the hologram.

Everly, standing in the door as it slid open, covered in blood. She had been about to step into the corridor, then put her hands to her mouth as if she realized her mistake. She had slammed the door closed and was turning away as that clear image vanished.

His blood, in the shape of her palm, was found on the door's control panel. Her footprints were all over the front room of the suite, although she ended up leaving her shoes behind.

She had cleaned up in his shower, then put on his shirt and some loose pants, as well as a pair of his slippers, and walked, like a furtive lover, back to her own quarters. She had stayed there for nearly two hours, apparently making a plan and altering the DNA in her personnel file.

Everly had known a lot about procedure, and once she had gotten past the emotions that had led to her murder of Harkness, she had implemented all that she knew with a coldness that still bothered Virji.

"It was clear that she killed him," Virji said. "It was even clear how she killed him. She was so organized afterward that it seemed to me she had done this before."

"Lost control and killed?" Nicoleau asked.

Virji shook her head. "Killed. I think the losing control part was new. I later learned she had killed at least fifteen times before. Each time, she had had a plan going into the murder and a plan coming out of it. I think the killing of Tom Harkness was the first time she hadn't had a plan going in. I think she surprised herself."

"What makes you say that?" Nicoleau was standing now. He looked as unsettled as she felt.

"All of her other murders, the ones we know about, anyway, they were efficient. I think she actually had feelings for Harkness, and he had angered her and she lashed out." Virji shook her head.

She'd been thinking about this for a long time. Not just the image of the woman at the door, but the bloody shoes, left behind at the death scene. So very neat. Side by side as if they were removed so that their owner could walk barefoot through the ship.

Everly had done it again—murdered in a moment of passion and then fled in a runabout.

What would she have done if the *Ijo* hadn't docked?

Or had the *Ijo* itself pushed her into it? The memories of the ship, the way that she had lived before.

"Was she here the last time we came for maintenance?" Virji asked.

"What?" Nicoleau clearly didn't follow her leap in logic.

"We've come here several times since she worked in the base," Virji said. "Someone would have recognized her. I wonder if she had arranged to be gone every time we showed up."

"We can check," he said in a way that made it sound like he didn't really care. It was a minor detail, at least at the moment.

Virji stopped pacing. She took a deep breath. She felt calmer for telling him.

"Why didn't you want to tell everyone in that room?" Nicoleau asked.

"Because they'll focus on the murders, not on the theft," Virji said.

He leaned his head back, clearly surprised. "Aren't the murders the important thing?"

"Not if we let her get away," Virji said.

He tilted his head just a little. "I hate to break it to you, Captain, but she *has* gotten away."

Virji shook her head. "I'm not so sure."

"You think she's still on base?"

"No," Virji said. "I think if your people determine that the runabout went into foldspace instead of destroying itself, then we have a chance to get her."

"I don't understand," Nicoleau said.

Of course he didn't understand. He wasn't a spaceship captain. He had probably never served on a ship. Ships came to him.

"We hook into the *anacapa*," she said. "We use the maintenance system. She wouldn't have known how to shut it off. She might not even have known it was on."

"And that will bring a ship out of foldspace?" Nicoleau asked.

"My small ships are all equipped that way," Virji said.

What she didn't tell him was that it was her interactions with Everly that had made Virji order that *every* small ship on the *Ijo*, no matter how insignificant, be outfitted with maintenance recall.

He was frowning at her, and she finally realized why. She was smiling.

"We have two ways to bring her back here," Virji said. "The maintenance mode, and that *anacapa* drive."

"I thought people got lost in foldspace," he said. "I've heard stories—"

"And they're all true," Virji said. "If we can't locate her, then she's lost. But if her *anacapa* drive is functioning, and if she's anywhere within range of this sector base, then we can pull her back here."

"I assume you mean 'if she's within range and not inside foldspace,'" he said.

Virji nodded. "Remember, she's smart. She knows the dangers of foldspace as well as the rest of us. The more time she spends there, the more danger she's in. She's been gone now for hours. No one remains in foldspace that long if it can be avoided. All she wants to do is escape, not travel incredibly long distances."

"You're making it sound like you know what she'll do," he said.

Virji smiled. "I've spent decades studying her, Gian. She's organized, smart, and efficient. She'll take the logical route unless her emotions overtake her. And they generally only seem to do that in the presence of a lover. We know she's alone."

"What if she's trapped in foldspace?" Nicoleau asked.

Virji's smile faded. "Then we don't get closure. We'll never know exactly what happened to her…."

She let her voice trail off. She wasn't sure she could live with that. Especially if she had been this close to Everly, and she had let Everly slip through her fingers.

Again.

42

Hranek sat on a chair in his office, pulling on his boots. He tried not to hurry—hurrying would only make him slip up and forget something.

He had lost track of time while performing the autopsy on the unidentified woman. Her body had been an eloquent indictment of her killer—and he had found it all fascinating.

The dead woman had been in good health before someone targeted her, so everything wrong with her body, as far as he could tell, was tied to her death.

She had not drowned. She had no water in her lungs at all. Her jaw was broken, which might have been the injury that incapacitated her. Then she was suffocated, probably by a strong hand covering her mouth and something else pinching her nose closed.

That kind of murder had to take a lot of strength. Someone unconscious would wake up—it was one of the body's automatic reactions—and start to fight. He found no evidence that the dead woman had been tied up or forced down in any way—nothing on the wrists or ankles.

There had been nothing in the lungs, either—no fibers, no nanobits, nothing to show what had been covering the mouth and nose—which was why he was assuming the killer had used a gloveless hand.

The killer had known what a death investigator would look for, which was probably why the mouth had been smashed in and the body tossed into the water. Water destroyed more evidence than it preserved, even water as cold as the water at the base of the Falls.

He suspected, but he couldn't prove, that the smashing of the face had more to do with a visual identification than with any attempt to conceal evidence. The killer had known that someone would try to identify the body from the clothing, build, and hair color.

Part of him hoped that the killer hadn't thought *he* would make such a mistake. And then he had smiled at his own hubris. He was worried about what a killer thought of him.

It was always best when killers *under*estimated him. He had to remember that.

He stood, grabbed his slicker so that he wouldn't get wet near the Falls, and scrounged for his kit. He had to focus on bringing the right equipment to the diving scene. The YSR-SR had recovered one body there without his observation, and that body turned out to be the unidentified body of a murder victim.

He had to assume the second body was, as well.

He hadn't touched his kit since the last time he'd been called to the Falls, nearly three weeks before. When he got back, he always replaced, replenished, and cleaned his equipment. He should have trusted himself, but he never did.

Because he might have been distracted (as he was this morning) or he might have forgotten a detail. It was always best to make sure he hadn't forgotten anything *before* he left, rather than become irritated with himself after he arrived.

Someone knocked on his door and then it creaked open. Mina Ansari peeked her head inside. She was his second-best assistant, after Okilani. She was small, with hair that she dyed a light pink that set off her light brown skin.

He hated Ansari's timidity, but he couldn't seem to force her out of it. And this morning wasn't going to help because he had no time for the niceties when he was running late.

"What?" he asked.

"I needed to tell you that we have an identification." Her voice was soft. She sounded almost hesitant and he knew, if he pushed her, she would apologize for bothering him even though he had told her that he wanted to know the identity of the victim the moment she figured it out—if she figured it out.

But he had also instructed her to remain with the corpse, clean it, and finish the small details of the autopsy. Either she had done that already (he doubted it) or the DNA hit had come in and she believed he needed that immediately.

"I'm assuming this is the woman we were working on all night?" he asked, as he set his kit on the chair. Because if it wasn't that woman, he was going to yell at Ansari. Any other identification could wait until he returned.

"Yes," she said.

He slipped on the slicker. "Well?"

"It just came through from Ynchi City," she said, backing into the information because she was so nervous. She was clearly trying to explain why she didn't have the information sooner.

"I'm in a hurry, Mina," he snapped.

"Right," she said, and made that half-smile, half-grimace she always made when he snapped at her. "Her name is Sallie Sumption. She's from Ynchi City. She came here on vacation and had rented a cabin near Fiskett Falls. She came alone. She was going through a divorce, so no one thought it weird that she didn't contact them, until a week went by. Then they found out she never spent a night at the cabin, even though she brought in food and her stuff. So they sent out DNA last night—"

"And you got a hit," he said. "Excellent. Are you working with the Ynchi City's police department?"

"I am," she said. "And the family."

"Have you told them she's dead?" he asked.

"No," she said. "I came to you first."

"Good. I'll take care of it, after I finish at the death site. We might have more information then."

"Shouldn't we let them know that she's dead?"

Of course Ansari would ask that. She was the most soft-hearted person on staff. She hated telling people that their loved ones had died or had died badly.

Hranek only let her handle cases where a few tears would improve the interaction the family had with the death investigator's office—and that wasn't very many.

"We're not going to let them know yet," he said. "The last thing we want is some liaison from Ynchi City to show up and the family to start interfering with our investigation."

"But they'll know we ran the DNA," she said.

She worried about the strangest things. He really didn't care what the police in Ynchi City knew and didn't know.

"Yes, they'll know." He put on his slicker and then slung his kit over his shoulder. "But they won't know what we compared it to, and they won't know the result. We can stall for a few hours."

Which was all he needed to oversee the dive before getting back here to work on the second corpse. At that point, he might be willing to release the information to the girl's family.

Or he might not. But he wasn't in the mood to decide now.

"Should I get someone to investigate what happened to her?" Ansari asked.

He stopped. There were so many ways that someone could screw up that investigation.

"No," he said. "I'll take care of it."

"But—"

"Finish up with her," he snapped. "I have to get to the dive."

Ansari sighed heavily, letting him know she didn't approve without saying a word. Then she stepped away from the door.

"All right," she said.

He resisted the urge to roll his eyes as he passed her. The one thing he couldn't instill in his people was that the dead didn't care about anything. They didn't care if their families found out this afternoon or next week. They didn't care if their murderer was caught or their body helped contribute to some weird scientific discovery.

The only urgency in anything to do with the dead came from the living, and as the death investigator of the entire Sandoveil Valley, he could control that urgency in most cases.

He could control parts of it in this case.

The rest, he was going to try to control as best he could, which was why he was heading to the dive site now.

He pushed open the exterior doors. The sky had lightened over the mountains. His clock said it wasn't dawn yet, but it would be in just a few minutes. And he hoped to hell that the YSR-SR kept to their promise that they'd dive at dawn and not before.

Once he got in his van, he would let them know he was on his way. Nothing in Sandoveil was more than fifteen minutes from anything else, so he wouldn't be that late.

The body had been underwater for hours, maybe days. It could wait a few more minutes.

His van was parked haphazardly at the edge of the parking lot, not anywhere near his usual spot. He hadn't been paying attention when he returned last night.

And there weren't a lot of other vans in the lot. Most of his staff took public transportation. Three of the death examiner vans were still in the lot, but the fourth was out. Apparently, Okilani was still gathering evidence.

He started toward his van when a woman called his name.

He almost didn't turn around. He didn't want to continue the argument with Ansari.

But he did turn, because she had to know that arguing with him about procedure was not a good idea. He was formulating his argument when he realized she wasn't behind him.

Bassima Beck was.

She looked tired. Her usually crisp uniform was rumpled, and her hair stuck out in clumps.

It took him a moment to realize that nothing had happened to her—just that she had been working as hard as he had, and apparently, she cared as little about appearances as he did.

"I know where Glida Kimura is," Beck said.

It took him a moment to figure out what she was talking about. He had forgotten that he had assigned her to track all the images coming in and out of that office near Main.

"You know where she is right now?" he asked.

"I think so," Beck said.

"*Think* isn't good enough," he said. "And I'm late. So when you know for certain—"

"I can't know for certain," Beck said, "and neither can you."

That stopped him. He could know anything he wanted. He had the best security clearance in the city. She had probably forgotten that.

"Why not?" he asked, hearing the arrogance in his tone and deciding he didn't care if she heard it too.

"Because she went into the sector base hours after she left the downtown," Beck said. "Her vehicle is still there. And I've looked at everything I can. As far as I can tell, she hasn't come out."

He let out a small breath. Could it be that easy? If so, why would Kimura go to such lengths to fake her own death?

Beck's news was so surprising he wasn't sure how to handle it at all. There had to be more to this.

"Could you link Kimura to the bodies found at Fiskett Falls?" he asked.

"Bodies?" Beck asked.

He forgot. She didn't know about the second one, and he didn't know if the second one was related to this case. Just because it was there didn't mean it was dumped at the same time as that fake Kimura body.

"Sorry," he said. "Body at Fiskett Falls."

"Not yet," she said. "Glida disappeared for a while, though, right in the proper timeframe. There's just not a lot of public footage for me to go through."

"She went to the sector base *after* she went to Fiskett Falls," he said, trying to process that.

"Yes," Beck said. "If she did go to Fiskett Falls."

He was preoccupied. Because he normally didn't make misstatements like that.

Nor did he make rookie mistakes, and yet he had. He never thought to check Kimura's place of employment to see if she was on the job. He had assumed she wasn't.

"I'm assuming you didn't check to see if she was at work?" he asked.

Beck straightened. "I didn't want to tip her off."

Which was a no. Beck hadn't checked Kimura's place of employment before crossing paths with Hranek. He wasn't the only one making rookie mistakes.

"Well, don't tip her off now," he said. "But make sure she's there."

Beck nodded. "I thought I'd tell you first. I'm going to arrest her, though, if she is. I have enough just on the footage to hold her on suspicion of murder."

He frowned. Such charges didn't always stick. But charging criminals was not something that he always had control over, unless he had direct proof from his own investigation. He wasn't far from that now.

Rather than tell Beck to stay away, he would slow her down.

"You realize you might have to work with Sector Base Security," he said.

"No 'might' about it," she said. "I *will* have to work with them."

Then she gave him a knowing look.

"Don't worry. I'll be discreet."

He hoped so.

His skepticism must have shown on his face because her expression grew fierce.

"I liked Taji Kimura," Beck said. "She didn't deserve to die, especially at the hands of the person she loved. I won't do anything to harm the investigation or an arrest."

Hranek nodded. The light in the morning sky had grown brighter. Now he was late, and he hadn't contacted the YSR-SR. He would have to.

"You'll have to trust me," Beck said.

"Yes," he said drily, wishing there was another way. "I suppose I will."

43

Bristol almost didn't hear them enter her lab. In fact, she wouldn't have heard them if she hadn't set a small vibrating alarm, on the bracelet she wore on her wrist, to notify her when something changed.

She had programmed that first, because there were still people in the storage room, doing whatever she had assigned them—work she had deliberately put out of her mind. She hadn't wanted to lose complete track of them, but she hadn't wanted to monitor them either.

And she had known she was going to get lost in numbers and charts and logistics and all the wonderful things she loved about research—the reasons she had started working with *anacapa* drives in the first place, even though they made her terribly nervous.

When her bracelet alarm went off, Bristol looked up, saw all the uninvited people in her lab, and felt a surge of anger. Captain Virji stood in front of one of the consoles, with five people that Bristol did not recognize.

Bristol had invited none of them. She had thought the lab invaders were done now that everyone had been assigned their various tasks.

Apparently, she was wrong.

These people, none of whom she recognized, were obviously Someones, because if they hadn't been, Virji wouldn't have gotten them past all the heightened security. But it would have been nice if one of the Someones had contacted Bristol.

Virji was consulting with another woman, who was gesturing at the various consoles. Some of Virji's people were scattering to the other consoles.

Bristol opened her mouth to stop them, then remembered just in time that she was dealing with a captain of the Fleet, one of the Elite. But just because someone was elite didn't mean she could just barge into Bristol's lab without permission.

"*Excuse me*," Bristol said, using as much bite as she possible could. "This is *my* lab." So much for diplomacy. "What *are* you doing?"

Virji looked over at her. "Ah, Ms. Iannazzi. Excellent. I was hoping you'd be here."

As if Virji hadn't seen Bristol when the group barged into the lab. As if Bristol wasn't standing *in the very middle of it*.

"This is my lab," Bristol repeated. "Of course I'm here. And I'm working. We all are."

Virji didn't seem to notice Bristol's distress, or if she did, she was ignoring it. Then Virji smiled, a cold smile that made it very clear she was the one in charge here, not Bristol.

Which just made Bristol angrier.

"Please stop whatever it is you're doing," Virji said. "We've figured out how to recall the runabout, and we would like your assistance."

Stupid way to ask for it, Bristol nearly said.

"No," she said, no longer caring about her job. "You cannot come in here and think you know how to deal with that runabout. It's—"

"I'm sorry," said the woman Virji had been consulting with, her tone as clipped as Bristol's. "You're just a tech, right? Yes, this is your lab, but it's in a sector base—"

"I am not just a tech," Bristol snapped. "I am an engineer. More importantly, I am this base's expert on *anacapa* drives, and on the way that *anacapa* drives work *here*, in this sector base, *underground*. I don't know what you think you know, but I can guarantee that it's wrong."

"I am Ionie Fedo, chief engineer of the *Ijo*."

Well, hooray for you! Bristol had to bite back that comment too. She was angrier than she had been in a long time. Some of that was due to her exhaustion, some of it due to her distress at all the violations that had occurred in her lab, but much of it was due to the disrespect she suddenly found herself faced with.

"I can assure you," Fedo said, "I know a great deal about *anacapa* drives as well, and what I know is not wrong."

"Really?" Bristol asked. "Because you want to come in here and *recall* the runabout, right? Do you even know what kind of condition it's in? Do you know where it is? Do you know *where* it will end up?"

"It will return to the *Ijo*," Fedo said. "All of our small ships are equipped with return mechanisms that we designed. They hook into the *anacapa*—"

"Which is sitting right here." Bristol touched the *anacapa* box. "That's where your runabout's *anacapa* is. *Not* on the runabout."

The entire team that Virji brought with her looked at Bristol with horror.

"You asked me to repair your runabout," Bristol said. "We ran several diagnostics, found that the *anacapa* drive was weak and possibly malfunctioning, and removed it."

"That's not possible," Fedo said. "An FS-Prime runabout won't operate without an *anacapa*."

Give a prize to the idiot engineer, Bristol wanted to say. Instead, she managed, "That's correct. Which is why we swapped out your *anacapa* with one of our reserve *anacapas*."

"And your reserve *anacapa* malfunctioned. Oh dear," Fedo said.

"No, it did not," Bristol said. *At least that we know of,* she added mentally. "This is a procedure we've done many times. We've used our reserve *anacapa* many times as well. We always test it before putting it into a runabout. *Always.*"

Fedo looked like she was about to argue, but Bristol wasn't going to let her, not yet anyway. Not until Bristol had finished.

"You know nothing about the reserve *anacapa*," Bristol said. "You have no idea when it was manufactured, what its capabilities are, or why we chose it to replace the runabout's regular *anacapa*. I do, and I know where and what could have happened."

"We don't need the original *anacapa* to bring her back, do we?" Virji asked Fedo. Clearly, Virji was discussing Glida Kimura now. Apparently, the people who had invaded Bristol's lab had a plan, one they had decided to use before they barged in here, one that Virji, at least, wasn't willing to give up. "We use maintenance mode, tap into whatever *anacapa* she's using, and—"

"Maintenance mode?" Bristol asked.

Fedo glared it at her. "I suppose you don't read your updates. All the small ships on the *Ijo* are equipped with a fail-safe in the maintenance system. Anyone who tries to steal the ship won't see this. It's a backdoor into the *anacapa* drive, one we can access from here."

"Even if the ship's in foldspace?" Bristol had never heard of any way that a Fleet vessel could communicate with another vessel in foldspace, not even through the maintenance system.

In spite of herself, she was intrigued. Because if the engineering crew of the *Ijo* had come up with something like that, they should have contacted everyone who worked with *anacapa* drives throughout the Fleet. Despite what Fedo said, Bristol did examine all of the updates, and she knew no one had ever sent this information.

She would have flagged it for her staff because it was that important. Finding better ways to pull ships out of foldspace was a high priority at all of the sector bases.

If the *Ijo* had a way to contact and rescue ships in foldspace, then it was imperative that the ship share that method. Because communicating with a ship in foldspace would be a breakthrough of massive proportions, even if that communication was as specific as the maintenance mode speaking to the *anacapa* drive.

That gave the sector base yet another tool in its arsenal so that it could rescue trapped ships.

Not that any of this mattered at the moment, because no one knew if this Kimura woman was trapped. And if she had stolen the runabout, she would not have activated the distress signal, not even if she really was in trouble.

Bristol stared at Fedo, waiting for her to answer the question about maintenance mode and foldspace.

Fedo's lips thinned.

It was Virji who answered.

"We haven't attempted maintenance mode in foldspace, although I was assured it would work." She glanced at Fedo. "Was that incorrect?"

If Bristol had felt kinder, she would have stepped in. If she understood what Fedo had been talking about, and if the whole maintenance mode gambit worked even in foldspace, there was still the issue of the *anacapa* drives.

Fedo had said the communication was between the maintenance mode and the original *anacapa*. *If* the *Ijo* could communicate through foldspace with the runabout, and *if* the maintenance mode got the message, it would still have to transmit that message to the *anacapa* drive.

The original *anacapa* was a hundred times more powerful than the replacement *anacapa*. Even if the communication got through to the replacement *anacapa*, the replacement *anacapa* might not have enough power to link with the *Ijo*'s drive and return to the *Ijo*.

Bristol ran through all of that in her head, expecting Fedo to actually be saying the same thing out loud.

Only Fedo was not speaking. She looked a little appalled, as if she wasn't quite sure what was going on.

Bristol's breath caught. She suddenly realized what was happening.

Captain Virji wanted to bring this Kimura woman back. Virji, who didn't have the *anacapa* expertise, had rousted her people to get Kimura one way or another. Virji figured she knew how to do it, with some half-remembered explanations of the maintenance mode and the *anacapa* drive. She had rousted her people, and if they had protested, then she might have said that Bristol could help.

Although Bristol doubted that. She was beginning to get the sense that Virji was one of those captains whose word was law, and no one dare contradict it. So if Virji believed that something impossible could happen, her people would do whatever they could to make the impossible happen—or, at least, to wave their hands and do their very best.

These five people, including Fedo, had probably convinced the captain to come to Bristol's lab because the runabout had left from here. They had probably hoped that the runabout would boomerang back here.

Or maybe they had been counting on Bristol to help.

Although, given Fedo's hostility, Bristol doubted that.

Fedo's uncomfortable look, though, caught Bristol, and made her realize that everything was about to come apart. If Bristol wanted to control this situation, now was the time to do so.

"I have no idea what your team told you about your maintenance mode workaround and foldspace," Bristol said to Virji. Bristol could see Fedo out of the corner of her eye.

The color had drained from Fedo's face, and Bristol suddenly realized how critical her words sounded.

"I suspect," Bristol said, modifying her tone just a little, "that whatever they told you about the runabout and the *Ijo* is correct, for that circumstance. But this circumstance is different."

Virji's eyes narrowed. She raised her chin slightly.

Even Bristol, who wasn't all that great at reading others, understood that movement. Virji was showing her resistance to whatever Bristol was going to say.

"Whatever you were told about the maintenance mode," Bristol said, "probably came from tests with the small vehicles in your bay. But those tests were invalidated for this runabout when I switched out the *anacapa* drives."

Fedo gave her a grateful look.

Bristol continued in a flat, even voice, "I doubt anyone who serves on a Fleet vessel knows that it's common operating procedure to swap out the *anacapa*s in FS-Prime runabouts when work proceeds on those ships, particularly if there are hints of *anacapa* problems."

Bristol glanced at Fedo, whose eyes had grown big. She shook her head ever so slightly. Bristol wanted to point at her, to get her to settle down.

But Fedo wouldn't settle down. She knew she had made a mistake. She had promised her overly demanding captain that she could do something that was impossible. Bristol knew it. She hoped that Fedo understood that Bristol held the future of the entire *Ijo* engineering crew in her hands.

They had screwed up. They had promised that they could communicate with a ship in foldspace without testing that promise. It was foolish, and egotistical, and probably never would have been discovered if the Kimura woman hadn't stolen the runabout.

"Because I didn't know about the workaround," Bristol said. "I did not hook up that *anacapa* drive to anything except the navigational system. That's all we needed to keep the runabout in proper working order."

Virji crossed her arms, but she had brought her chin down. She was now looking at Bristol directly.

Bristol was getting through. She had to tread carefully to make sure she didn't overpromise and she didn't ruin the small headway she was making with Virji.

"The reason I did that is that the runabout just needed to 'think' it had a functioning *anacapa*." Bristol shrugged. "So, even if you could figure out how to communicate with that runabout, wherever it is, your maintenance fail-safe isn't hooked up. The maintenance system was shut off the moment we brought that runabout to this lab."

Fedo was nodding. That was standard procedure on all repairs. If an automated maintenance system was left on, it would try to undo all the work a repair team was doing as the repair team was working.

"In other words," Virji said, sounding very disappointed, "we're not going to be able to recall Everly anyway."

Everly must have been Kimura. Or whatever her name was.

"I didn't say that." Bristol was still shaking from the interruption and the amount of emotional energy that had come at her. She wished Pereyra had been in this room when the team had come in. Pereyra would have handled this entire encounter with a lot less anger and a lot more finesse.

"Before you interrupted me," Bristol said, "I was already working on a way of recovering the runabout. We've managed a few foldspace rescues in the past. I was hoping to try one here."

Fedo tilted her head. She clearly had questions, but she wasn't willing to ask them in front of her captain.

Virji didn't seem to notice Fedo's reaction at all.

"I hadn't realized you had this well in hand," Virji said. "Yet you're working this all alone."

"Actually, I'm not," Bristol said. "My team is working on this at various points in the base. We're trying to figure out where the runabout is before we try to recall it."

"I don't understand," Virji said.

Fedo, who was standing slightly behind her, closed her eyes briefly, as if she couldn't believe what the captain was saying.

Bristol was a bit surprised she had to explain this, but she decided to do the best she could.

"The runabout might be in orbit around a nearby planet or it might be in foldspace. It might even be lurking in the asteroid belt at the edge of this solar system, waiting for the *Ijo* to leave." She added that last because she had a sense that Virji's overinflated ego liked the occasional massage.

Of course, Bristol was so bad with people, she might have been misreading that, but she wasn't sure.

"You can determine that from what, exactly?" Virji asked.

Standard scans, Bristol almost said and then decided against it. Virji clearly had the idea that the runabout would be hard to find, and right now, Bristol didn't want to dissuade her.

"There are a variety of things that we're doing," Bristol said. "And more that we could do."

As she spoke, her mind played with the maintenance mode idea that Fedo had described. There was something in that description that might help find this Kimura woman.

"I'll leave my team with you," Virji said. "You can direct them, and get them to help you—"

The last thing Bristol wanted was more people in her lab. But Fedo seemed bright enough, and embarrassed enough, to help a little.

"I just need her," Bristol said. "Everyone else can go back to the *Ijo*, maybe get me a history of where the runabout's been recently or something."

It was make-work, but it was the only thing she could come up with at the moment.

"It hasn't been anywhere," Virji said. "We don't use those runabouts."

She sounded tense.

Bristol didn't care about the inner politics of the *Ijo*. All she cared about was getting her lab back.

"Well, it's been places," Bristol said. "Maybe not recently, but once upon a time. And those places might be programmed into its drive. So if someone would check for me…?"

Fedo stepped forward, and for a moment, Bristol worried that she would leave. Instead, she turned to the four other people who had come into the lab with Virji.

"Head back to the *Ijo* and see if you can find records or anything that might help us here. Also, records of Everly's use of the runabout would help as well."

"Indeed," Virji said, as if she were the one giving the orders.

"Let me know if you find anything," Fedo said. Apparently she was used to that kind of interruption from Virji.

The four nodded, and headed to the door. Bristol made herself smile at Virji. "Captain, if you would like to go with your team…"

"No, I'll stay here," Virji said. "I'm sure I can be useful."

Fedo's mouth twisted as if she had swallowed something sour. Apparently, they weren't going to get rid of Virji any time soon.

"Well, then, take a seat," Bristol said. "Some of this will get very technical. And it might be dangerous, since we'll be working with an open *anacapa* drive."

Virji's smile was condescending. "We are used to danger," she said. "That's what the ships of the Fleet are all about."

Behind her, Fedo rolled her eyes.

Bristol was beginning to like her.

"All right then," Bristol said, because she couldn't do anything else. She turned to Fedo. "Are you ready to give this a try?"

"Yes," Fedo said. "Let's see what we can figure out."

And together they walked over to the *anacapa* drive casing to start the most dangerous work Bristol had attempted in years.

44

Bassima arrived at the sector base, unable to shake her own feelings of irritation. She knew that Hranek had few social skills, particularly when he was busy, but she had never had him treat her like such an idiot before.

After she saw him, she stopped briefly at the Sandoveil Security Office. She needed to see Amy Loraas before heading to the sector base. What Hranek didn't know—or maybe he had forgotten—was that the security office had to work in coordination with the sector base on anything that involved both of them.

Loraas was in, and receptive to everything Bassima told her. Of course, Loraas had to see what evidence there was. She believed, like Bassima, that there was more than enough to take Glida Kimura into custody. They would resolve the other issues later. Once they had Glida Kimura under watch, they would be able to slow down the investigation.

Loraas added one more wrinkle. She wanted the day crew to find out where Glida Kimura went after she left Taji Kimura's office. There was a short period of time that Bassima couldn't find footage on. Bassima suspected that was when Glida got rid of Taji's body.

Bassima might have fought to keep that part of the job if she hadn't struggled with that footage all night.

Bassima was slowing down, and she felt it. She needed a nap, if nothing else, and she would get it once Glida was in custody.

The exterior of the sector base was almost impossible to see from the road. Even the parking area was hidden under a shelf of rock that matched the mountainside. The rock was reinforced with nanobits so that it wouldn't come down.

But Bassima hated it nonetheless. It looked unstable to her, which was probably on purpose. Its very appearance made outsiders think twice before walking underneath it.

She parked her official aircar in the visitor's area, which was deliberately tiny. There were very few visitors to the sector base—or at least, very few that came by ground. Sometimes young locals just out of school or new arrivals to the Sandoveil Valley applied for work here.

They all had to be DNA tested before they could get a job here, which Bassima thought outrageously invasive. It was one of the many reasons she wasn't working here.

That, and she didn't want to spend her entire working life underneath a mountain.

Most of the new arrivals who visited the sector base, though, came from the Fleet. They either entered with that weirdo-magic drive she'd heard so much about, that somehow helped them appear under solid rock; or, on very rare occasions, the fake mountaintop above the sector base opened, and a ship went through it.

When that happened, the entire city got warning. The YSR-SR usually had to scramble to make sure no one had been hiking up there. It was illegal to hike on the fake mountaintop, but that didn't stop people from doing it.

In fact, a lot of teenagers had died up there over the centuries. It seemed that the word *restricted* was a magnet for anyone under the age of twenty-five. Bassima always thought it was a way that they could prove just how incredibly stupid they were.

But she wasn't allowed to voice opinions like that. Because more than once, she'd been the one to break the news to grieving families that their reckless teenage kid wasn't ever coming back.

She wiped a hand over her face, willing herself awake. She'd gone in the front door of the sector base only a few times since she started working for the security office. The last time had been more than a decade ago.

She finger-combed her hair and tugged on the shirt of her uniform, hoping she looked at least slightly presentable.

The entry was wide and cavernous, which she was certain was intentional. It was almost like she had entered a gigantic black cave. It was dark and uncomfortable, and she *knew* that was on purpose, because she had asked about the design once.

Anyone who balked at this part of the sector base couldn't work in any other section.

She didn't balk, exactly, but she understood. Her skin crawled, just like it had every other time she had come here. It was a sensation she apparently hadn't forgotten.

An opaque wall, with warnings written in more languages than she could read, faced her. The warnings told her this place was restricted and unless she had reasons for being here, she should leave.

She walked up to the door, stated her name and her position, then said she needed to discuss an employee. Part of the opaque wall slid back, revealing an even more cavernous space before her. It, however, was mostly light. There were skylights in the ceiling, although she doubted they actually showed the real sky. The light seemed like sunlight, though.

The floor was a reflective white, but the walls were made of black nanobits. She'd recognize that substance anywhere. Six short desks huddled near each other—three on the left side of the entry and three on the right. Each had a floating sign identifying the function of the desk.

She went to the desk with the word *Security* above it, even though a woman behind the desk with the words *Employment Matters* stood as Bassima went by, apparently thinking she would be coming there.

The man behind the *Security* desk didn't look happy to see her. Bassima understood why. He had once applied for a job at Sandoveil's Security Office, and she had convinced Loraas to turn him down.

Dwight Wilson was a groper, or at least, he had been when he and Bassima were in school together. He had grabbed her ass more times than she wanted to think about, and each time, she had either complained, shoved him back, or hit him in the stomach with her elbow.

She was rather surprised that he had gotten a job here. But maybe there was nothing about his proclivities on the record.

Or maybe he outgrew them, although she doubted that was likely. He was probably just more circumspect about his victims.

His lips twisted into a half grimace.

"Never thought I'd see you here, Beck," he said.

"Likewise," she said.

"We don't need any new security officers," he said, "although I'm not supposed to tell you that. You're supposed to go to the employment desk to inquire about working here."

His words were easy for her to hear, but the unique design of the room made them fade only a few feet away. She remembered that from an earlier visit as well.

That was why there were seating groups farther in, where people were having intense conversations, and some clusters of employees looking around as if they were seeing the place for the first time.

She had no idea what they were doing, but they all acted as if their missions were important.

"Well, good thing I'm talking to you, then," she said, even though she hated to use the word "good" and "you" in the same sentence when dealing with Dwight. "I need to inquire about an employee. I need to know, discreetly, if she came in to work today."

"Discreetly," he repeated. "What does that mean, exactly?"

"It means I don't want her to know that I'm asking about her. This is a security matter, and if she's here, I'll need to partner with the base."

His twisted expression eased, and he called up a holographic screen with an opaque back. She couldn't see what he was looking at unless she actually tried to peer around it, which she would never do.

He was all business, which she was grateful for and surprised by.

"Let me be clear," he said. "You're here in your capacity as an officer for the Sandoveil Security Office."

"Yes," she said, glad he had asked it that way. He had already called up the screen, which probably meant that he was recording their interaction. Which was also good.

"All right," he said. "The name of the employee?"

"Glida Kimura," Bassima said. "Her car has been here for days, but I see no evidence that she's left the premises. If you could—"

He held up a finger, stopping her from speaking, a frown creasing his forehead. "Glida Kimura," he repeated. He sounded very serious.

"Yes," Beck said.

"And this is connected to something outside of the base?" he asked.

"Yes," she said. She wasn't going to go into detail here.

His skin had gone gray. She'd never seen anything quite like it.

He looked up at Bassima and, if she had to guess, she would have guessed that he looked frightened.

"If you don't mind sitting over there…?" He nodded toward a seating arrangement near the wall that she hadn't seen when she came in. The long gray couch looked as if no one had ever sat on it before, and the table in front of it was a shiny black.

"Problem?" she asked, not moving.

"Please, just…sit. Okay? Someone will be with you in a minute." He was being polite and freaked out, two things she never would have expected from Dwight.

"All right," she said and wandered, slowly, to the couch. She made sure she walked at an angle, so she could see what Dwight was doing.

He was tapping screens—two of them at least—and then he'd bow his head as if he was talking to someone. Twice he shook his head, clearly worried. Once he glanced over at her.

She sank onto the couch, which was as uncomfortable as it looked. There was no give in the fabric. Maybe some brain-dead designer had thought that making a couch out of nanobits was a good idea—if this couch actually *was* made of nanobits. It probably wasn't. It just felt that way.

Dwight continued his comparisons of the screens, occasionally talking to someone, even gesturing once, although he didn't appear to be on a video conference. He was upset. And he kept glancing at her as if he expected her to run—or maybe level more accusations at him, or something.

Then she realized she wasn't being fair. He had treated her well since she came in here, and she had clearly upset him. Something was up with Glida Kimura, something important enough that a lower level flunky like Dwight knew enough to be freaked out.

Bassima leaned back on the couch, feeling the hard cushion dig into the small of her back. As she did so, she realized it was good that the couch was uncomfortable. She was tired enough to sleep despite Dwight's floor show.

She folded her hands together, watched Dwight flap around, and hoped that with all his consternation, he wasn't tipping off Glida Kimura.

Because Bassima needed the element of surprise. The last thing she wanted was for Glida Kimura to escape.

45

In the end, Hranek decided not to bring any other members of his team to the pool behind Fiskett Falls. If this were a normal day and a normal case, he would bring half his staff. Partly, he'd want to train them, and partly, he would want their assistance.

But this was not a normal day, and his best people were already working on the two deaths he knew about—figuring out what happened to Taji Kimura's body, and dealing with the body that YSR-SR had already pulled out of this pool.

Part of him wished he could be with Bassima Beck at the sector base. He wanted to catch Glida Kimura after watching her shadow on the environmental system in her wife's office.

Sometimes arresting the bastards was as satisfying as finding the evidence that would put them away. But he was too busy to indulge, at least today.

And he was running late.

The sun was already peeking over the mountains as he pulled the van into an unsanctioned parking area near Fiskett Falls. Several vehicles were already parked here, a few haphazardly, equipment scattered, and impressions on the dirt that showed where a body bag had been.

A body bag and several footprints. Death scene contamination already. And Marnie Sar wondered why he wanted to be here.

The YSR-SR never paid attention to death scene protocol. They were always concerned with information or lives or rescue—even when they knew (as they had here) that rescue wasn't possible.

He stepped out of his van, grabbing his kit as he did so. The Falls sounded louder here than anywhere else. The ground vibrated beneath his feet, something that he knew he would get used to as the morning went on. The air was filled with spray—just enough to remind him that the Falls were nearby, but not enough to get him wet. At least, not right away.

Ardelia Novoa stood at the beginning of the path that led behind the Falls. Her arms were crossed. Half of the white diving suit covered her legs. The remainder of the suit toppled back over her bottom like a coat tied around the waist.

Two towels wrapped around her neck, covering her torso. For a moment, he worried that she wasn't wearing anything else on top, despite the cold. As she stepped forward, though, he realized that she was wearing some kind of black sleeveless thing.

"I was about to give up on you," she said in a tone that let him know she wished he hadn't shown up. "You're late."

"Yeah." He would have apologized if she hadn't used that tone on him. Instead, he let his annoyance out. "I had to deal with a body that no one followed procedure on."

"Wow," she said. "You really are something, you know that?"

"I'm the one who is supposed to be in charge of death scenes," he said. "You should be following *my* procedure, and if I'm six hours late, then I'm six hours late."

"If you were six hours late, the body would be at the examiner's office and maybe someone would be working on it." She peered around him, her movement exaggerated. "I thought you were bringing a team."

"It seems we've had a mini-crime spree," he said. "My team is busy, but I'm here."

"Crime spree? Besides these two bodies?" Novoa asked.

"Yeah," he said, and did not elaborate. What was going on in his office was none of her business.

"Good lord," she said. "What's happening in Sandoveil?"

He wasn't sure if the question was rhetorical or not, so he chose to take it that way.

"You said we're running late. So let's get moving," he said.

She raised her eyebrows as if she found his determination to go forward annoying.

"When was the last time you were behind the Falls?" she asked.

His patience was nearly gone. "I don't know."

"Then there are procedures to review," she said, blocking his way.

"Procedures be damned," he said. "Let's go."

She glared at him. "You're here because you insist on procedures. Have you changed your mind about that?"

Anger surged through him. "Let me remind you that you're a volunteer," he said. "I *work* for the city of Sandoveil. I *need* to get to that site for my job—"

"And I need to make sure you get there alive."

"Then watch me," he said. "Because I'm going there without you."

He walked around her and hoped he remembered how to open the barrier that let him into the area behind the Falls.

She struggled to keep up, then passed him, reaching the barrier first. She didn't say another word, and he wondered if she had just provoked him to get him on record denying that he needed to review procedure.

He supposed the YSR-SR was doing that to cover its ass. He couldn't believe someone would do that to undercut him, although that little interchange would have done it.

She stood in front of the barrier and pressed, and poked, and did a few other things that he really didn't pay attention to, now that she was doing her job again. The barrier came down, and the black path appeared in all its nanobit glory, just like it used to be before the city realized how much money it was spending on rescuing tourists (alive and dead) who felt trapped behind the Falls.

The Falls were loud enough here that he could barely hear himself breathe. The air was filled with droplets. The water fell like a sheet to his right, and the ground had stopped vibrating under his feet. Now it bounced.

Novoa kept pace with him until the path narrowed and then he went first, picking his way over the surface, which was a little too slick for him.

And then, just almost like a surprise, he was on the other side of the Falls. The pool area, with its shallow outcropping, spread before him, and the water looked deceptively calm.

Marnie Sar stood near the entrance. Tevin Egbe wore all of his diving suit except his hood. He had an equipment bag over his shoulder. A woman stood near him. As Hranek arrived, she had pulled a hood over her face. The skin of her long hands was dark brown against the white of her suit.

She was tall and athletic, but most of the people who worked for the YSR-SR were both tall and athletic. Tevin Egbe was.

He glared at Hranek.

"Can we proceed *now*?" Tevin asked, his voice filled with sarcasm. "Or should we wait until the daylight reaches this little area?"

The daylight probably wouldn't reach the area in any effective way for hours yet. It was lighter here than it had probably been two hours ago, but it still looked more like twilight than daylight.

"I want to see what you have on the body first," Hranek said. "Where is it exactly?"

Tevin's jaw tightened. He looked like a man about to explode. Apparently his patience was gone too. And didn't he need patience to dive?

"We've reviewed the footage," Tevin said. "We know where the body is. We have told you what we saw. And we know how to recover a body. I don't need you second-guessing what we're going to do. You're here as a courtesy."

"Tevin," Marnie said.

"He's right," Novoa said.

"I am here to make sure procedure gets followed," Hranek said. "From your earlier report, we have a murder victim here, is that right?"

"Someone piled rocks on her and someone put her here," Tevin said. "I have no idea if she drowned here or if she was killed elsewhere, but this is definitely a death scene."

"All right then," Hranek said. "We'll get me set up on your comm and then you'll dive. I want the evidence removed in a particular way."

"You want us to keep the *rocks*?" the woman asked.

He hadn't thought of that. He was tired, and glad they had misunderstood him.

"Yes," he said. "In case one of them is the murder weapon."

Tevin rolled his eyes. "We're not doing that. We only have so much air time. We're going to bring you what we can—"

"We'll make a holographic representation," Marnie said. "That will work."

"*No*," Hranek said. "You will bring me the rocks, at least the ones small enough that a human being could use them as a weapon."

"Oh, well, that's *so* much better," said the woman in the suit.

He couldn't deal with this team much longer. He turned to Marnie. They were her people: she could corral them.

"Two bodies in this pool," he said. "One *mis*identified and *mis*handled by your people. That body, by the way, belongs to a tourist from Ynchi City. You can bet that her people will want a thorough investigation, which your people have already mucked up. So, you will do this my way or we will bring in another team who will. Or, if you prefer, we'll bring in a team from Ynchi City who understands procedure."

It was a bluff.

"Calm down, Mushtaq," Marnie said. "They'll bring your rocks and anything else they find."

"They don't get to determine what to bring me," he said. "*I* determine it. From here."

Tevin actually turned away as if this discussion was disturbing him. Novoa had her arms crossed again, and the woman who was already suited up shook her head slightly.

They seemed to think Hranek was being unreasonable, but he wasn't. They didn't know that he suspected Glida Kimura of orchestrating at least two deaths in the past week. He wanted to make certain she got punished for them.

"I know." Marnie patted her hand on Hranek's arm in an apparent attempt to placate him.

It took all of his strength not to wrench his arm away. He didn't want to seem *that* childish.

"You get to make all of the final decisions," she said. "That's why you'll be viewing the footage in real time."

"Which you could have done from your office," someone muttered.

He couldn't tell who had said that, or whether the voice was male or female. He didn't respond, because they wanted him to respond. Everyone seemed to be on edge.

But if he *had* responded, he would have said that *of course* he could have monitored all of it from his office. He just couldn't have influenced it. Here he would tell Marnie what he needed or tell Tevin directly, and if they didn't do it, he would push and push and push until someone did it.

He would even get them back in the water if need be.

His death scene. His responsibility.

He looked at all of them—Tevin with his jaw working as if he was chewing on something bad; the other diver, who kept shaking her head as if she couldn't believe what she was hearing; Novoa, who was pacing, and Marnie, who still held her hand near his arm, as if she were trying to stop him from doing something.

"Well," he said coldly. "Should we get started?"

His words hung in the damp air for a moment, and then Tevin let out a sound of disgust. The other diver put her hand on his arm—the exact same gesture that Marnie had tried to use with Hranek—and Tevin shook his head.

Marnie watched that as well, but her expression remained impassive as she turned toward Hranek.

"We'll get underway in a minute," she said. "Please, step back. If you need to do some setup, now is the time."

She wanted him out of the way. Apparently, he was irritating the team. Poor things. They couldn't take true instruction.

Hranek walked toward the stone walls that led up the mountainside. As he had predicted, the sound of the Falls had become background. But the ground kept vibrating, which he knew would throw off his equipment.

While they calmed themselves in preparation to do their jobs, he walked around the area, looking up, then peering at the pathway, then looking up again.

Bodies landing here weren't that unusual. He'd cleaned up more than his fair share of them. But he had never dealt with one covered in rocks before. Deliberately weighted down. Or the rocks placed on top of them somehow.

No one ever brought boats in here. It was too hard. And a blow-up raft would be at the mercy of the Falls.

There were footprints everywhere on this little patch of ground. Even if the killer had left her footprints behind, the footprints would be gone now. Completely gone. Buried under more footprints.

This was why he was here. Too late, of course. The YSR-SR had trampled the scene for over twelve hours.

Hranek stepped back and looked up. Then he looked at the pool. The divers were gearing up, taking their equipment, leaning toward each other the way that people linking up comms did. Marnie was bent over her equipment, as far from the water's edge as she could get, and another man—what was his name? Zhou?—had joined them. Like Novoa earlier, he wore half of his diving suit. Apparently, he wasn't going in the water with the rest of them.

There were rocks of all sizes at the base of this cliff. Most appeared as though they had been here for a long time, but several had darker surfaces than the others. Some of the ones with darker surfaces had mold growing up the sides that just stopped.

He walked around the edge, then looked up again. There was no way that anyone could place a body into this pool and fling rocks on top of it from above, not and do it accurately.

If the rocks were somehow attached to the body, well, then it would take someone freakishly strong to toss it over one of the overlooks. Or it would take some kind of equipment that was usually forbidden up here.

The simplest—and strangest—explanation was that someone had weighted down the body, and then piled rocks on it, from this vantage point, swimming into the pool and doing it laboriously, one rock at a time.

Hranek whirled around and watched the divers double-check each other's suits. They were standing in the water, with it lapping against their ankles. They wouldn't have to walk far to grab one of the rocks from beside the cliff face and take it into the pool.

He had no idea exactly where the body was, but it couldn't be too close to the Falls. They wouldn't have seen it or have suggested diving for it if it were buried under all that water.

So the actual effort to take and drop the rocks was not as great as he had initially thought. It would take work, yes, and a lot of risk. But everything he had seen from Glida Kimura in the past day had involved risk.

He doubted that stopped her.

But she would have had to come in through that barricade. And in theory, the barricade's passcode was only known to a few people. It was "tourist proof," or so he had been told repeatedly.

A thought itched at him. It had bothered him before, particularly when he stood here, and it bothered him now.

All those bodies he'd pulled out of this pool—or had the YSR-SR pull out of the pool—had come from above. Or so he had assumed. He had believed they had jumped off the overlooks or ridden down the Falls and tumbled sideways.

He'd only dealt with one body at a time back here. This was the first time he'd dealt with two, and he was only doing that because YSR-SR had been following his procedures.

He would have to thank Marnie for that, when he was less tired and less annoyed.

He walked over to her now. She was hunched over the equipment. The divers were finishing their rituals and wading into the water.

"Hey, Marnie," Hranek asked, "how many people have the passcodes for the barrier?"

"I don't know," she said without looking up. "Do you want me to put this on a holoscreen for you or can you watch from here?"

"My own screen, thanks," he said.

She started to set that up, and as she did, he realized she hadn't realized how serious his question was.

"Marnie, please, how many people have the passcode?"

"I don't know," she said a lot more forcefully. "You can either have me monitor what the team is doing or you can have me look up the esoteric information. Which do you want?"

He wanted both, but he wasn't going to get both. He would have to wait for the answer to his question until the dive was over.

"My screen, please," he said.

He noted that Zhou already had his own screen. He was sitting on a pile of rocks, away from the water, staring gape-mouthed at what the divers were doing. His equipment was beside him, except for the suit, which he now wore all the way up to his neck. The hood was tipped back, but at the ready.

Hranek realized that Zhou was the designated rescue diver, in case something went bad. Hranek couldn't remember ever seeing that before and wondered if it was because of the rocks they all had to carry or because this dive was a particularly dangerous one.

He wasn't going to ask.

A screen popped up beside Marnie.

"You can move it to the left," she said, "but not too far. We're working with limited resources here."

He didn't question that. Instead, he pulled the screen over. It was split between all three divers. The water was gray and filled with silt from all of their cameras. The suits gave water temperature, chemical components, and pressure.

"You're getting all the environmental details, right?" he asked.

"Yes," Marnie said.

"Make sure you make a backup of that for me," he said.

She let out an exasperated sigh. "I always do."

"You going to watch this dive or not?" Zhou asked from his corner of their little world.

Hranek didn't answer him. Instead, Hranek brought the screen up and combined all three images into one. The silt, moving in three different directions because of the combined imagery, made him slightly dizzy, and he was having trouble identifying what, exactly, he was seeing.

He had to change them back into a split screen, hoping one of the divers would end up being the primary one.

They would be in the water for some time. He probably should sit down, but he didn't want to at the moment. He felt oddly exhilarated and deeply exhausted.

And the day had just begun.

46

When Bristol usually worked with *anacapa* drives, the drives remained off. They looked cold and unassuming when they weren't in use, resembling nothing more than a hunk of black-and-gold rock that a stream had polished smooth. Small threads of color worked through the black-and-gold exterior, leading to different parts of the drive.

But when the *anacapa* drive was activated, it looked completely different. When the drive worked properly, it gave off a whitish gold-and-pink glow at rest, and a rich blue, laced with white and gold, when it linked with foldspace. When the drive was malfunctioning, those bright lights were laced with other colors.

Sometimes Bristol could diagnose by color alone. But sometimes she actually had to dig in to the drive. It was easier to dig in when the drive was completely deactivated, because the colors threaded through that black and gold sometimes leached gray. She could use *anacapa*-specific tools, open the tiny area where the leaching occurred, and do the repairs.

Even though the repairs were usually simple at that point, they could take weeks. She would have to determine why that portion of the drive had died, then figure out if she could simply reactivate it or if she needed to grow an entire new section of the drive. Reactivation meant finding the nanobit specific to that little section and turning on the piece that had shut itself off.

Reactivating that little portion of the drive would take constant monitoring, to make sure whatever problem had caused the *anacapa* to malfunction in the first place didn't repeat. Reactivation was chancy.

She usually grew new sections of the drive if she knew that the drive itself hadn't killed those nanobits. Growing new parts of the drive was what took all the time. She had to baby the parts along, make sure that nothing went awry, and hope that the drive would accept the newly grafted part.

When she discussed the drives with others, she spoke of the drives as things. But when she actually looked at the drives, they shared a lot in common with biological organisms. She had had some medical training, and privately, she thought that was what made her one of the best *anacapa* experts in the Fleet. She knew that the drives operated like the human body—the theory was the same for all drives, but each drive was so vastly different from the others that she often thought of them as different planets.

She always tried to be cautious, and test everything she could, because there was a mysterious component to the *anacapa* drive. She believed that the original founders of the Fleet had stumbled onto the *anacapa* drive accidentally while building something else. They harnessed the power they found, and built the Fleet around it.

Over the millennia, the Fleet learned a lot about the *anacapa* drive but never quite conquered the whole foldspace equation—what was foldspace, how did they communicate with foldspace, and what, exactly, could they do to create something else that interacted with foldspace.

She believed the answer wasn't just in the *anacapa* drives, it was also in foldspace. But she wasn't courageous enough to venture into foldspace to find the answer.

She'd gone to foldspace several times. Of course, she had. She couldn't do her job otherwise. But she had hated it, more than she hated being in conventional space. And conventional space didn't work for her well at all.

Which was why she was one of the most cautious *anacapa* experts in the Fleet. Because there were apocryphal stories of engineers opening an *anacapa* drive's protective case, activating an *anacapa* drive to work on it, and getting sent into foldspace—*without* a ship.

She personally couldn't find records of that, so she actually doubted it happened.

But it sounded so plausible that she thought of it each time she prepared to work on an activated drive, her back and stomach muscles tense like they were now.

Before Bristol opened the *anacapa* casing, she had asked Fedo to step back. Captain Virji sat in front of a console near the door, chair turned so that she could see part of what they were doing.

"I don't know if you looked at this drive before you got to the sector base," Bristol said to Fedo, "but it's a mess."

"I didn't look," Fedo said. "I would love to retire all the FS-Prime runabouts."

Bristol peeled back the *anacapa* casing to reveal the small drive. Over time, its polish had become a dull sheen. There were huge holes in the drive's center, and most of the drive's gold was gone. The remaining black had only three colors threading through it—a yellowish, puke green; a pale, lavender blue; and a startling orange pink.

Until she had started work on this drive, Bristol had seen none of those colors in an *anacapa* drive before. She was of the personal opinion that this drive was dying. But she couldn't express that sentiment in those terms to another engineer. Because most engineers did not consider *anacapa* drives to be living things.

"Holy…" Fedo said before stopping herself. "This was the drive that was *in* the runabout?"

"Yeah," Bristol said.

"What's the problem?" Virji stood and came toward them.

Bristol extended a hand, palm facing Virji.

"Captain," she said, "it's better if you don't come too close."

"I've been around *anacapa*s my entire career," Virji said.

"Not like this, Captain," Fedo said. "We're going to have to activate this one, and I would prefer that you leave the area. We'll call you back down when we think we can recall the runabout."

Her tone made it sound like she didn't think they could recall the runabout.

"Very well," Virji said. "I'm sure there are some things I can check on the ship itself."

She walked to the door. She tried to look at the *anacapa* as she did, but she wouldn't have been able to see it from her vantage point.

She let herself out, and Bristol let out a sigh of relief.

"Is she always that difficult?" Bristol asked.

Fedo grinned. "She's a captain. You don't work with them here, do you?"

"Sure I do," Bristol said. "All of them find their way to this base at one point or another."

"But you don't *work* with them. They're tough, demanding, and used to getting their own way," Fedo said. "Sometimes they listen to reason, but sometimes they don't, particularly when they're feeling guilty."

"Guilty?" Bristol asked.

"She feels responsible for Everly/Kimura." Fedo shrugged. "It's a long story, and I'd rather focus on this thing in front of us."

Bristol suppressed a sigh. Human beings were much too complicated for her. She'd rather work with the damaged *anacapa* drive.

"These colors," Fedo said. "I've never seen these colors before."

"Neither have I," Bristol said. "And I've only seen a few drives this damaged. All of the drives that had similar holes were extremely old, with connections missing. The problem with old *anacapa*s, though, is that their power usually flares as they die."

Fedo leaned back, that pale expression back on her face. "We had no flares registering inside that cargo bay."

She sounded certain. Bristol believed Fedo *was* certain. Those flares would have registered on all kinds of equipment, especially in a ship as large as the *Ijo*.

"Which means that the flares were contained," Fedo said, more to herself than Bristol.

Bristol nodded. "I've seen it before. We build great casings for the *anacapa* drives. I think the flares are what cause the holes in the drive itself. The problem is that anything hooked up to the drive will also experience the flare."

"The maintenance system," Fedo breathed. "Son of a bitch. I thought it was such a great workaround."

"It might be, for a healthy *anacapa* drive." Bristol mentally winced at the word *healthy* and hoped Fedo didn't notice. "But for one like this…"

"The *anacapa*s in the FS-Prime runabouts are hooked into the entire ship," Fedo said, clearly thinking out loud. She hadn't even heard what Bristol had said. Or if she had, she wasn't acknowledging it. "That runabout might not work at all."

"Well, it works," Bristol said. "We determined that it didn't explode. But what interacted with the *anacapa* I had put in there, we have no idea."

"Whatever route she'd programmed into that runabout," Fedo said, "might not even communicate with the *anacapa* you put in there in the way she intended."

"You people knew her," Bristol said. "Would she have simply tried to reverse the last command and put the runabout back on the *Ijo*?"

As Bristol spoke, a chill ran down her back. That old *anacapa* drive had taken the runabout from the bay in the *Ijo* through foldspace to the storage room beside her lab. They were all lucky that some kind of explosion hadn't happened at all, or a flare or *something* horrible.

That was it. She made a mental note to request that all of the model FS-Prime runabouts were removed from service purposely. She'd attach an image of this *anacapa* drive to the request.

"I don't think she would go back to the *Ijo*," Fedo said. "Given her history with us."

Bristol nodded. That seemed logical.

"The damage to this drive was probably caused by the fact it was never shut off," she said. "All the other drives only get activated when we're going to use them. They are rarely in rest mode."

"That's the theory," Fedo said. "In practice, some ships leave their *anacapa*s in rest whenever they go through hostile or unknown territory."

Which explained why drives from different DV-class vessels had different levels of wear.

"I hadn't known that," Bristol said. "I'll be honest. I was going to activate this drive and take information off its memory, to see how it interacted with the maintenance system on that runabout, but I'm leery about activating the drive at all."

"Plus, if the drive has flared and damaged the systems in the runabout," Fedo said, "then how this drive interacted with the runabout doesn't matter much."

Bristol stared at it for a moment. The leached colors, the gray parts, the holes. She frowned.

"Actually," she said. "It does matter. This drive will have a record of its flares, and we will be able to figure out what—if any—systems got hit."

Fedo's gaze met Bristol's over the drive.

"So we can figure out if Everly actually has control over the runabout or not," Fedo said.

Bristol nodded. "I'm going to double the containment field around the *anacapa*. We're going to have to work through the field. If you're not okay with that, then I can do this myself."

"I would triple the field," Fedo said. "I routinely work with a double field on the *Ijo*."

"Good," Bristol said. "Then we both have experience with it."

And, because she didn't want to sound too negative, she didn't add, *Let's hope that will be enough.*

47

Even though Tevin couldn't feel the water against his skin, he could sense the coolness, the pull of the current. His movements always felt elegant when he was underwater, as if he had become a professional dancer and the entire city watched.

He shut off information about the water temperature, pressure, and composition, and left only the warnings on. They would tell him if he was about to enter a riptide or if the current suddenly shifted so that he would be pulled toward the waterfall.

The undertow was the most dangerous part of this dive. Even though the surface of this pool looked calm, the water underneath was anything but. The force of the water coming down differed from day to day, by water volume, snowmelt (or lack thereof), and a whole bunch of other factors. Even a rock that slipped into the river above might change the flow of the Falls, which would then alter how the water hit the pool.

He'd seen the current go in so many different directions underwater that he couldn't keep track of it visually. He let his suit keep track of some of it, but he had made a rule years ago that none of his people would ever dive near Fiskett Falls without a free-flow barrier blocking passage from the dive to the Falls. He had insisted that the YSR-SR implement that rule before he ever took teams to the Falls.

He and Dinithi set up the barrier while standing in the pool. They released it, let it hit the ground and roll into place. He used the largest barrier they had for this pool, even though the specs called for a smaller one.

The barrier worked like a net. Water flowed through it, but humans caught in the undertow would hit the barrier and not get sucked under the Falls. Even so, it was difficult to get someone free of the water when they hit the barrier.

This particular barrier was his favorite, because it had a detachable section that could wrap around a diver, roll up, and yank the diver toward the shore.

The pool was so small here that the detachable section would get the diver to shallow water, where he could simply walk up and out of the area.

It still wasn't perfect, but it worked. He'd seen people survive who would have normally been sucked under the Falls and died. Whereas, he had seen more people than he wanted to think about die because they'd actually gone under the Falls.

He knew only one person who had survived a slip underneath the Falls, and that had been him.

It wasn't an experience he ever wanted to repeat.

The waterfall churned to his right. The water bubbled and foamed, pushing downward or outward or upward, shimmering and forming different colors as it moved.

From underneath, the Falls looked like clouds, coming in with a big wind behind them, building, and threatening storms of such severity that everything in the Sandoveil Valley would be obliterated.

If he ever saw clouds like that in the sky, he would run for cover. Here, there was no cover. Just the barrier.

This moment—this first moment when he saw the waterfall from underneath—always activated his fight-or-flight response. The suit noticed his panic, and warned him that he could not remain at this elevated level of adrenaline for very long.

He ignored that because he knew that, dramatic as it was, he would be able to stop focusing on the Falls in a very short period of time.

He started ignoring the Falls now, as he swam toward the rock formation they had seen with the probe.

He suspected, given the position of that body, that there wasn't much of an undertow there, but he had been wrong about rock formations before. He wasn't going to be wrong here. He was going in with caution.

He had briefed his team about the dangers of working with rock formations so close to churning water.

And now Hranek had thrown in his little orders, as if the pool really were calm and Tevin's team could walk in and out carrying rocks.

Tevin would bring only the rocks that looked important. If they were worth carrying. It didn't matter how much Hranek bitched. Tevin would make the decision based on the degree of danger to himself and his team.

He could feel the waterfall. It was like a drumbeat, constant and insistent, the vibration so strong that he could hear it, even through the suit and the water. In fact, the water probably amplified it.

The initial adrenaline had calmed. His suit stopped yelling at him to return to base. (It still thought it was in space: he had never changed that aspect of the suit. *He* would never go to space, but he loved the default language usage on the suit. It made him feel more worldly than he was.)

He glanced at his diving partners. They had dived near the Falls before as well, which reassured him. Everyone on his team had done practice dives in the bigger, easier-to-access part of Rockwell Pool. The safer pool.

But that way, he knew that his team understood the dangers and the risks of a dive like this.

Both women swam to his left. Novoa was the closest to him because she had worked in this pool before, although never at this depth. Dinithi had helped retrieve the first body, but not anything else. She was the one he was most concerned about.

He and Dinithi and Novoa had tested their comms before they left together to do this dive. Technically, he should have checked the comms one more time as the three of them descended, but he hadn't wanted to. He knew how much work it was to get his attitude right, with the Falls pounding beside him, and he felt it was safer to bring himself into focus.

Because he and the women were searching for anything unusual, they had all of their suit lights on, from the focused lights on the palms of their gloves to the diffuse lights all over their legs and torso. He also had a hood light, but he kept that a little dimmer than the women did. The hood light irritated his eyes, particularly as the silt flowed around him.

The pile of rocks showed up almost immediately. He should have expected that: it took less time for a human to cross a short span of water than it did for a small probe to do that.

The rocks seemed even more jagged than they had through the cameras, and his earlier observation had been correct: there was no visible sediment on the rocks at all. He couldn't see the necklace that had started all of this, though, partly because the water was so dark here, and partly because of the sediment.

His eyes weren't as fine an instrument as the probe had been.

"All right," Dinithi said through the comm, startling him. "Consider this the final comm check."

"Check," Novoa said.

"Check," Tevin said.

"Now," Dinithi said, apparently thinking that Tevin wasn't going to take control of the dive without some prompting. "How does Hranek want us to proceed? Rocks first?"

Tevin suppressed a sigh. Dinithi had believed Hranek when he said he was in charge.

"You'll follow my lead underwater," Tevin said before Marnie could cut in. He prayed she didn't have Hranek attached to their comm system, because that would piss Tevin off to no end. He never liked the man, but after this morning's display, Tevin was starting to loathe him.

"Sorry," Dinithi said, apparently taking that as a rebuke to her, not to Hranek.

"No need to apologize. I'll keep us structured," Tevin said. "So, to answer your question, we're going to follow standard procedure. We're going to examine the entire area, then figure out how to handle the body. If we need to move rocks, that's when we'll discuss those."

"Got it," Dinithi said. He wanted to believe she sounded relieved.

He paused, treading water, and the women paused beside him. He took in the entire structure.

The rocks weren't a formation like he had initially thought, at least, not at the top. The bottom was in a well that he had noticed on a previous dive. The well was deep, part of a trench that centuries of water coming off the mountain had carved into the ground.

Even though he trained his light downward, he couldn't see the bottom of that trench. He knew that some geologist at Sandoveil University had done a lot of work in these pools. He also knew the geologist had research on file with the YSR-SR, so *someone* probably knew the depth of this trench.

In fact, Zhou probably did, but they had elected to leave him on shore with the equipment.

For a moment, Tevin was tempted to ask Zhou to research the depth of the trench, then decided that could wait.

They just needed to see what they were dealing with first.

"Let's start with this side," Tevin said. "Let's go as deep as this thing will let us. In tandem."

In tandem for this team meant that they worked side by side. With beginners, he would have had them rope together or hold hands, but the two of them, as experienced as they were, only needed to be told.

They fell into a rhythm automatically, fanning out slightly so that they covered the entire rock pile, but remaining at the exact same level and in almost the same position as they worked their way down.

He turned on the lights on his shoulders and aimed them at the rocks. Novoa brightened her hood light, and Dinithi lit up every focused light they had.

The rocks came into clearer focus as the three of them increased the light. And it became evident almost immediately that the rocks were less of a formation and more of a pile.

The upper layer of the pile contained the body. The arms floated like seaweed.

"I don't like this," Novoa said. "It's weird."

They had all been cautioned, back when they were brought in to the YSR-SR, to be as clear as they could when they were on comms because comms could be part of the public record.

But *weird* was pretty accurate. And if need be, he would reinforce that on the record.

The rock pile was huge. It disappeared into the trench. He couldn't tell if it rested on top of an existing formation, but the idea of that made him frown.

If the trench hadn't been carved by the waterfall, then it was some kind of ancient lava trench or a split in the ground that had formed around something else. He barely remembered the geology he had studied in school, but the one thing he had learned since he joined the YSR-SR was that the sector base would never have been built beneath the Payyer Mountain Range if it had been an active volcanic range. It was simply too dangerous.

There was—according to Fleet geologists of several centuries ago—no chance that lava could burble up from beneath the ground and change the formation of these rocks.

"What the hell is this?" Dinithi asked as they swam deeper.

They still had nearly fifty feet to go before they reached the lip of the trench. Tevin's suit informed him of the increasing pressure.

And oddly, the farther down he went, the quieter the waterfall seemed. The vibration had eased, at least a little. He suspected that, if he looked up, the water storm would seem very far away.

"You seeing this?" he asked Marnie.

"Yeah," she responded, quicker than he expected. "In 2D it makes very little sense. What are you all exclaiming about?"

He didn't want to explain anything to her right now. He needed to focus on the dive.

"Just ask Jabari if this could be an avalanche zone," Tevin said.

Dinithi whipped her head toward him, as hard as the water allowed. The movement sent her backward and sideways and almost over the lip of the trench.

In fact, she would have gone over the lip if Novoa hadn't also seen the movement and caught Dinithi's arm. It took a visible effort for Novoa to pull her closer.

"Bad current?" Tevin asked.

"Yeah," Novoa said. "We have to stay back from the edge of that trench."

He wasn't feeling it on this side of the rock pile, so he suspected he had missed the current altogether.

"Tevin, Jabari here," Zhou said, even though Tevin would have recognized his voice anywhere. Zhou identified himself more for the record than he did for Tevin. "Mushtaq and I are measuring now, and looking at some historical records—"

Mushtaq? Tevin had no idea who that was. Then he realized that had to be Hranek. Wonderful. He didn't want Hranek involved, although he had no real choice.

"—we don't know definitively if you're in an avalanche area, but judging from your location, it would be unusual to have an avalanche pile there."

"Even from really high?" Dinithi asked. "Like one of the areas of the overlooks, maybe?"

"Some rocks would bounce outward, yes, but have you watched an avalanche?" Zhou asked.

Tevin stopped swimming forward. He indicated with his hands that the women should stop too. They were treading water, the light from their equipment illuminating the rocks.

"Not in person," Novoa said.

"Or any other way," Dinithi said.

"An avalanche is generally dirt and debris sliding down a mountainside. Not a pile of rocks tumbling outward like they were tossed by giants." Zhou paused, and Tevin could tell Zhou was pausing for effect. "To get the kind of rock pile you have there from an avalanche would mean that the entire area from the base of the mountain through the water to the trench would be covered in loose rocks."

"Plus, we would know about the avalanche," Dinithi said as if she understood.

"Not if it had happened hundreds of years ago, although the ground itself would give us that message," Zhou said. "Right now, Mushtaq and I have found no evidence of an avalanche on this side of the waterfall."

"Thanks," he said, and cut off the rest of the questions. He signaled that his team should swim forward and down ever so slightly.

Dinithi tilted downward, her body so lit up that the water around her looked almost white. She swam just a hair too close to the rocks, and as Tevin opened his mouth to warn her, she used the water to push herself backward in an almost involuntary movement.

She didn't scream—they were all too well-trained to scream—but her body screamed for her.

"What is it?" Novoa asked as she swam toward the rock pile. Then she sucked in air so audibly that it sounded like a gasp.

Tevin swam forward as well. He turned on his bright headlamp and pointed his chin downward.

Rocks, jagged and pointed, and lots of moving plants, growing in between. Moving plants and—

He let out a little puff of air, and his heart rate went up. His suit warned him that he was sensing danger.

He didn't want to correct it. Because the danger was long past. He was seeing something, not sensing anything at all.

Bits of cloth, bones. Skulls. Bodies, underneath rocks. Real rocks, maybe weighing the bodies down initially, or maybe just piled on them because—

Oh, hell, he didn't know why.

Bodies.

He counted at least five skulls. And there might be more going down deeper in that trench.

His mind couldn't quite handle the discovery. His heart rate had spiked, his breathing was uneven, and his fight-or-flight response was still active.

Primitive responses. He knew it, but his body still wanted him to leave.

He took a deep breath, then nodded at the women.

"We're going back up," he said.

48

"Bassima Beck?"

Bassima started, her eyes popping open. She had fallen asleep after all. She mentally kicked herself. It had been a long time since she had pulled an all-nighter, and she was clearly no longer used to doing it.

Dwight wasn't at his desk, but the people manning the other five desks were staring at her. Or rather, at the person who had spoken to her.

He was slightly behind her, beside the arm of the uncomfortable couch. Which, apparently, hadn't been uncomfortable enough.

She stood, quickly and awkwardly, and found herself towering over him. She could see the tiny bald spot on the crown of his head. His black-and-silver hair swirled around it, like spices in a particularly well made cupcake.

He looked up at her, clearly not uncomfortable with her height. And why would he be? He was probably used to people being taller than him. Maybe not looming over him the way she did, but taller nonetheless.

He held out a hand. "I'm Gian Nicoleau. I head security here at the sector base."

The *head* of security had come to see her? Now that was a surprise. Something very important was happening here.

She took his hand and shook it gently.

"I didn't mean to interrupt you, sir," she said. "I was making a simple inquiry about—"

"Yes, I know," he said. "And sometimes the simplest inquiries are the most complex. Please come with me. I need to speak to you in private."

She frowned. No one had ever offered to take her deeper into the base. If anything, they had tried to keep her away from the rest of the base.

"Sure," she said, wondering only half-humorously if she was dreaming. Because this was odd by any measure.

He waved his hand at the wall, and a small door opened behind him. As she stepped through that door, she realized it was extremely thick. In the city of Sandoveil, the door would be called a blast door.

The corridor he led her into was wide and arched. It had comfortable, light blue walls and more of that overhead lighting that mimicked sunlight. Compared to the entry, this part of the sector base felt accommodating.

He led her through three different corridors, all of which looked the same. Fortunately, she had had that small nap, so she could keep track of where she was. She had a hunch other people got turned around very easily here.

He opened a door that was opaque, like the wall in the main entrance, and revealed a small meeting room. A seating arrangement with several chairs huddled against one wall; another, with a round table and four chairs, stood near some cabinets.

Obviously, this wasn't his office. She was probably nowhere near the real security center in the sector base. This was a meeting area designed for outsiders who couldn't go in the restricted parts.

He swept a hand toward the table.

"Please," he said. "Sit."

She sat at the round table, in a chair with a view of the door. It was no longer opaque, but clear, so that anyone in the corridor could see the meeting going on inside here.

He sat in the chair closest to hers, so that anyone passing in the corridor could see that he was in this meeting.

"You were asking about Glida Kimura," he said. "May I ask why?"

Bassima almost felt like a suspect herself. And yet nothing in his tone implied it. Her feeling came from his posture, which was both on edge and wary, while pretending to be relaxed.

For a moment she hesitated, wondering how much information to share. Then she decided to play it by ear. He was the head of security here and she did have permission to loop him in, so she could tell him anything.

She would decide as the conversation progressed if he needed to know everything.

"We have reason to believe that Glida Kimura murdered her wife, Taji Kimura, two days ago," Bassima said. "I tracked Glida here. Her vehicle is outside, and as far as I can tell, she hasn't left here since she arrived."

Something twitched in his face. He didn't hide information well; at least, he didn't hide it well from people who knew how to observe.

She decided not to dance around. She was too tired for that.

"Am I wrong about that?" she asked.

"Well," he said. "It's a bit trickier than that. May I ask a few questions before I answer yours?"

"Sure," she said, and folded her hands on the tabletop. Two could play the *I'm completely relaxed even though I'm not* game.

"Are you certain she killed her wife?" he asked.

"As certain as we can be without a body," Bassima said.

"She disposed of the body?" he asked.

"Somehow," Bassima said, and then added another tidbit. "We are in the process of tracking that, and figuring out who the second murder victim was."

His mouth opened, and she realized he had been about to ask another question before he had heard her answer.

"Other victim?" he asked.

"It looks like Glida Kimura dropped a body—not Taji Kimura—into the pool behind Fiskett Falls. That body was supposed to make us think Glida had died and been dumped there, and it probably would have, too, if it had been discovered later."

He didn't look shocked. In fact, he looked intrigued.

"She planned that," he said, more to himself than to Bassima.

"Yeah," Bassima said. "But I can't figure out the end game or why she would come to work. The only thing I can figure is that there's some other exit from here that none of us in Sandoveil know about."

He shook his head so quickly that she thought he was covering something up.

"You know all the physical exits," he said. "It's the other exits that you haven't thought of."

Bassima let out a breath. The only other exit she could think of was impossible.

"I didn't think Fleet vessels took passengers," she said.

"They don't," he said.

"Then what—?"

"She tried to steal a ship," he said.

"Tried to?" Bassima asked.

He nodded. "We have no idea yet if she was successful."

"I don't understand," Bassima said.

"I know," he said. "I don't know exactly what I can tell you. I need to check a few things first."

He was going to check Bassima's background. That was what she would do in his place. But she didn't have time for screwing around.

"Listen," she said. "We only have a very short window here. If Glida tried to escape from this base, she'll try again. And we're looking at her for two murders. This is our best chance of catching her."

Nicoleau sighed. He looked as if he was about to say more, then he shook his head.

"Yeah," he said. "Today is our best chance of catching her."

His wording was odd. Bassima frowned, wishing he could tell her what he was holding back.

"If we do, we're going to have a jurisdictional nightmare." He looked down, as if he were considering something. "Can you speak for the Sandoveil Security Office?"

"As a security officer," she said.

"Legally," he clarified. "As someone who runs the office."

She felt cold, and she wasn't sure why. "I think you'll need Amy Loraas for that. Why? What's the jurisdictional problem?"

"I don't think I'm revealing anything classified when I tell you that not only will you have a case against Glida Kimura when we capture her, but so will the sector base, and so will the *Ijo*. And maybe other jurisdictions as well."

Bassima frowned. "Are you telling me she's committed crimes on the base, crimes against the *Ijo*?"

He shook his head. "It's worse than that," he said. "It's a whole hell of a lot worse."

49

Tevin pushed back his hood as he stomped out of the water.

"Tell me this is some kind of primitive sculpture," he said as he walked to the shore.

Dinithi had already reached the shore before him. She had gone to the rocky edge, as far from the group as she could get. She had her hood off, and she was losing whatever she had eaten for the past three days.

Novoa had kept pace with Tevin. She didn't look queasy or even frightened. She looked angry.

Hranek, Zhou, and Marnie Sar were crowded around screens, pointing and arguing. They didn't seem to notice Tevin.

"I said," he repeated, "tell me—"

"We heard you," Hranek said without looking up. "And since you opted to abandon the dive, we have no more information than you do."

"Actually, we do." Zhou stood up. He gave Dinithi a sideways glance, filled with concern. They had all lost their stomach contents on one recovery mission or another, and they all knew how embarrassing it could be.

Novoa grabbed some medicated water and walked past the entire group. Her body language told Tevin that she believed they should be tending Dinithi first, and only then discussing what they had seen.

He didn't care. He wanted to know what the hell was going on.

"Unless those skeletons are covered with some kind of preservative," Zhou said, "they are definitely not primitive. They could only have been in the water for a few decades at most. With that churn and the warming water temperatures from late-spring to mid-summer, those bodies would have lost any connective tissues relatively quickly. You would see some bones lodged against the rocks, but most of those bodies wouldn't be intact."

"They're recent enough to still have tissue?" Tevin asked, making sure he understood.

"Yes," Zhou said.

"You do not know that," Hranek said. "We cannot speculate, based on almost no evidence."

"*You* might not have evidence," Zhou said, "but I have plenty of it. I know how the currents work, I know how water destroys rock in that area alone. Think of bone as something not quite as strong as rock, but just as malleable. And tissue—well, you all know how tissue degrades."

"We have to conduct experiments—"

"For anything to have a legal ramification, yes," Marnie said, shutting down Hranek. He was good at his job, but he was good precisely because he was anal.

They didn't need anal here.

What they needed were members of the YSR-SR to deal with the situation at hand. Hranek wasn't a member of the YSR-SR. He was an *investigator*, with a focus on answering all the questions in an unassailable way.

Right now, Tevin needed rescue-and-recovery questions answered, not how-to questions. He needed to know if he and his team would continue to risk their lives for this…bone pile.

They needed to know if this bone pile was worth recovering.

"How do you want us to proceed?" Tevin asked Marnie.

"I counted five skulls in addition to the one you initially found, is that correct?" Marnie asked.

Tevin nodded. "And that was just on this side. We didn't go very deep."

"There's a nasty current on the edge of that rock pile." Dinithi added. Her voice was raspy. She took a swig of the medicated water, rinsed her mouth, and then spit the water out.

"You have to drink that," Novoa said softly.

"Baby steps," Dinithi said.

In spite of himself, Tevin smiled. He'd been there too. She was using taste to see if she could hold down the water.

"I don't understand the relevance of the current," Hranek said. "We're—"

"There's a lot to that current," Zhou said. "It proves my point about connective tissue."

"It also makes dives doubly and triply dangerous," Marnie said. "We need the team to investigate the bone pile, but it has its own undertows and surprise currents. We can put up a barrier, but that will hamper the investigation—"

"Which is why I came up here," Tevin said. "If we're going to recover all of those bodies, then we'll need a much larger team and a huge effort."

"We need to send in probes," Dinithi said. "Believe me, that current is so strong that I'm not sure how many probes will survive this thing. I know some people won't."

"She's right," Novoa said. "It took most of my strength to pull her back from that edge."

Tevin nodded. "Probes would work." He looked at Marnie. "This isn't something we can finish in one day."

"Yeah," she said, "I'm beginning to understand that."

Hranek sighed. Tevin looked at him, surprised. He would have thought that Hranek was the one who would want them to take their time investigating this.

"What's the hesitation, Mushtaq?" Marnie asked.

Hranek shook his head. "You're all correct. We need to take this one step at a time. I was simply hoping that I would solve at least one mystery today."

"And that is?" Marnie asked.

Hranek shrugged. He looked a little lost, something Tevin had never seen from him before.

"I thought I knew who that body belonged to," Hranek said. "I was so certain I knew how the body got here—"

"We don't have to rule anything out," Zhou said.

Tevin stared at Hranek. "I thought you didn't like to make assumptions."

Hranek gave him a bitter smile. "I don't, and this is why. Had I assumed, and had you not gone in with lights blazing, we might have proceeded from my guess, rather than from fact."

Hranek *approved* of the work Tevin was doing? That surprised him.

Marnie Sar was looking at the frozen image on all of the screens.

"We need to plan this like one of the most difficult rescues we've ever done," she said. "And, I'm sorry, Tevin, we can't go slowly."

He frowned at her. "Taking our time—"

"Oh, I would love to take our time," she said. "But this is the kind of thing that will bring out the crazies. We won't be able to protect this information and this site for very long, even with the protected entry behind these Falls. We need to work on mapping and recovering whatever the hell all that is for the next several days."

She looked around at the entire team. They all peered at the screens—everyone except Dinithi, who looked at the pool as if she expected something to launch itself out of the water and attack her.

"Does anyone disagree?" Marnie asked.

"I don't know how I feel about this." Dinithi punctuated the sentence by taking a swig of that water. She swallowed, winced, and took another sip.

Tevin watched her. She wasn't just recovering from her reaction. She was thinking about something.

"I mean," Dinithi said, her voice less raspy. "We saw parts of at least six bodies down there."

Her voice wobbled a little, and she swallowed again, this time clearly keeping something down. Her hand visibly tightened on that bottle.

"Six people, recent deaths," Dinithi said. "And then today's—yesterday's—floater. How come we didn't know that so many people had died in such a short space of time? I mean, Sandoveil is a small town. We should know this stuff, right? When someone disappears? When someone *dies*?"

Zhou looked up from the screen, and let his gaze skim the water as well. It felt to Tevin as though his team was searching the water for answers.

"A lot of strangers come through Sandoveil," Zhou said tentatively.

"Yes, they do," Hranek said, his tone businesslike. "But that's the cause of the problem, not the actual problem."

The entire team looked at him. His lips had thinned. He had deep circles under his eyes. Apparently he hadn't gotten much sleep in the last twenty-four hours either.

"The Sandoveil Valley has one of the highest death rates per capita on all of Nindowne," he said. "We also have one of the highest disappearance rates."

Tevin's stomach twisted. How come no one had ever told the YSR-SR this? Or did anyone need to tell them? After all, the YSR-SR should have been dealing with both the deaths and disappearances, at least in theory. Maybe the YSR-SR was just too busy to notice.

Or, more likely, as a primarily volunteer organization, the YSR-SR didn't have time to do anything extra, like track statistics. The YSR-SR was too busy rescuing, finding, and recovering people to pay attention to what was going on in some other community.

"And you thought it was okay to keep that a secret?" Dinithi snapped. Novoa put a hand on her arm, calming her down.

It wouldn't do to have any of them get angry right now. Their anger really wasn't at each other. It was at the situation, which had spiraled out of control.

"I wasn't keeping it a secret," Hranek said. "It was just a fact until a moment ago, one I always attributed to the terrain. We are the most heavily populated wild place on the entire planet."

"I wouldn't call Sandoveil heavily populated," Marnie said, almost under her breath.

"But it is," Hranek said. "Our population grows by factors of ten each time a Fleet ship lands. Sometimes more than one Fleet ship is at the sector base at a time. We don't usually have to worry about hotel rooms for the Fleet, but there are times when the crew must leave the ship, due to the repairs. We have enough hotel rooms and rentals to accommodate one DV-class vessel's worth of people, but not two. And that doesn't count all the tourists we get from all over Nindowne. We are one of the major tourist destinations on the entire planet."

Tevin frowned. He had known some of that, but he hadn't put it all together.

"The crews would know if someone was missing," Marnie said. She had crossed her arms.

"They would," Hranek said, "and they do. Sometimes they believe that their colleagues have deliberately left the Fleet, without saying a word. Apparently, that happens."

"It's common?" Novoa asked.

"It's not common," Hranek said. "But it happens. What happens most is that tourists either don't arrive here or don't make it home. We hear about it, but what can we do? The Sandoveil Security Office investigates, puts up notices, and lets nearby communities know that someone either didn't get home or didn't make it here. But for all we know, that person's plans changed and they went somewhere else. We rarely hear about the follow-up."

Dinithi took another swig of her water. Then she looked at the pool, her expression downcast.

Tevin looked too, but he wasn't seeing the surface of the water. He was seeing that pile of rocks and bones beneath it. That pile was huge and it went deep.

"You had an idea who did all of this," Tevin said. Even though he was speaking to Hranek, he didn't look at Hranek. Tevin kept staring at the pool, the pile superimposed over it in his mind.

"I did," Hranek said. "I must have been wrong."

"Did you think it was Glida?" Tevin asked.

Hranek didn't answer for a long moment. And no one else spoke either. The only sound was the thunder of the Falls. Spray hit Tevin's face so continually that he barely noticed it anymore.

Finally, Hranek spoke. "Why would you ask that?"

"The floating body," Tevin said. "It looked like Glida, but it wasn't."

He turned, wiping the spray off his face. Hranek's expression was flat. Novoa bit her lower lip. Zhou looked surprised. Only Dinithi hadn't changed her position.

"And the body, the one on top of that rock pile, that's Taji," Tevin said.

"I told you," Hranek snapped. "You can't do identifications without me. They're not always accurate—"

"This one's accurate," Tevin said. "I knew her. I saw the scar under her chin. She thought that scar was a badge of honor. It was Taji."

Now, it was his voice that wobbled. He hadn't expected to be emotional over Taji Kimura. They hadn't know each other that well, and he had had all night to contemplate her loss.

But somehow, saying it out loud made it real in a way that seeing her underwater hadn't.

"You thought Glida killed her and planted the other body," Tevin said. "Right?"

Hranek's lips moved for a moment, then he pursed them. "As I said, making assumptions is always a bad idea. Something else clearly is going on."

Dinithi drained the bottle, then set it in her kit.

"How would she have gotten here?" Dinithi asked.

"What?" Marnie asked.

"Glida, or whomever put these bodies in the water. How did she do it?" Dinithi frowned at all of them. "I've been trying to picture it. You can't throw them from above, not and get those rocks in position. You'd have to do it from here."

"Oh, God," Novoa said. "You're saying she *carried* the bodies in?"

"That would take someone really strong," Zhou said.

Tevin frowned. Then he shook his head. "All of it would require strength," he said. "Whether you tossed the bodies off a great height or carried them in, you'd need some upper body strength."

"And then you'd have to dive the rocks," Dinithi said. "Just like you wanted us to do."

She looked at Hranek, as if blaming him for what was going on.

"Only in reverse," he said. "I wanted you to remove the rocks."

"So, whoever did this was a diver."

"Or had access to equipment," Zhou said. "Some kind of robotic arm or something."

No one spoke again. The ground shook from the falling water. The YSR-SR had a lot of equipment designed to keep the humans out of dangerous situations. Robotic arms, some submersibles that had grappling capability. But none of them worked well in a pool of this size. It was too small. They were all designed to work in the ocean or in some of the deeper mountain lakes.

"Nothing we have could get in here," Marnie said. "Not from above or from the ground here. That's why we dive this pool. Because our equipment doesn't work here."

Everyone knew that, except Hranek. He nodded once.

"Well, speculation gets us nowhere. We need facts. And since Egbe here decided to abort the dive, facts are few and far between."

Tevin felt a rush of heat to his face. Anger. He tamped it back.

"Facts *are* few and far between," he said to Marnie. "We need probes. We'll probably lose a number of them in that current, but I think it's worthwhile."

"And we need someone to get the records from all the barriers around here," Zhou said. "We need to know who has been accessing them."

"The only people who can access them are YSR-SR," Dinithi said.

Her gaze met everyone else's, one at a time, almost as if she were accusing the entire team of murdering people and placing them in the pool.

"Yes, that's true," Marnie said.

"You think one of our people did this?" Zhou asked.

"I think Mushtaq is right," Marnie said. "Jumping to conclusions is a bad idea."

Tevin glanced over his shoulder at the path. It wouldn't be hard to get through that barrier. He couldn't remember the last time the codes were changed—if ever. And so many people had them. Including people who worked at the sector base.

But he wasn't going to say that. He was sick of speculation.

"You need to get investigators on all of the above-ground stuff," he said to Hranek.

Hranek nodded.

"And you need to ask yourself one other question," Tevin said.

Hranek frowned.

"It goes to the heart of your assumption earlier." Tevin knew he was toying with Hranek a little, but he didn't care. Hranek had given him enough grief over the years. He didn't mind paying it back.

"What does?" Hranek asked.

"If a person or persons unknown hid these bodies in the pool, and went through all the difficulty of placing rocks on them to hold them in place," Tevin said, "then why was the body dressed like Glida Kimura allowed to float?"

"The killer got interrupted?" Zhou said, apparently enjoying the speculation.

But Tevin hadn't asked that to speculate, and Hranek knew it. Tevin could see that from Hranek's face. They were still on the earlier conclusion.

They were missing an important piece. But it felt like they were missing only one important piece—and once they had it, everything would fall into place.

"You still think she's involved," Dinithi said.

"Yes," Tevin said. "I just don't know how."

"Speculation," Hranek said and turned away.

"More like an educated guess," Tevin said, and left it at that.

50

THE WORK WAS RELATIVELY SIMPLE: accessing an *anacapa* drive's memory was something Bristol did almost weekly. But because she didn't want to turn this drive back on a second time if she discovered she had not gotten enough information, she accessed every backup memory subroutine in the drive, and hoped that would be enough.

Once she and Fedo had powered on this drive, they worked quickly. Because the drive's resting colors were as odd as the colors it had when it was off. There was no white or gold in the light that came from this particular *anacapa*, something she had never seen before.

The light was the same yellowish, puke green as one of the color threads going through the drive when it wasn't on at all. A flat, brownish rust wove through the puke green, and beneath it all, a twilight gray throbbed.

The power readings were all over the chart. Fedo got different readings than Bristol did, so they both decided at the same time to get the information they needed and shut the drive off again.

As soon as they had, Fedo had leaned back and wiped sweat off her forehead.

"This thing is dangerous," she said. "And to think we carried it with us on the *Ijo*."

Bristol didn't comment. It wasn't her place.

Rather than converse with Fedo, Bristol investigated the drive's memory. Some of it was as hole-riddled as the drive itself, but with all of the subroutines, she could read where this drive had been, when it had been activated, and how long it had been in foldspace.

As she examined the memory, she started forming a theory. But she needed Fedo's help. So Bristol said, "I need you to double-check the years that Kimura—I mean, whatsername? Evers—?"

"Everly," Fedo said.

"—the years she served on the *Ijo*. See where this runabout went then," Bristol said.

"All right," Fedo said.

Bristol dug into the data while Fedo did her work. Then Bristol stepped away from that information and contacted her team. In particular, she wanted to know what Rajivk had found.

She pinged him in his own lab first.

He responded with a video image of his lab station. He was at the side of the image, head bent as he clearly worked a console.

"How can I help you?" he asked.

She loved the question, because the tone in which he delivered it was essentially, *Tell me what you need or leave me alone.*

"Were there problems when the runabout left the *Ijo*?" she asked. "Did the runabout end up in the storage room at the precise coordinates? Was there something unusual?"

Rajivk didn't even have to check his data. He had clearly been exploring this.

"It took longer than average to arrive," he said. "But by longer than average, I mean milliseconds longer. I wouldn't have found it if I hadn't been looking for anomalies."

"Did you find any other anomalies?" she asked.

"No," he said. "And I've been searching the base. We don't have a runabout half in and half out of phase, either."

She let out a small sigh. Apparently, on a subconscious level, she had been more worried about that than she had realized.

Fedo looked up at that, startled. Apparently that particular malfunction hadn't even crossed her mind until just now.

"Well, that's good news, I guess," Bristol said.

Rajivk shook his head ever so slightly. If Bristol hadn't been watching him closely, she wouldn't have seen it.

"Yeah, there's no one dying in our walls," he said. "That's a good thing."

She felt her cheeks warm. That wasn't what she meant. She would have liked to know where the damn runabout was, and if it were stuck in a wall somewhere, she would know.

She severed the connection without commenting, only to find Fedo watching her.

"He's your subordinate?" Fedo asked, with judgment in her tone.

"We don't follow military protocol here," Bristol snapped.

"Clearly," Fedo said.

She ignored Fedo and contacted the rest of the team. So far, they had found no evidence of the runabout in this solar system.

It was as she expected.

After she finished with them, she asked Fedo, "Did you find anything from the years that Everly was with the *Ijo*?"

"I'm not done yet," Fedo said.

Bristol felt a surge of irritation and tamped it down. Virji—Fedo's captain—had stressed the need to hurry. Bristol felt it. Why hadn't Fedo?

Or was this how fast Fedo worked?

"Give me what you have," Bristol said.

She only wanted to confirm something anyway. She had found an entire series of trips, one per week for a few years, that entered foldspace in the same way. The trips, as far as she could tell from the damaged *anacapa*, ended up in different places—different solar systems, different planets—but they always left the *Ijo* the same way, into a foldspace bubble that someone had created as a contained foldspace entry point.

Bristol had hoped to find something like that. Because if a ship used a foldspace bubble, the ship was likely to have a default set to that bubble on its navigational system.

But she thought she would check one more thing with Fedo.

"Is your captain the one who prefers the use of a foldspace bubble or does that predate you?" Bristol asked, head down. She tried not to sound judgmental. Foldspace bubbles sometimes attached themselves to small ships, and created little warps that made foldspace dangerous for larger vessels.

"No," Fedo said, sounding surprised. "*Ijo* policy expressly forbids the use of foldspace bubbles. The Fleet discourages it too. We've lost too many good people over the years because of the bubbles. We have always considered them too risky to maintain. Why? Have you found one?"

"For years, this runabout used a foldspace bubble," Bristol said. "I'm assuming nothing about that practice changed, at least for this particular runabout."

Fedo made a soft sound of disgust. "Why don't people listen?"

Bristol didn't know the answer to that, although she would assume that someone like Kimura wouldn't have listened no matter who had forbidden her to do something.

Then Fedo looked at her, eyes wide. "You think that runabout is in its foldspace bubble?"

"I think it tried to find the bubble," Bristol said. "I'm sure that Kimura or Everly or whatever you call her activated the navigational program that would send the runabout to the bubble. But I doubt she got into the bubble the way she wanted to. The navigational system might have been compromised, the maintenance system definitely was, and with a different *anacapa* in place, the ship wouldn't have some of its usual backups."

"Well, that makes it even harder to find her," Fedo said.

Bristol almost rolled her eyes. That settled it: Fedo simply wasn't of a caliber that would ever allow her to work for Bristol. Bristol wondered how Fedo had gotten her job in the first place.

Bristol hoped it was some kind of nepotism, because if Fedo was the best the Fleet had out in space, the entire Fleet was in trouble.

"Actually," Bristol said, "it just got easier to find her. We can narrow down the routes into that bubble."

"But you just said the ship wouldn't know them," Fedo said.

"I said that she wouldn't have gotten to the bubble the way she wanted to, and I mean that," Bristol said. "The ship might have taken a circuitous route. Or it might have found a quick way into the bubble, a way that punched the bubble. Or it might have missed by a few degrees. We don't know."

"That's what I'm saying," Fedo said. "We don't know."

"Ah," Bristol said, "but now we know where to look."

51

SHE HAD A PROTECTIVE SECURITY COVERING over her coat. Bassima had almost asked Nicoleau if the coating would ruin her coat's fabric, and then decided that sounded too self-involved. She really wasn't self-involved.

She was just scared to death.

She had always wanted to go deep inside the sector base, and now that she was here, she was wondering if it was a good idea.

Bassima had agreed readily enough. Nicoleau asked her if she wanted to be present when they captured Glida Kimura. Bassima had said yes. She had to clear her presence deep in the bowels of the sector base with Amy Loraas, but Amy had approved and had given Bassima permission to handle whatever came up.

Although Bassima was beginning to wonder if she was qualified to handle any of it.

She and Nicoleau had gone through five layers of security so far. Each seemed more draconian than the last. More people, more examination, more sideways looks.

Even though Nicoleau headed security for the base, his own staff questioned him the deeper the two of them got into the sector base. They would ask him if he thought it a good idea to bring a "civilian" to the most dangerous part of the base, as if he hadn't realized that Bassima even accompanied him.

Each time someone asked him, he would smile and say *Yes*. No justification, no explanation. Just a simple yes. He seemed unperturbed by the questions, the attitude, or the situation.

Bassima was perturbed by all of it. The base had a surprising sameness to its corridors and ceilings. They were made of some shiny black substance, probably the nanobits that the Fleet engineers had used to carve out various parts of the Sandoveil Valley, including the overlook where the shoes were discovered.

It was one thing to look at the shiny black nanobits covered with spray from the waterfall, another to see them deep below the largest mountain range on Nindowne. She knew the deeper she went, the harder it would be to get out.

She didn't say anything to Nicoleau, though. Instead, she listened to his concerns about Glida Kimura, whom he said the Fleet had known as Sloane Everly. He'd said Glida had killed people before, and that the captain of the *Ijo* wanted her captured, which was why he had asked Bassima if she could handle jurisdiction.

The more he spoke, the more Bassima wondered if she could. If what he said was true, there were going to be dozens of jurisdictions at play. There were three in the Sandoveil Valley alone—Sandoveil, possibly the Valley security force, and then the security team at the sector base. None of that counted this captain, who was apparently out for blood, or any of the places that the captain believed Glida Kimura had gone to murder people for sport.

Bassima wouldn't have believed any of that if she hadn't seen the footage from the night before and spoken to Hranek about Glida. Glida had seemed a little off, but not that far off.

Apparently, Glida had learned how to mask her abnormalities, at least somewhat. She had always seemed unusual—those colorful clothes, the occasional cold glance—but she had never seemed dangerous or even stranger than most people in Sandoveil.

Glida had masked her abnormalities long enough to appeal to Taji. To *live* with Taji. Until something had gone terribly wrong.

Bassima shook her head every time she thought of Taji. Taji seemed too nice, too normal to have married someone with Glida's history.

The last security checkpoint—or whatever they called it at the sector base—was in a roundish, bowl-like area, with corridors funneling off it on six sides. The guards down here seemed extremely serious. They made Bassima stand in the corridor while they argued with Nicoleau.

From what she could overhear, they weren't just worried that she might do something dangerous or illegal. They were worried that she would reveal secrets. Apparently, Nicoleau was trying to take her to a part of the sector base that most people who worked at the sector base couldn't go to.

Finally, he agreed to be the one to sign off on everything. The guards' names wouldn't be on any approval that had gotten Bassima through. If she did something wrong, Nicoleau would have to take the blame.

Which, apparently, he was willing to do.

She wasn't so much fascinated by the arguments the other guards had; she was fascinated by the fact that he couldn't just override them, even though he ran security.

Nicoleau waved her through. The security this time was tighter than the last—she had to go through various boxes and readers, and submit to searches with devices she had never seen before. She had to give up DNA and saliva, register a voice print, and have her retina scanned.

Only after all of that was she allowed to follow Nicoleau through the narrowest corridor spiraling off the security area.

None of the doors down this corridor were marked. A few seemed almost invisible, at least to her.

Yet Nicoleau seemed to know which door he wanted. He pressed a palm against a side panel and the door slid open.

A woman cursed, followed by, "This is not the time to bring in a crowd."

"I'm not bringing in a crowd," Nicoleau said, blocking Bassima's entrance with his body. "I'm bringing in Bassima Beck, with the city of Sandoveil's security office."

"Great," the woman said, voice rising with irritation. "Just great. I hope she knows the dangers."

The hair rose on the back of Bassima's neck. Dangers?

"She knows," Nicoleau said, but Bassima wanted to contradict him. What dangers? He hadn't mentioned any dangers.

"All right, then," the woman said, "but don't talk to us or touch anything. We're still not sure this is going to work."

Nicoleau stepped farther into the lab. Bassima followed, gingerly, still wondering if she could flee.

The lab smelled of sweat and recycled air. There was an underlying funk that apparently the environmental system couldn't get rid of, as if someone had actually lived here, and bathed only occasionally. Overlying that was a metallic tang that Bassima couldn't identify, except that she knew she had never smelled it before.

The walls were covered with screens, some active and some not. Consoles jutted out from them, but the two women in the center of the lab were working on holographic screens, the kind Bassima preferred.

People stood all over the lab, most of them watching the two women work. Bassima recognized only one of them, a lean man with brownish hair and a rather sullen mouth. She had seen him around a lot, not in the stores or the diner, but walking.

He was one of the people who hiked all over the city, and sometimes on the trails around the Falls. Whenever she was in a vehicle, hurrying to get from place to place, she'd see him plodding along, and feel guilty that she wasn't getting enough exercise.

A couple of people were talking quietly about some storage room. Everyone else was watching the two women work. They seemed involved in what they were doing, heads down, fingers moving quickly. They would consult with each other in single words and half sentences, as if they both understood what the other meant.

One woman stood apart. She had broad shoulders and a trim figure, with perfect posture. Bassima hadn't seen her before, but she had seen her type. That woman was a senior officer in the Fleet. She wasn't in uniform at the moment, but she looked like she would be more comfortable if she were.

Maybe she was the one who had spoken. She certainly seemed to be the kind who would take charge.

Her gaze met Bassima's, took her in, and then looked away as if Bassima were unimportant.

Nicoleau moved Bassima toward a wall where no one was standing. As he brought her down here, he had made it sound like they had already brought the runabout back. All they needed to know was if Glida was inside.

But that clearly wasn't the case. They were still working on bringing the runabout back.

Bassima sighed softly.

Had she known that, she would have insisted that Loraas come here, not her.

And then Bassima mentally smiled at herself. That wasn't true. She had wanted to go deep into the security base—until she had gone deep and realized just how scary it all was.

She moved closer to the wall but didn't lean, in case there were features that she couldn't see, things she would be messing with that she didn't understand.

Considering how hard it had been to get here in the first place, she doubted they would let her go back to the surface on her own.

But she wasn't sure how long she could stand here.

And then she realized she had no choice.

52

It took a long time to set up the probes. Part of the problem was that Marnie didn't want anyone new brought in to the death scene, as Hranek now called this pool. Marnie was afraid that she would get too many volunteers.

And Dinithi's point was a good one: the only people who had easy access to the pool were all volunteers at the YSR-SR.

Besides, who better than the YSR-SR to carry out deaths like this? Someone in the YSR-SR would know who was missing, who was hard to find, who didn't have help. Some of the volunteers worked alone, and all of them had YSR-SR identification.

While the identification didn't make them instantly trustworthy, it did help. That was one reason she insisted her teams all have identification.

Of course, the identification had to be earned. Everyone had to go through psych evaluations to make sure they could handle the stresses of the job, through physical training to determine their aptitudes, and then intern—for lack of a better word—at more than a dozen rescue/recoveries before ever becoming an official volunteer.

Marnie liked to think she knew everyone who worked at the YSR-SR, and she liked to think she trusted them.

If someone had asked her yesterday if she did, she would have said yes.

But today? No. She would have to say that almost everyone who worked for the YSR-SR was a suspect, at least in her mind.

She had to rule out this team. They were still working the pool, tirelessly, making certain all the details were correct. She had to think—making an assumption in a way that Hranek probably wouldn't approve of—that the team wouldn't be working this hard if one of them was involved in placing all the bodies here.

Besides, it was hard to fake a physical reaction like the one that Dinithi had earlier in the day.

Still, Marnie kept her eye on all of them, so maybe she wasn't being as trusting as she would normally be.

Zhou had set up monitors so that they could all watch the feeds coming from the probes Marnie planned to send into the pool. Dinithi had stripped out of her suit and was sitting in the sun, making sure all of the probes were linked up properly. She was also checking to make certain they could handle the currents below.

Tevin had reinforced the barriers. He still wore his suit, and went in and out of the water several times to plant some lights near the work area. The probes all had lights, but he wanted this thing flooded.

He also offered to drop some lights into the trench, but Marnie had overruled him on that. She didn't want the lights to bang their way down in the current and destroy something that might end up as evidence later.

Novoa had coordinated everything while Marnie went back to the YSR-SR to get equipment. The reason the team still seemed to function smoothly had little to do with Marnie or with Tevin, but with Novoa.

She had also helped Marnie carry the equipment into the pool area. Floating carts were useless back here. The spray from the Falls got into their mechanisms. Many floating carts got tangled in the waterfall itself.

Marnie had lost too many carts over the years to leave anything like that to chance.

She brought in two carts, but she and Novoa held them and didn't use the guidance systems or the autopilots.

"And there," Tevin had said as the first cart came in, "is how our killer or killers brought the bodies in here."

Marnie hadn't responded to any of that. Because the fact that the killer or killers had known how to maneuver a cart through these narrow paths meant that the killer or killers had some kind of working knowledge of how everything functioned back here.

Which, she supposed, the killer or killers could have gotten through their own personal experience.

But she kept thinking about the timeline—the fact that, as Zhou had said, the bodies still had some of their connective tissue—and she knew that whoever had done this, had done it in a relatively short space of time.

Marnie supposed anyone could learn in a short space of time, but in her experience, people didn't do things more than once if those things were hard.

Unless the person in question loved a challenge.

Marnie and Novoa had also brought in food, enough to last through the evening. Marnie had spent part of her trip back into Sandoveil trying to plan how this operation would work.

She figured they needed the information from the probes, and that would be what they focused on today. After that, they would have to bring in other team members.

Recovery was going to take days, longer if Hranek still wanted the rocks.

He wasn't here to ask any longer. He had gone back to Sandoveil to continue work on the body he had and the death scenes he was overseeing. Plus, he looked like a man who desperately needed some sleep.

By rights, Marnie should have needed sleep as well, but she didn't. She had trained herself to handle long jobs like this one. She wouldn't be handling all the detail work—she was going to leave that to the team—but she would still need to do some of it.

And, from what she gathered, she had gotten a little more sleep than Hranek had the night before.

"We're barely going to get coverage with ten probes." Zhou opened a holographic screen near her. It had a map he had drawn up. "Here's what we know of the currents near that trench and structure. I think we'll need five probes on that side of the pile all by themselves, rather than the two you've allotted."

"We're using two," she said calmly. She was used to being questioned like this. She wasn't even going to explain herself.

The first two probes on that side of the pile were sacrificial. They would show what the currents were now, as opposed to at dawn, and they would probably show what other dangers lurked on that side of the structure.

If the probes made it out all right, then she would send in even more, because Zhou was right: two was really not enough.

This operation was going to cost the YSR-SR a lot of money. She was already planning on losing two probes. She had a hunch she would lose a lot more before the day was out.

"I think we're good to go," Dinithi said. She had color in her face again. Earlier that day, Marnie hadn't been sure whether or not she should send Dinithi home.

But Marnie was unwilling to. She didn't want to let anyone out of her sight—hers and Novoa's.

Marnie had brought Novoa in on this instead of Tevin because Tevin had told everyone he had known Taji. That meant that he might actually have a motive to kill her, although if Marnie was pressed, she would say Tevin was uninvolved.

Of all the people she knew, Tevin seemed the least likely to murder anyone, even when provoked.

Novoa hadn't known Taji Kimura, or at least, hadn't known her well. Marnie wasn't an investigator and didn't know exactly how to ask her team if they were involved with the dead woman, without somehow leading them.

So she had decided to trust them as best she could.

Still, she had urged Zhou to keep an eye on Novoa, and Novoa to keep an eye on everyone else.

Paranoia was ruling the day out here, which irritated her to no end.

"Want me to double-check the probes?" Novoa asked Marnie.

"That would be triple-check," Zhou said. He sounded a little irritated.

Marnie decided to ignore that.

Tevin stood half in the water. He looked almost feral. His hair was dry, but spiky because it had been wet earlier. He still had the lower half of his diving equipment on, while the upper half just hung off his back. He was getting too much sun—or maybe his skin was always ruddy like this after exertion.

That, she had never paid attention to before.

He looked all right, though.

"The barriers are holding," he said, "and the light is good."

He swept a hand toward the pool. The sun had finally crested over the mountain peaks and hit the pool, making it look green and grainy. Considering how small this pool was, the sun wouldn't be here long, especially at this time of year.

He was right: they only had about two hours of sunlight on the water to work with.

Although the probes were going so deep into that trench, Marnie doubted sunlight had reached those depths in years. If ever.

Was that why the bodies were hidden here? And if it was, why leave one body floating, to point out that the others existed?

She only had one answer at the moment, and she didn't like it.

It felt like a giant arrow on the water, accompanied by the words *Ha-ha, idiots. Look at what you missed.*

And they *had* missed it. They had missed all of it.

Marnie took a deep breath. Finally, she understood the truth that Hranek had been expressing all along. They couldn't speculate. They didn't dare speculate.

Not only because they might be wrong, but also because it was so very demoralizing.

Right now, she needed to know what was down there. Then she would figure out how to deal with it all.

"All right," she said, bracing herself. "Let's send in those probes."

53

The lab was unusually quiet, and it felt stuffy. The environmental system here wasn't set up for so many people. Virji didn't know all of them. She knew Fedo, of course, who was working with Iannazzi to finalize the whatever they were going to do to recall the runabout. Fedo had tried to explain their change in thinking, but it had gotten too technical for Virji—and she was usually good with technical.

All of Iannazzi's team had returned, and all of them stood near consoles, clearly prepared to step in should something go wrong. Wèi and his team scattered throughout the room and then Nicoleau had brought in another woman—big, tall, and wide-eyed. Obviously, she'd never been in a lab like this one.

Virji wasn't going to ask for history on the Beck woman. Nicoleau thought it important for her to be here, which was good enough for Virji.

Virji's entire crew had returned to the *Ijo*. They now stood by.

She wanted her staff to be ready if the runabout boomeranged back to the *Ijo* instead of the storage room. She wanted someone to storm that little runabout and pull Sloane Everly off it. Virji wanted that woman in custody.

Virji rubbed her hands in anticipation, wishing this would get underway faster, yet knowing that something experimental like this was better if it wasn't rushed.

"All right," Iannazzi said as she looked up from the screens she had been working on. "We're a go."

"Now?" Rajivk asked. "What about—?"

Iannazzi held up a finger at him, silencing him. She was about to speak when Wèi said, "I'll take the security team into the storage unit."

Virji could almost see Iannazzi consider it. And the consideration wasn't one of safety: it was one of annoyance. Virji had felt that way many times throughout her career—if someone wanted to be stupid, she was willing to let them be stupid, so long as it didn't get them killed. Particularly if they annoyed her, as Wèi clearly annoyed Iannazzi.

"No," Fedo said forcefully, missing all of the interpersonal dynamics. "This runabout has a lot of damage. If it got lost in foldspace for a while, it might have other issues as well. We have no idea what's going to happen when it returns here."

"What do you mean, no idea?" asked one of Wèi's security personnel, a woman.

"Precisely that," Iannazzi said. "The runabout could show up and be just fine. It could boomerang just as we expected, ending up in the storage room. It could arrive slightly off-coordinates, and end up on a different part of the floor or in the wall."

Or out here, Virji added mentally, but didn't say since everyone seemed on edge enough.

"It could explode," Iannazzi said, "like we initially thought it had. There are a thousand ways this entire operation could go wrong. Including that it won't work at all."

No one spoke. Everyone stared at Iannazzi, as if they hadn't thought of any of that. Most of them hadn't.

In fact, the new woman, Beck, shifted slightly. Virji got a sense that Beck wanted to bolt right now, maybe even run screaming from the room. Clearly, she was not raised in the Fleet, nor would she ever qualify for it.

"But don't worry," Iannazzi said with a little more relish than Virji would have. "The blast doors should hold if there is an explosion."

Beck looked from side to side. Virji almost smiled. If Beck could have snuck out of the room, she clearly would have done so.

"If Kimura is in that runabout," Wèi said, "how do we prevent her from just firing the runabout back up and heading out before we even get into the storage room?"

Iannazzi gave him a withering glance. She clearly disliked him.

"She could do that whether you're in the room or not," Fedo said before Iannazzi could answer. "It's a risk we're all going to have to take."

Besides, Virji knew, they would simply boomerang the runabout back again. Or they would try. There were several tricks the sector base could use, with the help of the *Ijo,* if it came down to it.

She had an open comm link to the *Ijo* just in case. But she wasn't going to reassure Wèi either. Virji wanted Sloane Everly to face justice, but justice throughout the sector, not just justice on the base.

"We're going to watch the storage room live," Iannazzi said. "We'll see what happened this time. We've finally rigged cameras into that room so that we'll know what occurs with the runabout."

She moved her hand over one of the holographic screens. The wall screens all came on, half showing the interior of that storage room, and the rest showing some sort of space view. Virji frowned. Had they already connected with the runabout? Because sometimes space views showed what the ship that the system had linked to was seeing.

She had no real idea, and she wasn't going to question it. She didn't want her eagerness to show.

Virji had lived with the ghost of Everly for years.

This time, she would bring Everly to justice herself, make Everly pay for everything she had done. Everly would understand the agony she had put families through—the agony she had put the crew of the *Ijo* through.

No matter what the onboard psychiatrists said. They claimed people like Everly never understood the consequences of their actions, because their emotions were wired differently.

But Virji would prove them wrong. She would make Everly feel the pain she had caused.

Somehow.

All Virji wanted was the opportunity.

And it looked like she just might get it.

54

The probes streamed into the pool like big fat fish. Tevin watched them until they disappeared under the surface. Then he slogged back to the shore, where Marnie and his team waited.

Dinithi already had a hand over her forehead. Novoa had her arms wrapped around her waist. Zhou was fiddling with something in front of him, and Marnie was shaking her head.

Ten probes, ten pieces of information. Ten times the confusion.

Tevin had known that would happen, but he hadn't wanted to weigh in until everyone saw the problem. Solutions came quicker when everyone agreed about what was wrong.

"Unify the information streams," he said to Zhou, "and build a three-D holographic model. *Not* life-size."

Because life-size would take up the entire dry patch that they were working on, plus half of the cliff face. He knew that without doing actual measurements.

That pile spread out as it went deeper. If it filled the trench, it would end up being bigger than he ever wanted to imagine.

It only took a moment for Zhou to follow Tevin's instruction. Zhou had defined the information that would be in the 3D model so that it didn't include the swim toward the pile, which was smart. Tevin hadn't thought of that.

The model appeared between Zhou and the three women. It carved a human-sized image in the area around them, kind of an opaque shadow, one that Tevin recognized. Whenever the probes and computers did not have enough information, they built something like this.

Right now, all the probes had were the trench, its depth, and the top of the pile. So they knew how tall it was, and the hologram established that by creating a white space around it all.

As Tevin walked toward the group, no one moved. It was as if they couldn't take their gazes off that big patch of nothingness.

Then, as he got close, he saw that it had already formed into a bit of the pile. The top existed all the way around, a small mound, with rocks on the top, and Taji's body, bent and broken, one arm waving in the nonexistent water.

Her necklace floated upward, visible only as a small black line so miniscule that it seemed like a flaw in the image.

Tevin joined the others, watched as the pile emerged, layer by layer. Rocks and seaweed and strands of hair. Skulls and finger bones tapping away at the emptiness.

Zhou had been right. Most of the connective tissue still held everything in place, which was just plain creepy.

The probes continue to delve downward because the pile kept emerging. Femurs and pelvises and ankles—some of the feet missing.

Tevin swallowed hard. Now he was feeling just a little queasy, not because everything was so graphic, but because there was so much of it.

No one spoke. They just watched.

He walked around them all, looking at the entire model, stunned at what he saw.

He counted ten skulls, then eleven, then twelve. And he couldn't quite understand the layout—not where the rocks were placed, but how the bodies had been placed.

Some of the lower bodies had lost their small bones—the fingers were gone, leaving parts of the arm and sometimes not even that. The image grew darker as it went down, and he wasn't sure if that was because the information from the probes reflected the loss of the sunlight on the water, or because they had gone deeply into that trench.

As he walked around the mountainside of the image, something wavered, and then blanked out. The growing information stopped on that side entirely.

"Lost a probe," he said, since he was the only one on that side of the image at the moment.

"Yeah, I know," Zhou said. "Cherish, prep another for me, will you?"

"Two more," Marnie said. Her voice sounded strangled, as if it hurt her to talk.

They were all pretending to be professional, but there was nothing to be professional about. None of them had ever seen anything like this.

Novoa took a step toward Tevin, her own fingers white where they grabbed the black shirt she always wore under her diving equipment.

"This can't be the work of one person," she said, but she didn't sound convinced.

Of course it could be the work of one person, over a long, long period of time. But he didn't understand why anyone would do this.

"I mean, this couldn't be something from the sector base, or something, could it?" Novoa asked.

"No, it's not," Marnie said. "They handle their own corpses."

She had gotten blunt. Heaven help all of them when Marnie got blunt. Blunt meant she no longer cared about anyone's feelings. Blunt meant she had had enough.

"So even if one of their mighty ships blew up," she said, "and flung dead bodies everywhere, the sector base would deal with it all."

"And besides," Zhou said softly, "they didn't need to hide the bodies here. If they wanted to hide bodies, they could just send them into space."

Tevin looked away from the empty patch at Zhou. Zhou was right. That one little comment, that one little insight, confirmed something that had niggled at Tevin.

Whoever did this was a local. Someone with a lot of knowledge about the way everything worked in Sandoveil, the Sandoveil Valley, and in Sandoveil government. The person (or persons) would also have a working knowledge of the YSR-SR.

Tevin took a small breath. Those three details meant that it wouldn't be hard to find whoever did this. Because, as Dinithi pointed out earlier, there weren't that many locals in Sandoveil. And there were even fewer that knew the workings of the YSR-SR.

That didn't mean that whoever did this was a current or former member of the YSR-SR. Someone close to the organization, yes—like a spouse or a close friend of someone who volunteered.

But not necessarily a member.

He hoped.

"Got them," Dinithi said, and for a moment, Tevin thought she meant that she had figured out who had done this horrible thing.

She meant that she was releasing the new probes. He turned so he could watch.

They scuttled across the surface of the water until they reached the edge of the barrier and then they sank underneath it.

Something in their telemetry told them that this was a better approach than the ones the now missing probe had used.

The waterfall roared and pounded, the water spilling over the edges of that cliff, nonstop, relentless.

That was the problem: Tevin wasn't being relentless. He was looking at this as a gigantic tragedy for the town and for the YSR-SR. Not to mention the recovery teams that would dive it, and the people who would have to deal with the remains.

But there was another way to look at this entire thing. Now, at least a dozen families would get information, maybe even closure, about what had happened to their loved ones. And the Sandoveil Security Office would find the person or persons who did this and stop even more killing.

It wasn't the best solution, but there were no good solutions in situations like this.

There was only discovery, which would answer questions and bring something that had been hidden into the light.

If he pursued whoever had done this as relentlessly as that water spilled into this pool, he would make a difference.

He would help someone, even a little.

The missing part of the holographic image filled in, and he wished it hadn't.

Two more skulls, one almost on top of the other. A ribcage that didn't seem attached to either of them.

And more jewelry and bits of clothing, trapped under the rocks.

The entire base of this pile was still unmapped. The destruction looked like a sculpture carved on top of marble. A hideous, disgusting sculpture.

Novoa sighed beside him. "We're going to spend months on this, aren't we?"

He nodded, although "months" probably wasn't accurate. "Years" was more likely. And then procedures would change, because of this, and the casual nature of life in Sandoveil would go away, along with the base.

The world he had grown up in, the *community* he had grown up in, would no longer be something he recognized. Maybe not in thirty years, like he had expected with the base closure, but next year or the year after.

They couldn't trust each other anymore.

They had let a predator into their community, and now, everyone would pay.

55

Bristol looked at Fedo. They had become compatriots in this quest to get the runabout back. Fedo seemed pale, but determined.

Everyone else in the lab looked either frightened or a little too tough. Only Virji seemed unfazed by this. She leaned back, arms crossed, as if daring someone to anger her further.

Bristol took a deep breath, and nodded ever so slightly at Fedo, asking *Ready?* without saying a word.

Fedo nodded back, almost imperceptibly.

Then Bristol activated the program they had developed together.

It pooled all of their resources—the maintenance mode that Fedo had designed, the linked *anacapa* rescue system inside the sector base, and the educated guesses that Bristol had made about the runabout's location.

She waited, breathing shallowly, hoping that this would work. If it didn't, she wasn't sure what to do next.

People stared at the screens. Fedo watched her own holographic screen to see if the runabout turned up inside the *Ijo*. Bristol's screen ran a series of numbers along with all of the other coordinate information she had gathered, but so far she was getting nothing.

Nothing at all.

If they didn't capture this woman, someone would have to conduct some kind of search. If they didn't capture her, she would continue harming people everywhere.

Bristol would have to write some kind of program so that the sector base could continually search for the runabout, even once the base was closed. She'd make the search automated, and she'd make sure that Glida Whatever-hernameis would come back here, even if it were years in the future.

It would serve her right.

But Bristol doubted that would happen. She had a hunch they would all end up as frustrated as Virji, constantly searching for the ghost of a woman who had bested them a thousand times over.

Bristol wasn't even certain there was a good punishment for Glida. Everyone would fight over jurisdiction, and she'd be an old woman before someone decided to try her or imprison her.

She would get away with everything.

No one wanted that. But even with Bristol's limited knowledge of the way the various justice systems worked, scattered throughout the sector, Bristol had a hunch that Glida *would* get away with it all.

Glida was smart. She could play one group against another. She might even find another way to escape.

Not that she would need to, since it looked like she had already gotten away. It looked like Glida Kimura was gone forever.

Then the blast doors slammed against the wall, making the entire lab shiver. Nanobits rained down from the ceiling, something Bristol had never seen before.

The new woman—Beck?—looked up, startled, as if she were afraid the entire base would fall in on them.

Bristol glanced at the monitors.

The runabout sat in the middle of the storage room, ice fog rising off the surface. The temperature in the storage room had dropped almost fifty degrees in the few seconds since the runabout arrived.

"Is that it?" Wēi asked. "That looks like it."

He sounded excited. He gestured to his team and started heading toward the door.

"You wait," Bristol said with more command in her voice than she had ever used before. "We're checking the environment first."

Glida Kimura was a dangerous woman. She might have planned for a contingency like this. If she had, she might actually have some of the shipboard chemicals isolated and ready to deploy as a weapon outside the runabout.

That was what Bristol would do. She would attack any way she could—if she couldn't get the runabout out of the base a second time.

After all, Glida had nothing to lose. She had already killed people, so killing more wouldn't make that much of a difference. And it might buy her enough time to get the runabout ready to leave again.

Maybe.

The environmental system in the storage room had restored the temperature to normal. The system wasn't doing any extra work, according to the information Bristol was getting, so Glida hadn't deployed any makeshift weapons.

Bristol glanced at Fedo. Fedo shrugged one shoulder. She wasn't seeing anything.

Then Bristol looked at her team. They were all focused on their screens, except for Rajivk.

"See anything unusual?" she asked him.

"Yeah," he said. "Look at the exterior of that ship."

He meant the runabout. She looked, ran a composite.

The runabout was in much worse shape than it had been a few days ago. The exterior, which had been pockmarked before, seemed thinner. It looked like there might actually be a hole in its side.

Bristol couldn't get her equipment to examine that, not closely, and not given the limited resources she had in the storage room.

"Any way your people can detect life forms in that runabout?" Bristol asked Fedo.

Because Bristol hadn't thought to set anything like that up in the storage area. She never had need of major scanning equipment there before. What she did have was limited, even in the lab, because she worked on *anacapa* drives, not on ships.

The person who answered Bristol wasn't Fedo. It was Virji.

"I've already checked," Virji said. "We're not reading anything. But there seems to be some sort of interference with the *Ijo*'s scans."

"Because of a malfunctioning *anacapa* drive," Fedo said to Bristol, not to Virji. "It's acting as a low-level cloak."

Bristol's mouth went dry. Glida could have planned that. She might have booby-trapped the entire runabout.

"Is the *anacapa naturally* acting that way?" Bristol asked. "Or did *she* do it?"

"I think it's from the *anacapa* you installed," Fedo said, without blame. "I think that's how it's interacting with all those problems inside the runabout."

Maybe. But that was all speculation.

"I don't think it matters," Virji said. "We have to go get her before she manages to get that runabout functional again."

Bristol wasn't sure what functional meant. But she did understand the dangers.

"If anyone goes in there as she sets off that *anacapa* to take the runabout back into foldspace," Bristol said, "all of us could die. If the blast doors are open—"

"Then vacate the lab," Virji snapped. "Because we're going in."

56

VIRJI DIDN'T CARE ABOUT the delicate sensibilities of the planet-bound. They had no idea how to face any kind of danger, with their layers of security and their tiny worries about a base closure that would happen decades from now.

They were weak, and they were scared, and they were in her way.

She glared at all of them, mentally daring them to stay in the lab.

That Beck woman tugged on Nicoleau's sleeve. He shook his head once. Clearly she wanted to leave, and he didn't want to go. Since she was, apparently, reliant on him, she would have to stay too.

"If you want to go in, come with me," Virji said to Wèi. She'd let him take the arrest as the security of the Fleet's sector base. She'd argue jurisdiction later.

But she was going to have the satisfaction of taking that murdering bitch into custody. Virji wouldn't kill her, but Virji would certainly let her know just what kind of shit she found herself in.

Virji was trembling ever so slightly. Adrenaline. She wanted Everly in the worst way.

"If you're coming with us, Captain," Wèi said, "you'll have to stay toward the back. This is our op."

"*My* op," Virji said. "You're with me."

She didn't care about protocol. She only cared about getting Everly.

Virji shoved her way past the stupid lab spectators, most of whom still looked stunned at the idea that they might die this afternoon, and approached the blast doors.

"Open them," she said to Iannazzi.

Iannazzi didn't hesitate. She moved a finger, and some kind of command went through her screen to the blast doors. They shuddered, making more nanobits fall from the ceiling.

A couple people looked up, worried.

Virji was more worried about the way that the doors strained. They didn't fit their frame any longer. They had been warped by the *anacapa* field.

If she couldn't get in because the *anacapa* had destroyed the damn doors, she'd figure out a way to carve her way through the stupid wall. She was going in before Everly had yet another chance to escape.

Then the doors wobbled open.

The smell of burned dust wafted in, along with a hint of space-cold. Usually Virji loved the smell of space, frigid and clean and surprisingly familiar, but not right now. It felt almost contaminated by its contact with Everly.

Virji pulled her pistol. Wèi maneuvered around her and stopped at the doors, following procedure, doing a visual check to make certain that no one was waiting on either side.

Virji could have told him no one was. No one had left that runabout, and anyone who had been waiting inside that storage room would be dead right now. She didn't smell death, not from the storage room.

And she heard no sound except the shuffling of the people behind her and her own ragged breathing.

She wasn't as calm as she wanted to be.

She started to go in, but Wèi held her back. He shook his head.

"No captain is dying on my watch," he said.

She didn't care about his watch. She pushed past him. He didn't know how to get into the runabout, and he didn't know the way the vessel was laid out.

Besides, he couldn't open the runabout's door without her.

The runabout dominated the storage room. The air still had that slightly frigid feel as the environmental systems worked to equalize the oxygen and temperature levels.

The runabout looked unfamiliar. Oh, it was the right make, and it had the proper markings. It was her runabout.

But it looked damaged and gray and old, as if the nanobits had ceased working a long, long time ago. Something had scored the side of the hull closest to Virji.

"We're sending Tranh in first," Wèi said, pushing up beside Virji.

Virji glared at him angrily, but he didn't seem fazed by that. He moved the tall, dark-haired woman—Tranh, apparently—in front of both of them. Another of his team members—a man—flanked her.

It was the smarter play, even if Virji didn't like it.

She palmed the exterior of the runabout. It felt cold and clammy against her skin, not warm the way it should have after a few minutes in the new environment.

The runabout's exterior was badly damaged, and the damage didn't look like it had been done by another ship or a firefight.

A shiver ran through her. Foldspace was unpredictable.

She revised her expectations downward. They might not find Everly at all. They might find a completely empty runabout, with no clue as to where she went.

In fact, if Virji had to hazard a guess based on the evidence, that would be what she would expect now.

She let out a hiss of disappointment. Wèi looked at her oddly, but didn't say a word.

The runabout's door should have opened by now. Virji palmed the opening again, and nothing happened.

So she tapped in an emergency code—one of fifteen that the Fleet used to override protocols.

Still, the door didn't open.

"Let me," Wèi said. He pulled out a small, thin, metal tool Virji didn't recognize and inserted it between the door and the runabout's frame. "Now try."

Virji put her palm against the control panel, and this time, the runabout's door squealed. It opened only a half an inch, enough for Wèi and Tranh to get their fingers into it.

They braced themselves and pulled the door toward the other side of the frame, their muscles bunching, their faces turning red.

If Everly was inside, she certainly had enough time to prepare for them now.

The door's squeal grew louder, as if it were protesting the way it was being treated. Finally Wèi and Tranh managed to get it into the frame.

The air emerging smelled fetid. Virji would wager it wasn't even air, but some kind of leftover chemical component of the environmental system.

"Fitzwilliam," Wèi said. "I need clamps."

The bald male security guard who had been at Wèi's side since Virji first met them hurried forward. He was holding small door clamps in each hand. Apparently, he had been ready for this, or maybe some had been on the shelves in the back of the storage area.

Fitzwilliam and Wèi struggled with his side of the door, and then they both helped Tranh with hers.

The door to the airlock on the runabout stood open.

"It doesn't seem like anything's working in there," Wèi said.

Virji sensed the same thing.

"We're going to have to suit up," she said. "And then we'll see what we can find."

57

They heard every sound coming out of the storage room, which Bassima did not think was a good idea. Having the blast doors open wasn't a good idea, and coming down here had been a *terrible* idea.

The ceiling kept shedding nanobits, covering her in a layer of black dust. She wanted out, and Nicoleau wouldn't let her leave.

The next time she had the opportunity to step in for Loraas, Bassima would not do it. She would make a mental note about how horrible this experience had been, and she would call it to mind each and every time someone wanted her instead of Loraas.

If Bassima survived this, which she considered to be a really big *if*.

She didn't even have her pistol. They had taken it away from her at one of the security checks. She couldn't go to the blast doors and provide back up if Glida escaped.

Or if someone else was in that runabout, someone other than Glida.

And now, that horrid captain was asking for a suit. They needed environmental suits to go into the runabout.

Iannazzi cursed when she heard that and waved her fingers at one of her staff members, who looked at her and rolled his eyes. Bassima had no idea who he was, only that he seemed as unimpressed with the captain as she was.

He grabbed something out of a small storage area. As he carried it to the blast doors, Bassima saw that he was holding a thin, expensive environmental suit.

She hoped it would fit Captain Virji, because maybe this nightmare would end soon—however it would end.

With Glida coming out of the runabout with guns blazing or with the team going in and grabbing her, with the runabout disappearing (and no one getting hurt), whatever was going to happen, Bassima just wished it would happen and she could either die or get buried in rubble or scurry back to the surface.

Because she had answered her own interpersonal questions: she was *never* going to work in the sector base. Ever, ever, ever.

If she was lucky, she would never have to come back here.

If she was lucky, she would get out.

Because right now, she wasn't sure.

Right now, she was thinking that she was going to die.

58

They brought the suit to her in record time, and Virji slipped it on as if it were an old friend. It was as sophisticated as her suit, made of thinner material, and clearly newer. It hadn't been used much.

She double-checked her oxygen mix, flipped on the comm, and said to Wèi, "Ready?"

He nodded. His suit looked older than this one, worn and tired. Or maybe it looked that way because it had been piled in some corner. He had clearly worn it earlier and then discarded it.

The two other members of his team were wearing theirs as well. Only this time, Virji wasn't going to defer to them. If a captain died on Wèi's watch, so be it.

These people were amateurs. They had probably never stormed a ship before.

She had.

She stepped into the airlock. It was dark, and the information on the screen of her visor told her that the air from the storage room was slowly infiltrating this space.

When she stepped in, a light should have gone on. It did not.

Before she touched the backup keypad to open the interior door, she ran a gloved hand over the door itself.

A small blue light flared.

A tag: *Caution* written in two languages.

Followed by something in a single language her visor translated as *Property of* or maybe *Reserved for*…and then three more words that made no sense—one she couldn't understand and two that she might have mistranslated. *Ghost Corporation.* Or maybe, the translation program told her *Lost Souls Corporation.*

There was a logo attached, at least she thought that was a logo, and not another word.

"You ever hear of something called the Lost Souls Corporation?" Virji asked Wèi.

"No," he said, his voice tinny through the comm.

"Ghost Corporation?"

"No," he said. He sounded as confused as she felt.

She removed her laser pistol and held it tightly. Clearly, someone other than Everly had been on this ship. And they had marked it, for what purpose she did not know.

She had no idea if they were still on board or if they were gone.

She also had no idea if they had rigged it to blow up, or if they had stolen everything off of it.

Everything except the *anacapa*, of course.

"I'm not getting any readings from the interior of this ship," Wèi said.

Virji wished that she had her people here. Wèi was too damn unspecific. He didn't seem to know what to say in a situation like this.

How did a man get to be a security officer on a sector base, anyway? Did he do it by kissing up to his bosses or by saving someone? Did he have to have field training?

Those were all questions she should have asked long before she stepped into this airlock, and of course, she hadn't.

"What do you mean, readings?" she asked. The information she was getting from her suit was pretty specific. The only power the runabout gave off came from the *anacapa*. The environmental controls weren't working inside the ship either, and she wasn't getting any power signatures.

"Life signs," Wèi said.

So nice of him to be specific now.

"Yeah," she said. "I told the entire lab that piece of information fifteen minutes ago."

"I meant, that I checked again, and still nothing." He sounded flustered. Just what they all needed. Some flustered security guy.

She lifted her hand and typed in the backup code. No response. Just like the exterior doors. She sighed, typed in another backup code, and another.

No response at all.

She turned toward Wèi, about to say that he and Tranh would have to pry this door open as well, when the entire runabout shuddered.

Virji's heart sped up. She wasn't frightened, but she was startled. The runabout shouldn't shudder like that for any reason.

Then the door moved. It opened an inch, then stopped. Just as she was about to stick her gloved hand inside that opening, the runabout shuddered again, and the door moved three inches.

"What the...?" Wèi said. "Why is the ship shaking?"

Virji had experienced this before.

"Illusion," she said. "Just this part of the ship is vibrating, and it's carrying throughout this part of the frame. If we were in the cockpit, we might see a tiny shiver, but that's it."

Speaking those words out loud calmed her. She had to forget that she was with an inexperienced crew. She had to remember that there was a chance—however small—that Everly was inside this runabout, and maybe, for the first time in years, Virji would be able to capture her.

The door opened six more inches.

Virji flicked on a light on her wrist and pointed at the gloom inside. She saw shapes and some nanobits floating in the light, just from that little bit of movement.

The runabout was slowly disassembling itself, something she had read about but never seen.

Only really old ships did that—*ancient* ships. She felt her stomach clench. She didn't like the way this was going.

The door moved again, and as it did, she slipped between it and the frame, then pushed the door into its wall pocket, disturbing even more nanobits. They rose up off the floor, floating for a moment, before descending slowly back to the ground.

She turned on her other wrist light, then shone them both in different directions.

The runabout's small corridor was gray, the floor littered with nanobits. A hole in the wall just below the ceiling made her wonder what had been there. She couldn't remember.

But that looked more like a hole someone made removing something than a hole made by a weapon.

Still, she had hers out. She surveyed the entire corridor before stepping into it.

"I'll go first," Wèi said with annoyance.

"Stay out of my way," Virji snapped, and deliberately stepped in front of him.

She had been too intent on finding Everly. She hadn't expected anything quite like this. If she had, Virji would have had some of her people report to this part of the sector base.

It wasn't too late. She could send for them and seal up the runabout until they arrived.

But that wouldn't solve the possible problem of Everly getting the runabout running again. That wouldn't prevent Everly from leaving.

Although, judging by this part of the runabout, it hadn't run on its own power for a long, long time.

Virji didn't feel like losing Everly one more time. If she were playing Virji for a fool—again—then she would set up this interior to give the illusion of time and loss.

Virji wouldn't do it that way—Virji would attack and flee—but long ago, the interactions Virji had with Everly proved that Everly and Virji were nothing alike.

Virji stepped forward, moving cautiously as the nanobits rose around her.

"Captain, no," Wèi said, apparently trying to show some respect. "Let us—"

"Shut up and do as I tell you," she snapped. "Get your damn weapons out, and follow me. If one of you shoots me and I live, I will see to it that you will never work at any Fleet facility again. Are we clear?"

"Yes," Wèi said. The others either didn't respond or didn't have their comms set up right.

What a damn clusterfuck.

She moved slowly down the corridor. There weren't many places to hide in a runabout of this vintage. The crew cabins—all two of them. The galley kitchen, sort of.

And then there was the cockpit/inflight area, where everyone could sit together while the pilot took the runabout wherever it was scheduled to go.

Virji was heading there.

If Everly was hiding in the crew cabins, she would remain there. It was smarter to wait in the cockpit: she would retain control of the runabout that way.

And Everly was nothing if not smart.

Virji paused only to activate all of the suit's sensors. She mentally accommodated for the security team following her. The suit didn't like the nanobits that she kept kicking up. Clearly, everything had settled quickly once the runabout had arrived into this storage room.

Her heart had stopped pounding. She was calm, like she always was when she led a mission.

She couldn't remember the last time she'd actually been on the ground on a mission.

Her people would have fits when they realized she had done this. Ah, well.

She was breathing shallowly, even though it wasn't necessary. The suit itself prevented anyone else from hearing her breathe.

And she needed the suit. According to the readings she got, the environmental system had been off for a very, very long time. There was nothing breathable, at least where she was at the moment. The environment from the storage room was slowly seeping in here, just like the gravity had forced all those little nanobits onto the floor itself.

She reached the entrance to the cockpit area. Her mouth was dry. She couldn't hide from whoever was in there, if anyone was, because the nanobits were already rising from where she had disturbed them. Her lights probably let whomever know as well that she was coming.

So all she did was whirl, laser pistol held close so that no one could knock it out of her hand.

For a moment, she thought the cockpit was empty.

And then she realized that it was not.

59

PART OF HER WAS THRILLED that she was nowhere near that storage room, and part of her was more worried than she had ever been.

Bristol watched most of the action on the screens around her lab, but she stood just close enough to the blast doors that she could see the side of the runabout.

She knew when the security team, led by Virji, had gone inside, and she could see the runabout rock a few times as their weight distributed or something got activated.

Rajivk was working one of the stations, seeing if he could link up with the runabout's interior cameras, but at the moment, he couldn't access anything on that runabout. It appeared to be completely dead, except for the *anacapa* drive.

From what she could tell from her own analysis, based mostly on the energy signal it was giving off, that *anacapa* drive had lost 90 percent of the power it had had when she had installed it one week ago.

She had no idea how that happened. *Anacapa* drives lasted hundreds, sometimes thousands, of years.

Fedo was working her screen, trying to link up to the runabout as well, using all sorts of tricks, including that maintenance mode that she had initially bragged about.

So far, no one could get in.

Half the room seemed worried by what was happening just a few yards away, and the other half continued with their own work as if nothing strange were happening.

Bristol was somewhere in between. Inside that runabout was the woman who had hidden in her storage room for a full day, a woman who could have killed Bristol by activating that damn runabout while Bristol was in the lab.

But Bristol really wanted to work. She wanted data, and she had none, not at the moment.

Except that the runabout was dead, the *anacapa* was at 10 percent power, the runabout looked ancient, and it had come in from deep space.

She had a hunch that the runabout had been trapped in foldspace for a long time, or abandoned somewhere accessible through that foldspace connection.

What she didn't know about *anacapa*-to-*anacapa* contact bothered her, particularly at this moment, because she wasn't sure where, exactly, the runabout had come from.

Or when, exactly.

She stepped ever so slightly closer to that storage room. The runabout was inside it, but she wasn't sure there were answers in that runabout. She was worried that there would be more questions.

Not to mention the fact that something could still go horribly, terribly wrong. The runabout itself might be dangerously unstable in ways not immediately obvious.

Or Glida was inside, waiting to strike.

Or something else, much worse, was there.

Bristol glanced at the woman in the room she didn't know, that Beck woman who had come in with Nicoleau, the only person who seemed to express her extreme displeasure in ways that Bristol completely understood.

Bristol wasn't sure she would want to stand there either, waiting to see if they would all die.

Because that was the unspoken part of all of this. Would the *anacapa* malfunction? Would the runabout take off with the blast doors open? Would it explode?

Or was she worrying for no reason whatsoever?

She had no idea.

All she could do was wait.

60

Virji stepped into the cockpit. The pilot's chair faced the navigational equipment, the *anacapa* controls open at the side. A ragged sleeve hung near the controls.

Virji held her breath even though there was no need to. She took a step closer, Wèi at her heels. She put up a hand, holding him back. She didn't feel like talking.

The person in the pilot's chair did not move. Two of the other chairs were completely gone. The remaining chair was set in its reclining position, almost as if it had gotten stuck there.

Out of the corner of her eye, she could see the galley kitchen. It was empty. It also looked like it had been gutted in part as well.

She kept her pistol on the pilot's chair, staring at the back of it as if she expected it to swivel at any moment.

But it didn't.

She stepped to one side, pistol first, and gasped aloud.

A mummified body was strapped in, one hand reaching for the *anacapa* controls, the other resting on the navigational board as if the person was still flying the runabout.

Some wispy brown hair clung to the mummy's head. Its clothing was black, boots worn almost to nothing.

That was the odd thing: the clothing looked like it had been worn hard. The body looked like it had simply died in place.

In space, clothing did not decay—but this clothing had. Bodies did mummify in some environments, though. Virji had seen more mummies than she could count.

She let out a small breath.

"Clear the rest of the runabout," she said to Wèi, even though she knew that was not necessary. If someone else was alive on this runabout, they would have seen that person by now. If someone else was alive on this runabout, that person would have moved this body.

But it looked like it had been strapped in place for a very, very long time.

Virji approached it. Apparently, Wèi did not feel he had to follow her orders directly because he followed her.

"I told you to clear the runabout," Virji snapped.

"I sent Tranh and Fitzwilliam away." Wèi wasn't looking at her. He was looking at the corpse. "You think that's Glida Kimura?"

"I gave you examples of three different DNA samples that Kimura used," Virji said. "We need to test this corpse against those. Do you have the information?"

"Not in this suit," he said, sounding startled.

Oh, of course. Why would he do something sensible like carry anything with him? Virji let out an irritated sigh, keeping her thoughts to herself.

Planetside security. Inept and lazy. Anyone from her ship would have brought the DNA with them, because going back and forth wasn't just a waste of time, it was often *impossible.*

She made herself take a deep breath. She really wasn't angry at him. She had a lot of adrenaline and a huge desire to have a fight with someone, even if it was just a verbal tussle.

She had hoped for a firefight—and if she were honest with herself, she had hoped she would have been able to shoot Everly at least once.

"Do we leave it?" Wèi asked.

It took her a moment to realize he was talking about the corpse.

"Yes," she snapped. "We leave it. We'll need all kinds of techs to examine this scene."

She leaned back, looking. The navigational panel seemed surprisingly clean, considering the condition of the floors and walls. She walked over there, careful to avoid the corpse.

Someone had scraped it off. There was actually the impression of a glove on one side, like a handprint.

She would point that out to whoever took over the examination of this runabout.

She crouched and examined the area around the handprint, and saw a recent scratch, as if someone had ripped a device off the side.

"Look here," she said. "See what you find."

She pointed to the area around the panel.

"And record it," she added, because she had to. These people had the brains of a nanobit. "Be sure not to touch anything."

Then she moved to the other side of the chair, crouching again. The *anacapa* drive casing was open, and that too looked recent. A tiny tag glowed on top of the casing, warning, in those same letters she had seen on the door into the runabout, that the *anacapa* was dangerous.

She had her suit try to translate again, and again, she got the word Corporation, along with maybe Lost Souls or Ghost.

She had no idea what that meant.

Virji stood, hands on hips, and surveyed the cockpit.

If she had come on this in space, she knew what she would have assumed: she would have assumed that the runabout had been floating for some time. Years, decades. No power, and a single pilot who died, unable to get the runabout going again or to get to some sanctuary somewhere.

Then she would investigate.

She spun, deciding to examine the runabout herself.

"Captain?" Wèi asked. "What are we doing?"

"You are going to record everything, just like I told you," Virji said. "I'm going to walk through the runabout."

He started to say something else, something about his people, something about they were competent enough. She didn't care enough to listen.

She went back into the corridor, pistol in hand, feeling like she was finally thinking like a captain again. What she had seen in that cockpit was evidence of scavengers, scavengers who either found nothing or had been interrupted in the middle of what they had been doing.

Or the runabout had been completely scavenged, and she only saw the remnants. That Lost Souls Corporation or whatever it was might have seen the energy signature on the *anacapa*, thought it was something, and then realized they had no idea how to remove it, so they left it behind.

It was a malfunctioning *anacapa*, and sometimes people died near them. Which would explain the danger label.

It might also explain the corpse.

She felt that surge of disappointment again, and she pushed it down.

She checked the captain's cabin, such as it was, since it was only slightly larger than the other cabin. She looked in the closet, the tiny private bath, and moved anything that could conceal a person or the remains of a person.

Jammed into the ever-so-small closet, she found clothing that looked familiar—a dark, hooded sweatshirt and a pack that was in tatters—but nothing else. The blankets on the bed were tucked in military style, set for zero-g, like everyone in the Fleet had been trained to do.

Virji still ran her hands across the bed and registered nothing out of the ordinary.

She left the main cabin and went to the only other one, which was barely the size of a closet in her suite on the *Ijo*. Empty as well.

She let out a small sigh.

All they had found was an ancient, derelict ship, a mummified corpse, and evidence that someone who was not of the Fleet had been here.

Although she did wonder how those people got inside.

She turned and stared at the main door, then shrugged.

Probably the same way that Wèi had gotten into the airlock. With the right tools and a bit of muscle.

Virji held herself rigidly for a moment. She had to set aside the disappointment. She had so hoped that she would be able to confront Everly.

That clearly wasn't going to happen today.

But she would get some answers.

Whether or not she liked them would be another matter altogether.

61

Bristol kept one eye on the cameras from the environmental suits running through the security system. But she was also trying, just like the rest of the team was, to coax some life into the runabout, to find out what kind of records it had, what it knew, and where it had been.

She didn't like the corpse. The corpse could have been anyone.

Only it had been strapped in. That was strange in and of itself.

"Got something," Fedo said, still messing with her screen.

Bristol cloned it, then stared at the work Fedo had been doing. Fedo managed to activate something using that maintenance mode. The cameras had come to life on the runabout five days ago, according to the runabout itself.

Five days ago, the runabout had been sitting in the storage room where it was right now. But not according to the runabout itself.

Five days ago, it had been floating, derelict, no gravity, no environment. Ever so briefly, images of people floated by, wearing environmental suits that looked ancient, with extra oxygen on the waist.

The camera that had been activated was on the navigational panel, and it looked up at the corpse, which was (of course) oblivious to the entire thing.

The images were silent, and only lasted two minutes before they vanished again.

Scavengers.

Bristol closed the cloned screen, then rubbed the heel of her hand over her face.

"What's going on?" that Beck asked. Nicoleau put a hand on her arm, cautioning her, but she didn't seem to care.

"Do you know what foldspace is?" Bristol asked her.

"Kind of," the woman said. Bristol almost smiled at that. It was the appropriate answer for all of them.

"That runabout got trapped in foldspace," Bristol said.

"You don't know that for certain," Fedo said.

Bristol gave her a withering look. "For certain? With scientific evidence? Not yet. But your eyes can see it. So can mine. That runabout is decades, maybe centuries, older than it was when it left here."

"How is that possible?" Beck asked.

There were so many answers. Bristol didn't have the time for any of them. So she turned her back on Beck.

"There's some life in that navigational panel," she said to Rajivk.

"I've already found it," he said. "There's some old records buried in the system. They didn't decay. Those runabouts are well made."

"Yeah," Fedo said drily.

Then Captain Virji and the security team stepped out of the storage room. Virji's hood was down, her hair moist with sweat.

She looked at Nicoleau, not at Bristol.

"Your man Wèi finally managed to test the DNA on that corpse," Virji said, her voice dripping with contempt.

Bristol had no idea why Virji had said *finally*. They hadn't been inside the runabout for very long.

"It's Everly—Kimura—whatever you call her." Virji sounded almost disappointed. "She died in there. It looks like she was alone."

Trapped in foldspace. Bristol shuddered.

"Wait," Beck said. "She *died*. How could she die?"

Virji looked at her almost as if the woman were beneath her. Bristol recognized the look, and didn't quite like it. She knew she looked at people the same way sometimes.

"She left here," Virji said, "but the runabout wasn't working properly. It got her out of this base but, most likely, it trapped her in foldspace. She stayed there until she died."

"That happens?" Beck asked, sounding completely appalled.

Bristol wasn't sure if she was appalled at the way Kimura died or the fact that people could die in foldspace.

"It happens all the time," Virji said. "That's why everything needs to run at tip-top condition."

She looked at Bristol when she made that last comment. Bristol wasn't certain if it was an intentional insult, a reminder, or a compliment. Maybe a little of all three.

"God," Beck breathed. "That's why I don't go into space."

"Oh, you can go into space," Fedo said in her blithe way. "Just don't let anyone get you into foldspace."

Bristol ignored them and walked to the door of the storage room. She felt an odd relief. The woman who had disturbed her lab wouldn't bother it again.

"Well," said Nicoleau behind her, "we can go, Bassima. There will be no justice here."

Bassima must have been Beck.

"No justice?" Beck asked, her voice rising. "Are you *serious?*"

Everyone looked at her. Even Bristol turned around. Virji had her head tilted as if she couldn't quite believe what she heard.

"What are you people thinking?" Beck asked. "How long would it have taken her to die there?"

She addressed that last at Fedo.

Fedo shrugged. "We keep the runabouts stocked with enough supplies for four people for one year."

"So one person, four years?" Beck asked.

They all stared at each other. Bristol's stomach clenched.

"She was alone and *trapped*, unable to get out for *years?* And she knew it?" Beck shuddered. Bristol didn't blame her. She would have shuddered too. "Was she able to fix the runabout?"

"I don't know if *I* could have fixed that runabout," Bristol said. "I had planned to talk to the *Ijo* after I tested a few things."

"It doesn't matter," Virji said, her tone decidedly more friendly. "She didn't have the training—at least when she left the *Ijo*, she didn't have the training. Her training was not in engineering."

"And she didn't gain any of those skills here," Beck said. "So she had no idea what she was doing. She was just trapped there, poking at things, for *years*, waiting to escape. God. Can you *imagine*?"

"She would have been relieved if we had pulled her back," Virji said slowly. "I would have hated helping her."

"Exactly," Nicoleau said.

"She killed so many people," Beck said. "And Taji. She killed Taji."

"I brought Officer Beck here because we were going to have jurisdiction issues," Nicoleau said. "I figured we'd get started with the problems right away."

Virji let out a snort. "Jurisdiction." She patted the pistol on the side of her environmental suit.

Her message was clear—it had to be, considering Bristol understood it. Virji had wanted to kill Glida.

Bristol looked at Virji in awe. And yet, something disturbed Bristol about that solution.

It was like exploding a ship that was malfunctioning. The explosion might be cathartic, but it gained them nothing.

"That woman," Bristol said. And stopped. Only it was too late. Everyone was watching her.

She licked her lips. They were dry.

"That woman, Kimura. She was broken, right?" Bristol asked.

"And impossible to fix," Nicoleau said. "There have been people like her throughout human history."

Bristol nodded. She knew that. And she also appreciated the fact that Nicoleau knew part of what she had been thinking.

"Yes, there have been," Bristol said. "But the opportunities she had, to kill—"

"We didn't know until she had left our ship," Virji said.

Bristol raised her eyebrows. She hadn't been thinking of that, per se. She held up her hands.

"Opportunities here in Sandoveil and through the Fleet," Bristol said. "Those things can be fixed, right? If we find out what happened? How she functioned? We can figure how what she did, what things she exploited, and make it impossible for someone else to do so."

"People aren't as simple as ships," Virji said.

"But systems are," Bristol said. "We can modify systems."

No one spoke after that. Most of the people in her lab looked down, as if they thought she was embarrassing herself or being naïve.

Only the Beck woman kept her gaze on Bristol.

"I think you're right," Beck said. "I think we figure out what she did, exactly, to keep her hunting secret from all of us, and then we make sure no one else does it, ever again."

"Hunting?" Virji asked.

"What would you call it?" Beck asked. "Because that's what it looked like to me."

Virji stared at her for a moment, then frowned.

"Hunting," she repeated. "That makes as much sense as anything else."

You couldn't hunt anywhere on Nindowne without some kind of permit. Bristol almost said that aloud, then realized that most people wouldn't see that as helpful: they would think she was suggesting that people like Kimura get a license.

But Bristol wasn't thinking that. She was thinking about all the regulations and loopholes and the way that some hunters tried to go around them. She knew people who liked the challenge of hunting, but not the end result.

Her brain was already working the problem—the loopholes, the technicalities—even here, in the lab, which Kimura had broken into despite all the security.

Everything had to be fixed.

She let out a small breath, felt a lifting in her heart, and knew it for what it was. Relief. A way forward.

Something to fix.

She loved having things to fix. Her entire life was about that.

She looked at Beck, who was still watching her, and she nodded just a little, wishing she could invite Beck for coffee to discuss all of this.

Then Bristol stiffened. What would stop her from doing so? Aside from the moment here, where it was inappropriate. But outside the base. They could talk, and maybe work on the problem together, and find solutions—not for the Fleet. Virji and Fedo had to do that—not that Bristol was sure Virji would.

But here, in Sandoveil. She and Beck could work out all kinds of solutions, and in the lab too, solutions she could send to other sector bases. To the new base just starting up.

Improved security. More caution around the *anacapa*s.

Bristol's fingers trailed the closed *anacapa* frame. It would provide answers too, just like the *anacapa* in the runabout.

A thousand things to fix, even more to prevent.

She had work for the next ten years or more just because of this. Work that would benefit the Fleet, the sector bases, and the community.

She didn't say any of this. She didn't want anyone to know that her mood had gotten lighter.

She knew how she was spending the next several years—not watching the sector base close, but helping with the future.

And she liked that.

She liked that more than she dared say.

62

THE SUN WAS JUST STARTING to set over the Payyer Mountains as Rajivk made his way home. He walked the long way because he needed time to think.

So much had happened since the last time he had tried to go home, just a little over twenty-four hours ago. His entire worldview had changed. *He* had changed, and only because he had seen things that he hadn't thought possible.

He took the upper trails, even though they were partly blocked off by the YSR-SR. Most of the blockages remained from a few hours before, when everyone thought they would have to make a case against whoever had killed the single body floating in the pool.

And then they discovered an entire pile of bodies, all, they thought (or so they said), killed by Kimura over years. Working alone.

Hunting, Bassima Beck had said.

Which was probably right.

Rajivk had spent the last part of his extra-long day pulling together the video record of the runabout. None of the record was corrupted, but it was excessive.

Glida Kimura—or Sloane Everly, or whatever she called herself—had ended up in foldspace, trapped and alone. For four years she moved back and forth in that tiny ship, apparently doing her best to repair it.

She broke down a lot. Crying, pounding the walls. Clawing at them. It seemed, after a while, that she just gave up.

Then she seemed to gain a second wind. Tried a few things. Gave up. Tried some more, and paced. Walking that tiny ship like a caged animal.

Back and forth, back and forth, crying, calm, until she tried *something*, although he couldn't figure out what that something was, something she had to strap herself in for. And that *something* had cut the power to the environmental system.

She had died there, alone, and—according to Captain Virji—contemplating her crimes.

Rajivk didn't believe that. He didn't think people like Kimura could contemplate their crimes. And he agreed with Beck: the punishment that Kimura got was the only kind of justice she would probably ever have gotten.

He reached the overlook where Kimura had left those shoes. He stopped, his face getting damp from the spray of the Falls. He hadn't really heard them as he walked up—not because they had gone silent—but because he was so tired that parts of his body just didn't seem to function.

He was spending all of his time thinking, lost in his own world, not paying any attention. He used to make fun of tourists for doing that, thinking that was what would get them in trouble, make them fall off the trail or into the Jeleen River or get trapped in the mud flats.

He thought their lack of attention would cause some of them to disappear.

But now he knew: some of them disappeared because Glida Kimura had a system for finding loners, killing them, and dumping them in that pool.

She *liked* doing it. It had been a challenge for her.

He shoved his hands in the back pockets of his pants and stared at the water. The power of the entire planet in one gigantic waterfall.

And everyone who lived here had blamed the environment, not the human beings. Tourists died.

Now, Hranek had more work than he would know what to do with. He would have to identify all those bodies. The government of the city of Sandoveil would have to revise its cause-of-death statistics. The murder rate would skyrocket, and the accidental death rate would plummet.

Rajivk sighed, tasting the fresh spray. Water beaded on his face and along his clothing, but he didn't care.

No one would have known about all the bodies if he hadn't found those shoes. And it would have taken days before someone had seen the body floating in the pool.

Kimura had planned that. She wanted everyone to think that she was dead. She had apparently done the same thing in the *Ijo*.

People would have thought exactly what he had initially worried about—that Glida and her wife, Taji, had died together, either as a murder-suicide or a double suicide. And then, with the discovery of Taji's office and all the blood, the authorities would settle on murder-suicide, and not give it much more thought.

For her entire life, Glida had trusted the fact that people did not give the things she did much thought.

He ran a hand over his wet face.

Everyone in town had known she was a little off. Everyone had suspected her of being crazy in one way or another. And a lot of people had discussed Taji, wondering how she could live with Glida, because Glida was so odd.

But not murderous odd. No one had suspected that.

Just like they hadn't suspected Glida Kimura to be anything other than who she was.

He sighed. It was starting to get dark.

Light filtered up the waterfall in ways he had never seen before because of all those powerful lights planted near the pool. Marnie wanted to keep working on the body dump, as she had called it when he spoke to her briefly. She didn't want onlookers to show up, or others to get in the way of the recovery effort.

The original team had already gone home, except for Tevin Egbe, who wouldn't leave. He wanted to supervise the entire mission, and he probably would—even though it was going to take days and days.

Rajivk didn't envy him.

Nor did he envy those who were going to have to put the entire story of Glida Kimura into the record.

He had heard enough, between Captain Virji and the YSR-SR team. Kimura—Everly—whatever she was called—had been trouble from the start of her young life. She got a second chance and used it to hunt whenever she left the *Ijo*. And no one knew.

Until she lost her temper at her lover. Had he found out what she had been doing? Or had it been a lover's spat?

Rajivk wasn't clear on that.

But he was clear on one thing: she had used her skills in a fit of rage to murder the man she claimed she loved.

Then she had tried to fake her own death and she fled the *Ijo*. Somehow she had learned how to spoof DNA, and her name, her Everly name, never ended up tied to her Kimura identity.

She had used that trick to make the entire sector base her playground.

He shuddered. At least she hadn't murdered anyone in the base.

That he knew of.

He shook off the water as if he were getting out of the shower. If he was going to make it around the upper path before dark, he had to keep moving.

He gave the overlook one final glance.

She hadn't wanted to be caught. But she had wanted some kind of acknowledgement. She wanted the community to know that she was gone, maybe even wanted them to know that she had killed Taji.

Of course, Glida should have been long gone by the time the body was discovered. But she had had bad luck from the beginning of this one. She hadn't expected all the attention on the sector base closing. She hadn't expected the runabout to fail her.

And she hadn't expected to die, trapped, in foldspace.

He smiled just a little at that thought.

It had been horrible watching how frantic she had gotten as the days went on and she realized she could not escape. There had been no escape pods on this runabout, and even if there had been, where would she have gone?

And yet, when he thought of all that she had done, all of the lives she had ruined, all of the people she had killed, he shouldn't have considered her death horrible at all.

He should have considered it justified.

What did it say about him that even knowing all she had done, he felt twinges of compassion as he scanned through the images of the end of her life?

He shook his head and started up the trail. The sun had moved behind the peaks. It was gloomy up there.

His heart pounded, and he was tired. Exhausted, actually.

The exact setup for a misstep on the slick black trail.

He sighed, then smiled at himself.

He wasn't being honest with himself. He'd walked this trail in growing darkness, so tired that the rumble and roar of the Falls barely registered, many times before.

This time, he wasn't so much worried about a misstep or a tumble into the river.

This time, he saw the shade of a woman up there, a woman who saw people like him as fair game for the sport that she pursued.

Her sport probably wasn't murder. From everything he had seen, her sport was duping the people around her. She liked never getting caught.

But to never get caught, you actually had to do something.

Or encounter someone doing something.

He took one more step forward and then stopped.

He wouldn't be as haunted after some sleep. She wouldn't bother him at all. He would be able to put the events of the last two days in some kind of perspective.

He hoped.

And then he turned around, and took the safe route home.

Coming Soon!

The story continues with the return of Boss
in *The Runabout,* which will be available
in ebook, paperback and audiobook
from your favorite bookseller in 2017.

But for now, turn the page for a preview.

1

CHORAL MUSIC. SIXTEEN VOICES, perfect harmony, singing without words. Chords shifting in a pattern. First, third, fifth, minor sixth and down again.

I can hear them, running up and down the scales like a waterfall, their chorus twice as loud as the rest of the music floating through the Boneyard.

Of course, I know there is no music here. I am hearing the malfunctioning tech of a thousand, five thousand, ten thousand ships, all clustered together in an area of space larger than some planets. The sound is the way that my head processes the changing energy signatures, although, oddly, I can't hear any of it when I have my exterior communications link off.

Anyone with a genetic marker that ties them to the Fleet can hear this. Everyone else can't.

Although I've never really tested this assumption thoroughly. I don't know if those of us with the marker hear the same thing.

My mind is wandering, which is dangerous during a dive. I have just exited the *Sove*, a Dignity Vessel we pulled from the Boneyard months ago, and I'm heading toward a completely intact Dignity Vessel only a one-hundred meters away. I'm wearing an upgraded environmental suit, with more features than I've ever used before. I hate those, but I've finally gotten used to the clear hood that seals around the neck, instead of a helmet, like I used to wear.

We've sent a line from the *Sove*'s smallest bay door to the only visible door on the Dignity Vessel, and I'm clinging to that line by my right hand.

I'm facing the Dignity Vessel, when the sound catches me.

Elaine Seager, one of the original Six who learned to dive with me way after we discovered the need for markers, is slowly working her way toward the other Dignity Vessel. She's ever so slightly ahead of me on the line. I was the second one to exit the *Sove*.

Orlando Rea, another one of the Six, is waiting to exit the *Sove*. We have strict procedure about the distance between divers on a line.

In fact, we have strict procedures about everything.

The procedures keep us safe.

"What's the hold-up?" Yash Zarlengo asks from inside the *Sove*. She's monitoring us. She hates diving, and avoids it as much as possible.

She'll have to do a lot of it on this trip—she often has to dive when we're in the Boneyard—but she's going to dive only after we know what's inside our target vessel.

I snap to attention, still caught by that sound.

"I'm the hold-up," I say. "Orlando, you need to go around me and catch up to Elaine."

"Not procedure, Boss," Orlando says from behind me. His tone is half-amused, half-chiding. I'm the one who always harps on procedure.

But he does as I ask. He exits the bay door on the right side instead of the left, and grips the line.

I flip my comm so that Yash can't hear what I have to say to the other two divers.

"You hearing that?" I ask Orlando and Elaine.

Orlando looks around—up, down, sideways. There are ships everywhere. Different kinds, different makes, different eras. As far as we can tell, they're all Fleet vessels, although some of our team back at the Lost Souls Corporation hopes that we'll also found vessels of other makes.

There's a theory that these ships were stored here during a protracted war.

I think the theory's wishful thinking. Because I love diving ancient and abandoned ships, I've learned a lot about history. And one thing that unites human beings, no matter where they live, is their ability to take a historical fact and discard it for a story that sounds ever so much better.

The war sounds so much better than a ship graveyard, put here to store abandoned ships until they're needed—a kind of junkyard in space.

I've stopped arguing that point of view, though. I figure time will tell us what this place actually is.

I can't see Orlando's face through his hood. He has turned away from me.

I wish the new suits had one more feature. I wish we could monitor each other's physical reactions in real time. We send that information back to the *Sove* as we dive, but we don't give it to each other.

I didn't help with the design of the new suits, and that was a mistake. Yash designed them to handle the constantly changing energy waves we identified inside the Boneyard. The waves come from all the *anacapa* drives inside the Boneyard and, Yash thinks, from the Boneyard's *anacapa* drives as well. Each drive has a different signature, and malfunctioning drives have even stranger signatures.

We hit the waves as we move across the emptiness from one ship to another, sometimes one wave in the short distance, and sometimes three dozen waves.

Orlando's hand remains tightly wrapped around the line.

"Yeah," he says softly, in answer to my question. "I do hear that. I can't tell where it's coming from."

Elaine has stopped a few meters from us.

"Are we diving or not?" she asks.

That annoyed question went across the open channel, which means Yash heard it.

"Is there a hold-up?" she asks again. "Besides Boss?"

I decide to come clean. "We've got a strange energy signature."

"I'm not reading anything from your suits," Yash says.

I sigh silently. We're now getting to the thing she hates—the musicality of the Boneyard itself.

"I can hear it," I say.

"Me, too," Orlando says. He doesn't have to. I hope he's not protecting me.

Even though Yash represents the Fleet on these dives, I'm in charge of them. I still run the Lost Souls Corporation, even if I've delegated many of my duties to Ilona Blake.

I never go on dives where someone else is in charge.

"Well," Yash says, "whatever you 'hear' isn't important. Examining that ship ahead of you is."

She's right. We are salvaging ships from the Boneyard, and it takes a lot of work. We've taken seventeen Dignity Vessels so far, but not all of them work as well as we want them to. We've ended up using six of them for parts.

Orlando turns toward me, remembering, maybe at this late date, that I'm the one who gives the final orders here.

I nod, then sigh.

"She's right," I say. "We're on the clock. Let's keep moving forward."

Be the first to know!

Just sign up for the Kristine Kathryn Rusch newsletter, and keep up with the latest news, releases and so much more—even the occasional giveaway.

To sign up, go to kristinekathrynrusch.com.

But wait! There's more. Sign up for the WMG Publishing newsletter, too, and get the latest news and releases from all of the WMG authors and lines, including Kristine Grayson, Kris Nelscott, Dean Wesley Smith, *Fiction River: An Original Anthology Magazine, Smith's Monthly,* and so much more.

Just go to wmgpublishing.com and click on Newsletter.

ABOUT THE AUTHOR

New York Times bestselling author Kristine Kathryn Rusch writes in almost every genre. Generally, she uses her real name (Rusch) for most of her writing. Under that name, she publishes bestselling science fiction and fantasy, award-winning mysteries, acclaimed mainstream fiction, controversial nonfiction, and the occasional romance. Her novels have made bestseller lists around the world and her short fiction has appeared in eighteen best of the year collections. She has won more than twenty-five awards for her fiction, including the Hugo, *Le Prix Imaginales*, the *Asimov's* Readers Choice award, and the *Ellery Queen Mystery Magazine* Readers Choice Award.

To keep up with everything she does, go to kriswrites.com. To track her many pen names and series, see their individual websites (krisnelscott.com, kristinegrayson.com, retrievalartist.com, divingintothewreck.com, fictionriver.com). She lives and occasionally sleeps in Oregon.